"ANYONE WHO LOVES ROMANCE
MUST READ SABRINA JEFFRIES!"
—*New York Times* bestselling author Lisa Kleypas

"JEFFRIES'S ADDICTIVE SERIES SATISFIES."
—*Library Journal*

**Praise for the first book in The Duke's Men, the
enthralling new series from New York Times and
USA Today bestselling author
SABRINA JEFFRIES**

WHAT THE DUKE DESIRES

"A totally engaging, adventurous love story . . . with
a strong plot, steamy desire, and an oh-so-wonderful
ending."

—*RT Book Reviews*

"This unusual tale of interlocking mysteries is full of
all the intriguing characters, brisk plotting, and witty
dialogue that Jeffries's readers have come to expect."
—*Publishers Weekly*, starred review

**Turn the page to read rave reviews of the acclaimed,
"exceptionally entertaining" (*Booklist*) novels of the**

HELLIONS OF HALSTEAD HALL

"Another sparkling series" (*Library Journal*)!

Critics adore Sabrina Jeffries and her five wonderful installments of the Hellions of Halstead Hall!

A LADY NEVER SURRENDERS

"Jeffries pulls out all the stops. . . . With depth of character, emotional intensity, and the resolution to the ongoing mystery rolled into a steamy love story, this one is not to be missed."

—*RT Book Reviews* (4½ stars, Top Pick)

"Sizzling, emotionally satisfying. . . . Another must-read."

—*Library Journal* (starred review)

"Brimming with superbly shaded characters, simmering sensuality, and a splendidly wicked wit, *A Lady Never Surrenders* wraps up the series nothing short of brilliantly."

—*Booklist*

TO WED A WILD LORD

"Wonderfully witty, deliciously seductive, graced with humor and charm. . . ."

—*Library Journal* (starred review)

"A beguiling blend of captivating characters, clever plotting, and sizzling sensuality."

—*Booklist*

HOW TO WOO A RELUCTANT LADY

"A delightful addition. . . . Charmingly original."

—*Publishers Weekly* (starred review)

"Richly imbued with steamy passion, deftly spiced with dangerous intrigue, and neatly tempered with just the right amount of tart wit."

—*Booklist*

A HELLION IN HER BED

"A lively plot blending equal measures of steamy passion and sharp wit. . . ."

—*Booklist* (starred review)

"Jeffries's sense of humor and delightfully delicious sensuality spice things up!"

—*RT Book Reviews* (4½ stars)

THE TRUTH ABOUT LORD STONEVILLE

"Jeffries combines her hallmark humor, poignancy, and sensuality to perfection."

RT Book Reviews (4½ stars, Top Pick)

"Lively repartee, fast action, luscious sensuality, and an abundance of humor."

—*Library Journal* (starred review)

"Delectably witty dialogue . . . and scorching sexual chemistry."

—*Booklist*

Sabrina Jeffries

When the Rogue Returns

POCKET BOOKS

New York   London   Toronto   Sydney   New Delhi

Pocket Books
A Division of Simon & Schuster, Inc.
1230 Avenue of the Americas
New York, NY 10020

This book is a work of fiction. Any references to historical events, real people, or real places are used fictitiously. Other names, characters, places, and events are products of the author's imagination, and any resemblance to actual events or places or persons, living or dead, is entirely coincidental.

This Pocket Books paperback edition February 2014

POCKET and colophon are registered trademarks of Simon & Schuster, Inc.

For information about special discounts for bulk purchases, please contact Simon & Schuster Special Sales at 1-866-506-1949 or business@simonandschuster.com.

The Simon & Schuster Speakers Bureau can bring authors to your live event. For more information or to book an event, contact the Simon & Schuster Speakers Bureau at 1-866-248-3049 or visit our website at www.simonspeakers.com.

Manufactured in the United States of America

10 9 8 7 6 5 4 3 2 1

ISBN 978-1-4767-6539-6
ISBN 978-1-4516-9352-2 (ebook)

To the wonderful Dru and the crew at my local Starbucks who keep me well supplied with iced coffee and everything bagels. You are true gems, every one of you! Thanks for letting me hang out and write.

To my niece Isabel "Isa" Martin and my nephew Craig Martin, thank you for brightening my days.

And to my brother Daren Martin, whose sage advice at a crucial point in my marriage altered my life forever. Thank you, and I love you.

THE DUKE'S MEN SERIES
FAMILY TREE

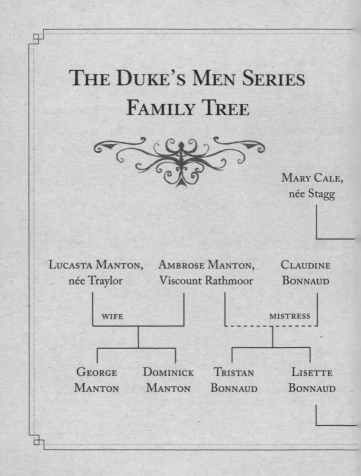

MARY CALE,
née Stagg

LUCASTA MANTON,
née Traylor

AMBROSE MANTON,
Viscount Rathmoor

CLAUDINE
BONNAUD

WIFE

MISTRESS

GEORGE
MANTON

DOMINICK
MANTON

TRISTAN
BONNAUD

LISETTE
BONNAUD

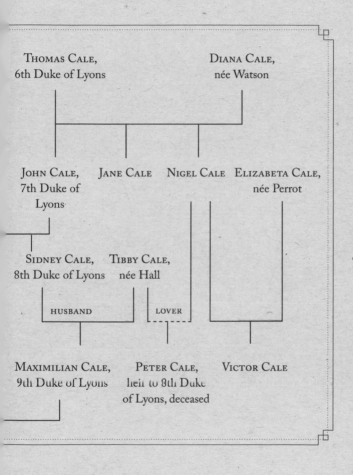

When the
Rogue Returns

PROLOGUE

Amsterdam
1818

DARKNESS HAD FALLEN a while ago. Eighteen-year-old Isabella Cale clung to her new husband Victor's neck as he carried her into her old room at her sister Jacoba's house. Isa hadn't wanted to come here, but it was safer than having Jacoba look after her in their apartment. She didn't want her sister nosing around for the imitation diamonds that Isa kept hidden from her husband. And Victor refused to leave Isa alone while she was sick.

She winced. She hoped this pretense of being ill succeeded. And that he never found out it was a sham. It had been hard enough to keep it up all day, when she was supposed to have been working at the jeweler's shop, but Victor's concerned glances now made it even more difficult. After only a week of marriage, the last thing she wanted to do was deceive him.

But she had no choice. It was for his own good. And hers.

"Are you sure she'll be fine?" Victor asked Jacoba as he laid Isa gently in her old bed.

"She just needs rest and coddling." Jacoba pulled the covers up over Isa. "She's had these awful sore throats since she was a girl. They never last more than a week. You were right to bring her here. It's not good for her to be alone."

Her older sister's soft words used to make her feel safe. But that was before their clockmaker father had died six years ago. Before Papa's apprentice, Gerhart Hendrix, had married Jacoba and taken them in. Before Gerhart had begun gambling.

Isa and Jacoba were no longer as close as they once were.

"I'm not so ill that I'll expire while you're at the shop," Isa told Victor in a raspy voice.

Victor worked temporarily as a night guard at the jeweler's where she was a diamond cutter. Since their conflicting shifts didn't allow them much time together, it had been pure bliss staying home with him today. Well, except for the pretending-to-be-sick part.

Shadows darkened Victor's lovely hazel eyes. "I'm sorry to have to leave you, but at least Jacoba can look after you."

Oh, how she wished she weren't too much of a coward to tell him the truth! But it would devastate her if it changed what he thought of her. Better to avoid the problem entirely.

If she could fool her sister and brother-in-law with her "illness" for just one night, it would all be over tomorrow. Then Victor would never have to learn of her family's insane scheme to steal the royal diamond parure from the jeweler's shop.

A lock of wavy hair the color of rich oak dropped over his brow as he bent to kiss her forehead. "I wish I didn't have to leave you alone, but with the prince's guard coming—"

"I know," she said, cutting him off before he could reveal that the royal diamonds would be leaving the shop tomorrow. Jacoba mustn't learn that the chance to steal them would be gone after tonight. "You may not have your post much longer, so you have to work while you can." His post would end in the morning, when the jeweler handed the royal jewels to the prince's guard.

"I *will* find work after this," he said resentfully, "even if the jeweler doesn't keep me on. Don't worry about that."

"I'm not," she hastened to reassure him. He was such a proud man, and she hadn't meant to wound him. Besides, who wouldn't hire Victor? And the jeweler was an old friend of his mother's; the man would surely find *some* way to keep Victor on. "I have faith in you."

Victor looked only slightly mollified by her words. "You're fretting over *something*. I can tell."

"Don't be silly." Had she been that transparent? Oh, Lord, she had to get him to leave, before she gave too much away. She forced hoarseness into her voice. "And if you don't go, you'll be late." His shift began at 8 P.M., when the jeweler went home. "Don't worry about me. I'm in good hands with Jacoba." She practically choked on that lie.

But he didn't seem to notice as he tucked the covers about her. "I'll come fetch you in the morning when I'm done with my shift, *Mausi*."

She winced at the German endearment. Victor often used foreign words—he spoke Dutch, Flemish, German, English, and French fluently, which impressed her. But she didn't like being called "little mouse."

Probably because she *was* a mouse, in every respect. She looked like one—nondescript brown hair that defied curling, boring brown eyes, and hips that were a touch too wide for her small bosom—and she acted like one, too. She would much rather cut diamonds or design jewelry than argue or make a fuss. It was how she'd landed in this mess in the first place.

It was also why she lay here silent while he headed for the door. She ought to call him back, tell him the truth, face the consequences. But it would be so much easier just to bluff her way through this night. Then she'd be free of her family's machinations forever.

Because she was *never* creating another imitation parure. She wouldn't have made this one if Jacoba and Gerhart hadn't convinced her that they could sell it as a legitimate copy and earn some good money out of her talent for creating false diamonds. If she'd known they would take it into their heads to use it to commit a crime . . .

Stifling a groan, she turned onto her side and watched as Victor went out with Jacoba into the hall, murmuring instructions on how to care for his wife. He was *so* handsome, her husband, and so kind. She lived in terror that he would find out about the Hendrixes' sordid plans and her part in them.

Her throat tightened. How had she even managed to snag his attention? He was a lion to her mouse. His many scars told her that he'd suffered a great deal during his three years in the Prussian army. And the pain of fighting at Waterloo still lurked beneath his clear hazel eyes. She suspected he had other dark secrets—he didn't talk about his childhood or his family—yet he took each day as it came, persevering through whatever agonies lay in his past.

Meanwhile, she lay here pretending to be sick. Oh, what she wouldn't give to be courageous and reckless, to stand up to Gerhart whenever he droned on about how he'd saved her and Jacoba from certain ruin after Papa died. It was true, but why should it mean that she had to risk her own happiness and safety? And why couldn't she just *say* that?

Because then Gerhart would shout at her and shout at Jacoba, and she hated the shouting. And the stony glances. And the reminders that she wouldn't even have her position at the jeweler's if Gerhart hadn't encouraged the talent for jewelry making and diamond cutting that she'd inherited from Papa.

She sighed against her pillow.

"So you're *not* asleep," Jacoba said, having padded back into the room with the quiet tread of a cat.

Isa tensed. "No, not yet. But I feel horrible, all weak and achy. And my throat hurts." Tamping down her guilt, she slanted a glance up at her sister, who, being seven years older, had been like a mother to her.

Once.

Jacoba laid her hand on Isa's brow. "You do seem a bit hot."

That's what came of lying under a pile of heavy covers. Though she prayed that the dampness of her brow wouldn't give her away. "I can't get warm," she lied in a husky whisper. "It always starts with the chills . . ."

"I remember."

Her sister cast her a hard look, as if she'd seen right through her farce, and Isa held her breath. Jacoba and Gerhart had been pressing her to substitute her imitation parure for the real one, now that the jeweler had finished it. All she'd have to do, according to them, was steal her husband's keys while he was asleep and get into the strongbox while the jeweler was at lunch.

Betraying her husband and everything she believed in.

She'd put them off for days. But last night Gerhart had threatened to bring up the matter with Victor and get him to do the switching. Isa couldn't have that; Victor would be horrified.

Let Gerhart rage about the injustice of her being sick on the last day she could have switched out the parure. Eventually he would resign himself to having missed his chance. He might even be able to sell the imitation parure, as he'd first intended, to some wealthy woman who wanted jewelry identical to that of the soon-to-be bride of the prince.

At last Jacoba seemed to accept Isa's ruse, and her

expression softened. "Well, then, you'd better get some sleep. I'll bring you something to soothe your throat."

"Thank you," Isa murmured, not bothering to hide her grimace.

She hated Jacoba's medicine. But when her sister returned with the vile tonic, Isa knew she had to choke it down. If she refused, Jacoba would be suspicious.

Afterward, her sister surprised her, sitting by her bedside and wiping her forehead with a cold cloth until she dozed off.

✦ ✦ ✦

IT SEEMED ONLY minutes later that she awoke to the gray dawn seeping into her bedchamber. At first she was groggy and disoriented. Where was she? Why wasn't she in her apartment? And where was Vic—

She bolted upright as last night's events came flooding back. It was always dark when Victor's shift ended at 6 A.M., but judging from the light, it must be well past seven now. He should be here. He'd said he would fetch her as soon as his shift ended!

A door opened and shut down the hall, and she heard voices. Before she could do more than throw her legs over the side of the bed, Gerhart and Jacoba entered her room.

"We did it, Isa!" Jacoba cried, her face flushed and her eyes bright as she performed a little jig. "We got them!"

When Isa stared in confusion, her brawny brother-in-law pulled a necklace from his pocket and held it up to catch the faint rays of morning light. "It's ours now. We'll break it down for the diamonds and sell them in Paris. I know a dealer who will pay us well for—"

"Stop it!" Isa said, horror growing in her belly. "What do you mean? You have the *real* diamonds?"

"Of course." Gerhart exchanged a glance with his wife. "With you ill, we had to act on our own. Surely you didn't think we'd let this opportunity pass? We made the switch ourselves."

Her mind raced. "But how . . . Victor would have had to let you . . ."

"Yes." Jacoba came over to lay an arm about her shoulders. "After I explained our scheme earlier, he agreed to help in exchange for our giving him the earrings from the parure. He and I left here to go look for the imitation at your apartment, and then he made the switch at the shop."

A chill coursed through her. Was that the reason for all the furtive whispers in the hall earlier? Jacoba had actually *spoken* to Victor about the scheme?

"We were more than happy to allow him a share," Gerhart put in, "given your part in the affair . . . and his. Sale from the earrings alone should provide the two of you with enough money to—"

"He wouldn't do that!" Isa cried through a throat thick and tight with dread. Shoving free of Jacoba, she rose to face them. "He would never steal. I know him."

"Apparently not as well as you thought." Gerhart headed over to the window and opened the curtains to let in the weak winter light. "I told you he would listen to reason if you only broached the subject."

Was it possible? Could she really have been that wrong about her husband? "I was waiting to mention it until—"

"Yes, we know," her sister said, her tone sharp. "I'm sure you simply forgot to tell us about the prince's guard coming this morning for the jewels. You weren't really planning to let it pass without comment."

"Of course not," she mumbled, unable to meet her sister's eyes. This couldn't be happening.

"Thank God Victor said something as he was leaving here," Jacoba said, "or we would have missed our chance entirely."

Dear heaven. "Where's Victor now?" Isa headed for the door. She had to find out if he'd really done this outrageous thing.

"He's gone." Gerhart tucked the necklace into his coat pocket. "He's the most at risk of being caught, so he had to head straight off to Antwerp as soon as his shift was over. They won't expect him back at the shop until this evening, and perhaps not even then, given that his post as guard ends today. Meanwhile—"

"You're saying Victor *left* me?" With her blood pounding in her ears, she whirled on them. "My husband left me?"

"Not exactly," Jacoba said, oozing sympathy and concern. "After he sells the earrings in Antwerp, he'll join us in Paris. That's where we're heading with the necklace, bracelet, and brooch. Victor suggested that we split up, in case anyone comes after us. They'll expect two couples traveling together. They won't expect you to go with us and him to go another way."

"Not that we think your imitations won't hold up under scrutiny," Gerhart said, "but it's better that we be well away, in case they don't. The jeweler won't expect you at the shop until tomorrow, since Victor already told him how sick you are—fortuitous for us. That gives us time to put some distance between us and here."

"And the beauty of it is that if your diamonds *do* escape notice, no one will ever even know about the theft!" Jacoba crowed. The unnatural light in her eyes made Isa shiver. "Victor left a letter behind with your landlord saying that you both got lucrative positions in Frankfurt. The jeweler will certainly find that plausible, especially with Victor's post coming to an end. It's the perfect plan!"

"Except that I wanted no part of it!" Isa cried.

Gerhart narrowed his gaze on her. "That's not what you said. You said you were waiting for the right moment."

Her mouth went dry. "Well, I—I lied. I don't *want* to be a criminal. I just want to cut diamonds and design jewelry and have a regular life."

"What kind of regular life do you think you'd have with a husband out of work?" Jacoba snapped. "How long do you think it would be before you lost your position to some man? And then what?" She jerked her gaze from Isa as if disgusted. "At least your husband saw the sense of our plan."

Determined not to be a mouse this time, Isa thrust out her chin. "I just can't believe that Victor would have agreed to—"

"He's not here, is he?" Jacoba pointed out. "And you heard him say he would be here to fetch you home. Yet it's well past the time for him to do so."

The truth of that struck her hard. "I still just don't—"

"How do you think we got the diamonds, you little fool?" Gerhart strode up to her in a temper. "We couldn't have breached the strongbox ourselves. The thing takes five men to lift, and the locks are intricate. It could only be opened with the keys. *Victor's* keys."

Isa's blood thundered in her ears.

He let that sink in, then added coldly, "He was more than happy to help when he realized it was the only way to make sure he could provide for his wife."

I will find work after this, even if the jeweler doesn't keep me on. Don't worry about that.

Tears sprang to her eyes. Had she sent him off to do this awful thing by making him believe she was worried about his ability to find another post?

"And I should *think*," Gerhart pressed on, "that you'd be grateful for all the trouble we have taken to provide for you. Instead, you stand here mewling—"

"Gerhart, darling," Jacoba said in soothing tones, "why don't you go pack our things and let me talk to my sister?"

Gerhart glared at Isa, who was clutching her stomach in a fruitless attempt to quell the fear roiling inside her. With a snort, he walked out.

As soon as he was gone, Jacoba came to Isa's side. "My dearest, I like Victor as much as you, but you must admit that you hardly know him. He rarely even speaks of his previous life. For all you know, he may have done this kind of thing before. Consider all those languages he speaks—has he ever even said how he knows so many?"

She swallowed. She'd never asked. He just seemed worldly, a man who'd learned things far beyond her ken, even though he was only two years older. "He *was* a soldier in the Prussian army," she pointed out.

"That explains his knowledge of German. But how does he know English? Or French? Surely not just from being a soldier. I daresay he did a few things during the war that required special . . . skills."

Since she'd often wondered about his reticence, she could hardly ignore that possibility.

"Besides," Jacoba went on, "soldiers are practical sorts. And since you never mentioned our plan to him, how do you know he wouldn't have embraced it?"

The words cut her right through. She didn't. She had only her instincts to go on, which said that Victor would never steal. But could she be sure? Or did she just believe it because she'd placed him so high in her esteem?

Worse yet, some facts were irrefutable. Jacoba and Gerhart couldn't have breached the strongbox without Victor. And a glance at the clock showed it was already 8 A.M. He would have been here long before now if he were coming.

That was the part that hurt.

"He didn't even say goodbye," Isa whispered.

Jacoba chucked her under the chin. "Why should he, silly girl? He'll see you in a few weeks. This is just temporary. He had to get as far away as he could before the time he'd be expected at the shop." She bent her head to touch Isa's. "And we have to as well, so come along now. Victor packed your bags, and we have to hurry to the dock."

Her heart faltered. "Can't I go back to the apartment?"

"We've no time, I'm afraid. The packet boat for Calais leaves very soon. We'll barely make it as it is, and the next one doesn't leave for hours." Jacoba squeezed her hand. "Don't worry—I gave Victor the address of the hotel where we mean to stay in Paris, and I daresay there will be a letter waiting for us the moment we arrive. Or one will come shortly afterward."

Isa hesitated, but what choice did she have? She could never go back to the shop now. Even if the imitations were never discovered, she would know they were there, and that would plague her until she told the truth.

Besides, she couldn't risk implicating Victor. Or her family. She was furious that they'd taken the matter out of her hands, but now it was done, and she didn't want to see them go to prison—or worse yet, be hanged!

She could end up in prison or hanged herself, just for making the parure. The thought sent a chill to her soul.

"All right?" her sister pressed.

She nodded. But as they raced about, preparing to go, she vowed that this would be the last time she let them bully her into doing something so despicable.

And once her husband arrived in Paris, she would find out what kind of man she had really married.

+ + +

FOUR MONTHS LATER, Victor still hadn't come or even sent word. And now she had his child growing in her belly. Dear heaven, what was she going to do?

Feeling particularly blue, she sat in the parlor of their very fine Paris town house and waited for the mail. She wasn't sure why she bothered. Clearly something awful had happened to Victor. It was easier to believe that than to think he might just have abandoned her.

A ray of afternoon sun flashed through the barely parted silk curtains, glinting off Jacoba's new gilded or-molu clock, dancing across Gerhart's recently acquired Persian rug, and bursting into sparkles in the cut-crystal bowl near her hand. But she could find no joy in all the costly newness.

With a sigh, she picked up that week's issue of the *Gazette de France* and flipped through it. An article caught her attention. Her French wasn't the best yet, but she could still decipher a bit of gossip that a local jeweler named Angus Gordon was leaving Paris to return to his native Scotland. His French wife had died, and he wanted to go home.

But what intrigued her was that the fellow had built his reputation by creating exquisite imitation jewelry.

She muttered an oath, something she was doing more and more lately. If her sister and brother-in-law hadn't been so impatient, the three of them might have built a similar business in Amsterdam.

No, that would never have satisfied them. Gerhart was already hinting that Isa should make more imitations to sell as real. So they could buy an even better house in an even better part of Paris, with better chances for social advancement.

She suspected that he just wanted more money to wager on wrestling bouts. He thought he could always win since he'd been a wrestler briefly himself, before he'd injured his knee. And the very thought of committing fraud repeatedly in order to provide Gerhart more money for gambling chilled her blood.

Jacoba wandered in, thumbing absently through a stack of mail. She looked different now, with her hair short and fringed about her face to change her appearance. Gerhart wore a beard now for the same reason.

Swiftly turning over the newspaper, Isa asked, "Anything for me?"

At the quiver in her voice, her sister's head came up. "It's just bills." She walked up to the table. "My dear, I hate to see you like this. Don't you enjoy being able to buy what you want and go to the theater whenever you wish?"

"That was always your dream, not mine." Isa's hands shook now, too. "I just wanted Victor."

Something like guilt flashed over Jacoba's face before her expression hardened. "Well, it's clear he's not coming. He took the earrings and left, the wretch, and there's nothing we can do about it. We don't even have a way to find him."

The truth of that statement struck Isa hard. "We wouldn't *have* to find him if you and Gerhart hadn't gone to him behind my back. He was probably so disillusioned to learn that his beloved wife was no better than a counterfeiter that he—"

"Has it occurred to you that perhaps he married 'his beloved wife' in the first place because of her post at the jeweler's?" Jacoba snapped.

Isa blanched. No, that hadn't occurred to her. But it should have.

With an oath, Jacoba hurried to sit beside her and take her hand. "I'm sorry, sister, I shouldn't have said that."

Misery choked her. Jacoba was merely voicing fears that Isa hadn't wanted to admit to herself. It was time she faced the truth. After all, it had never made sense to her that a fine, stalwart fellow like Victor would consider her worthy to be his wife. She wasn't tall and elegant and blond like Jacoba. She wasn't a good cook, which every man wanted, and she liked to spend her hours poring over design books and experimenting with smelly chemicals.

"Do you really think he married me because of . . . my post?" Isa managed.

"Of course. The jeweler constantly sang your praises. So if Victor married *you*, he knew he could stay on longer. The jeweler would have found something for him to do, if only to keep you there."

Isa's heart broke. She hadn't thought of it in that way,

but it made sense. Had she always been the mouse to him, someone to shoo off once he got what he wanted? Had she really only been a convenient means to an end?

How could she not have seen that?

But she knew how. She'd been so enamored of his sweet kisses, so caught up in the idea of healing his pain from the war that she hadn't seen the real him. All it had taken was those diamond earrings dangled in front of him, and he'd sold his soul to the devil.

And thrown away their marriage in the process.

"I'm sorry to be so blunt," Jacoba said softly, "but I thought you would have figured it out by now." She tightened her grip on Isa's hand. "You deserve better than Victor Cale."

Isa stared at her sister a long moment, then lifted her chin. Yes, she *did*. She deserved a husband who didn't hide his ulterior motives behind his reserve. Who didn't run off without saying goodbye.

Who didn't collude with her family to steal things.

"He only wanted to use you," Jacoba added.

Like you and Gerhart? Isa nearly said.

It was dawning on her that she also deserved better than to be used by her kith and kin. She had a child to consider. It was one thing to let them use *her*, but it would be quite another to let them use her child. And they would surely find a way to do it.

"Shall I fetch you something?" Jacoba asked, all soothing kindness now that she'd made her point. "You have to keep your strength up for the babe, you know. Perhaps some of those summer peaches you love?"

"Yes, thank you," she murmured.

As soon as Jacoba was gone, Isa flipped back to the article she'd been reading. Mr. Gordon had told the paper that his main regret in leaving Paris was that he had to leave his French apprentices behind. They didn't want to go to a land as wild and barren as Scotland. So now he would have to train new ones in Edinburgh, and that would take time.

Her heart began to pound. She tore out the article, then tossed the rest of the paper into the fire so Jacoba and Gerhart wouldn't figure out that she was planning something.

Was she? It was a mad idea at best, to think she could convince a stranger to hire her as his apprentice and take her with him to Scotland. How was she supposed to manage it?

By steeling her heart and swallowing her fears. It would take strength and courage to get away. And she had to get away. She dared not stay with her family any longer if she wanted to have a respectable future.

Papa had left her Mama's ruby ring, which might cover the cost of the passage if this Mr. Gordon wouldn't agree to pay for it. And she had her talent. All she had to do was show the jeweler what she was capable of, and be honest with him about what she wanted. If he had any heart at all, he might be swayed when she told him her soldier husband was dead.

It was almost true, after all. Victor might as well be dead to her, along with her old life and all it meant to her. If he'd wanted to find her, he could have, and so far he'd made no effort.

Tears stung her eyes, and she fought them back. No more tears allowed. No more waiting and hiding from life. If she was to save herself and her child, that must all end.

She would be *Mausi* no more.

1

London
September 1828

VICTOR CALE PACED the foyer of Manton's Investigations in an unassuming town house on Bow Street, praying that his longtime friend Tristan Bonnaud was here today. Tristan had to convince Dominick Manton, owner of the investigative concern, to try Victor out as an investigator.

It wasn't as if he didn't have useful skills—he was fluent in six languages, he had decent aim, and he'd already done some investigative work. It might even be considered an asset that he'd recently been discovered to be cousin to Maximilian Cale, the Duke of Lyons and one of the wealthiest and most powerful men in England.

Most important, Tristan wouldn't hold the crimes of Victor's father against him, which was refreshing. Sometimes he felt as if he wore his father's actions like a brand, even though Max never so much as alluded to them. Indeed, Max went out of his way to treat his newfound cousin well.

That was the trouble. Max seemed determined to show him off in high society, where Victor could never feel comfortable. A childhood spent in English regimental camps and three years in the Prussian army had hardly prepared him for such a life. Nor had his brief, ill-fated marriage to a lying thief.

He scowled.

"Mr. Manton will see you now."

Victor turned to find Dominick Manton's butler, Mr. Skrimshaw, standing there in a bright salmon waistcoat, blue Cossacks, and a coat so over-braided and frogged in gold that he looked like a soldier from some war of fashion. "I'm not here to see Dom," Victor pointed out.

"'Come, gentlemen, we sit too long on trifles.'" With that curt and curious statement, Skrimshaw headed for the stairs, clearly expecting Victor to follow.

Only then did Victor remember that Skrimshaw not only acted in the theater sometimes but had a penchant for quoting lines from plays. He wished the irritating fellow had a penchant for speaking and dressing plainly, instead. The man's coat was an assault on the eyes. Though perhaps it was a costume. One never knew with Skrimshaw.

When the butler ushered him into Dom's study, Victor relaxed to find both Dom and Tristan waiting for him. Whenever he saw the two half brothers together, he was struck by the family resemblance. Both men had ink-black hair, though Tristan's was longish and wildly curly, while Dom's was cropped shorter than was fashionable. Tristan's eyes were blue and Dom's green, but they were of the same shape and size. And both men had the sort of lean attractiveness that made women blush and stammer whenever either entered a room.

That was where the resemblance ended, however, for Tristan liked a good joke, a fine glass of brandy, and as many pretty females as he could tumble without compromising his work as an investigator.

Dom liked work and naught else. The man meant to make Manton's Investigations a force to be reckoned with. Apparently jokes, brandy, and pretty females were unacceptable distractions.

So it was no surprise when Tristan was the one who came forward to clap a hand on Victor's shoulder. "How are you, old chap? It's been a few weeks, hasn't it?"

"A few." Victor shot a glance at Dom, who remained seated. The man's expression gave nothing away.

He wished Dom weren't here, too. That might make this very awkward.

"Sit, sit," Tristan said as he leaned against the desk with arms crossed. "Tell us why you've come."

With a sigh, Victor settled into a chair. In for a penny, in for a pound. "It's simple, really. I was hoping you might take me on as an investigator." When both men looked surprised, he went on hastily, "You won't have to pay me, just cover my expenses. Max gives me an ample allowance. But I need something to do."

He'd spent enough time playing the role expected of him as Max's long-lost cousin. He had to get back into the world of investigations. To start looking for his betraying wife again.

Tristan exchanged a glance with his older brother. "Tired of the ducal life already, are you?"

"Let's just say that nobody warned me what it would entail. I've done naught but attend dinners and parties and balls where I'm bombarded with questions about my life abroad, none of which I can answer without bringing down scandal on the house of Lyons." Victor shifted in the small chair. "And when people aren't interrogating me, they're talking about fashion or who placed the latest wager in White's betting book. Or, worst of all, about whether waltzes really are morally reprehensible."

"What, you don't have an opinion about the moral implications of the waltz?" Tristan quipped. "I'm stunned."

"I don't like dancing," Victor grumbled. Especially since he didn't know how. Though one of these days he probably should learn.

"I loathe dancing myself," Dom put in, "but it's the primary way to meet ladies in good society."

"Victor doesn't need to meet ladies," Tristan said dryly. "They throw themselves at him. Always did. And he always ignored them. Of course, now that he's the duke's first cousin once removed, he's eminently more eligible."

Except for the fact that he was already married—though no one knew that. No one could *ever* know that.

He tensed as an image of Isa leapt into his mind, young and sweet and adoring. But it had all been an act.

She'd been setting him up for betrayal from the beginning, her and her scurrilous family.

After all these years, he could still hear his inquisitors in the Amsterdam gaol. *She used you, you besotted arse! Yet you protect her.*

He had . . . at first. He'd remained silent throughout his ordeal, thinking that she couldn't have been part of it. It had taken him years to admit to himself that she must have been.

So now he searched for her wherever and whenever he could. He'd suspended the search when he'd come to London, in hopes that finding his English family might enable him to forget her and make a new life for himself.

Except that he couldn't. The injustice of what she'd done ate at him. He had to find her. He *needed* to find her. He told himself it was because he didn't want his past with her coming up to harm his cousin unexpectedly, but deep down he knew that was a lie. Finding her was the only way to get some peace. Because she still, after all these years, plagued his dreams.

He gritted his teeth. It was all the fault of the damned duke and his new duchess, with their billing and cooing. Max and Lisette were so deeply in love that doves probably roosted in the canopy over their bed. Victor was truly happy for his cousin, but sometimes envy choked him.

Envy? Ridiculous. The only thing he envied was that their life was settled and his wasn't. If he didn't find Isa, he'd be tied to her until he died. He should probably divorce her—the Dutch laws were more lax than the

English ones—but he refused to set her free when he was still enslaved to her memory. Besides, he wanted to retain the power of a husband over his recalcitrant wife for when he found her. He wanted to be the one to bring her to justice.

The snide voices of the past intruded on his memories: *Tell the truth—it was your wife who made the imitations, who stole the real diamonds.*

His inquisitors had probably been right, damn them. And he would make her pay for it, by God, if it took him a lifetime to do so.

"The point is," he said curtly, "I have no stomach for this life of parties and such. I need a change."

He also needed to learn the tricks of finding people, something for which Dom was famous. Victor had gleaned a few from his cases with Tristan in Antwerp, but not enough. And now that he had financial resources, he could widen his search. The half brothers might even help him, if he proved himself useful to them.

"We do have that one case you were about to turn down," Tristan said to Dom.

"Why would you refuse a case?" Victor asked.

"Because it's odd," Dom said. "Pays well, but I don't know what to make of it. And it's going to take some time, not to mention travel."

"Victor would be perfect for it," Tristan pointed out. "He speaks Dutch, he's lived in Belgium . . . and he's good at picking out a lie from the truth."

"Tell me, what do you know about Edinburgh?" Dom asked.

Victor blinked. "It's a city in Scotland, filled with damned fine soldiers who make damned fine whiskey. Why?"

"How would you like to sample that fine whiskey straight from the still?"

Victor's blood quickened. "I would if it means you're offering to send me to Scotland on a case."

"Does your cousin know you want to do this?" Dom asked intently.

"Does it matter?" Victor countered.

Tristan laughed. "Dom isn't eager to involve the duke in our affairs any more than is absolutely necessary. He's still smarting over how everyone insists on calling the agency 'The Duke's Men,' even after all these months."

Max had been forced to give the press a rather convoluted tale of how he and Lisette had found Victor, and in the process the press had conflated Dom's agency with Max. Which annoyed Dom exceedingly.

"And how would *you* feel," Dom snapped at Tristan, "if the business you'd worked so hard to build were credited to a duke who did nothing?"

"Nothing?" Tristan countered. "He gained us the favorable press that is bringing us all these new clients." A sudden gleam entered his gaze. "Not to mention, he provided us with a free clerk."

"Don't let Lisette hear you call her a clerk," Dom shot back, "or you'll find yourself doing investigations at the back of beyond."

In addition to being Max's duchess, Lisette was

Dom's half sister and Tristan's sister. The daft female enjoyed organizing their office as a sort of hobby.

Manton's Investigations was a family business in every sense of the word.

Victor ignored their usual sparring. "Let me take care of Max. I assure you, he won't interfere with my involvement in Manton's Investigations. He has his life; I have mine."

Dom looked skeptical, but Tristan said, "Come now, Dom, what will it hurt to give Victor a chance? You were going to turn down the case anyway, and now you won't have to." When Dom looked as if he was wavering, Tristan added, "We do owe Victor, you know. If not for him and the duke, I'd still be back in France, wishing I could come home."

A long sigh escaped the older brother. "Fine. But only one case to start with. Then we'll see."

"Thank you," Victor said, a weight lifting from his chest.

"You won't thank me when you see what the case is." Dom hunted through a stack of files, then handed one to Victor. "It's the sort of unsavory work that I hate doing: investigating a man's prospective fiancée for his meddling mother."

Victor noted the signature on the letter on top. "The client is a baroness?"

"A dowager baroness, Lady Lochlaw. She isn't pleased with her son Rupert's latest love interest, a Dutch-speaking widow named Sofie Franke, who claims to be from Belgium."

Franke? That was the maiden name of Victor's mother. How odd.

"Apparently, her ladyship thinks that the widow is suspiciously lacking in a knowledge of Belgium," Tristan said. "Given your long sojourn there, you ought to be able to tell if she's lying."

Victor skimmed the letter, and his heart began to pound. "And this Mrs. Franke makes her living designing imitation diamond jewelry?" Surely not. How could it be?

"That's right," Dom said. "You can read through the entire file later, but the main points are that according to the records at Customs, she entered Scotland from France with her business partner, another jeweler, nearly ten years ago. And when we put Eugène Vidocq on the case in France, he discovered that the Paris address listed for her at Customs never had a tenant. Indeed, we can find no record of any Sofie Franke living in Paris before this woman got on a boat in Calais to go to Edinburgh. So you can see the problem."

He certainly could. Excitement growing in his chest, Victor flipped through the papers. "Is there any mention of the woman's age or what she looks like?"

"Why?" Tristan asked with lifted eyebrow. "Is how she looks important?"

"Perhaps," Victor said. *Though not for the reason you think, you sly dog.*

"The baroness described her as a 'grasping siren with her hooks in my son,'" Dom said dryly, "so I assume she's somewhat pretty. As for age, the baroness didn't mention it, probably because she doesn't know, but considering that the baron is only twenty-two, his lady friend can't be *too* old."

"Yes, but the woman is a soldier's widow," Tristan pointed out. "The Belgians haven't fought any wars since Boney—and that's been thirteen years. Depending on when her husband died, she could be well past thirty, easily."

A soldier's widow. Victor's excitement ratcheted up a notch. It made sense that Isa would stick as close to the truth as she could. "She may have married young." And she might know that her soldier husband was out for her blood.

What were the chances of there being *two* Dutch-speaking female jewelry designers with a penchant for imitation diamonds and soldier husbands? The timing was right, and Isa could very well have fled to Paris when she left him. There was also the fact that Mrs. Franke was at the very least hiding her real name and place of origin. And that she bore his mother's maiden name.

Still, it made no sense. The Isa he thought he'd known—shy and hesitant and reliant on her family and him for everything—would never have had the fortitude to travel across the sea and become a partner in a business.

And the Isa of his suspicions—a scheming thief who cared only about money—wouldn't have settled down in such a place as Edinburgh for ten years. She would have stayed on the Continent to live the high life under her assumed name. With her talent, she might even have gone on to more thieving, and that would have required moving around.

So how could Mrs. Franke be Isa?

"Soldier's widow or not," Dom said, "she has to be young enough to bear Lochlaw an heir."

Victor froze. "So the baroness really thinks her son and this woman mean to *marry*?" The irony of it didn't escape him.

"Her ladyship seems very sure of it," Dom replied. "Her son will inherit a great deal of money, and he has a title besides."

His blood chilled. Well, *that* would certainly attract a scheming thief. Still, ten years was a long time to plot to entice a baron, especially since she would have had to start when the man was only twelve. And would she really be fool enough to commit bigamy?

Though perhaps she'd assumed that Victor had gone to prison for her crime. With her false name, she might have felt certain that no one would uncover her past.

"We can't know the true situation for sure," Dom went on, "until you get there and assess matters. You know these dowagers—they always think unsuitable women are trying to reel in their eligible sons."

"Actually, I *don't* know these dowagers," Victor said. "Five months in London society hardly qualifies me as an expert. So you probably shouldn't play up that I'm the duke's cousin, because I'm bound to disappoint your client if that's what she's looking for."

"The baroness didn't hear of us because of the 'Duke's Men' connection," Tristan put in, "but because of a referral from someone in Edinburgh whose case Dom handled a few months ago. She may not even recognize your name." He cast Victor an amused glance. "So you can be as boorish as you please, old chap. She won't know you as anything but one of our investigators."

Victor let out a breath. "Good." Because if Mrs. Franke *did* turn out to be his missing wife, he would prefer that Isa not learn of his grand connections—not at first, anyway. The last thing he needed was for the thieving chit and her family—if they were still about— to try insinuating themselves into Max's life on the basis of Isa's marriage to Victor.

A marriage Victor meant to put an end to once and for all . . . assuming the woman in question was Isa. If he could prove that she really had been involved in the theft of the royal jewels, then no court in Europe would contest a divorce.

And he damned well *would* see her and her relations prosecuted for it.

The image of Isa's last stark note to him flashed into his mind:

> *Dear Victor,*
> *Our marriage was a mistake. I want*
> *something more than you can offer, so I've*
> *taken a position with a jeweler elsewhere.*
> *One day you will thank me.*
> *Isa*

Thank her? Even then, he'd known *that* would never happen, though he hadn't quite believed her note. Even after she didn't come home, even after her family disappeared, supposedly going off to look for her, he'd thought she was just suffering a case of new wife's nervousness. That she would come back to him soon.

All of that had changed a week later, when someone at the palace discovered that one of the commissioned parures was imitation. When the authorities had come after *him*, he'd realized that Isa had really left him. That she'd intentionally sent his life spiraling down into hell.

Only then had he looked back to see the little signs he'd missed. Yes, she'd been an innocent on their wedding night, but that had been the only truthful thing about her. And perhaps she'd lied about that, too, sprinkling pig's blood on the sheets or something. He'd been so stupidly in love that he would have believed anything she told him.

Not anymore. After her desertion—and his weeks of "interrogation"—his heart had grown hard as stone. He'd taught himself to be cold and thorough and unmoved by feminine wiles. So this time he would be prepared. He would turn the tables on *her*.

Perhaps then he could purge her from his mind once and for all.

+ + +

A FEW DAYS later, Victor arrived in Edinburgh. He hadn't been surprised to learn that Max owned a house here, but he'd been touched when Max offered to let him stay in it as long as necessary.

He'd almost refused the offer, in case his quarry found out his connection, but it was hard to say no to the cousin he was just getting to know, and even harder to say no to the man's meddling wife.

Fortunately, the house wasn't a large, imposing palace in the center of town, but a villa outside the city proper. He should be able to stay there relatively anonymously, especially after he made it clear to the servants that his presence in Edinburgh needed to be discreet.

As soon as he got himself situated, he headed off to Charlotte Square to meet his new client, driving a phaeton from his cousin's stables. But Lady Lochlaw proved to be not at all what Victor had expected, and not because of her relatively young age, either. Though the term *dowager baroness* might have led some to expect a doddering old lady, he'd known better. She was newly widowed, barely out of her mourning period, and with a twenty-two-year-old son; it made sense that she be in her forties.

He *had*, however, expected a woman very aware of her consequence and wealth. It was why she was hiring him to investigate her son's "friend," after all. And since describing another female as a "siren" generally showed a woman to be secretly envious, he'd also assumed she was unattractive.

Nothing could have been further from the truth. The moment he was shown into the drawing room of her fashionable town house, he was taken aback to find Lady Lochlaw tall and handsome, with honeyed curls, crystal-blue eyes, and a smile that would make any man feel at ease. Or the opposite, if the man happened not to be interested in what she was selling.

Which was why, when she ran her gaze down him familiarly while he was being announced, he had to grit his teeth. "My lady," he said with a little bow.

"Please, Mr. Cale, do not stand on ceremony with me," she purred as she approached to take him by the arm and guide him to a settee. "This isn't stuffy old London, you know."

When she sat down and patted the place next to her, he picked a spot at the other end of the settee and said firmly, "Ah, but you are still my employer, my lady. I wouldn't dare to presume."

It was a phrase he'd picked up at those London parties, though he'd never had to use it before.

"How very decent of you." She cast him a dazzling smile. "Still, if I'd had any idea that dear Mr. Manton would send me such a *braw* fellow, as we Scots say, I would have insisted that you stay here at the town house." With a fluttering of her lashes, she leaned forward to run a finger down his arm. "His letter of introduction said you fought at Waterloo. You must have been quite a sight on the battlefield."

Trying not to stiffen visibly, Victor managed a bland smile. "Since I was only seventeen at the time and wet behind the ears, I imagine I was." He made his tone crisp and professional. "Now, perhaps we should discuss the situation regarding your son."

She stared at him, then sat back with an exaggerated sigh. "I only mentioned the war because my husband and I toured Waterloo in later years. Since we'd traveled all over Belgium, I found Mrs. Franke's claim of being from Brussels rather suspicious when she didn't seem to know much about it."

That made sense. Isa had never been to Belgium. Assuming Mrs. Franke was Isa, that is.

"I see." He drew out a notepad and a pencil. "When did your son and Mrs. Franke first become acquainted?"

"Acquainted? I fear it's more than that. With her being so much older than Rupert—"

"How much older? Or do you know?"

"She looks to be thirty at least."

Isa would be twenty-eight. "And they've known each other how long?"

"Only a year. They met when my son brought my jewelry into her shop to be cleaned."

"But she's lived here for ten. Are you sure he didn't meet her before?"

"He was in school. He only came home after he reached his majority."

"Ah, of course." He scribbled notes in his pad. "Can you tell me anything else about Mrs. Franke that's not in the materials you sent Manton's Investigations? I gather, from your use of the term *siren*, that she is attractive."

Her ladyship examined her fingernails. "She's pretty in a vulgar sort of way. I'm sure you know what I mean."

"Not really." He began to dislike the baroness. And feel sorry for her son. "In my experience, women are either pretty or plain, and I find both sorts equally distributed in all walks of society."

Her gaze turned piercing. "Indeed? In *my* rather

more vast experience, vulgar women lack the fine features and graceful movements of a woman of true breeding." She leaned close again, as if to betray a confidence. "She walks like a man, as if she's always in a hurry to get somewhere." Her voice turned cynical. "And we both know where she's in a hurry to get: into my son's fortune."

He took out the file he'd brought with him and made a show of flipping through it. "My understanding is that she's a partner in a jewelry shop that does quite well."

"Exactly!" she said. "A woman in trade? The very idea is appalling!"

"My point is, madam, that she has no need of your son's fortune."

"Oh, please do not insult my intelligence." With an elegant roll of her eyes, Lady Lochlaw laid her arm along the back of the settee. "Any woman would leap to snag a rich young baron like Rupert, but especially a woman of her sort, grasping enough to go into trade."

Inexplicably, that raised his hackles. "What did you expect a widow to do after she was deprived of the husband who'd provided for her? Starve?"

The minute he spoke the words he regretted them, for her ladyship's gaze narrowed on him. And why was he defending the wife who'd deserted him, who had set him up to pay for her crimes? Mrs. Franke might not even *be* his wife. He must remember that, and stop antagonizing the woman who was going to pay Manton's Investigations.

"Forgive me," he said. "I have a tendency to speak

too bluntly. All those years in the army made me ill-suited for the company of ladies 'of true breeding' like yourself."

She softened. "I wouldn't go so far as to say 'ill-suited.'" Her gaze trailed down him. "Even ladies of true breeding sometimes enjoy a taste of wild game, if you take my meaning."

He stifled a sharp retort. "If you don't mind, my lady, I have a few more questions about the case."

Her eyes glittered briefly. Then she managed a smile. "You are all business, aren't you, Mr. Cale?"

"It's what I do best."

"Well, then, I hope that in the midst of your dogged pursuit of the truth, you will do me one teeny-tiny favor." As he stifled a groan, she bent nearer to whisper, "I need you to keep your true reason for being in Edinburgh secret."

Oh, *that* kind of favor. Thank God. "I assure you I am always discreet."

"Of course," she said hastily. "You see, I don't want my son to guess why I've brought you here. Technically, he holds the purse strings, though he loans them out to me without a thought. But I should not want to give him a reason to take them back."

"Right." He was beginning to get an interesting picture of this baron—young, impressionable, entirely under his mother's thumb.

Except for his interest in Mrs. Franke.

Lady Lochlaw flashed him her shark's smile. "But I need you to join us on several social occasions, so you can observe him and Mrs. Franke together. Tonight we three are going to the theater, and I'd like you to accompany us. I was hoping you could pretend to be someone . . . well . . . more appropriate."

"Like who?" he said coolly.

"Perhaps a distant cousin, come from London to visit me."

"Don't you think your son will know that I am not your cousin?"

She waved her hand dismissively. "He pays no attention to such things. I have a hundred cousins." A scheming smile crossed her lips. "And if you play one, then you can be the concerned male relation, asking questions that no other man could." Her eyes lit up. "Except, perhaps, a suitor. You could pretend—"

"No, my lady," he cut in. "I would never presume." Clearly he'd be using that phrase quite often with his new client. "And if a stranger suddenly appears in your life as a suitor, your son will not only grow suspicious, but may start investigating *my* suitability for *you*."

Her face fell. "I hadn't thought of that." She gave an exaggerated sigh. "Very well, a cousin it is. You needn't change your name—there must be a Cale somewhere in my line." She glanced at him. "You don't mind, do you? The client who recommended Mr. Manton's services said that your employer actually had to do a bit of playacting to find out his information."

"I'm accustomed to that," he said truthfully. "I used to serve as an agent for an investigator on the Continent." Only occasionally, though she needn't know that.

"But your story won't hold water for long if your son grows curious."

"It won't need to hold up long, because you are going to make sure the matter is resolved quickly. We're having our annual house party at Kinlaw Castle next week, and I want to have every bit of ammunition against Mrs. Franke by then." Her voice took on an edge. "In case my fool of a son decides to announce an engagement to her."

"I see," Victor said. "That's not much time, especially if I'll be spending part of my days and nights at social affairs, as you requested."

Then it dawned on him. If the widow and Isa *were* one and the same, Isa would know it was a lie.

Yes. She would.

A smile curled his lips. And she would wonder what he was up to, and she wouldn't be able to say a damned thing. He liked that idea. Let her shake in her boots for a while. That might prompt her to unveil her real purpose more swiftly.

"I'm sure you can manage it, Mr. Cale." The baroness flashed him a sultry smile. "It's what I'm paying you for, is it not?"

The butler appeared in the doorway. "Mrs. Franke is here, my lady."

Victor stiffened. What the devil?

"Send her right up, if you please." Lady Lochlaw smiled brightly at Victor. "When I got your message that you were arriving today, I invited Mrs. Franke to take tea with us. I thought you might as well get right to it, and form your first impressions without my son around and without having to resort to subterfuge. Clever of me, wasn't it?"

"Quite clever," he bit out.

His heart was hammering, and his blood had chilled. He'd thought he'd have more time before he came face-to-face with her. He'd assumed he would get a chance to see her without being seen, so he could be sure it was *her*. Then he'd have time to figure out her game before he revealed his presence.

Damn! If Mrs. Franke *was* Isa, he couldn't confront her publicly yet. He still had no proof that she'd ever stolen anything, so he couldn't take her prisoner. And if he claimed her as his wife, what was to stop her from fleeing on the next boat to America or Canada or Italy?

Besides, he wasn't ready to open his past to public scrutiny—it might damage Max, who'd done so much for him, or put a stain on Manton's Investigations.

He needed to play this very carefully.

Tucking his notepad into his pocket, he rose and went to the window, positioning himself where he might get a look at her before she spotted him, since presumably she would head right for her hostess.

As if through a fog, he heard the butler announce her, and he turned to see a woman enter. For one heart-stopping moment, Victor thought it *wasn't* Isa. Though the hair was the right color, the woman was too fashionably dressed. Isa would never have possessed the courage to wear such a vibrant red. This woman's breasts were bigger than Isa's had been, and she was a bit taller than he remembered.

Then she bent to press the hand of the baroness, who hadn't bothered to rise, and he saw the high heels of her half boots. The height came from those.

But the trim, pretty little ankles were hers—he would recognize those anywhere. So when he heard her murmur, "Good afternoon, my lady, I hope you are well," in a lightly accented voice, he wasn't surprised that it was Isa's—though her tone was more self-assured than he remembered.

"My dear Mrs. Franke," Lady Lochlaw said, "we have another guest for tea today, whom I thought you might like to meet. May I introduce my cousin, Mr. Victor Cale?"

With her back to him, Isa froze.

Good. He hoped he'd thrown her into a panic. He was looking forward to seeing her alarm at being caught, after all these years. Or better yet, worried about what vengeance the husband she'd betrayed might mete out.

She began to turn toward him slowly, as if in a dream. He just had time to glimpse the porcelain skin, full lips, and other sweet features he'd found so compelling nearly ten years ago, when her gaze met his.

To his shock, it was ablaze with fury.

2

ISA WANTED TO throttle him. She'd known something was up when Lady Lochlaw, who didn't seem to like her, had invited her for tea. But she'd never dreamed that the woman had somehow unearthed her worthless scoundrel of a husband!

How dared he show up *now*, after she'd finally accepted that he would never return? She had a good life. She and Angus Gordon had built their jewelry shop into one of the preeminent ones in Edinburgh; she had friends who cared about her; and, most important, her daughter, Amalie, was happy and healthy and doing well at an expensive boarding school in Carlisle.

Yet now, after years of abandonment, he meant to trample on all her achievements by insinuating himself into her life as her husband. As Amalie's *father*.

Oh, Lord, he could take Amalie away! It was his right under the law in every country. Especially if he revealed her part in the theft years ago.

Though he could hardly do that without implicating himself, could he?

Suddenly Lady Lochlaw's words registered—*May I introduce my cousin . . .*

Victor couldn't possibly be related to the baroness. He was Belgian, not English.

But what reason would the baroness have to lie about it? And as her sister had pointed out years ago, Isa didn't really know much about the man she'd once been in love with.

After a decade of parsing every interaction for clues to his real nature, she still didn't. But the cold, calculating look in his eyes told her that he had known that she was here. He had come here specifically for her, curse him to hell.

How had he found her? And how much did Lady Lochlaw know? Was Isa about to find her business concern compromised because the baroness had learned that she was living under a false name? Or worse yet, that her family had been involved in a crime?

If he revealed that, Amalie would be taken from her for certain. Oh, Lord!

She squeezed the reticule that held the hatpins she'd made for Amalie, who was to start her new school term on Monday. Sending the girl away tore out part of Isa's soul every time, but Edinburgh had no schools for girls, and she was determined to see Amalie well educated. Now she rejoiced that her daughter would soon be back in Carlisle, safe from her blackguard of a father.

Victor could *never* have Amalie!

Stay calm. He doesn't know about her, and nobody else may even know about those imitation diamonds. They could still be sitting undetected in the palace in Amsterdam. And if Lady Lochlaw knew who you really were, she would have done this with Rupert present.

She relaxed. His mother had some wild notion that Isa was after her son's fortune. So the fact that the baroness hadn't done this in front of Rupert meant she didn't know about Isa's past at all.

"Mrs. Franke?" Lady Lochlaw asked, a note of bewilderment in her voice. "Are you all right?"

"I'm sorry, my lady," she said swiftly. "I'm just surprised. Your son never mentioned that he had a cousin coming to visit."

"It was rather sudden," Lady Lochlaw said smoothly. "And Mr. Cale is a very distant cousin; I'm not sure Rupert even knows him."

"Well," Isa choked out, "any cousin of yours is a welcome addition to our society. I'm delighted to meet you, Mr. Cale."

Would he reveal their past connection? Her blood beat a fierce tattoo in her veins.

A second passed, then two. Then Victor gave an abbreviated bow. "It's a pleasure to meet you as well, Mrs. . . . Franke, is it?"

He was taunting her, but she didn't find that nearly as unsettling as hearing his voice for the first time in ten years. Especially since he was speaking English flawlessly, with no trace of an accent. As if he were English.

Perhaps he really *was* Lady Lochlaw's cousin.

Wouldn't that be a cruel twist of fate? She let out a breath. "Yes, Sofie Franke."

"My mother's maiden name was Franke," he said in a sharp tone.

That was why she'd chosen the name in the first place—so he might find her through it. But she'd never guessed it would take him nearly *ten years* to do so. Or that she would no longer wish to have him find her. Or that when he did, he would look at her with such anger.

What did *he* have to be angry about? Clearly he'd engineered this . . . this farce of a meeting. He had come here for *some* purpose, but what could it possibly be?

A horrible thought occurred to her. What if he'd decided to hunt her down and get her to make more imitation jewels? She wouldn't put it past him. The sale of those diamond earrings wouldn't have plumped up his pockets forever, especially if he'd lived extravagantly. Which he obviously had, judging from his fine attire.

Outrage seared her. She had to get him alone, figure out what he was up to. And if another thieving scheme was his purpose, she would threaten to expose him— even if it meant exposing her own part in the previous theft.

She swallowed. Surely it wouldn't come to that. It couldn't. She had Amalie to think of.

A servant appeared in the doorway carrying a tray, and Lady Lochlaw smiled. "Ah, there's our tea. Come, sit. We can all get better acquainted."

The last thing Isa wanted was to make small talk with her rogue of a husband, but she had no choice.

Her ladyship would be watching for unusual behavior.

Besides, for Rupert's sake, she should be polite. The poor man *was* her friend, and he had enough conflicts with his mother as it was. Lady Lochlaw's flagrant flirtations perplexed him, and her dislike of his focus on scholarly interests wounded him. The woman simply refused to accept that he would never be the dashing man about town that she kept pushing him to be.

Isa took a seat and Victor followed suit. As her ladyship poured the tea, Isa seized the opportunity to look Victor over.

He kept his hair shorter these days, and his clothes were the height of fashion. Gone was the rough soldier, and in his place was a fine gentleman. He looked a little older, too, which made him even more attractive, more . . . settled in.

Yet some things about him were exactly the same. She'd forgotten how tall he was, and how well he filled out his coat. She'd forgotten that he had the aquiline nose of an aristocrat and the warm eyes of a sensualist.

She'd forgotten his crooked mouth.

How could she have forgotten that, after all the times they'd kissed—secretly at the shop, heatedly in the alley beside it, passionately in their bed . . .

Drat him, she wouldn't let him do this to her again!

She tightened her grip on her reticule. No, she would take this chance to find out as much as she could about his purpose. "So, how long do you intend to remain in the city, Mr. Cale?" she asked as Lady Lochlaw handed her a cup of tea.

His brutally intense gaze speared her. "I haven't de-cided. It depends on . . . a number of factors."

"But he's staying at least through my house party," Lady Lochlaw put in. "Aren't you, my dear?"

He stiffened. "If that is what your ladyship wants."

Her ladyship clearly wanted quite a bit more, which sent a surge of jealousy through Isa that annoyed her exceedingly. She no longer cared whose bed her wretch of a husband shared. She *didn't.*

The baroness flashed him one of her not-so-coy smiles. "Don't be so formal, cousin. You must call me Eustacia."

"As you wish, my la—Eustacia," Victor said. But his eyes were on Isa, scouring her as if trying to flay the flesh from her bones so he could see every secret in her heart. "And shall I call you Sofie, Mrs. Franke? Or do you have some nickname you prefer?"

Her temper flared at his blatant attempt to bait her. Did he think she would crumble into weeping and con-fess her real name just because he was tormenting her?

Of course he did. He'd always thought her easy to get over. "My late husband called me *Mausi* when we were first married. I suppose he thought me so meek and helpless that I would endure any insult to keep his affection. But he soon learned I wasn't a mouse after all."

His eyes burned into her. "Was your husband Ger-man? Because just as the English endearment 'my lamb' doesn't really mean a bleating, four-legged creature, *Mausi* as a German endearment doesn't really mean 'mouse.'" A haunted expression crossed his face. "It means something small and fragile and innocent. Precious, even. Perhaps that was how he meant it."

The words made her ache for the way they had been, which was probably what he'd intended. "I doubt it, or he wouldn't have—" She broke off, horrified that she'd nearly said *abandoned me*. "My husband was Belgian, Mr. Cale. Or so I thought." Her tone hardened. "I really didn't know him very well. He didn't *let* me know him very well."

"My, my, Mrs. Franke," Lady Lochlaw put in, "while this is a very intriguing conversation, it is hardly suitable."

Isa pasted a smile to her face for the baroness. "I'm sorry. I forget that you're a widow, too. No doubt talk of husbands pains you as much as it does me."

It was clear from the woman's arch smile that it wasn't talk of husbands that pained her. It was the fact that Isa had diverted Victor's attention from *her*.

"So," Lady Lochlaw said, "how is your little business doing, Mrs. Franke?"

Isa gritted her teeth. "It's doing quite well, thank you. We're about to unveil some new designs for our imitation work. You should come to the shop sometime, and I'll show them to you before we offer them for sale."

Lady Lochlaw looked horrified. "My dear, what need have I of jewelry made with imitation jewels? I can afford *real* jewels."

"We have those, too," Isa said, undaunted, "but you

might enjoy our imitation ones as well. They look so real that half the women in town are wearing them, and no one even knows. These are no Vauxhall glass, I assure you."

"Is that what you do, Mrs. Franke, make paste jewelry to fool people?" Victor asked in that faintly accusatory tone that was beginning to get on her nerves.

She stared him down. "No. I make beautiful works of art for women who wish to dress well for dinner and the theater, but who would rather spend their funds on more important pursuits than adorning themselves."

"So you actually sell your imitations?" He smiled thinly. "I would have thought the only people making imitation jewelry are those who do it for some criminal purpose."

Rage boiled up in her. The blackguard had the audacity to hint at her involvement in the theft, after *he'd* taken advantage of her skills? "Actually, I learned from my father, a respectable clockmaker. He liked to embellish his works with gems, but not everyone could afford clocks so elaborately decorated, so he sometimes resorted to imitation diamonds made of a higher-quality glass called strass. He always delineated which was which, of course."

"Of course," he echoed with faint sarcasm.

She glared at him. "He taught me the rudiments of crafting them, but I soon learned there were ways to improve them. Which I did. And I, too, always delineate which is which in my shop."

"So they're clearly not intended for a criminal purpose," he said with a joking air, though his eyes weren't joking in the least.

"No," she shot back. "That would be wrong, sir."

"Certainly, no one here is accusing anyone of wrong-doing, are we, Mr. Cale?" her ladyship put in, clearly bewildered.

Isa feared she couldn't contain her temper much longer. Setting down her empty cup, she rose. "I don't wish to be rude, my lady, but if I am to attend the theater tonight, I must return home. My gown required some alterations, which my maid is working on, and she may need to make additional ones after I try it on. It's not every day I go out with such fine companions."

"I understand completely," Lady Lochlaw said. "And I do look forward to our little expedition. Mr. Cale is joining us as well. We'll make a merry party."

"I'm sure we will," she lied. If she could keep from throwing him off a balcony.

"How are you getting home?" Victor surprised her by asking.

"I'll take a hackney." Mr. Gordon had been kind enough to bring her here, but she didn't want to impose upon him for the return trip since he had things to do.

"You can't take a hackney around the city alone," he said. "You must allow me to accompany you. I have my phaeton waiting right outside."

That was *his* phaeton she'd seen? Lord, he really was living high. She was surprised he still had any stolen funds left.

Or perhaps he'd found a more lucrative way to add

to his income—like insinuating himself into the life of a rich and lascivious widow like Lady Lochlaw.

Hope filled Isa. What if he *hadn't* come for her? What if this was just a chance meeting born of some other scheme?

Well, she would find out. And she'd start by letting him drive her around a bit. She did *not* want him to know where she lived—not with Amalie still home.

"Thank you, Mr. Cale," she said brightly. "That is very kind of you."

3

VICTOR FOLLOWED ISA and Lady Lochlaw downstairs. Isa had said that she'd thought her husband was
Belgian. He'd forgotten that he'd never told her about
his parents, ashamed of his father's madness and his
mother's early life as a tavern wench. She'd seemed so
sweet and gentle that he hadn't wanted to reveal anything of his sordid past, afraid she would recoil.

But he saw nothing of that in her now. *This* Isa was
a stranger. Lady Lochlaw was right: She *did* walk like
a man, and it only made her more attractive. This Isa
was bold, fearless, independent. There'd been no panic
in her face when she saw him, just contempt. She'd actually acted as if *he* had been the one to wrong *her*. It
infuriated him.

It shook him.

And that wasn't the only thing that shook him.
In Amsterdam, she'd worn her lush brown hair in a
simple braid wound about her head. Now she wore it

in a confection of loops and ribbons that gave her an elegance he wasn't used to.

His Isa had been young and naïve and real. It was one of the things he'd liked about her—that she was so practical. That she hadn't looked down her nose at him.

This Isa, with her beaded reticule and her ladylike manner and her rigid posture, wouldn't have given an uncouth young soldier the time of day years ago.

Worse yet, she was even more beautiful than he remembered, if that were possible. Her skin was flawless, her mouth perfect, and the new defiant spark in her eyes . . .

A groan rose in his throat. He'd always remembered them as a melting brown that turned him soft inside. Now they were a mysterious and haunting brown that made him hard—everywhere.

He choked back an oath as he handed her up into the phaeton, all too aware of her attractions. He didn't know how she'd gained those slightly larger breasts—no doubt some fancy addition to her corset—but he liked them. How the devil was he supposed to interrogate her, when all he wanted was to tear her clothes off and see what else had changed?

Admit it—you let your cock convince you to help your charming wife steal the royal diamonds! his inquisitors had shouted.

And he'd defended her. Because deep down, he'd known that he *had* let his cock do the thinking.

Never again.

With grim purpose, he leapt into the phaeton and

took up the reins. After a curt farewell to her ladyship, he set the horses going. "Where are we headed?" he clipped out before they'd even turned the corner onto the main thoroughfare.

"It doesn't matter," Isa said. "I only wanted a chance to talk to you alone. I have to know—what do you want from me, Victor? Why are you here after nearly ten years?"

The way she acted, as if *he* needed to explain things, made him grit his teeth. "I'm surprised you're even admitting that you know me, *Mrs. Franke,* since I'm supposed to be dead. Hard to ignore the husband standing right in front of you, reminding you of the vows you made." He lowered his voice. "Of the number of times we shared a bed before you deserted me."

"Deserted you!" she cried. "*You* were the one to run off to Antwerp without a word."

"You knew I went to Antwerp?" he asked, stunned. If she'd already fled to Paris, how could she have heard that he'd gone to Antwerp after his life had been ruined?

Her eyes widened. "Oh, was I not *supposed* to know?" She sat back against the seat with a little huff. "Of course not. You intended to go on with your life, free of the mousy wife you only acquired to get to the royal diamonds. I suppose that's why you're sniffing around me again—you've spent all the money from selling your share, and you need your mousy wife once more."

His *share*? His hands tightened on the reins. So that was her tack: She was going to blame *him* for the theft of the diamonds. And why the devil did she keep harping on being a "mousy wife"?

"First of all," he growled, "I never considered you a 'mousy' anything. You came up with that all on your own. And I certainly never 'acquired' you to get to the royal diamonds." His temper must have conveyed itself to the horses, because they were dragging on the reins, wanting to be sprung. "I could claim the same thing about you: You married me to get access to that strongbox."

"You know I had nothing to do with that." She clutched the reticule she'd been mangling ever since his arrival. "I did nothing wrong!"

"Really? Is that why you're here in Scotland, living under an assumed name? Is that why you've run from me for years?"

"It wasn't you I ran from; it was my cursed family. Why else do you think I chose your mother's maiden name as an alias? My family didn't know it. And it would enable you to track me from Paris, since you knew where I was staying there." Her tone turned sarcastic. "It should have been easy enough. You used to be a soldier—didn't you ever do reconnaissance, or whatever you soldiers call it?"

He was still reeling from the idea that she'd somehow *expected* him to know where to find her when she added, "Of course, I never dreamed that you would wait ten *years*, until you needed something from me. And what *do* you need from me? Or will you keep pretending that you actually care about me?"

And let her know how deeply she'd dug herself under his skin, even after all this time? Not a chance in hell. "I need to know the truth."

"About *what*?" she cried. When people hurrying down the crowded street looked up, she dropped her voice. "Is this because you want a divorce? I'll gladly give you whatever you need."

For some reason, her eagerness to be free of him really pricked his temper. "Why, so you can marry your precious baron?" God, he sounded jealous. Which he wasn't. Not a bit.

She snorted. "Don't be absurd. I have no desire to marry Rupert, even if I could."

Yet she called the baron "Rupert." The intimacy that implied made him burn from the inside out. "I see. You're just content to be his mistress."

"*Verdomme,*" she muttered, surprising him with her use of the Dutch word for "damn it." "I don't know what *you've* been doing all these years, but I upheld those marital vows you referred to so glibly. Rupert is only a friend."

That took him entirely off guard. Especially with her pressed up against him, reminding him of how it had felt to have her beside him . . . beneath him. It made him yearn for what he could no longer have.

Which was probably exactly what she intended. "That's not what his mother says," Victor snapped.

"And you would listen to *her*, of course, since she's blond and pretty and rich."

The note of jealousy in her voice oddly cheered him.

At least he wasn't the only one falling prey to that dangerous emotion. "I hadn't noticed."

"Right," she scoffed. "Are you really Lady Lochlaw's cousin, or is that just some connection you're claiming so you can get close enough to her to . . . to . . ."

"To what?"

As he made a sharp turn into a quieter street, she grabbed the side of the phaeton. "Perhaps *you're* the one looking to marry. You didn't deny that you wanted a divorce."

"If I'd wanted that, I could have had it long before now. Dutch law allows me to divorce my wife for malicious desertion, and given the circumstances—"

"For the last time," she bit out, "I did *not* desert you! And if you try to claim that in a court, I will happily refute it. But given your part in stealing those diamonds, I'd think you'd want to avoid going anywhere near a court."

The audacity of the woman! She was *threatening* him. Bad enough that she and her scurrilous family really *had* apparently stolen the jewels, making sure he got the blame for it. But now she meant to drag him through it all *again*?

He growled, "You know damned well that I had *no* part in it. And if you even attempt to imply that I did to the authorities, I swear to God I'll—"

"Mrs. Franke!" called a voice from a passing curricle. "I was just coming to meet you!" It was a man's voice. And a very expensive-looking curricle.

Isa grabbed his arm. "It's Rupert. You have to stop!"

"Why, so you can introduce him to your *husband*?" he said snidely.

"His feelings will be hurt if you don't. And he won't understand."

"I don't give a damn," he ground out. But he reined in. He wanted to know what sort of man had caught her eye. What sort of man needed to have investigators hired to protect him from women.

The baron turned his curricle around and pulled up behind them, then handed his reins to his groom and leapt out to approach them on foot. Victor turned his head to get a good look at the man and got quite a start.

Lochlaw looked nothing like his mother. Dark-haired and spare, he wore wrinkled trousers and a coat with small holes in one sleeve. He had the rawboned features of a youth just coming into his own. But there was no denying how his eyes lit up as he came abreast of the phacton . . . and Isa.

It chafed Victor keenly.

"I'm glad I ran into you, Mrs. Franke," the baron said in a rush. "I went to your cottage to borrow Dalton's book, but your maid told me you'd gone to Mother's. So I figured you might need rescuing. I know how she can be." His gaze flicked to Victor, but though curiosity shone in his eyes, he was apparently too well bred to ask who Isa's companion was.

In his place, Victor wouldn't only have asked; he would have demanded an answer. But then, Isa *was* his wife, no matter how much she wanted to escape the connection.

"Rupert," Isa said hastily, "I've just been making the acquaintance of a cousin of yours." She shot Victor a taunting glance. "Mr. Victor Cale."

Lochlaw blinked. "My cousin?"

"Your distant cousin," Victor gritted out.

"Yes," Isa said. "Your mother introduced us. Apparently, he's here visiting your family. I suppose you haven't had the chance to meet him yet."

The young man looked intrigued. "I didn't know I had a cousin named Victor Cale. Though the name does sound familiar."

Thank God Manton had made Victor study the *Debrett's* entries for the Lochlaw family before he left London. "My mother was a Rosedale," he lied, "so our connection is very remote. I believe she was your third cousin, once removed. Or was it second cousin, thrice—"

"I shall look it up," the baron said brightly.

"No need to go to that trouble," Isa put in. Was she trying to protect her husband? Or herself?

"But it's no trouble at all," Lochlaw protested. "I enjoy looking things up. Almost as much as I enjoy experiments."

"Experiments?" Victor couldn't help asking.

"Rupert is a chemist," Isa explained. "A very good one."

The man colored to the tips of his ears. "Well, only an amateur chemist and not very good yet. But I hope to be." He cast her a worshipful glance that set Victor's teeth on edge. "Mrs. Franke inspires me."

To do chemistry? What did Isa know about chemistry? And why the devil was she "inspiring" this stripling to do it?

Lochlaw studied Victor. "I wonder why Mother never told me you were coming to visit. That's odd indeed."

Damn Lady Lochlaw for insisting that her son would never question her subterfuge. "It was a sudden thing. I had some business in Edinburgh, so I paid a call on her. Family courtesy, you know. Your mother and I actually only met for the first time today. She was kind enough to overlook the fact that my mother married beneath her and was cut off from your family."

That was sort of true, though in reverse. Victor's mother had married far *above* her station, and his father had been the one cut off from his family. Or rather, he'd cut himself off with his own unthinkable act.

Lochlaw was gaping at him now. "My mother overlooked that?" He eyed Victor more closely. "Are you sure you met *my* mother? Because that doesn't sound like her. She'd be more likely to give you the cut direct. Mother can be . . . well . . ."

"Unpredictable," Isa supplied, as if she performed such a service often.

"I was going to say rude," Lochlaw retorted, "but I suppose one shouldn't call one's mother rude. Even if she is."

Victor couldn't begin to know how to respond to that. The baron was proving even less what he'd expected than the dowager baroness.

"So how long do you mean to stay in town?" Lochlaw asked with seemingly genuine interest. "I'd be delighted to introduce you about, show you some of the sights, bring you to visit the Royal Society of Edinburgh. You could witness some experiments."

"Oh, I'm sure Mr. Cale has no time for that," Isa put in, a panicky note in her voice. "If he's here on business, he's probably going to be busy."

"Nonsense," Victor said, determined to be the fly in her ointment until he found out what he needed to know. "I can mix a little pleasure with my business." And he *was* supposed to be finding out more about Rupert's relationship with Isa.

"Wonderful!" Lochlaw said. "It's not often I have a cousin in town. They tend to avoid Mother, especially the male ones."

Victor actually found himself sympathizing with the man. "They're probably just intimidated by such a beautiful and elegant lady."

"No, I think they hate that she keeps touching them," Lochlaw said matter-of-factly. "They seem to find it uncomfortable."

"Rupert!" Isa chided.

He blinked. "Too direct?" He glanced at Victor. "I have a bad habit of saying what I mean, and not what I should. It gets me into trouble." He smiled shyly at Isa. "Mrs. Franke helps me with that, too."

Victor was flummoxed. The baron sometimes seemed more like a schoolboy than a man, but he was definitely infatuated with Isa.

Her feelings weren't quite as clear, though she and the baron were obviously close. And that irritated Victor more than he liked.

"It appears that Mrs. Franke helps you with quite a few things," he said through gritted teeth.

"Indeed she does," Lochlaw answered. "She's teaching me Dutch, so I can read Dutch articles about chemistry. There aren't many, but I hate to miss anything. I already know German and French, so Dutch isn't too difficult."

"Rupert is writing his own article," Isa explained. "He knows a great deal about something called atomic theory."

"Speaking of that," Lochlaw said to her, "I need Dalton's book. I plan to read it this evening and start work on my article tomorrow."

"You're not going to the theater?" Isa said.

"The theater!" Rupert slammed his palm against his forehead. "I forgot all about it. Is it Saturday already?"

"I'm afraid so. But if you would rather not go—"

"We have to," Rupert said firmly. "Mother insisted that I invite you. If we don't show up, she will be very vexed. I shall just have to read the book tomorrow. Can you loan it to me?"

"Certainly," Isa said, determinedly ignoring Victor. "It's best if you take me home anyway. I'm sure Mr. Cale has things to do."

"Nothing more important than squiring *you* about, Mrs. Franke," Victor said as he watched his quarry slipping between his fingers. "You can bring the book tonight, so as not to inconvenience his lordship."

"It's no inconvenience at all, cousin," Lochlaw said heartily. "I'm a regular visitor at Mrs. Franke's."

Victor clamped down on a hot retort.

Isa stood and nearly overset the phaeton. "Then it's settled." She held her reticule against her chest like a shield as she stared pointedly down at Victor, obviously waiting for him to let her out. "I don't wish to keep you, sir."

And it dawned on him why she was suddenly so eager to escape him. She didn't want him to know where she lived.

Unless she had another reason. Was she thinking of fleeing Edinburgh now that he'd shown up? His gut clenched at that possibility.

But no. She was too entrenched in Edinburgh society to just run off, and she was clearly up to something with young Lochlaw. He doubted she would give that up.

There was also the fact that she seemed to think she could once again make *him* out to be the one in the wrong. He would have to disabuse her of that notion.

Reluctantly, he descended and helped her down. Lochlaw was already heading back to his curricle, so Victor took his chance to have a word alone with her. When she tried to slip away, he caught her waist in his hands.

"Know this, Isa." He fixed her with a hard gaze. "If you attempt to leave town, I will hunt you to the ends of the earth. I'm not letting you off so easily this time."

Temper flared in her pretty brown eyes. "Nor I you," she surprised him by saying. "I don't know what it is you're up to, but I won't rest until I find out."

She thought *he* was up to something? The very idea made him want to shake her.

Or take her, over and over. Because now he was only too aware of her painfully familiar scent—violets and honey—and of the softness of her flesh beneath his fingers. Of the way her breath was quickening, as if she felt what he did—the echoes of their past reverberating around them.

"Mrs. Franke!" Lochlaw cried. "Are you coming?"

"Yes," she said lightly. "Right away."

Pushing free of Victor's hold, she said in a low voice, "One more thing. Do as you want with Lady Lochlaw. But if you hurt Rupert in any way, you will have to answer to *me*."

And with that peculiar statement hanging in the air, she left.

The hell Rupert was merely a "friend." She was protective of the man; clearly, she had deep feelings for him.

Victor had to restrain himself to keep from following them. But there was no reason to rouse the baron's suspicions; surely he could find out where she lived from someone in town. It was time to start doing what he'd been paid to do—investigating.

Now that she had as much as admitted her culpability in the theft, he meant to learn everything he could about what she'd done with the diamonds. There were a few hours before he must dress for the theater, and he would use them to study Mrs. Franke's life in Edinburgh. The next time he saw his wife, he would be better armed for the encounter.

4

ISA SHOOK UNCONTROLLABLY on the first part of the ride to her cottage on the outskirts of Edinburgh, and not because of Rupert's manic driving. Granted, he narrowly dodged hackneys and wheelbarrows at full speed, like a hare escaping a hound, but she was used to that. Thankfully, it made conversation impossible. After her encounter with Victor, she needed to settle her nerves.

It hadn't gone well, what with Victor insisting that she'd deserted *him* and looking daggers at Rupert and trying to bully her into letting him drive her home. In that moment, she'd known she had to escape him . . . and take Rupert with her.

For one very good reason.

"Rupert?" Now that they'd left Edinburgh proper and Rupert had finally slowed on the quieter country road, she could learn what she needed to know. "Have you ever told your mother about Amalie?"

"No, indeed." He clicked his tongue at the horses.

"She already disapproves of our association. If she knew you had a child, she'd make even more trouble over it."

Relief coursed through her. At least Victor couldn't find out about Amalie through Lady Lochlaw.

Then the rest of Rupert's words registered. "'Even more trouble'? What do you mean?"

He stiffened. "It wouldn't be gentlemanly for me to say."

Her heart stumbled. "I need to know."

"Oh, all right. She forbade me to invite you to the house party. And I told her that I wanted you there." A mulish look crossed his face. "I reminded her that I am lord of Kinlaw Castle, so I can invite whomever I please. So we compromised. She said I should bring you to the theater tonight, and she would judge for herself whether you could behave with propriety in good society. If you could, she wouldn't make a fuss over your coming to the house party."

Isa gaped at him. Lady Lochlaw never ceased to amaze her. The woman had one set of rules for her son and an entirely different set for herself. "I don't need to attend your house party. Don't invite me, and make your mother happy."

With a dark scowl, he flicked the reins. "I can't abide those things. If it weren't a family tradition, I'd refuse to have it. But if I do that, everyone will assume there's some horrible reason. We've only just recovered from the most recent outlandish tales about Mother."

Lady Lochlaw was rumored to have been caught in the bed of a notorious local rakehell, who happened to be married. Isa suspected that it was every bit the truth. Of course, Rupert didn't want to hear that. She wasn't even sure he would understand it. She wasn't always sure *what* he understood.

"I need you to be there," he went on. "Otherwise, I'll go mad with all the inanity."

She laughed. "Is that even a word?"

"Of course, and you should add it to your vocabulary, as it describes half of what Mother calls 'good society.' I *hate* good society; all they ever do is gossip. I never know whom they're discussing, and I never care, either. If I have to hear one more word about who is sneaking where with whom, I will shoot myself."

"You will not. You don't even like to go shooting at your estate."

"True." He slumped in the driver's seat, then shot her a sidelong glance. "Why do you ask if Mother knows about Amalie?"

She blinked at the abrupt change of subject. But Rupert never let go of a topic until he'd squeezed the facts out of it. Unfortunately, she couldn't tell him the truth; that she didn't want his mother revealing Amalie's existence to Victor. That Victor might use his rights as Amalie's father to force Isa into something.

"I like my privacy as much as you." She smiled thinly. "Why do you think I live so far out of town? If your mother knew about my daughter, she might say mean things about Amalie just to anger me. I can't have that."

"I understand." He sighed. "Amalie is a sweet girl— I'd hate for her feelings to be hurt by anybody." The baron had only met Amalie a few times, but he'd always been kind to her. "Don't worry; I won't mention anything about her to Mother if you don't want me to."

"Or to your cousin, either," she prodded as he pulled up in front of the cottage and helped her down.

"Whatever you wish," he said, though he watched her with burgeoning curiosity while securing his horses to a tree.

Avoiding his gaze, she hurried toward the cottage and prayed he would keep his promise. When Rupert was thinking of some new experiment, he paid no attention to anything. Just as Father used to do.

A lump filled her throat. She did have a fondness for oblivious men of science.

Before she was halfway up the walk, Amalie burst through the cottage door. "Mama, can I pack my new hat to bring to school with me tomorrow?"

"*May* I pack my new hat," Isa corrected her.

Making a face, Amalie fell into step beside her. "*May* I? It goes so well with my pink gown."

Rupert joined them. "Is that the gown with the spiders on it?"

"They're not *spiders*, my lord!" Amalie protested. "They're little fleurs-de-lis!"

"They seemed awfully spidery to me when I saw them last week. I'm not saying that's bad. I happen to like spiders."

Planting her hands on her hips, Amalie gave a dramatic roll of her eyes. "You're only saying that to torture me, since you know that I loathe spiders."

"Then why wear something that looks like them on your gowns?" he asked in all seriousness.

"They do not look—" She broke off with an exasperated sigh. "I don't know why we are even talking about this." One eyebrow shot up as she scanned his eccentric attire. "Clearly I know more about fashion than you, sir."

"Amalie!" Isa chided. "Don't be impudent to his lordship."

"She's right." Rupert grinned. "Fashion is not my purview. I prefer atoms to cravats any day."

Amalie eyed him askance. "How many men named Adam do you know, anyway? You're always going on about the Adams, but I've only ever met one in my whole life."

"My dear girl," Rupert said, looking genuinely shocked, "did you not even open your mother's copy of Dalton's book?"

"I opened it." Amalie sniffed. "And I closed it right back up. Honestly, sir, how do you read such nonsense? It makes my head hurt."

"Yet that monstrous new hat of yours does not?" he countered.

It was Amalie's turn to be shocked. "Monstrous! But big hats are all the rage!" When he burst out laughing, she blinked, then shot him a sly look. "Oh, I see what you're about. You're *torturing* me again. Well, it won't work. I *like* my monstrous hat." She turned to Isa. "So may I pack it, Mama?"

"Of course, dear. If you can do it without crushing

it." Remembering the hatpins, Isa opened her reticule to draw them out. "And I brought you extra adornment for it."

She'd never before made jewelry for Amalie, worried that the child might still be too young to take care of it. But her daughter was growing up, and she deserved something special as she went off to school. "What do you think of these hatpins?" Isa said, holding them out.

Amalie's eyes went wide as she took them, handling them with great reverence. "Oh, *Mama.*" She glanced up. "Did you make them yourself?"

Isa nodded. "Rupert isn't the only one who has noticed your affection for fleurs-de-lis."

"You see?" Amalie said saucily to Rupert. "*Mama* knows they're not spiders." With a look of awe, she ran her fingers over the ruby-and-diamond-crusted emblems.

"The silver is real, but the gems aren't. If you show that you can take good care of these two, I'll give you a pair to wear for important occasions that are made of gold with real gems."

"Mama!" she squealed, and hugged Isa tightly. "How fabulous!" *Fabulous* was Amalie's latest favorite word. "But these are perfect, too. I *adore* them. I'm going to try them with my hat right this minute!" She skipped back toward the cottage. "Maura and Danielle will be green with envy when they see my fabulous hatpins!"

As she disappeared inside, Rupert shook his head. "Does that girl ever *walk* anywhere?"

"Afraid not. Whirling dervishes have nothing on my daughter."

Isa still couldn't figure out how she and Victor had created such a boisterous creature. Or such a pretty one. Amalie had Jacoba's blond curls and Victor's height, but her eyes were an unearthly green.

And Isa had *no* idea where Amalie's sense of fashion came from. Isa had always been good with jewelry, but it had taken her ten years to figure out how to dress well—to pick the right gowns, find the right colors, combine the jewelry and clothing in interesting ways. Amalie had sprung from the womb knowing the right thing to wear. Perhaps Victor had a modiste in his family tree.

A sigh escaped her. What was she to do about him and Amalie? Of course, she had no intention of letting them meet until she was sure of his purpose in coming here. And then? Amalie believed that her father was a dead soldier. It would devastate her to learn that he was a live scoundrel.

They entered the cottage, and Betsy, her maid-of-all-work and sometime nanny to Amalie, asked if they needed anything.

"His lordship is just here to get a book," Isa explained.

"I looked for it when he asked about it earlier," Betsy said, "but I couldna find it."

"I know where it is," Isa said. "Were you able to finish altering my gown?"

"It's waiting for you on your bed, madam," Betsy said cheerily. She shot Rupert a knowing glance. "I'll just go get everything ready for you to try it on."

"Thank you," Isa said, suppressing a sigh.

Betsy had lofty dreams of Isa becoming a baroness. For that matter, so did Mr. Gordon. Neither of them could see that Rupert regarded her more as a teacher than as a lover. He liked to talk about science with her because she didn't scold him for it like his mother, or call him a dabbler like the local scholars who thought him too young to know anything. She wasn't sure Rupert even realized she was a woman. Victor had nothing to be jealous of, if he was indeed jealous.

A moment's fear seized her. Victor could easily destroy poor Rupert; the young man was very unsure of himself. For that matter, Victor could easily destroy *her*. If he started talking to Mr. Gordon and her friends, making them question her and her past, who knew what might happen?

Her business partner believed that her husband was dead. Desperate to escape Paris and her family, she'd thought he might be more sympathetic to a soldier's widow. Though the lie weighed on her conscience more and more through the years, it would be awkward now to explain. It might raise questions about her past that she could ill afford.

After all of Mr. Gordon's kindness to her, it would kill her to have him suspect her of thievery. Curse Victor. Why couldn't he have stayed away?

"I think I left the book in the parlor," she said to Rupert, eager to have him gone so she could figure out what to do about Victor.

As she headed into the room, the young man followed her. "Why don't you want Mr. Cale to know about Amalie?"

"Because it's none of his concern," she said, hoping that would be enough of an answer.

"Don't you like my cousin?" Rupert prodded. "He seemed nice enough."

"For a vulture circling overhe—" She caught Rupert staring and forced a smile. "I'm sorry. I merely worry that he is here to take advantage of you and your mother, now that your father has passed on."

Rupert's eyes got very round. "I hadn't thought of that."

"Sometimes poor relations swoop in to see what they can get, once the family is vulnerable."

A frown creased Rupert's pale brow. "I don't think he's poor. He drives a very costly phaeton. And while I don't know fashion, I can tell that his clothes are quite fine."

How could she possibly explain the tactics of a sharper to someone as oblivious of the world as Rupert? Gerhart had dressed finely in Paris, too. And all the while, he'd been plotting another theft. If she hadn't left when she had—

Good Lord, was *that* why Victor had thought she deserted him? Had he gone to Paris after she'd left? It would have been just like Jacoba and Gerhart to tell him some mean thing about how she didn't want him anymore.

She raised her chin. Well, she'd waited for him in Paris as long as she could. With the child growing in her belly, she'd had to act, and she would just point that out to him. *If* indeed he had gone there looking for her. She didn't trust a word he said. Not after his part in the theft.

"Are you even sure that he's really your cousin?" she ventured.

"Mother says he is, so he must be." Rupert cocked his head. "Besides, I know I've seen his name somewhere. Probably in the family tree. Or *Debrett's*. I never forget names, and Victor is an unusual one for an Englishman."

"Pay me no mind," she said. "I'm probably wrong about him." She found the book he wanted and handed it to him.

"I hope you are. Mother wouldn't like being taken advantage of."

"I imagine not." Though Isa suspected Lady Lochlaw could hold her own against fortune hunters, sharpers, and schemers of any kind.

Rupert stared down at the book for a long moment. "I want her to like you," he said suddenly.

Now, what had brought that on? "It doesn't matter," Isa said. "We can be friends whether or not she likes me."

"Friends," he mumbled, two spots of color appearing high on his cheeks. "Of course."

When he continued to stare at the book, she asked, "That *is* the one you wanted, isn't it?"

He looked up, his eyes oddly filmy. "Yes. Are you sure you can spare it?"

She laughed. "I can't make heads or tails of it, to be honest. My English is good enough for novels, but understanding a scientific book is beyond me."

"Then why did you buy it?"

"Because I thought I could glean some knowledge on using chemicals to alter the colors of imitation gems. But he never speaks of that. The book has no practical applications. It's strictly theory."

He eyed her askance. "Well, it *is* titled *A New System of Chemical Philosophy*. Philosophy tends to be theoretical."

She smiled. He could be so very literal. "I know. It was a foolish purchase." She headed for the hallway.

"You are never foolish," he murmured as he followed her.

Oh, she'd been foolish many a time. And the worst was when she'd given her heart to the man who'd trampled on it.

But no more. Tonight she would force Victor to admit his purpose in coming here, one way or another.

5

BY THE TIME Victor arrived at the Theatre Royal, he was fit to chew nails. He'd started his investigation of "Mrs. Franke" at her shop on Princes Street, hoping to speak to her seventy-year-old partner. But the place was apparently closed on Saturdays, which was interesting. Shops closed on Sunday, not on both Saturday *and* Sunday. Not unless they made very good money.

Judging from what those who ran the neighboring shops had to say, that was indeed the case. And apparently the other shopkeepers found Mrs. Franke a fascinating subject for gossip. Some praised her talent as a jeweler. Others commented favorably on her willingness to contribute to charitable causes. A few speculated about her past—whether she was Angus Gordon's illegitimate granddaughter, why she'd settled in Edinburgh, what battles her soldier husband had fought in.

None of them knew where she lived. Or if she attended church. Or anything about her family, beyond the fact that she was a soldier's widow. To hear the denizens of Princes Street tell it, Sofie Franke's life began when she arrived at her shop in the morning and ended when she left at night.

They did agree on one thing—the Baron Lochlaw was sure to marry her within the year. He visited the shop with great regularity, he spoke of her in glowing terms, and he was often seen trailing after her like a puppy. She would be a fool not to accept any offer he made.

And Mrs. Franke was no fool.

The past rose up to taunt him. *You don't expect us to believe that your wife, the talented diamond cutter, had nothing to do with the theft of those diamonds. She was no fool, your wife. She left you to pick up the pieces.*

Victor gritted his teeth as he entered the theater, an unprepossessing building with only a statue of Shakespeare for adornment on the outside. The very thought of Isa attempting to marry a rich baron made him want to smash a hammer into one of the marble pillars in the theater's surprisingly lush interior. It wasn't right that she should be *rewarded* for what she'd done.

And he was going to make damn sure that she wasn't—even if it meant exposing his own past.

Though the Theatre Royale was nicely fitted out, only thirty or so private boxes lined the walls, probably half of what might be found in a London theater. It took only one word with an usher, and Victor was promptly shown into the Lochlaw box.

Lady Lochlaw rose to greet him with a kiss to each cheek, making sure he got a good glimpse down her very low-cut gown. Her heavy perfume swirled about his head like steam rising from a harem's bathing room, but he only had eyes for Isa.

She was standing at the other end of the box under a sconce, perusing a program with the baron. She frowned as the lad tried to explain certain English words.

Lochlaw looked only marginally better dressed than he had earlier. There were no holes in his coat sleeve, but both his cravat and his hair were rumpled, and the creases in his trouser legs had already started to vanish.

But Isa was a goddess in human form. Her hair was ornamented with ostrich feathers and a glittering diadem, probably made of imitation diamonds, though it was no less beautiful for it. If that was an example of her work, it was no wonder she and her partner did well.

Her gown was far simpler than the baroness's heavily furbelowed one—white taffeta embellished with green piping, short puffy sleeves, and a respectable neckline— but the little it revealed and the way it nipped in at her waist reminded him of the last time he'd taken a gown off of her. Slowly, with the reverence of a hesitant new husband.

Now he wanted to rip it off of her with his teeth. Then cover her soft, pale flesh with his body and explore every inch with his tongue and hands and cock. He wanted to bury his mouth in the enticingly shadowed valley between her breasts, lick his way down her slender belly to the dark brown curls that covered the sweetness below . . . and drive himself inside her until she begged for more.

He fought an erection.

No wonder Lochlaw had stars in his eyes whenever he gazed at her. No wonder Lady Lochlaw saw Isa as a threat.

Just then the baron looked up and spotted him. "Ah, there you are, cousin!"

Lochlaw headed for him but Isa stayed in place, her eyes widening and her mouth flattening into a tight line that he wanted to kiss until it softened.

God, what was wrong with him? She had betrayed him, left him to deal with the authorities alone, to make apologies for *her* wrongdoing. She had left him without one look back.

And all of that melted away when he saw her in that gown.

"Good evening," he said as Lochlaw reached him. He nodded in Isa's direction. "Nice to see you again, Mrs. Franke."

She nodded, a flush rising in her cheeks.

"I'm glad you've come," Lochlaw said. "The opera is about to start, and you won't want to miss the beginning."

"Opera?" He stifled a groan. "I thought we were seeing some play called *The Iron Chest*."

"They refer to it as a 'musical play' in the program," Isa said. "But some of the reviews deemed it 'operatic.'"

Her gaze met his, soft with memory, and he was catapulted back to Amsterdam. Gerhart and Jacoba had dragged them to the opera once. He and Isa had only been able to afford the worst seats, and they'd spent most of it whispering together, since neither of them had liked the singing. His opinion of opera hadn't altered since then, despite attending a couple of them with his relations in London.

A bell rang, and Lady Lochlaw took Victor's arm to lead him to two chairs sitting side by side behind two more. Lochlaw seated Isa in the chair directly in front of the baroness, then took the one in front of Victor for himself.

As the orchestra tuned up, Lady Lochlaw leaned over to Victor to whisper, "You see what I mean about vulgar? That tiara is the height of bad taste; I daresay the diamonds in it aren't real."

Judging from Isa's stiffened back, she'd heard every word.

"I couldn't tell," he whispered. "And as I recall, in London many women wear tiaras to the theater."

Lady Lochlaw sat back with a sniff. A moment went by, during which time the music began. Then she leaned close again. "Clearly she knows nothing about opera. Why, she pronounced the word *aria* as 'area.'"

Just as he was about to point out that Mrs. Franke wasn't a native speaker of English, Lochlaw half turned to hiss, "Quiet, Mother. I want to hear the music."

And that was that.

Thank God, because Victor didn't think he could tolerate many more of the baroness's snide comments. But he did understand her reaction. Isa outshone her as a rose did a weed, despite the wealthier woman's finery and expensive jewels. That had to gall.

The first act of the opera turned out to be not as bad as he expected. For one thing, it had a decent story, with some interesting political notes. And for another, from his vantage point he had a good look of Isa in profile. He could feast his eyes as much as he liked on her glorious hair, her delicate ear, her glowing cheek.

He knew it was foolish to do so, but he let himself dwell on the times he'd kissed her just there, where her pretty neck met her shoulder, or had run his tongue down the hollow of her throat. By the time the first act ended, every part of him ached to touch her.

Bloody idiot—he wasn't here to take up with his wife again, damn it! He was here for vengeance.

No, not vengeance. Justice. That's all. He had a right to expect that.

As the interlude began, they all rose.

"How did you like it, Mrs. Franke?" Lady Lochlaw asked, casting Victor a conspiratorial glance. "The contralto's *aria* was lovely, don't you think?"

A mischievous gleam shone in Isa's eyes. "I didn't really notice. I was too busy admiring the gorgeous necklace she'd purchased from my shop. It sparkled so nicely in the gaslights."

Lady Lochlaw's smug smile vanished. "Did it have real gems? Or imitation?"

"You mean you couldn't *tell*?" Isa asked sweetly. "How odd. I would have thought it obvious to a woman of your discernment."

The laugh that rose in him unbidden caught Victor by surprise, and he nearly bit his tongue holding it back. A servant entered just then with a tray of champagne glasses, which was a good thing, since Lady Lochlaw looked fit to be tied. Feeling oddly cheered by that, Victor took a glass. But when the baron handed Isa one, and she smiled up at him engagingly, Victor's mood suddenly soured.

"So, Mrs. Franke," he said in a hard voice, "what made you decide to leave the Continent for Scotland?"

She sipped some champagne. "The death of my husband. I wanted to escape the bad memories."

"Of his death?" he bit out. "Or of your marriage?"

"Both," she said pointedly.

He gritted his teeth. So that had been an illusion, too. All the time he'd been besotted, she'd been resenting their marriage. Damn her for having hidden it so well.

Lochlaw began to frown, and even her ladyship looked wary, but Victor ignored them. "What was wrong with your marriage? Was he cruel to you? Did he mistreat you?"

"Neither," she shot back. "He didn't have to. He just acted as if I were his pet. He never told me anything of himself or his family, never let me see inside him. After he was gone, I realized I never really knew him at all."

That wasn't the answer he'd expected, though on that subject at least, she spoke the truth. He'd been afraid that if she learned the dirty secrets of his childhood, she would bolt.

In the end, she'd bolted anyway. "Perhaps you weren't married long enough to take his measure."

"Perhaps. But that's all the more reason I was stunned to learn how much he'd lied to me; how much he'd pretended to be one thing when he was quite another."

What the devil was she talking about? "You make him sound like a villain," he growled.

"See here, cousin," Lochlaw interrupted, "this conversation is becoming very rude." He cast Isa an uncertain glance. "Don't you agree?"

"Your cousin is perfectly aware that it is," Isa said. "But I'm happy to tell him whatever he wishes to know." Setting her glass down, she came toward Victor. "Still, Mr. Cale, we needn't bore Rupert and his mother with such nonsense. Perhaps you'd like to take a tour of the theater? I understand there are some very fine statues in the lobby."

"And I'll go with you," Lochlaw broke in with a scowl.

Lady Lochlaw put her hand on her son's shoulder. "No, you will not." When he glowered at her, she added, "You can't leave me here alone, dear boy. What would people think?"

"I'm fine, Rupert," Isa said as she took the arm Victor offered. "Your cousin and I will take a little walk and be right back. I need to stretch my legs anyway."

He'd succeeded in provoking her, thank God! He'd spotted an unoccupied box a few boxes over, perfect for a private discussion, so this time he would make sure she gave him solid answers.

As soon as they were in the hall, she said, "Speaking

of lies, you're not really her ladyship's cousin, are you?"

He wasn't about to reveal what he'd been hired to do, since that might spook her into fleeing. "You're the one who remarked that I never told you about my family," he said evasively. "You're right. I didn't."

"So you really expect me to believe that you're cousin to a Scottish baron." Her voice turned acid. "And not that you're insinuating yourself into her life for some devious purpose."

They'd reached the other box, so he dragged her inside and pulled her behind a pillar where no one could see them from the theater. Thrusting her against it, he braced his hands on either side of her shoulders to glare down at her.

"My devious purpose is to unmask my wife," he growled. "You can hardly blame me when I find her frolicking with a rich baron."

"*Frolicking?*" she exclaimed, half laughing. "Are you mad? I keep telling you, Rupert and I are just friends!"

"You're either blind or a fool." He lowered his head. "He watches you whenever he thinks you don't see. He stares at you as a man stares at a beautiful woman. Perhaps *you* consider him a mere friend, but I assure you, he does not. I'm a man—I can damned well tell when another man covets my wife."

Her stunned expression told him that she truly hadn't realized that Rupert's feelings for her ran that deep.

Then she steadied her shoulders. "Even if you're right, even if he does have an interest in me, why do you care? You don't want me, so—"

"Don't want you?" he said incredulously before he could stop himself. His eyes fixed on her mouth, and his heart began to thunder in his chest. "Now you really *are* a fool."

Then, driven by the rampant need that had been boiling up in his blood ever since he'd seen her this afternoon, he seized her mouth with his.

◆ ◆ ◆

ISA FROZE AT the touch of his lips on hers. She ought to fight. She ought to shove him away. But years of wishing for this very moment kept her motionless. His mouth was exactly as she remembered, tender and needy, driving her blood into a fever. His hands moved to grip her head and she covered them with her own, fully intending to push them away.

Instead, she rose into his kiss, parted her lips for him, let him slide his tongue into her mouth to tantalize and tease her. It was the most exquisite madness. And she didn't want it to end.

Suddenly they were young again, stealing kisses wherever they could, too hungry to wait for later, when they could be alone. He drank from her mouth with a slow knowing that roused her blood, and she let him, the way she'd always let him in the old days.

After a moment of heady, silken kisses, he whispered against her lips, almost reverently, "Isa, *my* Isa." Then, as if reminded of what stood between them, he said in a harder voice, "My little temptress."

And this time when his mouth took hers, it was no

longer tender. It was hard and fierce and raw, taking what it wanted with no apologies. The scent of him swamped her as he thrust his tongue into her mouth over and over, more savage than sweet.

Which thrilled her even more. The husband she'd once adored was here in her arms at last. He'd hunted her down, and he was kissing her as if ten years were but a pebble in the ocean. She exulted in it, mad fool that she was.

She slid her hands into his beautiful hair, holding him tight, not wanting to let him go. With a groan, he skimmed his fingers down her neck to brush her shoulders, then moved them lower to cup both her breasts.

A wild fever erupted in her brain. She pressed herself into his hands, and that was all the encouragement he needed to fondle her shamelessly. She felt it even through her gown and corset and shift, felt her nipples bead beneath his deft caresses. It had been so long, so very long, and he was here and she wanted him so badly she could taste it.

He must have felt the same way, for with a groan he undulated against her, his hardened shaft reminding her of the last time they'd made love, the last time he'd been inside her, the last time—

"Ah, *Mausi*," he murmured. "My sweet *Mausi*."

The word resounded in her brain, a chant from years ago that no longer held true.

She shoved him back. "Stop," she hissed. "I am not your *Mausi* anymore. If you wanted to keep your *Mausi*, you shouldn't have abandoned me."

His dazed expression gave way to hot, hard anger. "*You* were the one who called our marriage a mistake. *You* were the one who said you wanted more than I could offer, who said you were going off to find a better position." His eyes glittered at her. "When actually, you were running off to spend the money you made from those stolen diamonds."

She gaped at him. "What are you talking about?"

Pure rage flared in his eyes. "You know damned well what I'm talking about."

Her breath felt heavy, thick. "I don't. Truly I don't."

A muscle jerked in his jaw. "So you're denying the theft? Denying that you made that imitation diamond parure so you and your bloody family could steal the royal diamonds?"

Why did he keep talking as if the theft was her and her family's fault alone?

"I'm denying that I ever called our marriage a mistake," she said in a low hiss. "I don't know where you got such nonsense, but I never said any such thing. I was in love with you. Why would I have—"

Lady Lochlaw's voice drifted through the door from out in the hall. "I'm sure they're around here somewhere, Rupert. Do not fret so."

"But the second act is about to start," Rupert said peevishly. "We have to find them."

"Well, you can hunt for them if you must. I'm going back to the box."

"I'll meet you there."

Alarm seized her. She did *not* want Rupert speculating about her association with Victor, a supposed stranger. "I have to go," she murmured, turning for the door.

Victor caught her by the arm and lowered his head to whisper in her ear. "Tell me where you live, and I'll come to you later tonight. We have to talk."

"That's not what you want, and you know it." He wanted to kiss and fondle her to distraction, to slip back into her life so he could get her to make more imitations.

You *were the one who called our marriage a mistake. You were the one who said you wanted more than I could offer, who said you were going off to find a better position.*

She swallowed hard. He'd spoken the words with such conviction. But she'd never said any such thing to him! His memory was playing tricks on him.

Oh, why was she even listening to him? She *knew* what sort of man he was. She must hold fast against him. If he came to the cottage he would find out about Amalie and use her against Isa, too.

"Tell me, damn you," Victor hissed. "You can't keep running from me."

Rupert was calling her now, and the longer she waited to answer, the more curious he would become.

She stared up at Victor. "Tell me where *you* are staying, and I'll come to *you*."

He froze. Then, with a foul curse, he glanced away.

Anger seared her. He was hiding his purpose here, whatever it was. "That's what I thought." Wrenching her arm free, she headed for the door.

"We are not done, Isa," he growled.

"For now, we are." She called out, "I'm here, Rupert!"

The door opened, and Rupert thrust his head inside. The clear suspicion on his face made her stomach roil. Could Victor be right about him? Was the baron not as oblivious to her feminine attributes as she'd assumed?

"What are you two doing in here alone?" he demanded.

"The best view of the theater is from this box." Better to lie to him than risk hurting him. "And since it was empty, we thought to take a look."

He seemed to accept that. "Well, you'd better come along. The second act is about to begin." His gaze flitted behind her. "You too, cousin."

She could feel Victor's presence like a hot brand against her back, and for half a second, she feared he would say something to ruin everything.

Then she heard Victor release a breath. "I'll be along presently. I want to enjoy the view a moment longer," he said in that husky voice that made her stomach flip over.

That was the trouble. He could still reduce her to mush with just a word, which made him dangerous. Because once she let him into her life, once he knew about their daughter, there would be no going back.

Rupert whisked her from the room. "Are you all right?" he asked as soon as they were in the hall. "You look flushed."

She resisted the urge to press her hands to her hot cheeks. An idea struck. "Actually, I'm feeling unwell.

Would you mind terribly leaving the play now and taking me home?"

"I'd be happy to," he surprised her by saying.

She eyed him skeptically. "Are you sure?" Rupert tended to follow rules slavishly, and one of those rules was that people did not leave theaters before the performance was finished.

"Of course I'm sure," he said resentfully. "What sort of gentleman would I be if I forced you to stay here and suffer?"

"Thank you, then. It's very kind of you." She tamped down a niggle of guilt at deceiving him.

Tomorrow she'd take Amalie to Carlisle on the mail coach, and her daughter would be safe. Then, and only then, she could concentrate on finding out why Victor was so determined to invade her life.

6

VICTOR SPENT THE next day with the Lochlaws, because he had no way of finding Isa. The sly wench had slipped away from the theater while he was trying to regain his composure, so he'd been unable to follow her home. She might not like being called *Mausi* anymore, but she certainly had a mouse's talent for sneaking out of one's grasp.

But he would find her. Tomorrow he'd wait at the shop until she arrived, and then he'd *make* her give him answers.

I'm denying that I ever called our marriage a mistake. I don't know where you got such nonsense, but I never said any such thing.

Those words seared a hole in his brain even as he attended church services with the Lochlaws. There'd been no mistaking the shock on her face. No mistaking how she'd glossed over the theft to focus on his words about their marriage.

I was in love with you.

As his throat tightened, he cursed his easy reaction. He knew better than to believe her. She'd wanted access to the diamonds and had seen how he'd wanted *her*. In his life, in his bed.

He still wanted her. What was wrong with him? He wasn't some randy young idiot anymore; how could she still do this to him?

No doubt she'd said those words to distract him, to keep him from hounding her about the theft. Though it was odd that she hadn't denied making the imitation parure. Or at least pretended outrage at his accusation. That wasn't the behavior of a criminal avoiding culpability.

Still, she hadn't admitted to doing it, either. She'd danced around the subject, but the fact that she even knew of it meant she'd been part of it somehow.

Didn't it?

Damnation, the inconsistencies in her behavior, her character, were eating at him. He had to get to the bottom of it!

Sunday droned on into a dinner with the Lochlaws. Lady Lochlaw clearly saw her son as little more than a child to be managed, and in her presence, he became one—sulking at the dining table, mumbling answers to her barbed questions, and toying with his food.

Until her ladyship suggested that he and Victor take a walk about town. Once they were out of the house, Lochlaw's entire demeanor changed. He became friendly, expansive, chatty. He didn't even seem to be upset about finding Victor and Isa together the night before. Perhaps she'd been right. Perhaps the man really did just regard her as a friend.

They headed toward Edinburgh Castle, which Lochlaw insisted that he visit. "You can view the entire city from the Battery," the young baron gushed. "And you should also see the regalia, which is on display. The crown itself . . ."

Victor could barely attend the man's prattling. All his thoughts were for Isa—where she was, how he could find her.

He waited until they'd visited all the public areas of the great castle and were walking down High Street toward the Palace of Holyrood House before he broached the subject.

"Where is Mrs. Franke today?" he asked, trying to sound casual.

Lochlaw turned instantly nervous. "I dunno. I never see her on Sundays. Mother insists I spend Sunday with her."

"Ah."

They walked a moment in silence. Then Lochlaw surprised him by asking, "What do you think of Mrs. Franke?"

"She seems lovely," Victor said through gritted teeth. *She's my wife, damn it! Keep your bloody hands off of her!* But he couldn't stake his claim to her publicly yet. Not until he figured out what she was up to. The last thing he needed was her trying to paint *him* as the thief.

Caution was the best course of action, yet he had this visceral need to proclaim her his wife. Especially after last night's kiss, when she'd melted in his arms, reminding him of how they'd once been.

Of how *she'd* once been, generous with her soft, sweet kisses and easy acceptance of who he was. Though in truth, she hadn't really known who he was back then. After the war, he'd been so eager to calm the heavy turmoil in his soul that he'd seized on her as his oasis. Instead, she'd proved to be his Waterloo. And he'd never been the same.

Lochlaw was watching him. "Mrs. Franke *is* lovely." But he said it as if it were a curse.

Very curious. Might as well find out about the baron's feelings for Isa while the lad was willing to talk. "Your mother worries that you mean to marry her."

"And what if I do?" Lochlaw said with sudden belligerence. "Mother has no say in it. I'm the baron. I can do as I wish."

"So, is that what you wish?" Victor's gut clenched. "To marry Mrs. Franke?"

"She's the only woman who's ever really been nice to me. And since I have to marry to sire an heir . . ." A look of despair crossed Lochlaw's face. "But even if I did wish to marry her, she would never have me."

Oddly enough, the young man's woeful expression tugged at Victor's sympathies. He remembered all too well the torment he'd suffered working himself up to ask for Isa's hand, sure that she would see only a worthless soldier with no fortune, no family, and no permanent position to commend him.

"You're a man of wealth and high rank," he pointed out. "She'd be a fool not to have you."

Lochlaw shook his head. "She doesn't care about all that."

"Trust me," Victor said cynically, "every woman cares about all that."

"Not *her*."

"How do you know?"

"Because I've spent most of my life with a woman who *does* care. Mother rates flowers by their cost. Roses are 'splendid'; daisies are 'cheap.' A man who drives a phaeton or a cabriolet is 'important'; a man who drives a curricle is 'unfashionable.'"

Which was probably why Lochlaw drove one.

"But Mrs. Franke rates flowers by color, which makes more sense. She likes hydrangeas and violets because they're purple. She doesn't care about carriages, because she likes to walk."

Victor was growing annoyed that the lad knew so much about Isa's likes. Though he hadn't mentioned dahlias. Those were her favorites. Victor definitely remembered that.

Then Lochlaw added, "And she prefers red oxide of lead to white."

"Red oxide of *what*?"

"Lead. It's a chemical she uses in her work. She says it's very pretty." Lochlaw sighed. "But when I brought her some as a gift, she merely said thank you and acted as if it meant nothing."

"You brought her red oxide of lead instead of hydrangeas?" Victor said incredulously.

"Why would I bring her hydrangeas? They weren't

in season." Lochlaw blinked. "Oh, Lord, should I have brought her hydrangeas? Or perhaps some walking shoes? I don't know where to get walking shoes for ladies. I suppose at a cobbler, but—"

"Don't bring her walking shoes," Victor snapped. "Trust me on that one."

That deflated poor Lochlaw. "I'm not good with women. They're like foreign creatures to me, even Mother."

"Ah, lad," Victor said dryly, "every man the world over thinks the same. But we all muddle through somehow."

Lochlaw gazed at him beseechingly. "You're older and know more. Will you help me court Mrs. Franke?"

Victor's reaction was instant, raw, and fierce. "Absolutely not."

Lochlaw looked wounded. "Why?"

Because she's mine! "Because every man has to find his own way with a woman." He choked down anger. "And I barely know her."

That had begun to seem very true.

God, he couldn't take another minute of this. He changed the subject, and as soon as he could politely make his escape, he did.

He spent that night in restless dreams, plagued by memories he'd banished years ago. Now he dredged through them, trying to find the Isa he used to know, before he'd erected a replica of her to throw stones at. As always, she eluded him.

So, the next morning he entered the shop on Princes

Street as soon as it opened. Inside, it looked much like the one where he'd served as night guard, with glass cases flanking the sides and a door set in the back wall that probably led to the work areas.

But this shop had some feminine touches: paintings of laughing ladies dripping with gems, black velvet in the cases, a nicely upholstered settee. And vases of purple dahlias. He smiled. Clearly Isa had laid her hand on the place.

As he entered, he was greeted by a dapper old man wearing a natty wool coat, a waistcoat of figured silk, and a pair of trousers that Victor's ducal cousin wouldn't be ashamed to don.

Isa's partner? He had to be.

"Good morning, sir," the shopkeeper asked. "May I help you?"

"Actually, I was hoping to speak to Mrs. Franke."

"She's not here today, I'm afraid."

Victor's blood began to pound in his ears. Surely she hadn't fled, damn her.

"I'm her partner, Angus Gordon," the old man went on. "Perhaps there is something *I* could help you with?"

"It's a personal matter, actually," Victor snapped. "Where is she?"

"She'll be back tomorrow," Gordon said blandly. "Perhaps you should return then."

"Back?" She really *had* fled. "Did she leave town?" he demanded, throwing caution to the winds. "Where did she go? Why?"

Gordon's eyes narrowed. "And who might you be?"

Victor forced himself to calm down. He would get nowhere by antagonizing the man. Time to change tacks, and soothe Gordon's suspicions.

Somehow he managed a smile. "I'm Victor Cale, cousin to the Baron Lochlaw." Lochlaw was a popular figure around here. "Since Mrs. Franke isn't here to answer my questions, perhaps I could speak with you about her?"

"Ah, yes. The Lochlaws' cousin. I've been hearing about you." Gordon looked him up and down, dissecting him with a thoroughness generally reserved for dead frogs. "You roused quite a flurry of gossip with all your questioning of the shopkeepers on Saturday."

"I'm merely concerned about his lordship's future. I want to know what sort of woman he has taken up with."

"And of course your interest is purely selfless, borne of naught but your concern for the baron," Gordon said with a faint Scottish brogue.

Victor ignored the dollop of acid in it. "Exactly."

Gordon stared hard at him. Then he shouted, "Mary Grace!" and a slender young woman hurried into the shop through the door in the back. "Could you watch the front for a while, lassie? I've business to conduct with this gentleman."

"Certainly, Uncle," she mumbled into her chest, which wasn't hard to do, since she stood hunched over as if afraid someone might see her freckled face. She was also doing her best to hide her flaming red hair, for it was scraped up beneath a mobcap, with only a few curls peeking out to betray its color.

As Gordon led Victor into the back, which did indeed prove to be a sort of workshop, he murmured, "Mary Grace is my brother's granddaughter. She comes to the shop to get away from her plague of a mother, who's always going on about her making a splash in good society."

They passed through a labyrinth of locked cabinets and worktables, skirted a large furnace, and finally entered a cozy little room containing a leather-topped mahogany partner's desk with brass fittings, two Windsor chairs on either side of the desk, a large cabinet, and a small fireplace.

Gordon closed the door, then gestured to one of the chairs. As Victor took a seat, the man went to stoke up the fire. From behind, Gordon resembled a priest with a tonsure, his gray curls surrounding a circlet of shiny bald pate.

"So," the old fellow said, "you want to know about Mrs. Franke."

"I understand that she and the baron have a . . . more than friendly relationship."

"Humph." Gordon sat in the chair opposite the desk from Victor. "You've been talking to his lordship's mother."

"What makes you think that?" As Tristan was fond of saying, *Answer a question with a question if you don't want to answer with the truth.*

"Her ladyship is obsessed with getting the poor man out of Mrs. Franke's so-called clutches. Don't know why. Mrs. Franke is a fine lass. The young baron would be lucky to have her."

"But would she be lucky to have *him*?" Victor countered, before he caught himself.

"Why should you care?"

Victor suppressed a curse, aware of the old man's gaze on him. *Steady now, you dolt. Stop letting your emotions rule your head.* "I don't. But I confess I was wondering what she could possibly see in the man. Aside from the obvious."

"The obvious?" Gordon asked.

"His title. His fortune. His connections."

"Ah." Gordon's gaze chilled, though when he spoke again, his tone was mild. "How well do you know Mrs. Franke?"

"I just met her yesterday." That was certainly true. "Mrs. Franke" hadn't existed for him until then.

"Then I should correct the impression of her that Lady Lochlaw has obviously given you. Mrs. Franke doesn't care about title, fortune, or connections."

Was every man who knew Isa completely smitten? Why did they all see her as such a saint, when she most certainly was not?

"Then what *does* she care about?" Victor snapped.

"Her—" Gordon paused. "Her work."

Victor had a sneaking suspicion that the man had started to say something else. "You mean, her work making fake jewels."

The Scotsman glared at him. "I mean, her work

designing beautiful jewelry, and attempting with every new creation to surpass the last."

Victor flashed on a memory of Isa bent over a table in the jeweler's shop in Amsterdam, her eyes alight as she manipulated tiny diamonds into an intricate brooch. Through the years he'd imbued that enraptured look with a certain greed, part of his way of explaining to himself how she could have chosen a set of royal jewels over him.

But had there really been any greed in her face? Or had that just been his rewriting of the past? "Isn't it odd for a woman to be satisfied with work alone?"

"Not when the woman is extraordinarily talented, no. Have you seen an example of her work?"

Even now, Victor remembered how lovely the imitation royal parure had been, so perfect that until the palace had forced the jeweler to make a closer examination of it, the man had missed that it was a fake. "Yes, I have."

That seemed to take Gordon off guard. "Oh? When?"

"Last night at the theater," Victor said swiftly. "Mrs. Franke told us that she had designed the necklace worn by the opera singer."

Gordon's face cleared. "Ah, yes. A beautiful piece."

"The tiara Mrs. Franke wore was her own work, too, I presume."

"It was." Gordon stared hard at Victor. "Why do you think I took her on? When she came to my shop to beg that I hire her, she brought a ruby ring left to her by her family. She'd refashioned it, using the most amazing imitation diamonds I'd ever seen. It was exquisite. I hired her as an apprentice on the strength of that ring alone."

"I gather from what Lady Lochlaw said that she's from the Continent. How did she end up in Scotland?"

Gordon looked confused. "You misunderstand. I didn't hire her *here*. She traveled with me to Edinburgh after I hired her in Paris."

That flummoxed Victor. She'd stolen a fortune in diamonds, and then gone begging for a position from Gordon? That made no sense.

And if she'd been trying to escape being captured, why not just pay for her passage with the proceeds from the theft?

"Why was she seeking work with you?"

"Why do you think?" Gordon said testily. "She had to live somehow. After her husband died in the army, she was left destitute." He scowled. "I suppose you're one of those who think a woman is better off starving than going into trade."

"Not at all," Victor said, trying to find his way in this increasingly odd conversation. "I'm just surprised that you would hire a woman you barely knew and pay for her passage to Scotland, merely so she could work for you as an apprentice."

Gordon sat up straight. "What the devil are you implying? That I had some other motive in hiring her? That I took advantage of the woman? That I'm some lecher who—"

"No, forgive me," Victor said hastily. The Scot was quick to take insult. "I'm saying this badly. But jewelers do tend to be circumspect about whom they hire. It was kind of you to take on a widow about whom you knew so little."

The man's glare faded a bit. "Well," he grumbled, "I needed an apprentice. She needed a position. There weren't many Frenchmen who wished to travel to Scotland."

"So you were in a bit of a pickle. Perfectly understandable." He chose his words carefully. "Did your wife mind that you were hiring a woman?"

A shadow crossed Gordon's face. "She's dead," he said softly. "That's why I came here. After my French wife was gone, there was no reason to stay in Paris. I missed my home."

And Isa might have offered to share a few of the diamonds with Gordon if he helped her start a new life.

But then why go through the nonsense about being his apprentice? Why not just live off of the money from the jewels? Or steal more? Victor was missing something in all this. He just didn't know what.

Gordon was staring at him now. "Her ladyship put you up to finding out about Mrs. Franke, didn't she?"

Victor tensed. "You can't blame her for worrying about her son. By your own account, you took in a stranger without knowing a thing about her except the tale she spun about her soldier husband. How can you be sure that she didn't come to you simply because she needed to leave Paris quickly? Because, perhaps, she'd been using her ability for creating imitation diamonds in some criminal pursuit?"

The shock on Gordon's face had barely registered before the Scotsman burst into laughter. He laughed so hard he nearly fell out of his chair.

Not the reaction Victor had expected. "What's so amusing?"

It took the man a minute to compose himself. "Mrs. Franke . . . leaving Paris quickly . . . a *criminal* pursuit?" He gasped out one last laugh, then drew out his handkerchief to wipe his eyes. "Och, now, I needed that."

"I confess that I miss the humor in it," Victor muttered.

"You . . . you honestly think an eighteen-year-old girl was sneaking about Paris, breaking into . . . some mansion to run off with a fortune in jewels." He started laughing again.

"You're the one who called her imitations 'amazing,'" Victor grumbled.

"Yes, but that's a far cry from stealing real ones. The woman was timid as a rabbit when I met her—hardly the type who pick locks and break into houses. And why would she have come to me if she'd owned a fortune in real jewels?"

Ignoring the logic of that, Victor pressed the man harder. "Because finding a buyer for stolen diamonds isn't that easy."

Gordon's humor vanished. He rose from his chair to round the desk. "Are you implying that *I* was her buyer? That I started my business concern here with ill-gotten jewels?"

Victor crossed his arms over his chest. "Well? Did

you?" Sometimes anger made people blurt out things they wouldn't say otherwise.

"I damned well did not!" He drew himself up with a dignified sniff. "And you have insulted me and Mrs. Franke long enough. This conversation is over. Time for you to leave."

He'd pressed too hard. Victor rose, too. "I beg your pardon, sir. I didn't mean to imply—"

His accent thickening by the moment, Gordon said, "If you think I'll stand here letting you disparage my character and that of my partner in our own shop, ye're as mad as that woman who sent you over here to dig up imaginary secrets on Mrs. Franke." He held the door to his office open. "Good day, sir."

Victor tamped down his irritation and headed through the door.

The testy codger followed him into the workshop. "And I'll have you know I was one of the wealthiest jewelers in Paris because of my trade in imitation jewels. *That* is why Mrs. Franke came to me—because she knew I'd appreciate her skills."

"I see," Victor said, surprised. But then, his only experience in the jewel trade had been his few short weeks as a guard.

They passed out into the shop, and Gordon followed him to the front entrance and out into the street.

The Scot glanced around, then growled, "And you can tell that cat, Lady Lochlaw, that I willna stand for her spreading lies about thieving and such just to separate Mrs. Franke from his lordship. She ought to be ashamed of herself, trying to part two lovers."

Victor froze. "Lovers? *Are* they lovers?"

Gordon blinked. "I only meant that they're *in* love. Not that they behave scandalously. They're respectable in their dealings, to be sure."

His heart thundered in his ears. "But you're certain that Mrs. Franke is in love with the baron."

Looking uneasy, the Scot glanced away. "All I'm saying is she's no fortune-hunting female like her ladyship would paint her. And she's certainly no thief." His voice hardened. "That witch of a baroness knows better than anyone that my partner is a good woman, reliable and trustworthy. Did she tell you how her son met Mrs. Franke?"

"Yes. He brought in some jewelry to be cleaned for his mother."

"Not just any jewelry." Gordon crossed his arms over his chest. "The Lochlaw diamonds, a necklace renowned throughout Scotland for its value and beauty. It's easily worth seventeen thousand pounds. Lady Lochlaw sent it to our shop without a qualm. Would she have entrusted them to us if she'd feared thievery? That lying she-devil had no trouble with Mrs. Franke at all until her son became smitten."

But Victor had honed in on the words *Lochlaw diamonds*. He'd been wondering what Isa might be after—and now he had his answer.

Except that it made no sense. Why wait ten years to steal again?

Perhaps she'd run out of money from the first theft.

Cleaning the diamonds would have given her the opportunity to study them and make an imitation. Then all she had to do was wait for a chance to switch them with her copy. And getting close to the baron might provide that.

No, that made no sense, either. She would be the first to be suspected once the copy was discovered.

Unless it never was. Lady Lochlaw had already proved she couldn't tell imitation diamonds from real. That might explain why Isa had been letting young Lochlaw court her. The upcoming house party would provide the perfect chance to switch out the necklace.

He was still thinking it through when he caught Gordon staring at his phaeton. The man's gaze snapped back to Victor. "Yer equipage?"

Victor's guard went up. "While I'm in town, yes. Why?"

A carefully blank expression crossed the man's face. "It's a handsome rig. Very nice. Very *expensive*."

"It belongs to my host," Victor said warily.

"Ah." Gordon nodded to it. "Well, perhaps you should drive back to wherever you came from. Because ye'll find no scandal here for smearing Mrs. Franke."

Victor stared him down. "I only want the truth. If you'd just tell me where she lives, I could get all the answers I want from her without bothering you again."

Gordon lifted an eyebrow. "If his lordship hasna told you where Mrs. Franke lives, and Lady Lochlaw doesna know, then I damned well won't invade the woman's privacy. Ye're on your own with that, laddie."

"Then you can expect to see me here first thing in the morning, when Mrs. Franke returns."

With that, Victor climbed into the duke's phaeton and drove off. But as he made his way back to the villa, he wondered if Isa had already slipped the net.

No, she wouldn't leave until she got what she wanted. And if what she wanted was the Lochlaw diamonds, she wouldn't get away with it this time.

7

FOR THE FIRST hour of her trip home from Carlisle, Isa did nothing but cry. It was always so hard to leave her baby at school. Oh, she knew it was necessary, even more so with Victor in town, but it still broke her heart every time.

Amalie never fussed over being left, which only made it worse. Was she just being stoic? Was she secretly grieving the loss of her mother and her home for three more months? Or was she so happy to be back at school that she'd already forgotten her mother?

That thought sent Isa into another bout of tears. Fortunately, she wasn't the only one crying. Two other inhabitants of the mail coach had left their children at school, so they commiserated together.

By the time she reached Edinburgh, she'd found some measure of peace. In truth, it was much better for Amalie to be away just now.

It was dark when the mail coach pulled up at the inn. Mr. Gordon was waiting for her, the dear man, as he always did. He'd offered before to drive her and Amalie to Carlisle, but she wouldn't hear of it. No point in closing the shop on a day they were generally open.

He helped her down. "How's our girl? Settling in well?"

"She was her usual buoyant self. I swear that she . . ." She trailed off when she noticed he wasn't paying attention. The look in his eyes definitely boded ill. "What's wrong?" she asked as he led her to his carriage. "Has something happened?"

"A man came looking for you today at the shop."

Her heart sank. Victor. It had to be. What if he'd revealed himself as her husband? "Who was it?"

"Some damned cousin of the Lochlaws by the name of Cale."

Mr. Gordon surely wouldn't call Victor a Lochlaw cousin if he knew the truth.

Her partner scowled. "You know he's been asking the other shopkeepers about you, don't you?"

"No, but I'm not surprised." *Blast him.*

"You know him?" Mr. Gordon asked as he handed her in.

You could say that. "We've met. What did he want?"

By the time Mr. Gordon got done relating the entirety of their conversation, Isa wanted to scream. How *dared* Victor hint at the old theft? Was that his sly way of threatening her? Was he implying that if she didn't cooperate with whatever his blasted plans were, he would ruin her?

Oh, she was going to throttle him with her bare hands the next time she saw him!

"I didn't tell him about Amalie, though," Mr. Gordon added. "No point in letting that witch Lady Lochlaw learn that you have a child. She would never approve a marriage between you and her son then."

Not bothering to remind him yet again that she and Rupert were merely friends, she let out a long breath. "I appreciate your discretion."

After Amalie was born in Edinburgh, Isa had kept private the fact that she had a child because she'd wanted to establish her credentials as a jeweler. It was hard enough for a woman to be taken seriously, and people also assumed that a mother would be more slack with her business than a man would. Only Mr. Gordon knew her situation, and he had no concerns.

Once a few years had passed and Victor hadn't followed the bread crumbs she'd left for him, she'd had a different reason for caution. After so many years of ignoring her, he would only show up if he wanted something from her. And she'd been determined that the something wouldn't include her daughter—not until she knew she could trust him.

Keeping her life private hadn't been hard. She and Amalie lived in a cottage outside Edinburgh proper, and Mr. Gordon was circumspect by nature. Betsy had been with her since Amalie was born, and she, too, was discreet. And Rupert had never mentioned her daughter to Lady Lochlaw.

So, thank God, Victor still didn't know about Amalie.

But if he kept pressing her friends and acquaintances, he might find out. It was time she reminded her husband that *he* had something to hide, too—and if he tried to interfere in her life, he would ruin himself in the process.

Mr. Gordon settled back against the squabs. "Don't you go worrying about what that fellow will say to Lady Lochlaw. I made sure that he understood how things were with you and his lordship."

Oh, dear. "What did you tell him?"

"That the two of you were in love, of course."

"Mr. Gordon!"

Her old friend thrust out his chin. "Well, I couldn't let him think you were after the baron's money. I couldn't have him looking down his nose at you. Especially when Mr. Cale has even loftier friends than the Lochlaws."

Her eyes narrowed. "What do you mean?"

"I recognized that phaeton he was driving. Belongs to a duke."

She gaped at him. How could Victor possibly know a duke well enough to borrow his phaeton? "Are you sure that it wasn't Mr. Cale's?"

"Yes. I asked him right out. He said it belonged to his host. I recognized it from years ago, when the heir to the duke came to the shop to have a bracelet repaired for his mother. Everyone on Princes Street came out to have a look at that phaeton, since back then there weren't too many hereabouts. We were all mightily impressed."

"I don't remember that."

"You weren't there. It was around the time Amalie was born. Anyway, rumor was that the family had come up to stay at their villa in Edinburgh while they consulted with some doctor on account of the duke's going mad. Turned out to be true."

Victor knew a duke. Oh, Lord. "What was the duke's name?"

A frown knit Mr. Gordon's brow. "Kinloch, as I recall. No, that was the son's title. The duke's was Lyons." His face cleared. "That's it. The Duke of Lyons. Though I think he's dead now, and his son has the title. The young heir couldn't have been any older then than Lochlaw is now. He looked a sight, poor lad, so troubled. Must be hard to have a father lose his wits like that."

Isa tightened her hands into fists. Yes, it would be hard. And a newly minted duke in such a difficult situation might be vulnerable to someone as clever as Victor. Someone looking to further his own interests once he realized the proceeds from those diamond earrings wouldn't go very far.

Was that what Victor had done? Insinuated himself into the Lyons household by implying that he was a distant cousin? Was that what he was doing with the Lochlaws now? She wouldn't put it past him. She knew better than anyone how he could show two faces at once—that of a loving husband *and* that of a conniving thief.

Well, all that was about to change.

"I presume that Mr. Cale is staying at the duke's

villa, since he referred to the owner of the phaeton as his host. Do you know where this villa is?"

Mr. Gordon went still. "Why?"

"I think it's time I speak to Mr. Cale and find out what he's up to."

"You can speak to him in the morning. The fellow said he'd be there to greet you when we opened, and I don't doubt that he will."

She didn't, either. The trouble was, she did *not* want to have this conversation in front of anyone else. It needed to be private.

"Besides," Mr. Gordon went on, "I know what he's up to, and I set him straight. Don't you worry."

"I *am* worried. What if he goes running off to Lady Lochlaw to whisper poisonous accusations in her ears? I'd like to know where he lives, at least, just in case that happens. Please, Mr. Gordon? This is my future we're talking about." She steeled herself for the lie. "My future with Rupert."

Mr. Gordon let out a long breath. "Very well. My coachman may remember from delivering the bracelet all those years ago, after it was repaired. I'll ask him when we get you home."

"Thank you."

The full moon was high by the time they reached her cottage. It had to be nearly nine o'clock. She was exhausted from her trip, yet she knew she wouldn't be able to sleep while this was unsettled.

To her relief, Mr. Gordon's coachman *did* remember where the Duke of Lyons's villa was. Best of all, it was on her side of town but farther west, near Calton Hill. Indeed, she'd seen the Palladian mansion a number of times and wondered to whom it belonged, since it was so lovely.

Leave it to her wretch of a husband to latch onto such a wealthy host.

Mr. Gordon accompanied her inside, where Betsy was waiting to take her cloak. Isa could smell supper cooking; Betsy always had a warm meal ready when she returned from these trips, and Mr. Gordon sometimes joined them.

Isa forced herself to offer him supper, relieved when he said he'd already eaten and was heading home. As he bade her good night, she kissed his papery cheek and whispered, "I do so appreciate your finding out where Mr. Cale is staying. I know you think I'm being silly, but I will sleep much better knowing that I can call on him if I need to."

"I don't think you're silly," he said gruffly. "I think you're mad. Then again, since you're generally sensible, I suppose you can be allowed to be daft once in a while."

She laughed. "Thank you, I think."

"See you in the morning?" he asked as she saw him to the door.

"Of course."

She waited until Mr. Gordon was well down the road, then told Betsy, "Have Rob saddle my mare." Isa rushed upstairs to change. When Betsy followed her, obviously bewildered, Isa explained, "I have to pay a call on someone."

"*Tonight?*" Betsy said, clearly shocked.

"Something urgent has come up. Help me into my riding habit."

Though Betsy did as she was bade, Isa could feel the older woman's disapproval like a chill wind.

"I hope this don't got naught to do with the baron," Betsy said as she finished. "Wouldn't be fitting for you to meet with him at night."

"Betsy!" she cried in her best tone of outrage. "Surely you are not implying what I think you are." She headed out of her bedchamber.

Betsy hurried behind her. "I'm just saying that it's a sad day when a woman as respectable as you starts going about late at night paying calls."

"Not that it's any of your concern," Isa bit out as she hurried down the stairs, "but it's nothing of that sort. It's something having to do with Amalie, and it will not wait until tomorrow."

"Well, then," Betsy said, her entire tone changing, "if it's for the little mite, you'd best be going." She caught Isa's arm. "But first you must eat something. Can't have you fainting in the saddle."

When Isa started to protest, Betsy added, "I'll see to rousing Rob, and by the time you've got something in you, he'll have your horse ready to go."

"Fine," Isa said with a sigh. When Betsy got her mind set on something, there wasn't much use in fighting her. And it probably *would* help to have some fortification before she confronted her husband.

Still, when she rode off half an hour later and the

moon was lower in the sky, she wished she hadn't lingered. The last thing she needed was to be stuck at the duke's villa once the moon set and there was no light to ride by.

But she had to settle this once and for all. If she ended up being turned away by the duke's staff and spending the night in some haymow, she would survive. She always survived.

That thought cheered her a bit. When she knocked at the door of the villa and a stiff-necked butler opened it to scour her with a critical glance, she held her head high.

"I'm here to see Mr. Victor Cale," she announced.

The man glanced to where she'd tethered her horse. "And who should I say is calling?" he asked, his voice dripping with condescension.

"Mrs. Sofie Franke. A relation of his."

She let down the hood of her cloak and the butler's gaze fixed on the jewelry she still wore. Though she wasn't fool enough to wear diamonds when she traveled, her small earbobs were gold with real emeralds.

Clearly the high-in-the-instep butler could tell quality when he saw it. "It is very late, madam," he said, his tone a trifle less condescending this time.

She forced hauteur into her voice. "Trust me, if Mr. Cale is in, he will see me. And if he hears that you turned me away, he will not be happy."

The man took in her cloak of good-quality wool and her fashionable hat, then stepped aside to allow her to enter. "I shall see if Mr. Cale is in to visitors."

Relief swamped her. She'd breached the fortress.

And what a fortress it was. As a jeweler, she'd seen plenty of grand halls, but this went beyond grand. The floors and staircase were of fine Italian marble, the curtains were of damask with gold threads, and the chandelier sparkled so brightly that it could only be crystal.

She couldn't help gawking as the butler left. Was that a Rembrandt? She tried to look casual as she strolled over to look at it. She'd seen a Rembrandt once at a museum, but she wasn't that familiar with fine paintings.

"Where the hell have you been these past two days?" demanded a hard voice from the stairs.

Isa stiffened, then turned to face her husband. "Why, good evening, Mr. Cale." She cast a meaningful glance at the servants. "It's nice to see you, too."

Victor went rigid. Which had to be difficult, since he was already stiff as a starched cravat. Sadly, it only made him look more dashing. Despite the fact that he wore only a figured blue banyan over his shirt, waistcoat, and trousers, he looked every inch a man of distinction as he came down the last few steps.

It would be too much to hope that he had turned out to be a long-lost duke, and wanted to be rid of her so he could marry someone more appropriate. That would suit her nicely.

"Jenkins," he barked as he marched toward her. "Mrs. Franke and I will be upstairs in my sitting room. We have urgent business to discuss, and we do not want to be disturbed."

The butler didn't so much as lift an eyebrow. "As you wish, sir."

Well. Victor certainly had the aristocratic arrogance down pat.

Pausing only long enough to let the footman take her cloak and hat, Victor grabbed her arm and urged her toward the stairs. "You and I need to talk."

"I couldn't agree more, so there's no need to manhandle me," she snapped as she wrestled free of his grip.

"Forgive me," he said acidly. "I forgot how independent you've become."

I had to be; my husband left me, she wanted to retort, but the servants were listening with obvious interest.

"How did you find me?" he asked as they ascended the stairs.

"Mr. Gordon recognized your phaeton as belonging to the Duke of Lyons, with whom he'd once had dealings. He directed me here." She shot him a sideways glance as they reached the next floor. "How do you know the Duke of Lyons?"

"He's a friend," he said tersely, but he wouldn't look at her.

"He must be quite a good friend," she said as Victor showed her into a well-appointed sitting room.

She spotted a bedchamber through an open adjoining door, and realized that the sitting room was part of a large suite. No doubt there was a dressing room connected to it as well.

"Very impressive," she murmured. "How did you manage to make a duke's acquaintance?"

Ignoring the question, Victor shut the door, then rounded on her with a black look. "Where were you today? Attempting to flee me?"

She glared at him. "I had business out of town. It had nothing to do with you—the trip was planned long before you came here. I wasn't going to put it off simply because you decided to show up and make trouble."

"What sort of business? Where?"

The suspicion threading his voice inflamed her. "Where were *you*?" she countered. "Oh, wait, I already know. You were at my shop, attempting to poison my partner against me."

Victor scowled. "Is that what he told you?"

"He told me you made all sorts of wild speculations about how I was breaking into houses and stealing diamonds and trying to sell them to him."

He had the good grace to look uncomfortable. "I didn't say that . . . exactly."

"Then what *did* you say, 'exactly'?"

"Nothing that wasn't true." He raked his fingers through already mussed hair. The gesture was so familiar that it sparked a reaction deep in her belly.

She forced herself to ignore it. "You mean you told him the parts of the story that would make me look bad, and left out anything about yourself. Because you hoped that if you went around spreading rumors about me, you could bully me into doing your bidding. Why else would you wait years to come after me?"

Eyes alight, he stalked up to her. "I waited years because I didn't know where the hell you were." He seemed oddly sincere. "Your note said you were leaving me. You didn't bother to mention where you were going. So how the devil was I supposed to—"

"Note?" she broke in. "What note?"

He glowered at her. "The note you left for me in our apartment that night you were sick. The note that said our marriage was a mistake, and you wanted something else out of life than being my wife."

He'd muttered the same sort of accusations the night of the play. "Victor," she whispered, "I never left you any note."

Shock lit his face. Then his eyes narrowed. "Don't lie to me. It was written in your hand."

"It's not possible, I tell you!" Her mind whirled. "I would never have written such a note, I swear."

He crossed his arms over his chest. "It was sitting on our bed. Jacoba fetched me at the shop in the middle of the night. She said you'd left her house to return to our lodgings while she was asleep. When she woke to find you gone, she went there but you wouldn't let her in. She said she was worried about you, afraid you might be delirious from the fever. So I hurried back to our apartment. But you weren't there. And that's when I found it."

"A note saying I'd *left* you?" she asked incredulously. What he was suggesting was unbelievable. Who would have written—

"Jacoba . . ." she whispered. Could Jacoba have forged such a note? Could she have feigned Isa's hand well enough to persuade Victor?

Her distress seemed to sink in, for he stiffened. "Stay

here," he ordered and headed for the door to the bed-chamber.

"Where are you going?"

"To get the note."

"You . . . you kept it?"

"Of course." His eyes darkened to a smoky brown. "Did you think I would have thrown the evidence away? I kept it so I would remember," he growled, "and learn from my mistake in ever trusting you."

With those harsh words, he went into the other room. She sank onto a nearby settee, her hands shaking. His words pounded in her ears. *It was sitting on our bed . . . Jacoba fetched me . . . you wouldn't let her in . . .*

Would her sister, her own sister, have lied to her face about him? Torn her purposely from her husband without a whit of remorse?

When Victor reentered, Isa shot to her feet. "No," she said firmly. "I don't believe you. You're lying! This is just a ruse to get you back into my good graces so you can use me again." She fisted her hands against her stomach.

"*Use* you? The way you used me?" He thrust a sheet of paper at her.

She took it with shaking hands. Yellowed with age, the paper had clearly once been crumpled, then flattened out. The cruel words written on it, though faint, were still readable.

They just weren't hers.

"I didn't write this." She lifted her gaze to him. "It's not my handwriting, I swear!"

"It damned well looks like yours," he ground out.

"I know. It's a close approximation. But not mine."

She hurried over to a writing table with a quill and inkwell atop it. Finding some paper, she scribbled the same words as in the note. Then she returned to hand the two sheets to him.

When he stared down at them, the blood drained from his face. "You're toying with me. You made your writing different."

"You know it's not that easy." She stared at him. "Think, Victor—how often had you seen my penmanship when you got this? Once? Maybe twice? It's not as if we were writing notes and letters to each other. When we weren't working, we were in each other's pockets. And you only courted me a few weeks before we married. We were . . . hasty."

"True," he clipped out.

"I've never seen this note before today. I most certainly didn't write it." When his eyes still smoldered with suspicion, she added, "I swear it on my father's grave."

That, at least, had some impact. A muscle jumped in his jaw. "*Someone* wrote it. If not you, then who?"

"Jacoba, probably." The thought of her sister betraying her so horribly stopped the breath in her throat. "She used to imitate Papa's hand, too, so we didn't have to bother him while he was working. He hated being interrupted for what he called 'silly things' like paying bills."

Victor's breath came in hard, short bursts. "You're saying that you never left me."

"Yes. Until this moment, I assumed that you'd left *me*."

"I don't . . . understand," he said in a guttural voice. "How could she . . . *Why* would she—"

"Destroy us? Separate us?" A vise tightened around Isa's chest. "To get what she wanted. Or rather, what Gerhart wanted."

Awareness dawned in his face, turning his features to granite. "The royal diamonds."

With a nod, she sank back onto the settee, the note in her hand. "They told me you were gone. They said you took the earrings from the parure in exchange for helping them get into the strongbox; that you wanted us to travel separately to thwart whomever might come after us. They claimed that you planned to meet us in Paris." She lifted her gaze to him. "But you never came."

"I never came because I never knew where you'd gone," he ground out. "And I damned well never helped them get into the bloody strongbox!"

He seemed genuinely outraged. But there was one detail he hadn't explained. "So how did Gerhart and Jacoba get the jewels?" She searched his face. "Answer me that."

"I can't. When I left the shop to check on you, Jacoba stayed behind. I wasn't worried about that because the cases and the strongbox were all locked up. They were still locked when I returned. If she stole the diamonds while I was gone, I don't know how."

He glanced away. "I eventually came to think that you must have switched the jewels out while at work. I had no other explanation for it. Your 'abandonment' of me seemed to be tied to the theft of the jewels."

"I would never have stolen anything!" she protested.

His gaze shot to her. "But you might have made a false key from *my* keys and given it to your family."

"Right. Because I was such a master criminal at eighteen," she said bitterly.

"*Someone* fashioned those imitation diamonds," he pointed out. "Neither Jacoba nor Gerhart had the ability. Are you trying to tell me you had nothing to do with that, either?"

She stared down at her hands. The only way to get through this was to unravel the past—and that meant telling the truth. Or as much of it as she dared.

"I think it's time you tell me what really happened that night," he said in a cold voice. "Because you and I clearly have very different versions of it."

8

VICTOR PACED BEFORE the settee, his thoughts racing. Isa hadn't written the note. She hadn't left him. Or so she said. And it was hard not to believe her, when she looked as stunned as he felt.

He stiffened. It could still be all an act. She could still be trying to rewrite the past so he wouldn't take vengeance on her. There *had* been a theft, after all, and clearly she'd had something to do with it.

But she'd also been very forthcoming so far. If she was trying to allay his suspicions, wouldn't she just pretend not to know anything about the theft?

Her eyes looked tormented as she met his gaze. "Before I tell you what happened, I need to clarify one thing. Are you saying you had absolutely nothing to do with the theft of those diamonds?"

He drew himself up stiffly. "Until the fakes were discovered, a week after the parure was taken to the palace, I didn't even know there had *been* a theft."

She gaped at him. "The imitations were discovered

that soon? But I never saw anything in the papers about it—"

"You were in Paris, remember?" he growled. "You were already living off the spoils."

When she flinched, he muttered a curse, then strode to the fireplace and back, trying to calm himself. He would get nowhere if he didn't control his feelings. If he reacted emotionally, it would be too easy for her to slip something past him. He had to behave as an investigator. He had to interrogate her with logic and reason.

Though that would be a great deal easier if he weren't interrogating the only woman who turned all his logic and reason into pudding.

He frowned as he came to a halt in front of her. Not this time, damn it.

"It wasn't in the papers," he said tersely. "The royal family didn't want to look like fools, and the jeweler didn't want his reputation damaged. Since no one could be sure whether the jewels had been switched at the palace or at the jeweler's, they didn't want to reveal the theft publicly until they found the thieves. Which they never did. Without any evidence, they couldn't even prosecute anyone."

"So they never knew it was my family?" she said incredulously.

"Not for certain. At first, *I* wasn't even sure." His voice hardened. "I thought my wife had deserted me, because she was afraid that I would lose my post and she'd end up having to take care of me."

Anger sparked in her eyes. "I would never have—"

"You were upset when I left you at Jacoba's that night, if you'll recall." He stared down at her. "You were worried about my not having a position."

She jumped to her feet. "I was worried about trying to get you out of there before you told Jacoba that the jewels were going to the palace the next day!"

That threw him off guard. "Why?"

"Because I knew what they were planning, and I was trying to prevent it."

Now he really *was* all at sea. "By insulting me?"

"No!" She muttered a Dutch oath. "Of course not. I had a great deal on my mind. They'd been pressing me to switch the imitations for the real ones, and I'd been stalling. I didn't want to do it." Her gaze swept him and softened. "I was so happy with you. I wanted no part of stealing any jewels. But they just kept badgering me and badgering me—"

"So you gave in."

"*Verdomme,* no! I played sick. I knew it was the last day for the diamonds to be in the shop, but I was fairly sure Gerhart and Jacoba didn't know. They must have found out somehow. My sister said that you told her, but most of what she said was lies, so—"

"I did tell her," he said ruefully. "We were in the hall, and I was concerned about you. I assured her that she wouldn't have to worry about taking care of you beyond that night, because the jewels were leaving the shop, and the jeweler had already said that I could have a night off after the royal commission was done."

Isa let out a long breath. "Oh, Lord, and I was trying so hard to keep it from them. I thought if I could just put them off until the next morning, it would all be over and they couldn't do anything about it." Her voice grew taut. "I never dreamed they would take matters into their own hands."

He stared her down. "You're saying you had nothing to do with it. That you didn't help them get me out of the way so that the diamonds could be stolen."

"No!" She wrapped her arms about her waist. "I was asleep while all that was happening."

Something horrible occurred to Victor. "So you were still at their house when I went to our lodgings to find that note. You never left."

She shook her head. "I slept until long after your shift ended."

"But after I went home, I went to their house next, praying that you might be there. I pounded on the door. No one answered."

"I never heard you. Jacoba had given me something for my supposed sore throat," Isa said, her expression wrought with betrayal. "It must have had laudanum in it."

A dark hum began in his ears. "They planned it," he bit out. "They planned the theft, they planned to separate us."

Her face went ashen.

"They had to have guessed you wouldn't switch out the parure." He went up to her as she shook her head in denial. "Come now, Isa, they *must* have planned it. How else did the forged note get into our apartment?"

"Our apartment was hardly secure. And if they'd asked the landlord, he would probably have—"

"They didn't—I questioned him a number of times. But let's say they got in through the window or something, and planted the note. That still doesn't explain how they breached the strongbox at the shop. Jacoba must have had a copy of the key, which meant they got hold of my keys somehow before that night." The hum in his ears rose to a roar. "Unless *you* gave them my keys."

"Blast you, no! I told you, I wanted no part of it!"

"Then why did you make the imitation parure?"

She blinked. Then she seemed to collapse into herself. Pressing her fingers to her eyes, she turned to wander the room. "It didn't start out as a scheme to steal anything, I swear. Jacoba had read about how popular fine paste gems were becoming, how people liked to own jewels that looked identical to those of their betters for a fraction of the cost. So when the jeweler gained the commission to create the royal jewels for the prince's new bride, Jacoba figured that if I could copy part of them, we could sell the copies for very good money."

"I didn't even know you had that particular talent," he bit out.

"Yes, I realize that," she said with an edge to her voice. "You always thought me a quiet little mou—"

"Don't say it," he snapped. "If I'd had any idea that you hated me calling you *Mausi*, I never would have." He stepped toward her, fighting the urge to touch her. "And don't put words in my mouth about what I thought of you, either. I was in love with you then, too."

The words hung between them, making him regret he'd said them. Except that they were true, and she needed to hear that he had never *used* her. Not the way she'd implied.

"Meanwhile," he went on, his tone sharpening, "your sister and brother-in-law were developing a plan to steal diamonds, and you were designing fake royal jewelry, and apparently you saw no reason whatsoever to let me in on the secret. Your own husband. Whom you'd promised to love and obey."

That was the crux of it. She'd kept secrets from him the whole while.

"I was afraid of what you'd think of me, damn it!" she cried.

The irony was painful. He'd been afraid of the same thing—what she would think of *him* if he told her about his past.

Her voice dropped to a whisper. "I hoped I could make it all go away, and you'd never have to know what they were plotting. Never have to know that my family considered thievery an acceptable choice."

"You were protecting them."

"No." She scrubbed her face. "Yes. I don't know." She cast him an imploring glance. "I created that parure before you even started courting me. I'd always helped Papa craft the imitation jewels to adorn his clocks, and I was good at it. They made it sound so simple— I would fashion the fake, then they could sell it and make enough money to lighten our troubles. That's what Gerhart said."

"And you went along with whatever he said," he grumbled, remembering how her sister and brother-in-law had treated her.

She faced him, taking a belligerent stance. "Jacoba and I owed Gerhart our very lives. You don't know what things were like for us after Papa died. No one would frequent a clock shop owned by two girls, and Papa hadn't left us much money. Then Gerhart married Jacoba and gave us both a home. If not for him—"

"You and I would have had these ten years together. So don't make excuses for him," Victor said in a hard tone.

All the starch went out of her spine. "I'm not," she whispered. "I'm making excuses for *me*. For why I agreed to make the parure in the first place."

He saw the guilt on her face before she pivoted away, and it tore at him. He caught her arm to turn her toward him. When she just stared down at the floor, it drove a stake through his heart.

"That isn't entirely your fault," he said hoarsely. "Gerhart played on your feelings of indebtedness. What you don't seem to understand is that he didn't marry Jacoba and take you in out of the goodness of his heart. He did it because he saw that he could use both of you to his own advantage. I always thought so."

She still wouldn't look at him. "You never said that."

"No, and I should have. It was just . . . I was coming into a new family, and I didn't want to create trouble between you and them." He brushed a strand of her hair out of her face. "And you seemed to think well of them."

"I loved my sister," she said fervently. "She was the only mother I ever knew. And I was grateful for what Gerhart had done. I owed him the clothes on my back, the food in my belly—"

"For the first few years after your father died, perhaps," Victor said, his temper flaring. "But after that, Gerhart got what he wanted out of you. He sent you out to work at the jeweler's when you were only fifteen. When I met you, you were already earning an excellent income while he played cards with his friends in the shop, letting it run into the ground. You did more than your part in supporting those two."

"Not according to them," she said in a dead voice. "According to him and my sister, I was an ungrateful little whiner who couldn't see how lucky I was to have them looking after me. And I believed them!" Her tone grew anguished. "I never guessed that she would ever be so . . . cruel as to drug me and tell me the lies she did that night. How could she have betrayed me so? How could I have *let* her?"

She finally lifted her gaze to his. "I regret that more than you can imagine." Her breath came in tortured gasps now, as if she fought tears. "I regret that I was such a stupid little . . . mouse of a girl . . . that I never even saw—"

"Shh," he murmured and pulled her into his arms. "Shh, *lieveke*."

The endearment seemed to do something to her, for she tensed in his arms. "I'm so sorry. So . . . very . . . sorry . . ."

If she'd been weeping and protesting her innocence, he might have kept his heart hardened against her. But when she was blaming herself and struggling not to cry, he couldn't take it. He'd always been a softhearted dolt when it came to her, and apparently that hadn't changed.

Later he would make her tell him what she and her family had done with the jewels, why she'd come here alone. But for now, he needed to comfort her. To hold her.

To kiss her.

The moment his lips met hers, she froze. Then, like snow in sunshine, she melted, her mouth just as sweet as he remembered, soft and giving and warm. While he was kissing her, he could forget the past, forget why they'd been torn apart, forget that he'd come here for vengeance and justice. He could lose himself in her and pretend that nothing had changed between them.

She jerked back, her eyes dark and startled, her lips trembling. "Wait—I have questions, and I know that you must have some, too."

"Not yet. Not now." He dragged her fully against him. "Let me have this first."

He kissed her again. And again and again, savoring the mouth he'd forgotten he'd missed, smelling the violet water in her hair. It was like sinking into a hot bath after a long day.

Except that instead of relaxing him, it drove him into a frenzy. Every inch of him was already hard for her, and she made it even worse by arching up against him, grabbing his head in her hands and kissing him back, feeding on his mouth as he was feeding on hers. She still wanted him, too.

She was *his*. Still his.

"Oh, Victor," she whispered against his lips, "we shouldn't do this."

"Why not?" He backed her toward the settee. "We're married."

"Yes, but . . . I'm not the same woman you knew."

"You look the same." He sat down on the settee and dragged her onto his lap so he could brand her neck and her shoulder and her throat with hot kisses. "You taste the same." He cupped her breast, reveling in the moan she gave before she leaned into his hand. "You feel the same."

When her nipple tightened beneath his caress, he realized that there were no enhancements in her riding habit to make her breasts seem bigger. "Well, mostly the same." He stroked her other breast, too. "These are a bit larger than I remember. However did you manage that?"

Her eyes shot to him, looking startled, even frightened. "What do you mean?"

"I'm teasing you, that's all," he murmured, not wanting her to withdraw from him again.

"Oh." She dropped her gaze to where his hands fondled her shamelessly. "Well . . . I . . . I was young when we parted. I guess I grew a bit."

"Trust me," he said as he kneaded her breasts, enjoying the feel of them and the way her cheeks flushed, "I'm not complaining."

"What man ever would?" she said dryly.

He laughed. It wasn't something the old Isa would have said. "True. And you're right—you aren't the same woman. But I'm not the same man, either."

Sadness spread over her face. "No, you're not." She seized his hands as her eyes met his. "There was always a darkness in you, and I accepted that because I knew it came from your service in the war. But you were never hard, as you are now. What happened to make you so hard?"

He stiffened. "My wife deserted me, that's what happened. I was left to pick up the pieces and be accused of—"

When her expression turned troubled, he could have bitten off his tongue. Right now he wanted her in his bed. He didn't want to dredge through the past.

"Accused of what?" she whispered. "If you *didn't* leave Amsterdam the way Jacoba and Gerhart said, then you must have been around when they found the imitations at the palace."

"I don't want to talk about it." He tried to pull her close for another kiss, but she twisted free and left his lap to stand staring down at him.

"Tell me what happened," she said firmly. "I need to know."

"Why?" he snapped. "So you can be sure that I kept your secret? That no one is searching for you and your family?" When she recoiled, he rose from the settee with a curse. "I'm sorry, Isa. I didn't mean that."

She held her ground, though he towered over her. "I think you did. But I suppose you have good reason." She lifted her hand to stroke his cheek. "Please, Victor, I have to know what they did to you. Did they blame you for the theft? Or did you leave before they could? You said you went to Antwerp."

"After my life had been destroyed." Shoving her hand away, he stalked past her to the fireplace. "Since no one was ever going to hire me in Amsterdam again, I had to try to find work elsewhere."

"Because of me."

"Yes, damn you!" he growled, whirling on her. "Because of you."

9

ISA WENT COLD. "So it's my fault you've become such a hard man," she whispered. "You blame me for what happened to you." How could he not? She'd let Jacoba and Gerhart convince her that he would do something entirely contrary to his nature.

And he'd had ten years in which to curse her name, ten years to turn into the bitter man who faced her now.

"I did blame you. But now I don't know what to think, who to blame."

At least he was as confused as she was. "Do you think I'm lying about not being directly involved in the theft?"

"Of course not." He scrubbed his hands over his face. "It's just . . . Damn it, I don't understand how you could have trusted them! How you could have thought, even for one moment, that I would help them steal something?"

"You thought the same thing of me. How is that any different?"

"But I *didn't* believe it," he said fiercely. "Not at first."

She swallowed hard. "What do you mean?"

"Since there was no evidence for a week that anything had been stolen, I thought you'd left me and that was all. Out of embarrassment, I kept quiet about the reason for your disappearance. I told the jeweler that you and your family had gone to Brussels to take care of an ill relative."

He clenched his fists at his sides. "I couldn't accept that you'd deserted me. I thought—I hoped—you might still return. I would have gone to look for you, but aside from the fact that I didn't know where to look, and had no money for the search, there was the problem of my position. The jeweler had kindly allowed me to stay on—so I didn't dare risk that, when I thought the entire reason for your leaving me was my lack of a post."

"Oh, Victor . . ." she murmured, regret stabbing her yet again.

Ignoring her sympathy, he glanced away. "Besides, your family had supposedly gone to look for you, and I was certain that they would convince you to do your duty by your husband." He muttered a curse. "I should have known better. They'd left no address, no way to reach them. The whole thing had the markings of a nefarious scheme. But they'd also left their furnishings behind in their house, so I assumed that they would return eventually."

"It was all mortgaged to the hilt, even the furniture," she admitted sheepishly.

"Yes, I found that out later, when the creditors came

looking for your family and thought I might know where they'd gone." His jaw went taut. "They weren't the only ones."

Her heart began to pound as the ramifications of that sank in. "Because the imitations had been discovered."

His gaze was bleak and accusing. "Yes."

"So they *did* blame you."

"What do you think?" he snapped, echoing her earlier words. "I was the guard. Either I or the jeweler was in charge of the diamonds until they were taken to the palace. And I'd never told anyone that I'd left the shop briefly in Jacoba's care. I'd had no reason to; I thought it was a private matter between my wife and me. So I became the main suspect—the one they were convinced had made the switch and kept the real jewels."

"Oh, Lord, no." She ached over how that must have mortified a proud man like him. "But once you told them about Jacoba, surely they shifted the blame to her."

He gave a bitter laugh. "Perhaps they would have, if I'd told them. But I didn't."

"Why in heaven's name not?"

"Because it would also have shifted the blame to *you*, since all three of you were missing. And you were my wife. They believed you to be under my control. If there was any suspicion that you'd stolen the jewels, then it would become my responsibility, too."

"But that's not fair!"

"Perhaps not, but the law is rarely fair." He threaded

his fingers through his hair. "In any case, I would have seemed even more culpable if I'd admitted that I'd left Jacoba alone in the shop at night. And that would have led to questions about why I'd done so, and the truth would have come out about your leaving me, which would have led them to think there was some plot afoot . . ."

His gaze fixed on her. "I couldn't risk it. Especially since I wasn't sure that you'd stolen anything. I was still praying that the three of you would return to defend yourselves. It didn't make sense to risk my life—or yours, for that matter—on my uncertain suspicions, when I knew the authorities couldn't prove anything."

"So you covered up Jacoba's involvement?" she said incredulously. "And mine?"

A steely note entered his voice. "I did what I had to, to save myself. I told them the same lie about your going to visit a sick relative in Brussels. I knew they had no evidence linking me to the crime. They searched our apartment, the Hendrix house, and your father's shop and found nothing—no tools for creating false diamonds, no money, nothing to incriminate any of us."

"Jacoba took all of that with us," she said quietly.

"Of course. And without evidence, and the real diamonds, they couldn't very well prosecute anyone—not when there was still the possibility that someone had broken into the palace to make the switch. I figured it was better to be taken for a dupe than for a complicit dupe. Holding firm and pretending ignorance when they questioned me was the only way to save myself."

"And us."

He dragged in a heavy breath. "Yes."

In all her wondering about what had happened to him, she'd never imagined that he'd been fending off authorities who'd tried to blame him for the theft. No wonder he'd looked fit to throttle her when he'd first seen her. "And they believed you."

"Eventually." There was a wealth of bitterness in that word.

"What did they do to you? Did they put you in gaol?"

The ache in her voice must have registered, for he got a lost look on his face that sent a dagger to her heart.

Then his eyes iced over. "I don't want to talk about it. It's in the past."

"Clearly not, given the things you've said."

He walked up to snag her about the waist. "It doesn't matter."

"It matters to *me*," she said, straining away from him. "I have to know what my actions wrought."

He leaned close to nuzzle her hair. "Your actions wrought nothing. You've made it clear that your family was responsible, not you."

She could tell from the edge in his voice that he still didn't quite believe that. Neither did she, entirely. "But I let them use me. Use *us*. I believed them when they told me you had agreed to help them. Meanwhile, you—" A sob choked her. She clasped his head between her hands, forced him to look into her eyes. "Meanwhile, you were what? I can't know how much I have to make amends for if I don't know what happened."

He stared at her a long moment, features rigid, breath coming fierce and fast. Then his breathing slowed, and something more frightening than anger sparked in his gaze. "You want to make amends?" he said in a harsh rasp as he moved her hands to his neck before gripping her waist. "Then share my bed. Tonight. Now. Prove to me that my memories of our marriage aren't false. That you really did care for me once."

The dark glitter in his eyes told her he was serious.

So did the terrifying thrill along her spine. And the idea of being with him again sent a yearning through her that made her belly tighten and her throat go dry.

"Making love never solves anything," she protested weakly.

A smile ghosted over his lips before he bent to rake kisses along her ear, her cheek, her throat. "It always worked for us." Then he paused, and his hands tensed on her waist. "But perhaps it didn't work quite so well for you and some other man."

"There's been no other man in my bed since you," she admitted.

He let out a long breath. Then dragged in another. "Right. And your 'Rupert' is just a friend," he growled, a distinct note of jealousy in his voice.

She jerked back to eye him askance. "You've met Rupert. You've seen us together. Do you really believe there's more than friendship between us?"

He gazed steadily at her. "Angus Gordon says you're in love with the fool."

"Mr. Gordon *wants* me and Rupert to be in love. But it's wishful thinking on his part, nothing more. He assumes that I'm free, which we both know isn't the case." She forced a smile. "Even if I were, can you imagine me as a baroness? It's absurd."

He didn't laugh. "Not absurd at all," he said solemnly. "You'd make a splendid baroness. Just not for a boy like Lochlaw." His gaze scoured her, rousing heat in whatever part it touched. "You belong in a man's bed, not a boy's. You belong in *my* bed."

"Vic—"

He cut her off with a devouring kiss that shook all her defenses.

She couldn't fight him. She was engulfed by the essence of him—scent, taste, heat. It fogged her mind, destroyed her good judgment.

He gripped her arms, lifting her up on tiptoes for hot, ravenous kisses that stoked her own need, and she slung her arms about his neck to keep from teetering. She'd forgotten how strong he was, how much she used to love the very size of him. She'd forgotten how he dwarfed her with his height and broad shoulders and powerful chest.

Reminded of those heady days before they were torn apart, she couldn't help wanting him. This very moment. She'd been secretly craving this ever since he'd found her.

Blast him for having such a hold over her. He was a randy rogue and a silver-tongued devil, and she didn't care—as long as he was *her* rogue, *her* devil.

He tore his mouth from hers to murmur, "Come to my bed, Isa."

He dragged openmouthed kisses down her jaw, leaving her gasping for air. Or sanity. She didn't remember him being so demanding. It probably would have frightened her back then.

It excited her now. "I don't think that's wise."

"Of course it's not wise. Neither was your showing up here late at night alone, but you did." Grabbing her hand, he started for the open door to his bedchamber. "Surely you knew this would happen."

"Certainly not." But had she? Had a small part of her, the part that still remembered the joyous days of being his wife, come here to seduce him?

Determined to deny it, she slipped her hand from his. "No," she said, "I didn't." She told herself to be strong, to hold out until things were more settled between them. Until she could be absolutely certain she could trust him. "And I definitely don't think I should go in there with you." She almost sounded convincing.

The corner of his mouth lifted. "Fine. If that's what you want."

She squelched a quick disappointment. "It is."

He gave an exaggerated shrug. "Then I suppose we'll just have to settle for staying here." With a knowing smile, he began unbuttoning her riding habit jacket.

"Stop that!" She grabbed his hands. "That's not what I meant, and you know it! I meant I don't intend to come to your bed."

"You're not," he said blithely. "You're coming to

my . . . er . . ." He glanced about. "My settee. That's perfectly respectable."

"Not with what *you* want to do on it," she grumbled. "And it's not *your* settee. This isn't even your house, for pity's sake."

When she tried to move away, he pulled her back, eyes gleaming. "My host won't mind, I promise." Swiftly, he undid the rest of her buttons. "If we ruin anything, I'll replace it."

"You can afford that?" she said dubiously.

He shoved her riding jacket off and tossed it aside. "I can afford whatever it takes to have you again, *lieveke*."

Little sweet one. The Flemish endearment reminded her powerfully of her homeland, and it melted her as *Mausi* never had. She really ought to stop him. She really ought not to be standing here like a ninny, smelling his musk oil scent and gazing at his crooked smile.

His crooked, seductive smile, which destroyed the rest of her objections. She remembered how it had curved his lips whenever he'd come toward her in the tiny bedchamber in their apartment. She remembered seeing it and knowing what it meant, and thrilling to the promise of it.

Blast him.

Breath quickening, he untied her chemisette and tossed it away to expose her far-too-revealing riding corset, with only a hint of chemise peeking above it. She went still as his gaze drifted down to where her bosom was half-uncovered. He skimmed the back of his hand along the swells of her breasts with a tenderness that made her heart flutter.

Foolish heart. No matter how much she lectured it, it was still ridiculously susceptible to him.

As if he'd guessed it, his eyes locked with hers. "Tell me you don't want me as much as I want you. Tell me that you never once missed our marital bed in the past ten years, and I will let you walk out of here right now."

She closed her eyes, hoping that not seeing him would make it easier to lie—but his fingers felt like fire on her skin, and the scent of him, so close, made her head swim, and she could no more speak than she could run from the room.

"That's answer enough for me," he rasped, then he turned her swiftly around so he could work loose her corset ties with frenzied movements.

Swaying against him, she felt the rigid bulge of his arousal against her bottom, but before she could even react, he'd slipped his arm about her waist to pull her into him more firmly.

"I wanted to do this Saturday night," he murmured in her ear as his hands pushed down her corset enough to close over her breasts, kneading, teasing. "I wanted to strip you naked and take you right there, against that pillar; to claim you as mine before God and everyone."

"That would have sparked a public riot. What would your family have said?"

"My family?" He slid one hand down her skirts to cup her between her thighs, and his tone sharpened.

"Ah. You mean the baron." He rubbed her roughly, making her gasp, then squirm. "Who whisked you away from me while I was still trying to get control over myself."

A control he was denying her now, by inciting her with wicked caresses. One hand tormented her above while the other pleasured her below.

Exquisite torment. Dangerous pleasure. Both she could ill afford.

She dug her fingers into his muscular thighs, but she couldn't make herself shove free of his grasp. "Rupert brought me home . . ." she managed, "because I . . . asked him to."

"Because you were too much a coward to face me." He tweaked her nipple, and the piercing pleasure made her moan. *Verdomme*, he'd always known how to rouse her.

Turning in his arms, she untied his banyan and shoved it from his shoulders. "I'm facing you now," she whispered as she shimmied out of her loosened corset and tossed it aside.

With a groan he untied her chemise and pulled it down just enough to bare her breasts, then bent to take one in his mouth, then the other, tonguing her and teasing her and driving her to distraction. A growing urgency made her undulate against him and he backed her toward the bedchamber door, halting only long enough to dispense with her skirt, petticoats, drawers, and stockings, which he dropped into a heap about her feet.

"I missed you," he murmured as he ran his gaze over her. "I missed this."

The wildness in his eyes called to the wildness in her heart, reminding her of the Victor she remembered, the one who couldn't keep his hands off her, whose gaze ate her up like a dragon feasting on virgins.

Except that she was no longer a virgin, even if she felt like one after so many years of abstinence. And with him standing in front of her, tempting her, it was hard to be cautious.

Part of her had to know if their lovemaking had been as perfect as she remembered. The Victor she'd created over the past decade was crumbling, but she still wasn't sure how much of him, how much of her *marriage*, had been illusion and how much had been real. She had to find out.

All the same, even *she* was surprised by her next words. "Take your clothes off." That throaty voice didn't even sound like hers.

Heat and surprise flared in his face. "Grown bold, have you?" he rasped, but he practically ripped the buttons from his shirt in his haste to remove it.

"Yes." She let her gaze drink him up as he shucked off his trousers. "I had no choice but to change if I wanted to take care of myself. I'm a different woman now. Are you sure you can handle that?"

The savage intensity in his look made her pulse jump. "Perhaps you should be sure you can handle *me*." Without warning, he scooped her up in his arms and carried her into the other room to lay her on a very elegant bed. She was still lying there, stunned, when he covered her body with his.

Planting his hands on either side of her head, he loomed over her to add, "I'm different now, too."

When he coupled that with a thrust against her below, a frisson of fear and arousal slid along her nerves. This new Victor could be very dangerous. She still didn't know how he'd found her, why he'd come here, if he was here for revenge. All of that should give her pause.

Yet it merely emboldened her further.

"Really?" With a coy smile, she slid her hand inside his drawers to cup the hard length of him. "You don't feel any different."

He hissed through his teeth, his member hot against her palm. "Some things never change, wife. And I begin to think that wanting you is one of them."

Before she could exult in those words, he seized her mouth with his.

After that, she was all instinct and urges, rising to the kiss and letting him explore whatever parts of her he wished. Better yet, she was exploring whatever parts of him *she* wished, something she would never have dared to do in the week after they married.

Some things *hadn't* changed—his body, for one. He still had a nice sprinkling of hair across his chest, and solid muscle still roped his abdomen. She'd barely been brave enough to touch those muscles when she was young, but now she couldn't wait to kiss and tongue them.

To her delight, his muscles flexed and rippled beneath her mouth, his skin went taut, and his caresses of her grew bolder and hotter and harder, until she was shimmying beneath him.

"I want you, too," she whispered. "Victor . . . please . . ."

With a growl, he slid out of his drawers and began drawing up her chemise. "When did you turn into such a temptress?" he said hoarsely.

"After you left me." She nuzzled his roughly whiskered jaw. "When I realized that I hadn't seized what I wanted when I should have."

His gaze was raw need. "Seize it now. Show me what you want."

"You." She pulled her knees up to allow him to settle between her thighs. "Inside me."

His eyes blazed down at her. "Thank God." And with a guttural groan, he entered her in one hard thrust.

She tensed at the suddenness of it, and he froze.

"Too rough?" he choked out.

"No," she whispered and reached around to fill her hands with his bare buttocks. His exceedingly firm buttocks. Dear heaven. She squeezed, taking a feminine delight in his moan and the way he hardened even more inside her. "Too long since I lay with you, that's all. But I'm ready now."

When she punctuated her words by writhing beneath him, his gaze turned a molten gold. "I've been ready for a decade."

He began to move, slowly at first, as if gauging her response. But as she rose to his thrusts, he quickened his motions until all she could do was grip his shoulders and hold on for dear life.

She couldn't believe she'd forgotten what it was like to be filled by him, to be plundered by a man who wanted her, *needed* her. To have his heat against her skin, his hands all over her.

To have him driving into her so deeply that she could see only the fine sheen of sweat on his skin and the glitter of his hungry gaze as he took her, feel only the intimate press of his body to hers as the whirlwind swirled up from somewhere hidden to seize her and take her higher . . . farther . . .

"Come for me," he gasped as he plunged into her. "Come for me . . . as you used to, my beautiful . . . temptress of a wife . . ."

And she did. Her release hit her like lightning, splitting her present from her past in one blazing flash and hurtling her into the future. With a hoarse cry she arched up into him, and he came, too, spilling himself inside her before collapsing atop her.

And as the whirlwind slowed, the room stopped spinning, and her body slid from pure pleasure to pure contentment, she realized one thing. Her memories had definitely *not* been an illusion.

10

VICTOR FORCED HIMSELF to roll off of Isa, since his weight must be crushing her. But he wished he could linger forever with her beneath him, and he felt bereft the second he was on his back staring up at the canopy. What insanity had made him think that bedding her would purge the obsessive need for her from his soul?

It had only made it worse. He could still smell the violet water in her hair, feel the softness of her against him.

He wanted her again. And again, and again, until he could be sure this was real. That she was truly his once more. That he could trust her with his life. His future.

Still breathing heavily, he glanced over to see her lying there flushed and beautiful and seemingly content. The top of her chemise was pulled down nearly to her belly and the bottom pulled up nearly to her mons. He hardened just to see her looking so luscious, with the candlelight turning her exposed breasts golden and highlighting the tops of her thighs before disappearing into the dark shadows between them. It made him want to reach over and unveil the umber curls just hidden beneath the bunched-up fabric.

But before he could act on the impulse, she straightened her clothing to cover herself more. When she rolled to face him, his breath caught in his throat. For the barest moment, she looked at him exactly the way she'd done when they were first married—as if he were the knight come to save her.

Then the look faded, and he choked back a curse. He *hadn't* saved her, after all. He'd barely saved himself. And now all those chickens were coming home to roost . . . and leave droppings all over her life.

Yet when she spoke, it was about *his* life. "You have so many scars." Running her hand over his chest, she fingered a healed gash along his collarbone. "As I recall, this was done with a bayonet during the war, right?"

"Yes." One that had narrowly missed his heart. He swallowed convulsively. "I can't believe you remember that."

Her hand continued to skim his chest. "You'd be surprised what I remember. These whorls of hair. This tiny mole near your underarm." She flashed him a shy smile. "The way you kiss."

That brief glimpse of the old Isa made him kiss her again . . . and cup her breast and nuzzle her neck as she ran her hands over him. He was just wondering if it was too soon to seduce her once more, when she drew back with a frown.

Her fingers had found two scars along his ribs. "These are new." Her brow furrowed as she touched a small round patch of skin on his other shoulder. "And this. It looks like that other one you have on your back, where you were shot with a musket at Waterloo."

With a sigh, he threw himself against the pillow. Clearly she was done with seduction for now. "That's because this one was made by a musket ball, too."

Her gaze filled with a stark concern that made his throat tighten. "How? Why? There haven't been any wars for you to serve in. What have you been doing all these years, that got you shot?"

"Looking for you," he said truthfully.

She eyed him askance. "On the wrong end of a musket?"

Covering her hand with his, he brought it to his lips to kiss. "I had to make a living, so I hired out my services. Sometimes the work was dangerous."

"How dangerous?" she whispered.

He shrugged. "I got shot a time or two. Gained a knife wound here and there. All in a day's work."

She pressed a kiss to the scar on his shoulder, her eyes troubled. "Who were you fighting?"

"Why does it matter? It's in the past."

"Is it?" She glanced around the room. "You're clearly a close enough intimate of a duke to be given his finest guest suite. You must have done something to earn his friendship."

"Trust me, it's not his finest." The servants had wanted to give him the best one, and he'd refused. It made him . . . uncomfortable. Sometimes he felt like an impostor when people tried to toady up to him. He might be a duke's cousin, but he *felt* like a criminal's son. "There's a much finer one down the hall."

"That's not the point," she said tersely. "How do you know a duke? Why did you come here?"

He hesitated, on the verge of telling her about the Duke's Men and his newfound relations, about being hired by Lochlaw's mother. But he couldn't bring himself to trust her that much yet. There were still holes in her story, and before he unveiled all his secrets, he needed to know more.

"Tell me why *you* came here," he countered. "Once you realized I wasn't joining you in Paris, why didn't you return to Amsterdam to look for me? Or Antwerp, if you thought that was where I'd gone?"

"*If?*" She drew back from him with a wounded look. "You still don't believe me."

"That's not . . ." He jerked the sheet up to his waist and turned to face her, some of his decadelong resentment rising in him again. "I'm just trying to understand how you could throw away our marriage on the word of your family. Why you didn't even attempt to look—"

"How was I supposed to manage that? I had no money unless I used the 'spoils' of the theft, as you called them, which I refused to do. And my family wouldn't have given me the money to go looking for you, anyway. They kept saying I was better off without you."

He tensed. "And you believed them."

She shifted onto her back with a haunted expression. "I didn't know what to believe. You were always so reticent, and I can see now that Jacoba played on that. She pointed out that you never talked about your family, that I barely knew you. All of that was true."

One day he was going to make sure Jacoba Hendrix paid for every deceitful word she'd spoken to her sister.

"And I wasn't even sure where you were," Isa went on. "Was I supposed to roam the Continent like a penniless nomad, searching for my husband? Or did you expect me to find some post where I could earn my living, in hopes that I might stumble across you one day?"

"Of course not," he clipped out, conceding the point. "Finding work is easier for a man than for a woman, anyway."

She stared at him. "Not to mention that I thought you were running from the authorities, just as we were. My family had convinced me that you were as culpable as they, so I couldn't return to the scene of the crime without risking being caught and made to admit what I believed was your part in the theft."

"Or yours or your family's," he said acidly.

She tensed. "Yes. Once it was done, I wasn't keen on being hanged for it. Like you, I did what I had to in order to save myself. But apparently *my* doing so is some kind of crime." She sat up as if to leave the bed, and he rose to catch her by the arm.

"*Lieveke,*" he said in a low voice, "I'm not accusing you."

"Aren't you?" Her lovely brown eyes darkened with sorrow. "You think I should have tried harder, should have looked for you, should have roamed the Continent searching for the man I thought had betrayed and abandoned me—"

"No," he cut in, reminded yet again that she'd been made to believe a lie. He still had difficulty remembering that her family had been as callous with her as with him.

Drawing her resistant body into his arms, he pulled her back down on the bed. When she lay rigid beside him, he stifled an oath. He was handling this very clumsily. But he had never expected that she'd thought *him* the villain of the piece all this time.

Propping his head on his hand, he stared down at her jutting chin and mutinous expression. "I see why you couldn't look for me. Why you felt compelled to go off on your own." He laid his hand on her belly. "But to run off to Scotland? It never occurred to me to search beyond the Continent, because I would never have thought you'd travel so far from your home."

She met his gaze imploringly. "I had to get away from them, don't you see? They wanted me to create more fakes so they could pass them off as real, to make money. I couldn't . . . I wouldn't . . ."

"Ah," he said, beginning to understand. "They wanted to turn you into a criminal, too." She'd really meant it when she'd said she'd been trying to escape her family. "So where are they now?"

"Still in Paris, I hope." She relaxed slightly against him. "I haven't seen them since I took my chance to get away from them."

He caught his breath. He could write to Vidocq in Paris and have the man find them there, then keep an eye on them until Victor could get there. "I suppose they're using false names."

She nodded. "They did so from the moment they booked passage on the ship in Amsterdam. And they took other measures to change their appearance— Gerhart grew a beard and Jacoba and I cut our hair."

Which explained why neither he nor anyone else had been able to track them after they left their lodgings.

"Gerhart had some friend who'd been a spy for the French in the war and knew how to create false papers," she added. "That's how I learned that such things could be obtained for a price."

"So the name you used to come here isn't the one you used to leave Amsterdam and enter France."

"Of course not. I didn't want Gerhart and Jacoba to find me, remember? It took a bit of doing, but I was able to discover someone in Paris to create false papers for me, as Gerhart's friend had done for them."

Nothing showed how much she distrusted her family more than the fact that she'd gone to such lengths to evade them. Then again, perhaps she'd simply been worried that her family would be caught eventually, so she'd changed her name to make sure *she* wasn't.

But in that case, she wouldn't have chosen his mother's name. So far, her version of events was much more plausible than any of the conjectures he'd made. Which meant that the villains of this piece were definitely Gerhart and Jacoba.

He forced a nonchalant expression to his face. "So what names did they take?" he said casually.

Apparently that didn't work, for her gaze shot to his. "Why?" When he didn't answer right away, the color drained from her face. "Victor, what do you intend to do?"

He played dumb. "I don't know what you mean."

"Oh, yes, you do. Now that you're certain my family and I were behind the thefts—"

"Not you," he broke in.

"I made the parure," she corrected him. "The authorities will consider me culpable. Why, *you* practically do, even knowing what happened."

"That's not true."

"Hear me out." Her breath grew ragged. "It's clear that you want vengeance—"

"Justice," he shot back. When she flinched, he cupped her cheek. "Don't you want that, too, after what they did? Don't you want to see them punished?"

"I would, if there was any way to do it without punishing me as well. And there is none." She shifted to face him. "If you capture them and haul them back to Amsterdam to stand trial, they will blame me for the theft. It will be their word against mine. And as you said, they didn't have the skills to make the parure. I did—a point they are sure to make. I could very well hang, and they could get off scot-free."

His breath stopped in his throat. He hadn't thought of that possibility. Of course, until this night, he'd assumed she deserved the same punishment they did. But since she didn't . . .

"Nonsense," he rasped. "Once I testify, there will be no question that they were guilty and not you."

"You're my husband, and you were once a suspect. Do you really think that the authorities will trust your word over my family's?"

Perhaps if he brought his cousin into it to vouch for his character. But that would mean dragging Max through another scandal. And during a trial, all the nastiness about Victor's father would come out, and that, too, would affect Max and Lisette.

Damn it all. It had been far easier seeking justice when he thought *she* deserved it.

He gritted his teeth. "You can't expect me to just forget what they did—to me, to you, to both of us. They deserve to suffer."

"Oh, believe me, I agree," she said softly. "But I don't see how they can be made to suffer without ruining my life. And possibly yours. Which would be patently unfair, since neither of us did anything wrong."

But Dom and Tristan had resources he did not. They might be able to build a case without damaging her interests—or involving Max.

"Surely the truth will count for something," he protested. "We have the note, which isn't written in your hand. A good examiner of documents—and I happen to know one—could easily affirm that it was forged. That alone throws suspicion on them and off of you. The very fact that they've been living the high life in Paris while you struggled to build a business here also adds to their guilt."

She lifted an eyebrow. "Does it? You were telling Mr. Gordon just this morning about how I either used the money to build the business or I fled to keep from being caught. My coming here clearly didn't eliminate my guilt in *your* eyes. How will it eliminate it in the eyes of the court?"

God, he hated it when she made sense. "So you're saying that I should just sit here and let them get away with it."

"I'm saying that whatever you do is bound to hurt me as well."

"I don't believe that!" When she stiffened, he moderated his tone. "I only want to do some preliminary investigation, to see if I can build a case. If we take Gerhart and Jacoba by surprise, we may even find evidence in their lodgings. Just tell me their aliases, and—"

"No," she said, her eyes wary. "I dare not risk it."

His temper rose. He couldn't believe she would thwart him on this! "Now that I know what city they're in," he said, fixing her with a hard glance, "I can probably find them without the names, especially since I have connections to the French secret police.

I'm giving you the chance to make it easier for me—but that doesn't mean that if you don't tell me, I won't pursue it."

Fear lit her eyes briefly before she wiped all expression from her face. "You do what you have to do." Slipping from the bed, she began to gather up her clothes. "But I will not put my neck in the noose for your vengeance. I have too much to lose."

A curse left him as he watched her slip on her drawers and stockings. This wasn't what he wanted. And he doubted that she wanted it, either.

He left the bed to draw her into his arms. "Don't you trust me to protect you, *lieveke*?" he asked softly. "I would never let anyone harm you, I swear it."

She remained rigid. "You may not have a choice. Once you pursue vengeance—"

"Justice, damn it!" he growled. "If I wanted vengeance, I would exact my own punishment."

Her eyes lifted to him, large and luminous in the firelight. "Is that why you came here? To exact your punishment against me?" When he just stared at her, wondering how much to admit, she said, "Why *did* you come here, Victor? How did you even find me after all these years?"

He tensed. "Does it matter?"

She gazed steadily up at him. "You say I should trust you to protect me. You want me to throw myself into your hands, but you won't tell me something so small as how you found me. Or why you're grand friends with a duke. Or even whether you're really Lady Lochlaw's cousin. Clearly you don't yet entirely trust *me*."

"That's not true." Except that it was.

If he told her about the duke, that still wouldn't explain why he'd come here. If he told her about the Duke's Men, he'd have to admit that he'd been hired to find out her secrets.

Then she could threaten to tell the baron about the dowager's actions. Since Lochlaw was about as discreet as a four-year-old, the man would instantly plague his mother over what she'd done, and his mother would complain to Dom about Victor's lack of discretion.

And if Dom were angry enough over it, he would refuse to help Victor bring Gerhart and Jacoba to justice—especially if there was a chance it might embroil the duke and Dom's half sister in scandal. Then Victor would be stuck trying to capture the Hendrixes without help.

Out of nowhere came the voices of his inquisitors. *Admit it—she learned the truth about you and your father, learned how low you really are, and she aspired toward more. You were the guard, you besotted arse—that's why she chose you. And like a dolt, you helped her.*

Damnation, *that* was the real reason he didn't want to reveal his high connections. No matter how much he told himself that everything the prince's guardsmen had said was a lie, part of him feared it wasn't. Part of him still wanted to be sure that she wanted him for him, not for his connections or anything else.

Isa regarded him expectantly a moment longer, but when he offered nothing more, she sighed and returned to dressing. "It's late, Victor. I have to be at the shop in the morning, so I must go. We can discuss this more tomorrow." She slid her corset down over her chemise and turned her back to him. "Would you lace me up, please?" she said in a prim voice that annoyed him.

He strode up behind her to catch her about the waist and pull her back against him. "I don't want you to go," he murmured into her silky hair. "Stay here tonight."

"You know I can't." Her breath was coming quickly. "I have a life in Edinburgh. If I stay out all night, my neighbors will notice, and I'll be the subject of gossip."

"Because you spent the night with your husband?" he bit out.

"They think my husband is dead, remember?" She faced him, her expression once more wary. "Of course, if you choose to tell them otherwise, there's not much I can do about it. But then they'll know that I lied about my past. And if you tell them why—"

"I wouldn't do that to you, damn it." He caressed her cheek. "Honestly, *lieveke*, I don't want the world knowing about the theft any more than you do."

She dropped her gaze to his chest. "You can't avoid that if you pursue justice for Jacoba and Gerhart. The whole world will learn of it then."

"You've made your point. And I admit it's a good one. But there must be a way to solve this. I just need to think, to decide what to do."

"I understand." A small smile graced her lips as she met his gaze once more. "But you won't get any thinking done if I stay."

"That's an understatement," he muttered.

Already he was rousing again, wanting her again. It seemed he couldn't be sensible or reasonable or even logical when it came to her.

"Fine," he added and turned her so he could lace her up. "I'll take you home."

"No," she said quickly. Too quickly. Even as he scowled at her back, she added, "That's as bad as my staying here the night." She glanced at the clock. "If a mysterious gentleman brings me home at midnight, my neighbors will almost certainly talk."

He jerked the ties of her stays hard enough to make her gasp. "I daresay the baron has brought you home late a time or two."

"Not that late. And my neighbors and my servants know him. They don't know you."

She had an answer for everything. But that didn't change one essential fact.

He tied off her corset, then turned her to face him again. "They *will* know me eventually, *lieveke*—I promise you that." He clasped her head in his hands. "I refuse to lose my wife again. We will figure out how to manage it so we can be together, without ruining what you've built here. But let me make one thing clear: I'm not letting you go."

The yearning that flashed across her face was unmistakable. "I don't want you to." She covered his hands with hers. "But unraveling this will take time. And I prefer to maintain my respectability until we can settle matters."

Although he knew she was only protecting herself, it chafed him to watch her leave. "I'm beginning to miss the old Isa," he grumbled, "the one who deferred to her husband."

She grew solemn. "I hope not. She was the one who didn't believe in you when she should have. Who didn't stand up for herself."

"Who was sweet and shy and guileless—"

"Not guileless," she said earnestly. "I hid the imitation parure from you. I hid my family's greed. I didn't tell you what they wanted from me."

"True." Back then he had thought he knew her, but he'd been wrong. He wasn't even entirely sure he knew her now. She was still hiding things from him. He didn't know how he knew it, but he did.

Or was he just so used to distrusting her that he simply didn't know how to begin trusting her again?

"So I don't want that Isa back," she said. "And you shouldn't, either."

The fact that she clearly regretted so much of what had happened made it hard for him *not* to trust her. And he had to admit that he did like his new, bolder wife.

"Very well. We'll put the old Isa to rest," he said, running his thumb over her lower lip. "But the new Isa had best get used to my being around. Because I'm not going anywhere ever again. You're still my wife, and that isn't going to change. Young Lochlaw will just have to look elsewhere for a bride."

"As if Rupert could ever be a match for you," she said lightly, then brushed her lips over his.

With a growl he drew her back for a longer kiss, reveling when she wrapped herself about him like a tree putting down roots.

She might not yet trust him completely, and she might have doubts about how he wanted to handle the matter of her relations, but one thing was certain. She desired him as much as or more than the old Isa.

And that would be his way back into her life.

11

ISA KNEW SHE was in trouble when she allowed Victor to take her back to bed. How did he send her good sense right out the window when he kissed and caressed her? As he made love to her fast and hard and raw, she lost herself in it with such abandon that she forgot everything that still stood between them.

Only afterward, when he fell into a doze, was she brought back to her senses. She looked over at him and sighed. When he was asleep, he looked so much like his old self. How many nights had she dreamed of him like this, only to awaken to the loss of him? How many years had she yearned fruitlessly for the husband who never came?

And now he was back, and she wanted nothing more than to take up where they'd left off. Except for one thing.

Amalie. She should have told him about her tonight. He deserved to know he had a daughter.

But what if his burning urge for revenge on Jacoba

and Gerhart couldn't be assuaged? What if he insisted upon a trial, insisted upon dragging her back to Amsterdam? What would happen to Amalie? Would he be willing to give up his vengeance for his daughter? Or would he insist that he could manage a trial and investigation without harming any of them?

Isa wanted to believe in his ability to save them. He'd said he'd looked for her all these years, and tonight he'd seemed to accept what she'd told him about the past. But what about in the morning, after he'd had time to think about it? How could she trust him when he still kept so many secrets?

Until she knew why he was here and what he intended to do, she had to leave her choices open in case she had to flee again. In case he got so angry over her hiding his daughter from him that he lashed out and tried to assert his rights to the girl.

Because once he knew about Amalie, everything would change. For one thing, if he realized exactly how much Jacoba and Gerhart had taken from him, he might be so furious at them that he could no longer proceed with caution. It had become clear to her that when Victor was angry, he didn't think straight. So before she put her life—and the life of her child—in his hands, she had to know what she was up against.

Slipping from the bed, she halted when he mumbled something and turned over. She stood with her breath tight in her throat until he slid back into sleep; then she edged away.

Creeping into the other room with her clothes, she

dressed quickly and put her hair back up as best she could. Then she found her reticule and headed downstairs. To her surprise, the butler came out of a little room off the foyer to greet her.

"Is my horse still out front?" she asked, wondering if he'd had it stabled while she was upstairs.

"I would imagine so, madam," he said stiffly. "You left no instructions regarding its disposition."

She started to leave, then thought of something and turned back. "Excuse me, Mr. Jenkins, but would you tell me something?"

"If I can," he said warily.

"Do you happen to know how Mr. Cale and your master, the duke, are connected?"

His stare was as frigid as the winds off of the Firth of Forth. "I'm afraid you will have to ask Mr. Cale that, madam."

She'd known the man would probably be circumspect, but she had to ask. It worried her that Victor was keeping his presence in Edinburgh so mysterious. Something odd was definitely afoot.

As she rode for home, she couldn't for the life of her think of what it might be. If Victor had been searching for her, what had prompted him to look here? Or was he really Lady Lochlaw's cousin, and his appearance here sheer coincidence?

Tomorrow she would hunt up Rupert and ask him if he'd ever consulted *Debrett's* to unearth his connection to Victor. Perhaps she should just consult it herself. The subscription library might have a copy.

By the time she reached home, she was so exhausted she could do little more than fall into bed. And when Betsy came to wake her the next morning, she had to drag herself from the bed to perform her ablutions, dress, and have a cup of chocolate before heading off to the shop.

But as she rode toward town, sore in every muscle, she couldn't help but smile. It had been a long time since her body had been so well used, but she couldn't regret it. Last night had been even more amazing than she remembered. Hard to believe that Victor could have become even better at lovemaking.

Unless . . .

She frowned. He'd never said whether *he'd* been faithful. Had he sought companionship in some other woman's bed? For all she knew, his connection to Lady Lochlaw was an intimate one.

No, she wouldn't make herself frantic over such thoughts. She had to focus on the important things— what he meant to do and how she was going to deal with it. So she was glad that no one else was there when she let herself into the shop, an hour before they usually opened. She could use some time to prepare herself in case Victor did seek her out today.

She needed to work. It was her salvation for any of her troubles—nothing settled her more than manipulating softened gold or creating strass or losing herself in the planes of a beautiful uncut diamond.

She headed into the area behind the shop, then sat herself at her worktable and took out a bowl for mixing up the metal salts she needed for painting on the back of her paste. As she stirred, her mind sifted through all that had happened.

What was she going to do about Victor's determination to seek vengeance against her family? The situation was more complicated than he would admit. Somehow she had to make him understand the consequences of what he planned.

After a while, she heard Mr. Gordon enter the shop out front. As usual, he busied himself with preparing for opening and didn't venture into the back to greet her. He knew she preferred solitude in the early mornings, needing the time to create while business was lighter.

As she continued the monotonous task of mixing salts, her mind fixed on Victor once more. It would help if she knew what he'd gone through in Amsterdam after she and her family had fled. But how was she to learn that if he wouldn't tell her?

She wasn't sure how long she'd been working and fretting when a ruckus out front dragged her from her thoughts.

"So ye're back, are you?" Mr. Gordon's accent thickened as his voice rose. "Ye're nay welcome here. I willna have you bothering Mrs. Franke!"

She shot up and hurried through the door into the shop. "It's all right, Mr. Gordon. I don't mind speaking with Mr. Cale."

"You see?" Victor said to her partner, though his unreadable gaze was on her. "Mrs. Franke knows I'm no threat to her."

Mr. Gordon snorted, and Isa nearly did, too.

"I'm in the middle of a complicated task," she lied for the benefit of Mr. Gordon. "Why don't you join me in the workshop, Mr. Cale? We can talk while I work."

Victor lifted an eyebrow but gave her a terse nod and walked toward her.

"Are you sure about this, Mrs. Franke?" Mr. Gordon asked as he followed Victor. "I dinna like this fellow troubling you."

"It's no trouble. I have a few things to say to him, that's all."

Her crisp tone must have conveyed to Mr. Gordon that she wanted privacy for the conversation, for the man halted. He glanced from her to Victor, then nodded. "If you need me—"

"I'm not going to ravish the woman, for God's sake," Victor muttered, making Mr. Gordon bristle and start forward again.

"Of course not," she said with a warning look for her partner. "This way, Mr. Cale. You might find it interesting to watch me work."

"I might indeed," he drawled and followed her into the workshop, closing the door behind him. They had only gone a few steps when he added in a low voice, "You have a bad habit of vanishing in the middle of the night, Isa."

As heat rose in her cheeks, she drew him to the very back of the workshop. "You were asleep. I didn't want to wake you."

"Liar," he murmured. Then he dragged her into his

arms and began kissing her with a hard passion that sent her senses spinning.

For a few moments, she indulged herself in the sweet, hot pleasure and wanting that swirled between them. Then she forced her mouth from his. "Not here." She pushed him away. "Anyone might see us."

His eyes glittered darkly. "I woke to find you gone, and even Jenkins couldn't tell me where. I thought . . . I was sure . . ."

"That I had fled town?" She ventured a smile. "You won't get rid of me that easily."

Hunger flared in his eyes, and he reached for her again, but she darted away. "Not. Here," she repeated as she put a table between them.

"Fine," he said with a sigh, then glanced about. "So this is where the straw is turned into gold, is it?"

She chuckled. "How I wish *that* would work. I would never have to deal with the gold merchants again." Seating herself at the worktable nearest the back, where they couldn't easily be overheard, she began to insert a small imitation topaz into the last setting of a ring she was designing.

Victor came up to stand before the table, and she slanted a glance at him. Today he wore a velvet frock coat and trousers of Egyptian brown, along with a waistcoat of white figured silk, and she wondered yet again how he could afford such costly attire. What had he been doing all these years?

But before she could ask, he said, "Tell the truth. Why did you leave me last night?"

"You know why. Because we both needed time to think about what we're going to do."

"I know what I'm going to do," he said softly. "I'm going to take back my wife."

Ignoring the thrill that his words sent coursing through her, she fought to concentrate on her task. "Beyond that. We both need to decide how we mean to go on." *And how far we can trust each other with our lives after so many years apart.*

He gestured to the table. "And this helps you to decide? Playing with gems in some musty workroom?"

She dared to tease him. "It's better than playing with you in your bed." Staring up at him, she smiled coyly. "You make it very hard for a woman to think."

His eyes gleamed at her. "Good. I don't want you thinking your way out of our marriage. I want you accepting that we belong together." He reached across to chuck her under the chin. "Fate threw us back into each other's laps for a reason, *lieveke.*"

"Fate?" she said with a lift of one brow. "Or something else you refuse to tell me about?"

He stiffened, then stared down at the table once more. "Are those gems real?"

Stifling a sigh, she returned to her work. He was the most stubborn, secretive fellow, and it was beginning to irritate her. "You and Lady Lochlaw have quite an obsession with what is real and what is not."

"I'm just astonished that people will pay good money for fake gems."

"I don't know why that surprises you. You should

know better than anyone that real gems are beyond the reach of the average tradesman. And this ring I'm creating for a merchant has seven such gems."

"Seven? Then they have to be imitations." He peered at the ring. "Why wouldn't the man just buy one fine emerald or ruby instead of seven gems?"

"This is an acrostic ring," she explained. "The initial letters of the gems spell out words. The merchant wants it for his wife's birthday this week. In order for it to spell out 'dearest,' I need a diamond, an emerald, an amethyst, a ruby, another emerald, a sapphire, and a topaz."

"Ah." He watched in silence a moment as she gingerly closed the tines around the topaz. "Do you make many acrostic rings?"

"We do, actually. Occasionally even with real gems. Acrostic jewelry is all the rage these days. We do bracelets, rings, brooches . . . whatever someone requests."

She heard Mr. Gordon greeting Mary Grace out front. The young woman had been hanging about at the shop more and more lately. Apparently, despite her shyness, she preferred being with her great-uncle to dealing with her strident mother.

Neither Isa nor Mr. Gordon minded. She could be useful to have around when they needed someone to fetch them tea or help arrange the display cabinets.

"Looks like you've got everything but the diamond in the setting," Victor said.

"Yes, the strass for the diamond is giving me trouble." She pulled out a chunk of the glass. "It's too milky.

I don't think it's the pulverized rock crystal in the mix, although sometimes that can make the glass *too* white. I suspect that it's the fault of the oxide of lead. If even a particle of tin gets into that, it ruins everything."

"So how do you fix it?"

"Fixing it is impossible, I'm afraid. I'll have to throw out the paste and start over. Which means my customer won't be getting his ring for another day. The strass mix must be heated slowly over many hours to get the sort of glass I need."

Taking out her special crucible, she measured more pulverized rock crystal into it, along with white lead, potass, and borax.

When she rose to put the new mix in the furnace, Victor said, "How on earth did you do this in Amsterdam, if it requires a special furnace and crucible and tools?"

She set the crucible into the unlit furnace. "We had all of that at Papa's shop. You probably just never noticed." After hunting through their wood to find the driest pieces, she started a blaze going beneath the crucible. "You tended to avoid Gerhart, if you'll recall."

Victor snorted. "I never liked him, I'll admit. I like him even less now."

"To be fair," she said, meeting his gaze, "when he first came into our lives after Papa's death, I was just happy we had someone to run things, someone who could keep a roof over our heads."

"He did a damned poor job of it," Victor growled.

"In the end, yes. He hadn't been an apprentice long

enough, I think, to realize how much work such a clockmaker's shop requires." Her tone turned cynical. "And Gerhart was never fond of hard work. Then, once he began to gamble . . ." She shrugged.

Returning to her table, she scored the milky strass so she could cut it. Victor moved around behind her to watch over her shoulder. She could feel the heat coming off of him, making her dizzy. Making her want to throw caution to the winds and announce to the world that he was her husband. Except that she dared not.

"I thought you said that the glass was no good," Victor remarked.

"For diamonds, yes, but it's all right for paste rubies. So I'm cutting a piece that will fit into one of my faceted gem molds."

He leaned forward to look over her head at what she was doing, placing his hand on her shoulder as he did so. Like heat reaching the strass mix in the crucible, it set off a chemical reaction that had her blood rising and her skin growing warm.

"How does that work?" Victor asked.

My arousal? she nearly said, before she remembered what they'd been talking about. "The molds. Right. Well, I lay the chunk of strass into the mold and heat it just enough to melt it, so it can take the shape of a faceted gem. Then I remove the paste stone from the mold when it cools."

"Where do you get the molds?"

"I make them from real faceted stones that pass through the shop."

"Real stones," he said with a sudden peculiar edge to his voice. "Like jewels that you've been asked to put into new settings, for example."

"Exactly." She tapped the tool she'd set into the grooved glass.

His fingers tightened on her shoulder. "Or ones that are being cleaned."

"Sometimes," she said, perplexed by his interest in her molds.

He was quiet a long moment, watching her break the glass into manageable pieces. Then he asked in a hard tone, "So tell me, Isa. Did you happen to make molds of the Lochlaw diamonds?"

12

WHEN ISA TENSED beneath his hand, Victor knew he'd gone too far. But damn it, what did she expect after she'd gone slinking off like some thief in the night while he was asleep? He'd awakened to an empty bed and a sinking fear that she'd left him again. That their entire night's discussion had just been a way to lull him until she could escape.

Of course, once his reason had asserted itself, he'd realized that was absurd. If she hadn't fled the first day he'd shown up in Edinburgh, she wasn't likely to flee now. And *she* had been the one to hunt him down at the villa. That was hardly the behavior of a guilty woman.

But it still rankled that she could run away from him so easily. "Well?" he asked. "Did you make a mold of the Lochlaw diamonds?"

"I did," she said in a clearly defensive tone. "There were several perfect gems in the necklace that I knew I could use copies of. It didn't hurt the gemstones to take an impression, especially since I was going to be cleaning them. It's not like they were . . ." She pivoted in her chair to glare at him. "Why should I explain this to you? I've done nothing wrong."

"I never said you did."

"No, you just gave me that accusing look of yours." She crossed her arms over her chest. "And how did you even hear about the Lochlaw diamonds, anyway?"

He pasted a bland expression onto his face. "Mr. Gordon mentioned them yesterday."

Anger glinted in her eyes. "And then you assumed that I was plotting to steal them."

Ah, she could read him so well. He hesitated, but opted for the truth. "Yes." When she sucked in a shocked breath, he added, "At the time, I thought you were a jewel thief, remember?"

That seemed to mollify her only slightly. "So you decided that I had switched out the Lochlaw diamonds with imitations, is that it? That I had risked my livelihood and that of Mr. Gordon for a fortune in stolen jewels?"

"Not exactly." He met her irate stare with an even one of his own, although her clear outrage began to make him uncomfortable. "I figured that you were going to switch them out at the house party. That way you wouldn't be suspected if the change was ever discovered."

She jumped up. "*Verdomme*, you were painting me to be quite the master criminal!" Her eyes narrowed on him. "Or perhaps you *still* think I'm a thief. Is that why you keep refusing to explain how you found me and why you're here?"

"Of course not." That was the absolute truth. It was just that her guarded behavior in running away while he slept had put him on edge. It meant she didn't trust him enough to let him know where she lived. It made him want to poke at her until she gave up her secrets.

When she just kept staring expectantly at him, however, he softened his voice. "Forgive me, Isa. Until we spoke last night, the Lochlaw diamonds were the only explanation I could come up with for why you would get close to the baron."

"Because it couldn't be something as innocuous as an innocent friendship between two like-minded people interested in science," she snapped. "Not in *your* suspicious eyes."

"At the time, no. I know better now."

She looked skeptical. "I didn't set out to get close to Rupert, you know. He's the one who became friendly with me."

"Because he's infatuated with you."

Her chin lifted. "So you say."

"You know it's true."

Resentment shone in her face. Then she sighed. "If you're right—and I'm not saying that you are—it's nothing I can help."

"I know."

"And it wasn't as if I ever encouraged any infatuation. Rupert just kept coming to the shop and asking questions about the chemical aspects of my work, and I—"

"Took him on as a pet," he said dryly.

"No!" When he arched an eyebrow, she muttered a Dutch oath. "All right, perhaps it was a bit like that. But I really did feel as if I was giving him something important—a friend who would neither berate him, like his mother, nor scoff at him behind his back, like everyone else. Rupert needs someone with whom he can discuss the subject he loves best—chemistry. And he really seems to enjoy watching me work. It's rather . . . well . . ."

"Flattering?"

A rueful smile crossed her face. "Do you really think me that vain?"

"No. Just that lonely." He understood loneliness very well. It was one reason he'd been willing to go along with Tristan when the man had suggested coming to England to look for Victor's family.

She released a long breath. "Lonely. Yes. I enjoyed talking to someone close to my age who regards me well." She gazed steadily at him. "But for me, Rupert has always been just a friend. Nothing more, nothing less. No matter *what* Mr. Gordon says about it."

"I believe you." The rational part of him did, anyway. The irrational part of him still growled every time the young baron began sniffing around her. "I believe that you consider him only a friend."

"Good." Then her expression turned mischievous. "So you thought I planned to steal the Lochlaw diamonds at the house party, did you?"

Beginning to wish he'd never brought it up, he muttered, "I told you, that was before I realized—"

"That I was *not* a master criminal?"

"I never said you were a master criminal."

"No, indeed," she said, eyes gleaming. "You merely said you thought me capable of making false keys and breaking into strongboxes and creeping into Lady Lochlaw's bedchamber in the dark of night to unearth her diamonds."

It sounded ludicrous when she put it like that. "You have to admit I had good reason to be suspicious."

She conceded the point with a smile. "I suppose. Though you've developed quite the wild imagination in the years since I knew you. You see thievery everywhere you look." Her voice turned mockingly dramatic. "And you seem to see *me* as some sly enchantress setting out to seduce young Rupert so I can get close to the Lochlaw diamonds."

"Don't even use the word *seduce* and *Rupert* in the same sentence," he countered, only half joking. Especially with her looking so fetching in that flouncy green-striped thing she was wearing, which nipped in at her slender waist and showed her new, more ample bosom to good effect.

She chuckled. "Don't be such a jealous fool. If I tried to seduce Rupert, he'd probably scream and run the other way."

"I doubt that. He wants to marry you. He told me so himself."

That seemed to startle her. "Really?" Her brow knit in a frown. "But he's never said . . . He never even hinted . . ."

"He says he's not good with women. But that doesn't mean he doesn't want one. That he doesn't want *you*."

She chewed on her lower lip. "His mother would never allow it."

"How well I know." When her gaze shot to him, he added quickly, "In any case, you should discourage him. This may seem a tad old-fashioned to you, but I take umbrage at having other men court my wife."

Though laughter glinted in her eyes, she nodded. "I'll have a talk with him."

"*Soon*, Isa," Victor said firmly. "Otherwise, *I'll* talk to him, and he might end up rather the worse for wear."

She snorted. "You know perfectly well you wouldn't harm a hair on that boy's head. You like him. Admit it."

He did like him, damn it. That's what made the whole thing more difficult.

"Besides," she said with a calculating glance, "you wouldn't harm your own cousin, would you?"

He groaned. Perhaps it *was* time he told her the truth about how he'd come to be here.

He was saved from having to answer when the door between the shop and the workshop opened and Gordon came in. "You have another visitor, Mrs. Franke," he said in jovial tones. "His lordship is here."

"Speak of the devil," Victor ground out, ignoring Isa's exasperated look.

Lochlaw entered behind Gordon, then stopped short when he spotted Victor. "Cousin! What the blazes are you doing here?"

Victor forced a smile. "After witnessing the beauty of

Mrs. Franke's imitation jewels at the theater, I thought I'd come see if I could get her to share her secrets. I've never seen such impressive paste jewels."

His explanation seemed to satisfy Lochlaw. "I know—aren't they magnificent?" As Gordon returned to the shop, Lochlaw headed their way. "But no matter how much you watch her, you'll never catch the hang of it. Mrs. Franke is an artist."

"So I gather," Victor said blandly. He glanced to where Lochlaw held a box wrapped up with pretty pink paper and a purple ribbon. "And so, apparently, are you."

Lochlaw colored. "This?" He tugged at his cravat. "I wasn't the one to wrap it. They did it at the shop."

"The shop?" Isa asked gently.

Lochlaw's eager look made Victor want to roll his eyes. "I bought you something I thought you could use at the house party."

As Victor began to bristle, Isa hastily stepped forward to take the box. "Thank you, Rupert." Sparing a warning glance for Victor, she opened the box and then stared into it, a look of complete bewilderment on her face.

Victor leaned over to see what Lochlaw had brought her. Inside a nest of satin lay a pair of delicate half boots in purple kid, with pink laces and a little red rosette on each toe. They were the most vivid shoes he'd ever seen.

They were also the smallest. Hmm.

"They're for walking," Lochlaw explained cheerily. "Since you enjoy it so much. And we'll probably be walking a great deal on the estate."

"Oh, I see," Isa murmured. "They're lovely, thank you."

"And colorful," Victor said, fighting to keep the amusement from his voice.

"You see, cousin?" Lochlaw said, triumph in his voice. "I know you were against the idea of walking shoes as a gift, but there were no hydrangeas to be had anywhere, and clearly she likes the half boots. Don't you, Mrs. Franke?"

"They're quite beautiful," Isa said with a thin smile.

"Yet sturdy enough for walking," Lochlaw said. "I was most particular about that when I saw them for sale at the cobbler's yesterday." He nudged the box. "Put them on. I want to see how they look on you."

It was all Victor could do to keep a straight face. "Oh yes, do put them on, Mrs. Franke."

Sparing a murderous glance for Victor, Isa smiled at Rupert. "I would hate to ruin them. They're so pretty, and the workshop is so . . . full of chemicals and dirt."

"Not at all like the outdoors," Victor quipped.

Blatantly ignoring him, she told Lochlaw, "I'll try them on later, when I'm at home."

"Nonsense," Lochlaw said. "My cousin is right. The outdoors is far dirtier than here."

With a sigh, she faced Lochlaw, who was watching with happy anticipation. "I'm afraid I can't put them on, Rupert. They won't fit."

Lochlaw blinked. "What do you mean?"

Victor leaned back against the worktable. "They're too small." And if he knew one thing about his wife, it was that she did *not* have particularly small feet.

A look of horror crossed the baron's face before his gaze shot down to her shoes. "They can't be. Mrs. Franke's feet are dainty. All women's feet are dainty. That's what the cobbler said."

Because he was trying to sell you a pair of shoes he couldn't get rid of.

Victor didn't have the heart to say that. "In theory, perhaps," he drawled, "but in reality, women's feet come in all shapes and sizes. And Mrs. Franke's are not . . . er . . . dainty."

"Thank you for calling attention to that particular flaw of mine," Isa told Victor dryly. Then noticing Lochlaw's crestfallen expression, she added, "But they really are very pretty shoes. I'm sure I can find a use for them."

"Perhaps they will fit Amalie," Lochlaw said, a hint of desperation in his voice.

Isa froze.

"Who's Amalie?" Victor asked.

The blood drained from Lochlaw's face. "Um . . . well . . ."

"My servant," Isa broke in. "She does happen to have very dainty feet."

Lochlaw's head bobbed. "Very dainty. I know they'd fit her." He looked absolutely terrified as he cast Isa an imploring glance. "They would, surely they would."

"Of course they would," Isa said quickly, and bent to pick up the shoes so she could restore them to their box.

The two of them seemed a bit afraid of this Amalie.

Victor would have to meet the dainty-footed servant who could frighten both Isa and Lochlaw.

The door to the shop opened and Mary Grace slipped in. She kept her head down as she approached, but he noticed that her cheeks were a bright red. "Mr. Gordon wants to know if he should send round for some tea for his lordship."

Lochlaw was staring at the shoes, as if still trying to gauge if they really were too small. "No, no tea." He frowned. "I wonder why the cobbler sold them to me," he said to Isa. "He had them in the window and I thought they were perfect. He asked your size, and I said your feet were about this big"—he demonstrated with his hands—"and I think he just didn't listen."

"Probably," Isa said in a soothing tone.

Mary Grace was edging back toward the door when Lochlaw called out, "Miss Gordon!"

She froze with the look of a startled doe before squeaking, "Yes, my lord?"

He grabbed the shoes from Isa and walked up to show them to Mary Grace. "Do these look small to you?"

The poor girl swallowed convulsively. "Um . . . it . . . well . . . it depends on who they're for. You have to measure the woman's feet to be certain."

He slumped. "I should have done that. I didn't think I'd need to, though. Women's feet are all small, are they not?"

"Well, mine are," she ventured, her blush creeping up to the tips of her ears, "but my mother's aren't, so it depends."

"Of course it does," he mumbled. "I should know that. I'm such a dullard."

"Not at all!" Mary Grace protested. "You're just not used to buying women's shoes. When you go to the cobbler for shoes for yourself, he probably does the measuring for you."

"Actually, I don't go to the cobbler," he admitted ruefully. "Some fellow comes to the house and Mother tells him what to make and they wrap a string around my feet." Awareness dawned. "Ohhh, that's what the string is for. Measurements." He stared down at the shoes. "Some man of science I am."

"Oh no, but you're brilliant!" she cried. "Who cares about shoes? You understand *atomic theory*. That's far more important than shoes."

Lochlaw's eyes lit up. "You know about atomic theory?"

She blinked, then dropped her gaze again. "Only a little. I read most of Dalton's book, but I—I got a bit confused by the part about chemical synthesis."

"That's not as complicated as it seems at first glance." He turned the half boots round in his hand. "I could . . . explain it to you sometime. If you want."

Her eyes shot to him and her blush crept down her neck. "That would be lovely. Just . . . lovely." From behind her, Gordon called through the doorway, and she mumbled, "I'd better go. Uncle wants me."

When she turned, Lochlaw said, "You and your uncle should attend my house party. Mrs. Franke is already coming, and I see no reason why you couldn't all come. It would just make it more complete."

She halted, the redness now showing on the back of her neck. "If Uncle says it's all right," she said, "that would be quite . . . lovely." Obviously Mary Grace wasn't terribly articulate when it came to young gentlemen. Unless they were discussing science.

Victor glanced over at Isa, only to find her looking from Lochlaw to Mary Grace. When he raised an eyebrow at her, she whispered, "I've never heard her say that many words at one time in all my life. I didn't even know she knew about atomic theory."

"What *is* it?" Victor whispered back.

Isa shrugged. "No idea. I couldn't understand one jot of that Dalton book. It was all numbers and proportions. I know about how to use chemicals, not what makes them work."

"Well, I have no knowledge of chemistry at all," Victor admitted. "That was one subject Father didn't know enough about to teach me."

"Your father taught you?" she asked.

Only when her carefully nonchalant tone registered did he realize he'd revealed more than he'd intended. "Some. We . . . er . . . traveled too much for me to have formal schooling."

"I never knew that. Why were you traveling? Where did you go? What subjects *did* your father know?"

The baron was heading back toward them, looking pensive, and Victor seized with great relief on the chance to abandon the topic of his father. "Lochlaw, perhaps you should take those shoes back to the cobbler." *So Isa and I can have some privacy.* "Clearly he

ought to have told you that you needed measurements before he sold them to you. I'll bet if you go
now and tell him what happened, he'll make good his
mistake."

"That's a fine idea," Lochlaw said and turned for the
door. But before he got very far, Isa called out, "Tell me,
Rupert, did you ever look up Mr. Cale in *Debrett's* as
you said you were going to?"

Damnation. She wasn't going to let that go, was she?

Lochlaw halted. "I forgot all about it." He steadied
his shoulders. "I shall do that after I'm finished at the
cobbler's. I'm sure Mother would wish to know. And
we must have a *Debrett's* in our library somewhere."

Flashing Victor a self-satisfied smile, Isa said, "If you
don't, there's probably one in the subscription library."

Victor strode forward. "I'll go with you, cousin. I'd
like to see *Debrett's* myself."

Isa's smile faded. "We should all go."

"Don't you have a piece of jewelry you have to finish
this week?" Victor pointed out smugly, trying not to
laugh when she glared at him. He took Lochlaw by the
arm. "We'll leave you to it. Besides, it'll give me and my
cousin more time to get acquainted, eh, Lochlaw?"

And perhaps in the process, he could find out exactly *what* Isa was hiding. It was becoming clear that
he had a better chance of that with Lochlaw than with
his wary wife.

Lochlaw brightened. "Oh, yes, that would be grand."
But as soon as they'd left the shop, Lochlaw said, "You
have to help me, cousin."

"I wouldn't know the first thing about where to find a *Debrett's*."

"No, not that," Lochlaw said with a roll of his eyes. "You have to help me get another present for Mrs. Franke. So she doesn't think I'm a dullard."

"I'm sure she would never think that," he bit out.

"She would never admit that she does. But who wouldn't think it after I bought the wrong-size boots?"

Victor sighed, feeling sorry for the fellow despite everything. "Miss Gordon clearly doesn't."

Lochlaw's expression grew troubled. "That's just it, don't you see? Miss Gordon was only trying to be polite. She's always polite. But if I don't get Mrs. Franke a better present and show her that I'm capable of pleasing a woman, Miss Gordon will be secretly convinced that I'm an idiot. And she'll never speak to me again."

"I seriously doubt that," Victor said dryly.

"She's never spoken to me before today," he pointed out. "Until now, I thought she didn't like me. She's often there when I come to the shop, but she never talks to me. And she always seems to get so flustered around me."

Victor bit back a smile. "That's because she *likes* you."

Lochlaw cast Victor a hopeful look. "Do you really think so?" Then his face fell. "No, that can't be true or else she would talk to me."

"She's shy, that's all. And with a shy woman, the more she likes someone, the less she is able to show it. That sort of woman needs a lot of encouragement before she'll reveal her true feelings."

Isa had been like that, once. Victor wished he had seen it better then.

Lochlaw stared off across the street, a frown spreading over his brow.

"Do you like Miss Gordon?" Victor asked.

"I always thought she was very pretty," Lochlaw admitted, "but once I heard her talking about atomic theory . . ." His shoulders slumped. "Now that I know she's clever, I like her even more. And that makes it even more hopeless than with Mrs. Franke."

"I don't follow."

"A clever sort like Miss Gordon will see at once that I'm terrible with women."

He considered pointing out that a clever woman would "see at once" that he was rich and titled, but it felt wrong to poison the baron's budding feelings with such cynicism. "If she likes you, she won't care."

The baron thrust out his chin. "You don't even know for sure that she does. That's why I have to get Mrs. Franke a better gift. And you have to help me!"

"You're making no sense, lad. If it's Miss Gordon you like, then why not get *her* a gift?"

"Now *you're* being a dullard," Lochlaw chided him. "Miss Gordon isn't married. Even *I* know that an unmarried gentleman can't give an unmarried woman a gift. It's just not done."

"So you're going to give one to Mrs. Franke instead?" Victor said, still bewildered.

"She's a widow, so I can do that. And if it's good

enough, she'll be so impressed that she'll tell Miss Gordon, and I'll look like quite the man about town. Mother always says that women like you better if they see that lots of other women like you."

That sounded exactly like something Lady Lochlaw would say, because she didn't want him fixing his attentions on Mrs. Franke. "Really, lad, I think you're going about this all wr—" Victor broke off as something occurred to him. "You know what? You might have a point. You should give Mrs. Franke a truly spectacular gift. And make sure that you have it delivered to her house."

Lochlaw blinked. "Why shouldn't I just bring it to the shop?"

"Women are always more impressed by gifts that are delivered to their homes," he said, feeling only a modicum of guilt over his little deception.

"They are?" Lochlaw said. "Why?"

"Who knows? But there's a reason men are always having flowers sent over to women's houses. Because women love that sort of thing."

"That makes sense," Lochlaw said. "So you think *I* should get flowers?"

"Certainly." Now he just had to make sure it didn't occur to Lochlaw that while gifts between unmarried gentlemen and unmarried ladies were unacceptable, flowers were perfectly fine. It would do Victor no good if Lochlaw had flowers sent to Miss Gordon instead of Isa. "Let's go order lots of flowers to be delivered to Mrs. Franke's house. That will impress her greatly."

"And it'll impress Miss Gordon, too, when Mrs. Franke tells her of it?"

"Most assuredly."

Then Victor would *finally* find out where Isa lived.

13

ISA HAD SPENT her entire day working on the merchant's ring when Mr. Gordon wandered back to the workshop.

"So," he said, taking a seat across from her worktable, "his lordship has invited me and Mary Grace to attend his house party."

"Yes, he told me."

"I'm just wondering why."

She concentrated on the setting she was working with. "I would imagine it's because he finds you both interesting."

He snorted. "It's not a crotchety old man like me that he has his eye on. Anyway, I can't leave the shop—not if you're going."

"I don't have to go, either," she said quickly. It would certainly simplify matters.

"You do if Mary Grace is to attend. She'll need a chaperone."

"Oh. Of course."

And Mary Grace desperately wanted to go. Isa had learned that at lunch when she'd quizzed the young woman. It had never occurred to her that Mary Grace might have a tendre for Rupert, but apparently she did. Once Isa prodded her a bit—and hinted that Mr. Cale, not Rupert, was the man who'd snagged Isa's interest— Mary Grace became positively voluble.

His lordship was so brilliant. His lordship was so handsome. His lordship was the finest man in all the world.

"Well, then," Isa said, "I'm happy to play chaperone." Especially if it solved the problem of Rupert finding a spouse who was not *her*.

Mr. Gordon gazed steadily at her. "But if I am to encourage the girl's father to let her attend, I'll need to know the extent of his lordship's interest in her. If he has his eye on you and merely thinks to make you happy by inviting her—"

"I don't think that's it. I think she intrigues him."

"He damned well intrigues *her*," Mr. Gordon said dryly. "She couldn't stop going on about him today." He shook his head. "Though if his interest turns serious, it will send his mother into apoplexy."

Isa chuckled. "It certainly will." She sobered. "But it's not as if Mary Grace came from the gutter. Her father is a well-admired coffee merchant and she has a substantial dowry."

"All of that means nothing to a wealthy peer, and you know it. Her father is still in trade, as are the rest of her relations."

"More money is more money, even to a peer. Besides, Rupert isn't like other peers. He needs a special kind of woman as a wife, no matter what his mother thinks. Mary Grace might never be good enough for Lady Loch-law, but as long as Rupert is happy, it doesn't matter."

"And do you honestly think he *would* be happy with my niece?" he asked earnestly. "She's not you."

"I know. But even if he may have . . . fancied me a little, I think his affections are already shifting. They might shift more if she gives him any encouragement. And it's not as if there could ever be anything between me and him." She met Mr. Gordon's gaze. "I will never marry him."

Mr. Gordon searched her face. "Because of Mr. Cale?"

She blinked. "Why do you say that?"

"I'm no fool, Mrs. Franke. Any man with eyes can tell that the two of you have known each other before. I would even venture to guess that you have known each other very well."

The sudden clamoring in Isa's chest made it hard for her to breathe. She should have realized that Mr. Gordon would start to wonder about Victor's interest in her.

Perhaps it was time she revealed the truth. He deserved to hear it, especially when so much was at stake. And she'd prefer that he heard it from her. Then he could prepare himself for whatever consequences came of Victor's thirst for vengeance, if she couldn't convince her husband to be cautious.

"There's something I need to tell you," she said softly. "Years ago, I lied to you when we first met in Paris." She drew a steadying breath and prepared herself for his shock. "My name is not Sofie Franke. It's Isabella Cale. Victor Cale is my husband."

✦ ✦ ✦

IT WAS PAST 6 P.M. by the time Isa closed up the shop, long after Mr. Gordon had left. He'd been surprisingly understanding of her situation. She'd told him everything—even down to informing him of her family's crime.

He hadn't seemed as shocked as she'd expected. Victor's odd questions had partly been responsible for that, but unbeknownst to her, Mr. Gordon had also had suspicions of his own, born of her insistence on keeping her life so private. Having worked in the diamond industry, he knew how many unscrupulous characters were out there. He said that he also knew she wasn't one of them.

Tears sprang to her eyes. He was so good to her, and she'd been so lucky. It humbled her that he could take her past in stride. And that he believed her when she said she'd had nothing to do with the theft.

He'd been no help, however, in advising her what to do about Victor. He saw her side, but he also saw Victor's side of the problem.

The truth was, so did she. And the more she was near Victor, the more she wanted what they'd once had. But her life was entirely different now. And she didn't even know *what* his life was like.

She locked the door, then jumped as a man stepped from the shadows. "Rupert!" she cried. "You nearly gave me heart failure. What are you doing here?"

"We have a problem," he said in a doleful voice.

"What sort of problem?"

He followed as she walked toward the livery that boarded her horse during the day. "Mr. Cale isn't really my cousin."

As if that were any great surprise. "He wasn't in *Debrett's*?"

"Yes. No. I mean, he was in an addendum that was shoved into the copy of *Debrett's*. But it was not for *my* family. It was for the Duke of Lyons. It turns out that Mr. Cale is the duke's first cousin once removed."

Her heart stumbled. How could that be? And why hadn't Victor just said that? "Is he really?" she managed.

"It gets worse."

"I can't imagine how."

"When I saw the listing for the duke, I remembered where I'd seen Mr. Cale's name—in a newspaper article some months ago, about him and the duke. The minute I remembered that, I had the librarian help me find the article. It took half the day, but we finally uncovered it."

Her pulse began to pound. "What was in the article?"

"It seems that my cousin—I mean, Mr. Cale—was discovered in Antwerp by some company called Manton's Investigations. I gather that it has connections to Bow Street as well as to the Duke of Lyons. They call it the Duke's Men."

Bow Street. Oh, heavens. Even she knew about the Bow Street Runners.

"It seems that the duke didn't know Mr. Cale existed until five months ago. Apparently, Mr. Cale's father was an English soldier estranged from the Cale family, though the article didn't say why. But this Manton's Investigations went looking for him on behalf of Lyons and brought him back to England. He's been in London all this time with his real cousin, the duke."

"Until he came here," she whispered. Victor must have hired the same people who'd found him to find her. He would finally have had the money and resources to do it.

But how had they found her? Victor claimed he hadn't even known she'd gone to Paris, and he'd certainly been unaware of her life in Scotland. These investigators must be awfully good.

Which meant they might know about Amalie already!

No—surely Victor wasn't so accomplished at deception that he could have hidden that from her.

Why not? He's hidden half his life from you.

And she'd hidden Amalie from him. But she'd had good reason. What possible reason could *he* have for hiding his connections from her?

Might his duke cousin have something to do with it? Lyons might wish to see Victor married respectably and thus have wanted Victor to find her and divorce her.

No, that made no sense—Victor didn't need her

presence to get a divorce in Amsterdam, as he'd pointed out to her.

So perhaps the duke wanted something else—to have the man's thieving wife dealt with? These great men never liked scandal besmirching their families. Though there was no way of knowing for sure until she spoke to Victor.

"Of course, I realized at once what was up," Rupert went on, anger edging into his voice.

She tensed. Rupert had figured out the truth about her and Victor all on his own? "And what is that?"

"Mother hired Manton's Investigations to find out all about you, so she could separate us. And the agency sent Victor."

Relief coursed through her. Rupert hadn't guessed the truth. "Nonsense. If he's cousin to a duke, he doesn't need to work as an investigator."

"Then why is he friends with Mother? Why has he been asking questions about you around town? If he's my cousin, that makes sense, but if he's not . . ."

She caught her breath. Rupert had a point. If this had just been Victor hunting her down, either on his own behalf or the duke's, then why involve Lady Lochlaw? Could the baroness have hired Manton's Investigations? And then they had notified Victor that they'd stumbled across his wife?

Her mind raced. That would certainly explain how Victor had found her. He'd said that "fate" had thrown them together. Perhaps he'd really meant that.

But then, why was he still hiding his reason for being here if he meant her no harm?

"What did Mr. Cale say when you confronted him with this?" Isa asked.

Rupert stared at her blankly. "I didn't confront him. I discovered all of this after he left me."

"What do you mean?" She could have sworn that Victor had gone off with Rupert precisely to prevent the baron from digging into his own affairs. "Are you saying that you parted as soon as you left the cobbler's?"

"We didn't go to the cobbler's. I figured I'd hold on to the shoes in case . . . well . . . some other lady might want them."

She was too worried about Victor to care if he meant Mary Grace. "So you parted as soon as you left my shop?"

"No, first we went to—" He scowled. "It doesn't matter."

"If Mr. Cale went with you, it most assuredly matters to me. You have to tell me, Rupert."

"I can't." A flush had risen in his cheeks. "It's a surprise."

"I don't need any more surprises, believe me." She searched his face, then softened her voice. "There are things you don't know about me, things that Mr. Cale is probably here to uncover. I can't figure out how to deal with him if I don't know what he knows."

"He doesn't know anything from our visit to the flower shop!" Rupert protested. "I was very careful to hide your address when I gave it to the florist." He scowled again. "Oh, blast, I wanted it to be a surprise."

Her heart dropped into her stomach. "You're saying that you arranged to have flowers delivered to me."

He hesitated, then nodded.

"Whose idea was that? Yours? Or Mr. Cale's?"

"Mine, of course." Rupert screwed up his face in thought. "Well, it was his idea to have them delivered." When she paled, he said, "I know what you're thinking, but I was too clever for him. I didn't let him see where I was sending the flowers."

"And he left you directly after that?"

"Yes. He said he had business to attend to."

Following the deliveryman, no doubt. Of course, it wouldn't occur to Rupert that anyone would be so devious.

She forced a smile. "Well, thank you for the information you discovered. You're a dear." She headed into the livery. "I have to go."

Most Edinburgh florists made deliveries in the evenings. If she left now, she might beat the deliveryman to the cottage and be waiting for Victor, so he couldn't question her neighbors or Betsy and find out about Amalie before she could tell him.

It was time to tell him—she *had* to tell him—but first she had to know what he was up to.

Rupert followed her into the livery. "Wait, what are we to do about Mother?"

"Nothing." She cast him a thin smile as the groom went to fetch her horse. "Rupert, *you* are in charge of your own life. And that means you can do as you please, no matter what your mother says. Leave her to her machinations; they will do her no good. I will deal with Mr. Cale. You just take care of yourself, and everything will be fine."

Rupert sighed. "I really thought he was my cousin. I asked him for advice. I *trusted* him."

"I know. And I truly believe your trust wasn't misplaced." She prayed that it wasn't. "He thinks kindly of you. Of that I'm certain."

The groom came up with her horse, and she allowed Rupert to help her mount. "I would love to talk to you more about this, but I must go. It's important." When his face fell, she said, "And you have to make plans for the house party, don't you? It's the day after tomorrow."

"You're still going to come?" he asked anxiously.

"Of course. I wouldn't miss it."

As she took up the reins, he said, "And . . . er . . . Mr. Gordon and Miss Gordon? Will they come?"

She stifled a smile. "Mr. Gordon said that although he couldn't leave the shop for that long himself, he would speak to Mary Grace's father about it. But he saw no reason why she couldn't go, as long as I was there to chaperone."

A brilliant smile lit Rupert's face. "Wonderful." As she rode out of the stables, he called after her, "I hope you like the flowers! And that you tell everyone about them! *Everyone!*"

With a shake of her head, she waved and prodded the horse into a trot. She would have thought Rupert was trying to play her and Mary Grace off of each other, if she hadn't known he was incapable of such a game.

She frowned as she sent the horse racing out of Edinburgh toward her cottage. Victor, however, was excellent at playing games. And at manipulating poor Rupert. She would give him a piece of her mind about that as soon as she saw him.

There was more traffic than usual along the road to her cottage, but she kept an eye out for the florist's deliveryman. When she never saw him, she breathed a sigh of relief. That gave her a little time to prepare Betsy for Victor's arrival.

So it was with surprise that she rode up to the cottage to find Victor waiting out front for her. He was leaning against the wall and watching her with that devouring gaze of his, and despite everything, she caught her breath to see him looking so stalwart and handsome.

She leapt down from the horse and handed it off to Rob. Waiting until the fellow disappeared into the barn, she approached Victor warily. "Well, aren't you the clever one, tricking poor Rupert into revealing where I live?"

That seemed to startle him. "You talked to Lochlaw?"

"Yes. It seems he found a *Debrett's* after all and learned that you're not his cousin." When Victor tensed, she added, "But that wasn't the real surprise. That came when he discovered that you're the Duke of Lyons's cousin."

As alarm rose in Victor's face, she added, "So tell me, Victor, are you here on behalf of yourself, Lady

Lochlaw, Manton's Investigations, or your cousin the duke?"

A curse escaped him. Then he shoved away from the wall. "All but the last. My cousin doesn't even know you exist. Yet."

She swallowed hard. "So Rupert was right. His mother hired you."

"His mother hired Manton's Investigations. And I was in their office when they showed me your file." He thrust his hands into his coat pockets. "It didn't take much for me to figure out that Sofie Franke and you were one and the same."

She struggled to breathe. He'd come here for her from the very beginning. "Why didn't you tell me?"

"You know why—I thought you were a criminal at first. I was hoping to find evidence of that."

Rubbing her clammy hands on her skirts, she said, "And after you knew how we had been tricked? Why not tell me then?"

"For the same reason you wouldn't tell me where you lived—because I was still trying to figure out what to do. How we were to go on, now that our lives are so different."

"You mean, now that you are cousin to a duke who might not approve of a wife like me."

"I don't care if he approves," he said fiercely. "He has nothing to do with it."

"But Manton's Investigations does. I knew there was something suspicious about how you found me, but I never guessed that you'd been sent here by the English authorities. If you've told them about me already, then you will have to give me over to them."

A scowl knit his brows. "They're not the authorities, devil take it! They work for themselves, and I didn't tell them a damned thing. They only know that Sofie Franke is being courted by the Baron Lochlaw. They don't know about you and me. I didn't want to say anything until I was sure that Mrs. Franke was you."

"But you'll have to tell them eventually," she pointed out, "when you give them your report. And then they will learn about the theft and I'll be hauled off to gaol."

"Damnation, Isa, no one's hauling you anywhere!" He came up to her and lowered his voice. "Surely you can't think that after all we have shared, I would let you be arrested."

"I don't know *what* you would do anymore. You hid your purpose from me even after we shared everything. Tell me the truth, Victor. Did you come here for vengeance?"

A muscle flexed in his jaw as his gaze caught hers. He stared at her a long moment, then released a hard breath. "I did. But that's in the past."

"Is it?" she asked tremulously. "What are you going to tell your employer?"

He tipped up her chin with one finger. "That I found the wife I thought I'd lost. Which makes Lady Lochlaw's reason for having you investigated rather pointless. We'll work out the rest, I swear. I refuse to lose you again."

When he bent his head as if to kiss her, she pulled away. "Not out here, where anyone can see us."

Though he muttered a curse at that, he followed her as she hurried into the house. But she didn't get far, struck dumb by the sight that greeted her just inside the door.

Her foyer was filled with purple dahlias. There were seemingly hundreds of them—arranged in vases with baby's breath, done up as nosegays, laid casually in bunches upon her front table. She had never seen so many dahlias in all her life.

Tears sprang to her eyes. She couldn't believe that Victor still remembered her favorite flower after all these years. Or that he'd told Rupert about them.

With her heart quavering, she turned to cast Victor a questioning glance.

"Don't worry," he said. "Though I encouraged young Lochlaw to order them, I returned to the florist after the baron left to ask that the bill be sent to me at the villa. And that I be allowed to deliver them myself." A faint smile touched his lips. "One advantage to being a duke's cousin is that florists are willing to bend the rules for me. Thank God. Because no man but me is going to send my wife flowers."

His eyes bore into hers, full of heat and yearning, making her throat constrict. And that was when she knew for certain: He meant it when he said he wasn't here for vengeance anymore. He was here for her, only her.

She cast him a blazing smile that he returned easily.

But before he could pull her into his arms, Betsy came hurrying up the hallway.

"You're home!" Betsy cried. "Isn't it marvelous? I know the baron must have sent them, but the brash fellow who delivered them insisted on waiting until you arrived. I wouldn't let him in here, mind you, but—" She came to a halt in the foyer, her eyes going wide as she caught sight of Victor. "Oh. I see that *you* let him in."

Victor stared at Isa with one eyebrow raised, and she hesitated. But though she could trust Betsy, she needed to tell Victor about Amalie before she presented him as her husband. And she had to do that now, privately.

"Betsy, this is Mr. Victor Cale," she said. "We are well acquainted from when I lived on the Continent. It's a long story, and I promise to tell you all of it later, but first I need to speak to him privately. Afterward we will want some dinner, but for now we'll be in the parlor, and we don't wish to be disturbed."

Though Betsy looked bewildered, she nodded. "Whatever you wish, madam. I'll just go make sure there's enough dinner for two."

As soon as Betsy left, Isa drew Victor into the parlor.

"Still not ready to claim me as your husband?" he said tightly as she closed the door.

"It's not that. But before we can go any further, I have to tell you something."

She paced, wondering where to start. How would he feel to know that he had a daughter? And how angry would he be to learn that she'd kept it from him?

"The thing is—" she began. The sound of voices in the hall made her pause.

Then a knock came at the door to the parlor. She bit back an oath as she strode to open it.

Betsy stood there wide-eyed. "There's a lady here to see you, madam."

"Just get rid of her," Isa said irritably. "I told you, we do not wish to be—"

"I know. I haven't let her in." Betsy glanced nervously down the hall toward the entrance door. "But I thought you might want to know about it because . . . well . . . she claims to be your sister."

Isa froze. "My . . . my sister?"

"Aye. It was hard to make out her words, since she barely speaks English, but I'm fair certain she said 'sister.' Oh, and she gave her name. Mrs. Hendrix. Jacoba Hendrix."

Lord help her. After all these years, her family had found her. And now there would be hell to pay.

14

VICTOR'S BLOOD RAN cold, then hot. Hadn't Isa said— "You told me they were still in Paris," he accused as he came up behind her.

When she faced him, her skin the color of ash, he realized she was as astonished and upset as he. "I swear this is the first time I have so much as heard her name in a decade."

He dragged in a heavy breath, belatedly realizing that the servant hadn't seemed to know who the woman at the door was, which didn't exactly imply that Isa and her sister were seeing each other regularly.

Still, he had to be certain. Leveling a steady look on Betsy, he asked, "Have you never met this woman before?"

Betsy glanced to Isa, who said, "Tell him the truth."

"No, sir," Betsy said, obviously perplexed. "To my knowledge, Mrs. Franke don't have a sister."

How he wished she didn't. But at least it proved that Isa hadn't been lying to him about her family.

"You'd better send Mrs. Hendrix in," Isa said softly.

As the servant nodded and headed back down the hall, Isa's unsettled gaze met his. "We have to see what she wants."

"True." Though he could probably guess—the damned bitch wanted to ruin Isa's life. And his. Again. "We also need to know how she found you."

Isa grimaced. "That too."

A few moments later, Betsy showed Jacoba into the parlor and left. The minute Jacoba saw Victor standing there, her eyes went wide. "V-Victor!" she stammered. "I thought you were at the duke's vil—" She halted, obviously realizing she'd revealed more than she intended. "I mean, I didn't expect you to be here."

She was speaking Dutch, so he did, too. "No, I would imagine that you didn't." It took all his control not to throttle the woman . . . or haul her off to the nearest magistrate.

But he could do nothing until he had settled how to keep Isa safe from prosecution. Besides, it was Gerhart he most wanted, so he'd have to bide his time if he wanted to get them both.

He moved forward to stand beside his wife. "I'd say that it's nice to see you again, but that would be a lie." He glanced beyond her. "And where's your scoundrel of a husband?"

Jacoba thrust out her chin. "I came here alone. Gerhart isn't feeling well."

"Good. Perhaps he'll die. It's what he deserves."

"Victor," Isa chided in a low voice. "Provoking her won't accomplish anything."

"Perhaps not, but it's certainly satisfying," he shot back. He turned his hard gaze on the sister-in-law, whom he hoped would rot in hell alongside her husband one day. "Why are you here?"

Now wary, Jacoba glanced from him to Isa. "I wish to speak to my sister. Alone."

"That will never happen," Isa said firmly. "After what you did to me and Victor, you'll have to deal with us together. I'm never giving you the chance to lie to me again." She took Victor's hand in hers. "It's both of us or nothing."

He squeezed her hand, then left her to go loom over Jacoba. Time to put his investigative skills to good use. "How did you find Isa?"

With a mutinous glance, she set her shoulders. "Does it matter?"

"Most assuredly," he countered. "If you can find her, so can others—like the authorities in Amsterdam, who are *still* wondering if she stole the diamonds that you and Gerhart actually took." He flashed her a thin smile. "They're looking for the two of you, too."

Jacoba cast him a resentful glance. "Don't be thinking you're going to haul us back to gaol, Victor. The four of us are all in this together."

"The hell we are!" he growled, taking another step toward her. "Now, tell me how you found her, damn it!"

Fear flickered in her eyes. "How do you think?" she cried, backing away from him. "We followed *you*."

He froze. "What do you mean?"

"The story of your new cousin, the duke, appeared in the Paris papers because of that Vidocq fellow's involvement. When we learned that you were in London, we traveled there. Then we just watched you and waited. We figured it was only a matter of time before you hired the Manton's Investigations people who found you, to find your wife." She shrugged. "So after you met with them, we followed you to Edinburgh."

Fear fisted around his chest. He'd led them straight to Isa. "You couldn't have followed me to this cottage today. I would have noticed that."

"No," Jacoba said. "Isa is the one who led me here."

Isa gasped. "When?" she asked, her voice edged with alarm.

Why did *that* matter?

"If you must know," Jacoba said with a sniff, "it was last night. I waited around, hoping to speak to you alone, but you had that Mr. Gordon with you. Then you rode off on a horse so quickly I couldn't keep up with you, not knowing the roads. After I waited here a bit I gave up and went back to town, and came back tonight when I knew you'd be here." She glared at Victor. "I didn't know you would have *him* here."

"Yes," Victor snapped, "I'm sure you would have preferred that I go on believing that my wife deserted me. After all, you're the one who set me up to believe it in the first place. The one who forged the note I found in our apartment."

She paled. "I—I didn't forge anything," she protested, though she avoided his gaze.

"Jacoba," Isa chided. "We know you did it. And if you won't tell the truth, there is nothing left for us to talk about. So you might as well—"

"All right, all right," Jacoba said irritably. "I forged the note. But only because I had to. It was the only way."

"To do what? Separate me from my husband?" Betrayal sounded in Isa's voice. "So you and Gerhart could live well for the rest of your lives?"

"You owed us that!" Jacoba cried. "We took care of you after Papa died, and all we asked—"

"Was that I become a criminal." Isa strode up next to Victor and leveled an accusing look at Jacoba. "You wanted me to turn *him* into a criminal, too. And when I refused to entertain the notion, you forced my hand and turned me into a criminal against my will. Then you separated me from my husband."

"I did what was best for you," Jacoba said stoutly.

"How do you figure that?" Victor growled.

Jacoba's eyes glittered at him. "Back then you didn't have two guilders to rub together!" she spat. "And your temporary post at the jeweler's was about to end. How were you going to support her without a post?"

"You didn't seem to care about that when you gave your approval to our marriage," he clipped out.

"That's because . . . well . . ."

"Because even then you were planning on using him to get into the strongbox, weren't you?" Isa said. "That's the only reason you encouraged the marriage." Her voice grew choked. "Victor was sure that you two planned the theft from the beginning, and I didn't want to believe him. But he's right, isn't he?"

Jacoba's mouth flattened into a grim line. "If we hadn't acted and you had stayed with him, the two of you would have been poor as church mice all your lives." She waved her hand to indicate both of them. "And look at you now. Thanks to us, you have a fine business and Victor has discovered he's a duke's cousin."

Victor took a menacing step toward her. "You two had naught to do with *that*."

"Those investigators found you in Antwerp, didn't they? That's what the papers said. And you would never have gone to Antwerp if we hadn't—"

"Destroyed my life? Set me up to take the blame for *your* crime?"

"We didn't do that!" she said. "Not . . . exactly. We just . . . thought that no one would ever discover that the diamonds were fake."

"And you made sure that if anyone did, I'd be blamed for it." He glared at her. "How did you get the keys to the strongbox? Did you steal them out of our home when I was asleep one day and make a copy? Is that what you did?"

When Jacoba colored, he knew he'd hit on the truth. "You conniving, devious—"

"I don't care what you think of me!" She glanced to Isa. "I did it for you. I *saved* you!"

"From a happy marriage?" Isa said incredulously. "Don't you dare take credit for anything we cobbled together from the ruins of your machinations. You didn't do a blasted thing for me; you did it for yourself. Because you wanted to dress in fine clothes and drive a costly equipage and live like a queen in Paris!"

"And what's wrong with that?" Jacoba crossed her arms over her chest. "Everyone wants that."

"Not me!" Isa cried. "All I wanted was to be a good wife to Victor. To spend my days with the man I loved. Yet you separated us for your own purposes." She slid her hand into the crook of his elbow. "Well, we're together again, despite all your attempts. And there isn't a thing you can do about it."

Covering Isa's hand with his own, Victor stared Jacoba down. "What do you want, anyway? Why go to all this trouble to find Isa? And don't tell me any nonsense about missing her, because we both know that would be a lie."

A bleak expression crossed her face. "You're wrong."

"Is he?" Isa's cynical laugh seemed to rattle Jacoba. "Don't even *think* to come sniffing around me now, begging my forgiveness. Not after what you did."

"Isa, please," Jacoba said in a low voice. "Just give me a few minutes to speak to you alone."

"Not a chance," Victor cut in. "And if you won't

say why you've come, then it's time for you to leave."

Jacoba stepped forward to place her hand on Isa's arm. "You would let him throw out your only sister?"

Isa jerked her arm away. "As far as I'm concerned, I don't have a sister."

"You don't mean that," Jacoba said in a pitiful voice that made Victor grit his teeth.

"Every word," Isa said. "And Victor's right. You might as well go."

Victor let out a breath. Isa had certainly told the truth about one thing. She wasn't a mouse anymore.

"Please, Isa—" Jacoba began.

"Now!" Isa hissed. "Before I throw you out myself."

When Isa took a step toward her as if to make good her threat, Jacoba cried, "Gerhart is dying!"

Isa tensed.

God help him. Would his softhearted wife fall for *that* ploy?

"The doctor's bills are enormous," Jacoba went on hastily when she saw she had her sister's attention, "and the money is running out. You *have* to help us. You have to help *him*."

"Because the two of you took such fine care of *me*?" Isa said in an acid tone.

When Jacoba looked taken aback, Victor wanted to crow. His softhearted wife was no longer a fool when it came to her manipulative sister, thank God.

"You have so much now, what with that fine shop of

yours," Jacoba complained. "And Victor is cousin to a duke! I don't know why you can't just—"

"Give you some of it?" Isa said in clear outrage. "After everything you did to us?" She narrowed her gaze on her sister. "My partner and I built that shop with the sweat of our brows. I worked for *years* to get to the point where I don't have to worry about my next meal and the rent for this cottage. If you think I'll give you and Gerhart a single penny, just so he can gamble it away, you're out of your mind."

Jacoba's face flushed in shock. Then her gaze turned calculating. "I wonder what Mr. Gordon would say if he knew that you created a fake parure used in a crime. Or what Victor's cousin the duke would say if he knew Victor's wife had a criminal past."

With a low growl, Victor lunged for Jacoba, but Isa grabbed his arm. "Let me handle this."

She left his side to bear down on her sister. "You have the audacity to *threaten* us?"

Jacoba blinked, then backed away as it finally dawned on her how angry her sister was.

Relentlessly Isa stalked her. "If you so much as *hint* to anyone what happened in Amsterdam, I'll report you to the Dutch authorities myself, even at the cost of my own freedom. I'll see you both hang before I allow you to blackmail me!"

Jacoba came up against the wall, and anger flared in her face. "And what will happen to your child then?" she said hotly. "Tell me that, dear sister!"

Isa froze, and Victor's heart plummeted into his stomach. Surely he hadn't heard Jacoba correctly. "Child? What child?" When Isa turned toward him, her face awash in guilt, he growled, "What the devil is she talking about, Isa?"

"Don't you know?" Jacoba said, glaring at her sister. "When Isa left us in Paris, she was carrying your child in her belly. Lord only knows what she's done with it."

Victor gasped.

With a growl, Isa whirled on her sister and stalked over to swing the door open. "Get out, you scheming bitch!" she hissed. "Get out of my house before I strangle you with my bare hands!"

Clearly taken aback by Isa's vehemence, Jacoba said plaintively, "There's no reason to get upset. Can't we all discuss this like civilized people?"

"Out!" Grabbing her sister's arm, Isa dragged her toward the door. "Get. Out. *Now!*"

Victor could only gape at them, his mind racing. He had a child? Where? What *had* Isa done with it? And why hadn't she told him?

Jacoba was protesting so loudly that Betsy came running, and Isa cried, "Get her out of here before I kill her!"

When Betsy tried to take Jacoba by the arm, Jacoba snatched it free and flashed Isa a hurt look. "We'll speak again when you're calmer. I know you don't mean what you're saying. You wouldn't abandon your family."

"Watch me." Isa took a step toward her.

Jacoba's eyes went wide. Then she turned and ran for the door.

"And don't you dare come back here, you . . . you leech!" Isa shouted, running into the hall after her.

Victor rushed out just in time to see Jacoba leave through the front door, slamming it behind her. Before he could even question Isa, she turned to Betsy and said, "Have Rob saddle my horse."

When Betsy headed for the door, Victor called out, "Wait just a moment, Betsy!" He turned to Isa. "Where the hell do you think you're going?"

"To follow her to wherever Gerhart is," Isa said resolutely.

"Not until you tell me about my child, you're not," he ground out.

Panic showed in her face. "We need to know where those two are hiding. Surely you must see that!"

"I do. But someone else can follow her. Indeed, that's probably best, since she wants to get you alone and may lie in wait for you if you run after her."

He walked up to Betsy. "Tell your stableboy to go after the woman who just left here and find out where she's lodging. And tell him to make sure she doesn't see him doing so."

Betsy blinked, then glanced beyond him to Isa. "Madam?"

Isa came up to stand beside him. "Do as he says."

The servant frowned. "But madam, why are you listening to this . . . this . . ."

"He's my husband, Betsy," Isa said tersely.

Poor Betsy looked as if someone had just slapped her. "Your . . . your *husband*?"

"Yes," Isa said. "And the woman who just left here is indeed my sister. I will tell you everything later, but for now, all you need to know is that my sister separated me from my husband years ago. And probably means to do it again, if she can."

Betsy's shocked expression gave way to one of anger. "Does she, now?" she snapped. "Well, then, we'll just see about that! I'll follow her myself if I have to."

"No, let Rob do it," Victor put in. "He's less likely to be noticed."

Betsy took his measure in one swift glance. "Very well, sir." She marched off like Joan of Arc hunting down her first Englishman.

The door shut behind her, and the hall fell eerily silent. Isa faced him then, her cheeks as pale as death, and he all but forgot about Jacoba. He had a child. A *child*.

He stared her down. "I take it that your sister told the truth about my . . . my . . . Devil take it, I don't even know if it's a boy or a girl!"

"You have a daughter." She drew a ragged breath. "She's nine years old, and her name is Amalie."

His gut twisted into a knot. "Your dainty-footed 'servant' Amalie?"

Eyes darkening, she nodded.

Fury roiled up in him like smoke billowing out of an inferno. "When the hell did you intend to tell me?"

She flinched. "I was about to when Jacoba showed up. You may recall that I said I had something important to relate, before we could go any further in our plans."

"That's the understatement of the decade," he snapped.

He raked his fingers through his hair. He had a child. A *daughter,* for God's sake. And Isa had kept it secret from him all these years.

Something suddenly occurred to him. "That's why you wouldn't let me know where you live. Because you were afraid I would find out about her."

"Yes," she said stiffly. "You had already questioned my fellow shopkeepers about me. Fortunately, I always kept my daughter's existence fairly private, so they didn't know about her. But I knew if you questioned my neighbors here, you would learn the truth."

Fighting for calm, he scanned the hall and glanced up the stairs. "So where is she?"

"She's away at school right now. There's no school for girls in Edinburgh, so I had to enroll her in one just across the border in England. That's where I was for the past two days—taking her to school. The term began yesterday."

So his daughter had actually been in town the day he'd arrived. And Isa had hidden her from him!

"I want to see her," he bit out.

"You can't," Isa said.

That sent him over the edge. "The hell I can't! She's my daughter!"

"Do you want to keep her safe?" she cried. "Because if you do, you have to leave her alone as long as Jacoba and Gerhart are loose in Edinburgh."

That gave him pause. "Damn it, Isa—"

"I know. It's not what you want. It's not what I want, either." She took several steadying breaths. "But until we can deal with them, it's safer for her if they don't know where she is."

A sudden terror for the girl he'd never even met engulfed him. "How can you be sure they don't already know?"

"Jacoba called her 'your child.' Wouldn't she have said 'your daughter' if she'd known?"

He gritted his teeth even as he acknowledged her logic. "I suppose."

"Besides, she said she followed me out here last night. That was after Amalie had gone off to school, so she wouldn't have seen her. No one in town knew about Amalie. And Mr. Gordon certainly wouldn't have mentioned her to a stranger—not without telling me."

Mr. Gordon *was* quite a determined advocate for Isa and obviously more than capable of protecting her privacy.

Isa softened her tone. "You know that if we go running to England just so you can see her, they'll follow us. And I don't trust them within a mile of her. I don't think they'd hurt her, but . . . but I don't want her to know them. Do you?"

"Not if I can help it," he growled. "But I can keep them off our trail."

"As you did in coming to Edinburgh?"

He muttered a curse. She *would* bring that up.

"It's safer this way," she said. "You know it is. Besides, it's better for her to stay where she is until we decide what to do about our marriage, and how to handle Gerhart and Jacoba. After everything is settled, we can tell her our plans."

He considered that a moment. "So where *is* this school of hers?"

"I'm not telling you," she said softly. "Not until I'm sure you won't go running off there and lead them to her."

That roused his temper all over again. "Damn it, Isa, you can trust me not to do anything that might hurt her."

Just then Betsy came in, frowning as she overheard his cursing. "Rob says he'll stick to the woman like a barnacle, he will."

"Good," Victor clipped out, his eyes still on Isa's ashen face. "Thank you, Betsy."

When the servant nodded and then looked expectantly at her mistress, Isa said, "Forgive me, Betsy, but my husband just found out that he is a father, so he and I have a few matters to discuss."

To say the least.

"Oh, Lord, that's right!" Betsy cried. "Poor little Amalie! She thinks her da is dead. She'll be so happy to hear she's got a father."

Isa swallowed. "I certainly hope so."

So did he.

"You're a lucky man, sir," Betsy said earnestly. "That girl is a dear, has been since she was a wee thing. Rather rambunctious, if I do say so myself, but clever as can be. She'll make you right proud of her."

Regret roiled in his belly. Even the servant knew more about his daughter than he did. He was never going to get those years back, never going to see her as a baby. He would be a stranger to her.

It made him want to throttle Jacoba and Gerhart. How dare they steal his chance to see his daughter grow up? How *dare* they?

With a worried glance at him, Isa said, "We'll be in the parlor if you need us, Betsy. But for now we really need to be alone."

"Of course, madam, of course. I'll just go make sure dinner stays warm for you."

His mind racing, Victor followed Isa as she headed back into the parlor.

She closed the door, then faced him warily. "I know you must have questions—"

"Oh yes, wife of mine, a great many." He scowled. "Like why the hell didn't you tell me about my daughter when I first got here?"

She tipped up her chin. "At that point, I thought you were a thief, remember? I wasn't about to let you anywhere near her. In my mind, you were as bad as Jacoba and Gerhart."

And he would make them pay for that. Thanks to them, his daughter had been fatherless for nine bloody years! They'd stolen those from Amalie, too.

Amalie. He had a daughter named Amalie. How would he get used to that?

"Everything I've done has been to protect her, to save her," Isa whispered. "I came here so she would be as far away from my family as I could manage. I kept the truth from you so you wouldn't be able to corrupt my child—"

"*Our* child!" he cried.

"Whom I raised alone!" With a shuddering breath, she turned to pace the room. "Try to put yourself in my place, if you can. I was carrying your child, and I thought you had abandoned me for the illicit riches my family had paid you off with. When Mr. Gordon took pity on me and hired me, Amalie was the only thing that kept me going through the pain of . . . of your abandonment."

"The abandonment that I did *not* instigate," he said in a hollow voice.

"I know." She faced him again. "But I didn't know that when you came here. All I knew was that you had left us to fend for ourselves, and now you thought to step back into our lives as if nothing had happened. Except that I also knew that English law always awards custody of a child to the father. So does Dutch law."

Her breath came in hard gasps. "I couldn't risk the possibility that you would try to take her from me. Not when I thought you were a thief. Surely you can understand that."

He supposed he should be glad that she was such a

fierce protector of their daughter, but resentment of all that he'd lost still beat a bitter tattoo in his veins.

So did the words of his inquisitors all those years ago. *Your wife is no fool. Why would she trust a bumbling oaf like you to take care of her?*

He thrust the memory back with a curse. "What about *after* you knew I wasn't a thief? Last night, you didn't say a word about her. And today, when Lochlaw mentioned her—"

"I had to be certain that you weren't here for vengeance, don't you *see*? Because taking my daughter— our daughter—would be the best revenge you could ever visit upon me."

Pain made it hard for him to breathe. "You thought me capable of that?" he choked out through a throat gone raw. He strode up to her. "You truly believed I could rip our child from the only home she's known, out of some desire to strike at you?"

"I didn't want to think it. But I hardly knew you anymore. When you first came here, you were so angry. And you had good reason. You still do. I took your child from you. My family took your reputation from you, and who knows what else. Any man would want revenge after that."

He hated that he perfectly understood her reasoning. "Not against *you*," he protested. "Am I angry that I lost ten years with you, and nearly that many with our daughter? Yes. Am I furious that it was because of your family's greed? Certainly. But not at you."

"But I'm the one who trusted them. I'm the one who chose to believe my family when I should have believed in my husband. I know you blame me for that, as well you should. My only defense is that I barely knew you then."

"And I barely knew you. Otherwise, I would have realized at once that you could never have deserted me. So we were both at fault in how we handled their lies. But now that ten years have passed—"

"I know you even less now!" she cried. "Can you blame me for being cautious when you're practically a stranger to me?"

"Is that the real reason you won't bring me to my daughter?" he ground out. "Because you don't trust me to be a good father to her?"

"Of course not. I just want to protect her from Jacoba and Gerhart." Her gaze met his, softly pleading. "But you must give me time to ease her into it. Please, Victor."

He stared at her, his heart thundering in his chest. "I can wait until we root out Gerhart. But know this, Isa: I want my family back. You *and* her. You told Jacoba that you and I are together now. I hope you meant it."

"I do." Her gaze softened. "I want you back, too. You cannot know how much."

At the look of hope on her face, his throat tightened. "You called me a stranger. But I'm the same man I was then—the husband who could never hurt you, the lover who never forgot you. Not for one second. You can trust me, *lieveke*."

When her breath quickened and her eyes filled with longing, he murmured huskily, "So you know me better than you think."

Then he covered her mouth with his.

15

LOOPING HER ARMS about Victor's neck, Isa lost herself in his kiss. In this, at least, he wasn't a stranger to her. He could always make her burn, always make her desire him. She'd spent half the day reliving every velvet touch and hot caress from last night, wanting him all over again.

But was such volatile passion good for a marriage? Or as dangerous as cheese in a trap to a mouse?

He broke the kiss to murmur, "I know *you* better than you think, too." His hands roamed her, untying and unbuttoning and unfastening. He nuzzled her ear, then breathed deeply. "I know that you rinse your hair in violet water, and prefer satin to silk."

She couldn't believe he remembered that. "That's because satin is shiny," she whispered. "Like diamonds."

"Or stars." His hand skimmed her cheek. "You used to know all the constellations."

"I still do." She caught his hand to press a kiss to his palm. "And you used to know the name of every regiment that fought at Waterloo. I remember your reciting them for me."

His eyes darkened. "Now, *that* is something I prefer to forget." He drew off her gloves, then lifted one of her hands so he could run his tongue along her index finger. "I would much rather remember how you licked your fingers whenever you finished pressing the almond paste into the *banketstaaf*."

She blushed. "I would rather you *didn't* remember that. I was very unrefined."

"You were refined enough for me. I miss your *banketstaaf*. I hope you'll make some for me soon." A teasing note entered his voice. "But don't make your tea. You used to put far too much honey in it." Catching her by the hand, he pulled her toward the sofa.

"That's because you didn't like tea. You always preferred coffee, black and very strong."

"Ah, you remember that, do you?" he said with a grin. "It was a taste I acquired in Spain as a lad."

She gaped at him. "I didn't know *that*!"

When he hesitated, she feared he would brush past his childhood again. To her surprise, he admitted, "Although my mother was Belgian, my father was an English soldier. I spent most of my childhood in regimental camps across the Continent. One of those was in Spain."

Tears stung her eyes. It was more than he'd ever told her about his family. She opened her mouth to ply him with questions, thirsty to know everything, but he cut her off with a long, passionate kiss that left her thirsty for something else entirely.

Next thing she knew, he'd dropped onto the sofa and pulled her astride his lap. He'd already opened her clothes enough to free her breasts, and as he filled his hand with one and his mouth with the other, she cried, "Victor . . . oh heavens, *Victor* . . ."

"I know what excites you," he murmured, tonguing and teasing her nipple so enticingly that she clutched his head to her breast, wanting more. Always more.

After lavishing both breasts with attention, he pulled back to flash her a knowing smile and slipped his hand deep beneath her skirts until he found the slit in her drawers. When he fondled her there, she gave a low moan.

His eyes gleamed at her. "I know what makes you wet."

Daringly, she laid her hand on the bulge in his trousers. "And I know what makes you hard."

"You," he growled. "*You* make me hard."

Only me? she wanted to ask, but she couldn't bear to spoil this moment by asking if there'd been other women over the past ten years. She wanted to know, and she didn't. How could she bear knowing?

He fumbled with the buttons of his trousers until he got them open, but was so impatient to undo his drawers that he couldn't manage it, so she brushed his hands aside and did it for him while he shamelessly caressed her breasts.

When his shaft sprang free, she took it in her hand and began to stroke. "I remember this eager truncheon of yours," she teased.

"A fitting companion for my new Isa," he said hoarsely. "My bold, wanton Isa. My wife." Taking her hand, he leaned forward to rasp in her ear, "Touch yourself, *lieveke*."

"T-touch myself?" Surely he couldn't mean . . . He couldn't know . . . She drew back to eye him warily. "What are you talking about?"

He dropped his gaze to look at her below. "I always wanted to watch you caress yourself. Back then, you could barely share my bed without blushing, much less try something so naughty as to take your own pleasure—but I imagined it countless times."

Casting her a challenging glance, he pushed up her skirts, then laid her hand between her legs. Lord help her.

"Don't tell me you don't know how," he said in a guttural voice. "All these years alone, you never touched yourself intimately? Never thought of me as you put your hand inside your nightdress—"

"Victor!" she protested, though the thought of having him watch her while she did *that* made her decidedly hot and bothered.

He simply arched an eyebrow, and she knew she couldn't lie to him. "If . . . if I did happen to do it, once or twice, it doesn't mean I could . . . that I would ever . . ."

"Do it for me?" A wicked look of knowing crossed his face. "Not even a little?" When she swallowed hard, he added, "I'll do it for you, if you'll reciprocate."

That *really* got her hot and bothered. "All right." The

words were out of her mouth before she could stop them.

But his smile of satisfaction kept her from taking them back. He grabbed his aroused shaft and began to stroke, harder and more roughly than she would ever have dared to do. She watched, fascinated, as his flesh lengthened and grew darker.

"You too," he rasped, nodding to her hand.

"Oh. Right."

At first she did it only to oblige him, moving her fingers mechanically over the slick folds she'd learned to know so well—*too* well for a respectable woman—during all those achingly lonely nights.

But the more heated his gaze on her became, the more aroused *she* became. There was something so delightfully carnal about having him watch her and revel in her pleasure. Before long, she was panting and wriggling and feeling the rise of her release just beyond her reach.

With an oath, he lifted her onto her knees, urging her to rise up over his rampant arousal. "Come down on me," he commanded. "Take me inside you, Isa."

That was definitely not something they'd done together, but it didn't take much imagination to figure out what he wanted. As she impaled herself on him, he let out a coarse cry that sent delicious shivers along her spine.

He began to move at once, grinding up against her. "Ride me, *lieveke*. Oh God, please . . . ride me . . ."

So she did. And it was glorious. She could control

the motion and set the pace, make him gasp or make him growl. She felt like a queen of old, able to seize and hold whatever she wished. In no time at all, she felt herself hurtling right to the edge.

He must have felt it, too, for his jaw went taut and raw heat shone in his eyes as he rose to meet her every motion. "Yes . . ." he hissed. "That's it . . . Oh yes, wife . . . *My* wife. Always."

"Always," she echoed.

Her release came with a thunderous explosion that rocked her to her very soul.

Then she collapsed on top of him, spent and limp. He clutched her to him, both of them breathing hard. She could feel the racing of his heart against her breast, where her own heart clamored like the Scottish drums at a military tattoo. His hands stroked her bare thighs, calming her, settling her.

When at last his breathing slowed and his heartbeat steadied, he pressed his mouth to her ear to whisper, "And now I know what makes you come."

A laugh bubbled up inside her. Turning to kiss his stubbled cheek, she whispered back, "And I know the same for you."

He chuckled. "Then I hope we'll be doing this more often."

"We'll see," she said, flashing him a coy smile.

The kiss he gave her then offered promises that she prayed he could keep. Because there was still so much unsettled between them. So much to worry about.

When the kiss ended, the first of those things burst

out of her. "I suppose you've had a lot of experience at doing this with women," she murmured, smoothing back a lock of his hair, unable to meet his gaze.

He stilled. "What do you mean?"

"It's been a long time since we . . . Surely you weren't . . . celibate all that time."

"Would you believe me if I said I was?" he asked softly.

Her gaze flew to his. "I don't know. You did think I had abandoned you, so—"

"You thought the same of *me*," he pointed out. "Yet you remained faithful."

"I'm a woman. It's . . . different for me."

"Is it?" A faint disappointment showed in his eyes. When he set her off of him onto the sofa so he could fasten up his drawers and trousers, she thought he wasn't going to answer her.

But as she put her own clothing to rights, he draped his arm about her shoulders. "Perhaps it's time I tell you about my family." Then he drew her close. "My mother's name was Elizabeta. She was a tavern wench in Ostend when my father, a duke's youngest son, met her. He got her with child—me. Fortunately for her, he agreed to marry her, so that I could be born on the right side of the blanket."

"That was fortunate indeed, for both you and her," she murmured, astonished that he'd never told her this. "Not to mention rather surprising for a duke's son. I would think that a man with his connections would just pay her to keep silent."

"I wonder about that, too. But he didn't. I'll never really know why. He claimed to love her, though he enjoyed throwing her low connections up to her whenever they argued. But I know for certain their marriage was legitimate—the first thing my cousin the duke did when he found me was confirm that."

She snuggled against him and waited for him to continue.

"Still, Father was no saint in his salad days. From what I understand, he sowed his wild oats liberally. By the time he married Mother, he'd already contracted syphilis during an earlier encounter with a whore."

"Oh, Victor," she whispered.

"The pox wasn't too virulent and had no lasting effects, or so we thought. Mother said he showed no signs of it when they married. I only know of it because of what happened when I turned thirteen, and he . . . he . . ." He dragged in a hard breath. "He tried to stab Mother."

Isa froze. "*What?*" she said incredulously. "Whyever for?"

"The reason he gave was that she burned his potatoes. But the real reason was the syphilis rotting his brain. At least that's what one of the doctors at Gheel told us when we brought him there."

That stunned her. For all of her life in Amsterdam, she'd heard of Gheel. Out of devotion to the Irish saint Dymphna, its inhabitants took care of the insane. "You brought him to the Colony of Maniacs?"

"Some call Gheel that, yes," he murmured. "It was

certainly fitting for him. That's where he lived until his death when I was sixteen."

Three years. Victor had endured his father's madness for three years! A chill went through her. The poor boy. His poor mother! Isa had lost her father at twelve, so she knew how difficult that was. But at least Papa had fallen prey to an illness she could understand, and she'd had him there in spirit until his death.

Victor had been forced to watch his mother suffer through the loss of his father in spirit and sense long before the man's body had wasted away. How horrible for Victor! It created an ache in her chest that would not be banished.

She laid her hand on his knee. "Why did you never tell me?"

His gaze shot to hers, wrought with pain. "That my father went mad because of his whoring? That the rest of us were forced to work long hours in a neighboring village so we could afford for him to be fed and housed and kept from killing anyone? At twenty, it still mortified me to even think of it. I certainly wasn't going to tell the woman I'd convinced to marry me."

"I would have understood," she said softly.

"Really?" he asked, his voice suddenly distant. "Your family convinced you that I had a suspicious past solely because I never talked about my background. Imagine how much more convincing their tales would have been if you'd known of my father's sordid life and death. They would have made much of that, of my mother's being a tavern maid and my father's going mad."

"Or they would have latched onto you as the descendant of a duke," she pointed out.

"I didn't know about that then."

"Oh, right, I forgot. Rupert said it came out only a few months ago."

Victor nodded. "As far as I knew, my father was an English soldier who'd paid for his whoring days by dying insane at Gheel." His voice grew ragged. "And who made us pay for them, too."

Suddenly she understood why he was finally telling her all this about his family. "So you're saying you really did remain celibate all those years. And this is why."

"Yes." His jaw tautened. "Although at first it didn't have that effect on me. When Mother wasted away from grief and then died herself, I joined the Prussian army because I knew the regimental life, and because I knew they would take me even at seventeen."

"So that's how you ended up fighting at Waterloo."

"Yes. Father had instilled in me a hatred of Boney, so I was itching for glory, glad to be part of the fight against the French. And like any soldier, I played as hard as I fought, making frequent use of the camp followers."

He laid his hand on hers and gripped it tightly. "But then a friend of mine caught the clap from one of them, and that brought it all back to me—Mother's suffering, Father's madness—and I realized how dangerous a game I was playing. I stopped consorting with camp followers then and there."

Both of his hands now clutched hers. He stared

down to where they were joined, and his voice dulled. "After you left . . . I considered it again. I was so lonely that even a whore—" He choked off the words. "But I could never blot the image of Father trying to stab Mother from my mind."

Tears clogged her throat, but she was careful not to let them out. Some instinct told her that he would not endure pity from her.

"Then I considered taking a mistress," he went on, threading his fingers through hers. "Until I realized how lucky Mother had been, that when she found herself with child, Father was willing to marry her. I couldn't marry anyone I sired a child upon; I was still married to you." He cast her a sidelong glance. "In the end, I figured it was better to pleasure myself. Less risky."

She could hardly breathe. "So . . . no other women."

"No." He caught her by the chin. "Not since you."

His kiss was gentler this time, more like the kisses of their youth, and rich with memories of all they'd been to each other and a promise of what they could be, if they put the past behind them. It made her wish she could linger forever in his embrace. When he drew back, it was to settle her more firmly in his arms, with her head tucked beneath his chin.

"Tell me about Amalie," he said.

The yearning in his voice made her heart twist in her chest. How she hated that her family's actions had torn him from his child. *Their* child. "Oh, Victor, you'll adore her. She can be willful at times, like any child, but she has a knack for seeing the good in everyone."

"That can be a curse," he said, and she knew he was thinking of her and her family.

"It can also be a blessing. Any disparaging remarks she hears about her mother who's in trade or about her lack of a father roll right off of her back." When he tensed, she added hastily, "She tells me that those people are just jealous because I'm so brilliant and they have boring, regular mothers."

As she'd hoped, that made him chuckle, and the rumble of it settled her anxiousness over wanting him to like Amalie, to be proud of her and see her for the wonderful girl that she was.

"Does she have her mother's talent for chemicals?" he asked.

"Not a jot. She says chemicals are messy, nasty things." She nuzzled his chest, drank in the scent of his musk oil. "But if I have anything to say about it, she won't need to learn a trade to survive. Not only is she pretty, but thanks to her schooling, she's so accomplished she'll have men clamoring to marry her."

"As did you."

She lifted her head to eye him askance. "You were the only one who wanted to marry me, if you'll recall."

"I was merely the only one who dared to ask," Victor said dryly. "The jewelers' apprentices all had their eyes on you."

"Nonsense. They were hateful to me."

"Only because you ignored their attempts at courtship."

She stared at him. "*What* attempts?"

Amusement showed in his face as he smoothed a lock of her hair from her cheek. "Their posturing. Their bragging about their prowess at shooting or hawking, and their talk of their connections to men of rank."

"That was courtship?" she said, incredulous. "I just thought they were all braggarts."

He shrugged. "Some men think that's how to court a woman, by preening and showing their feathers for her."

"You didn't," she said softly.

"I had no feathers to show. I was a rough-and-tumble soldier who'd witnessed too much hard death in battle to brag about my shooting skill." His gaze met hers. "And you were an angel whom I thought too good to be true."

"I thought the same of you, you know," she whispered. "To me you were a noble, brave hero who'd helped to rout Boney. I could scarcely believe that you wanted me." Her throat tightened. "Which is why it was so easy for Jacoba to play on my fears and convince me that you didn't."

His face darkened. "I swear, I wish I'd throttled her while I had the chance. I can't believe she tried to justify why she ripped you from me." His voice grew strained. "And the daughter you won't even trust me with."

"Victor—"

"Forgive me," he said tightly. "I'm still having trouble taking it all in."

Isa swallowed. "If I . . . tell you where Amalie is, will you swear not to go there until I can introduce you properly to her?"

Pain slashed over his face, but he nodded. "I have no more desire to see her harmed by them than you do."

"I know that." She tensed. "And speaking of my relations—assuming that Rob finds out where Gerhart is hiding, what do you mean to do to him and Jacoba?"

He froze a long moment. Then he rose to pace before shooting her a determined glance. "I mean to get rid of them once and for all."

16

VICTOR WANTED JUSTICE and, yes, vengeance. It was all he could think about. He wanted to be done with them for good.

Isa looked wary. "How do you propose to do that? You can't yet even prove that you and I had no part in their theft."

"Which is why I'm not going to try prosecuting them. I'm going to call Gerhart out. It's simple and effective, and it will rid us of them once and for all."

Shock spread over her features. "Don't be ridiculous," she said sharply. "You are not going to duel with my brother-in-law."

"Why not?" He stalked toward her. "He took my wife from me. He took my *daughter* from me. He can rot in hell—and I'm more than happy to help him get there."

Tucking her legs up beneath her on the sofa, she pointed out, "My sister had a part in it, too."

"We both know she would have never come up with

such a scheme on her own. She always did what he wanted. I would wager my life that he was the instigator."

"I don't hold Jacoba quite as blameless as you do," she said, "but even if I did, I wouldn't let you duel with Gerhart. You could be killed!"

He snorted. "He could no more win a duel against me than Rupert could."

She huffed out a breath. "Fine. Let's say you won the duel and killed Gerhart. The law would consider that murder, and you would be hanged."

"Not if I fled to the Continent." Never mind that he'd be leaving his new cousin behind, and a potential position with Manton's Investigations. It would be worth it to see that wretch pay for what he'd done. It would be worth it to keep his family safe. "We could return to the Netherlands, the three of us, and be free of them at last. Once Gerhart is gone, Jacoba will come to heel."

Isa flashed him a skeptical glance. "Or she'll hound you to the gallows in revenge for taking her husband from her." She rose to place her hand on his arm. "Come now, there can be no dueling. I don't fancy seeing you dangling from the end of a noose, now that I finally have you back. And we cannot drag Amalie off to the Continent if there's any chance that Jacoba might try to get us arrested."

He crossed his arms over his chest. "If we don't find some way to be rid of them, they'll attempt to blackmail us either into helping them, or into paying for their silence. And paying and paying and paying . . ."

She shook her head. "They can't make us do anything

we don't want to do. I say we call their bluff. If they threaten to expose our past, we'll threaten to turn them in to the authorities in the Netherlands. Surely they'll back down if they think we'd really do it. They have as much to lose if things go against them as we do."

"Do they?" he said. "Unlike us, they have no children to worry about."

A frown knit her brow. "You don't know that. They could have had children by now."

He scoffed at her. "Don't you think Jacoba would have used her 'poor defenseless children' to play on your sympathies if she'd had any?"

"Verdomme," she muttered. "You're right about that. And we certainly can't risk Amalie's being left alone if we're carted off to prison."

The sight of her consternation made his throat constrict. "Amalie is the reason you wouldn't entertain having them prosecuted when we discussed it last night. Isn't she?"

She nodded.

He scrubbed his face, then went to stand before the fire. Staring into the flames, he considered and discarded several solutions, all of which ended badly. "Since you won't let me shoot Gerhart," he grumbled, "we need to rid ourselves of them legally without landing either of us in gaol and leaving Amalie without family."

"I say we should just hold fast to our determination not to give in to them," she said earnestly. "They're both cowards at heart, Victor. You saw how Jacoba ran when I threatened her. Once she accepts that exposing us would mean exposing them, too, she'll back down and disappear."

"And escape justice in the process. I can't let them do that. Besides, I think you underestimate them." He faced her, squaring his shoulders. "We need help and legal advice. We need Dom and his brother."

Alarm sparked in her eyes. "The Bow Street investigators?"

"They don't work for Bow Street; they work for themselves. Dom studied law long enough to know it very well, and Tristan used to work for Eugène Vidocq, whose expertise with criminals is legendary. Between them, they can help us determine how to scuttle any attempts your family makes to ensnare us in their nasty plans."

"No, Victor, you mustn't speak to them." She hurried up to him. "The minute we involve the authorities in any way, we're taking a huge risk."

"They're not the 'authorities,' damn it! They're my friends. They won't do anything to make matters worse. And I daresay my cousin Max, the duke, can make sure your family is dealt with. Though I hate to involve him, I will if I must."

Her mouth flattened into a grim line. "He's not going to want that kind of scandal. And what if his response is to urge you to divorce me? It's not as if we have to do anything right away," she pleaded. "We can wait and see how much of a problem Gerhart and Jacoba become. They may do nothing more than make vague threats they can't carry out."

"Isa," he chided, "you're a fool if you think they'll

give up trying to get money from us. They followed me all the way from the Continent. That's not the behavior of people who will roll over and play dead."

"At least give me a chance to talk some sense into Gerhart."

He scowled at her. "You're not going anywhere near that bastard. I'll deal with him myself. Alone."

"By calling him out? Or worse, threatening to send investigators after him? That will only provoke him! We have to be cautious."

"Your *caution* is what got us into this mess in the first place!"

When her face fell, he could have kicked himself.

"I'm sorry, Isa," he murmured. "I don't mean that."

"Yes, you do," she said, wringing her hands. "But I have survived all these years by being cautious. You can't expect me to throw caution to the winds just because you have come back into my life."

"And you can't expect me to go on with this cloud hanging over our heads. We have to act—"

A knock came at the parlor door.

They exchanged a glance. Then Isa turned for the door. "Yes?"

"Rob is back, madam," Betsy said through the door. "I thought you'd wish to know."

Isa hurried to open the door. But when Victor saw Betsy's crestfallen expression, he knew that the news was bad. "I take it that the lad didn't find out where they were staying," he said tersely.

"I'm afraid not, sir," Betsy said.

Victor released a low oath.

"You can question Rob if you wish," Betsy went on, "but this is what he told me. Even though Mrs. Hendrix had a hackney waiting down the road to bring her back into the city, he was able to keep up on horseback. But once they reached town and the traffic became thicker, he thinks she jumped out somewhere without his noticing. She wasn't in the hackney when it stopped, and he couldn't find her after that."

"Damn it all to hell," Victor muttered.

Isa was watching him warily. "Now what?"

"I'm not going to sit around waiting for them to make another move." He headed for the door. "I was sent here as an investigator, and I'm going to investigate. A Dutch couple that speaks poor English won't have gone unnoticed. I'll root them out somehow."

"I'll go with you," Isa said.

"No. I can move faster without you." When she shot him a mutinous glance, he softened his tone. "Besides, people will be more likely to speak freely if I don't have a lady with me."

She searched his face. "Just promise me you won't—" Her gaze shifted to where Betsy was listening with great curiosity. "Er . . . fight with him."

He cast her a rueful smile. "How about if I promise not to do anything that will get me hanged? Will that suffice?"

Relief showed in her face. "Yes. And you must also promise to let me know what you discover as soon as you find them."

"It may take me a few days."

"I know. Do whatever you must."

Betsy stepped forward. "Begging your pardon, madam, but does that mean you're not going to his lordship's house party?"

Isa blinked. "*Verdomme*. I forgot all about it."

"You don't have to go," Victor pointed out. "I'll explain as much of the situation to Lady Lochlaw as I dare; we can avoid the thing entirely." A grim smile crossed his lips. "She won't mind, if it means that you're unavailable as a wife to Rupert."

"Oh, Lord," Isa said. "I *have* to attend! I promised Rupert and Mr. Gordon that I would serve as chaperone for Mary Grace."

"Ah, yes. Rupert's latest love." He mused for a moment. "Actually, it might be better if you're at the house party, anyway."

Her gaze narrowed on him. "And why is that?"

Because it would give him time to summon Tristan and Dom. He supposed she had some reason for being afraid, but he needed to know more about his avenues of legal recourse from someone he could trust.

But he couldn't tell her that. She would fly up into the boughs again, worrying herself over nothing.

So he said, "It will make it harder for your family to get you alone and try to work on you."

A scowl crossed her brow. "Do you really believe I would ever fall in with their plans again?"

Belatedly, he realized how that must have sounded. "Of course not. But while you think they'll merely make vague threats against us, I'm not so sure." He stepped near to take her hand. "I don't want anything to happen to you."

"I doubt that either of them has the courage to do more than whine," she said lightly.

"If you thought that, you wouldn't have fled Paris ten years ago to get away from them."

She sighed, acknowledging his point. "What will you tell Lady Lochlaw about us?"

He squeezed her hand. "I'll tell her that you and I were separated by relations who lied to both of us, and made us think we had each abandoned the other. That I took this case precisely because I suspected that you were my long-lost wife. And that we have since discovered how your family lied to us, and are ready to restore our marriage."

"What about the fact that I was going under a different name?"

He shrugged. "You were in fear for your life from me, thanks to the lies your family told you. She doesn't need to know the whys and wherefores of it all. Just enough to make her accept that you are out of her son's life for good. That's all she cares about."

With a furtive glance at Betsy, Isa said, "I've already told Mr. Gordon the whole story."

That startled him. "Everything? Even about what happened in Amsterdam?"

She nodded.

"That was very brave of you. What did he say?"

"He was quite kind, and more sympathetic than I

expected." She shook her head. "But that was before I knew that Gerhart and Jacoba followed me here. He might not be so kind if he learns that they are lurking about."

"Which is why we have to make sure they *stop* lurking about," Victor said stoutly. Lifting her hand to his lips, he kissed it. "And why I must go. The trail grows colder by the moment."

As he headed for the door, Betsy called out, "Shall you eat something first, sir?"

"I'll get something in town." Then he strode out the door.

Truth was, he had no appetite, not with Gerhart out there somewhere plotting against them. But he would find whatever rock the man had crawled under. And when he did, Gerhart would learn what vengeance Victor had in store for him.

17

TWO DAYS LATER, around noon, Isa placed the last few items she'd need into her trunk for the house party. She couldn't get her mind off of Victor. She hadn't seen him since he'd gone off to investigate, and she felt the loss of him like the loss of a limb.

He'd said he wanted them to be a family again, and the sparkling hope of that had kept her going despite all their problems. Whenever she thought of him making love to her so sweetly, so fiercely, the problems became as nothing.

But if she didn't see him soon, she would go mad! Any minute now, Mr. Gordon was supposed to come by with Mary Grace to drive them out to Kinlaw Castle. She'd feel better if she knew that Victor was all right, first.

Betsy appeared in the doorway. "His lordship is here."

Isa blinked. "Rupert? Why?"

"I don't know. But he looks none too happy about

something. Do you think he's heard that Mr. Cale is your husband?"

"It depends on whether Victor has spoken to Lady Lochlaw yet."

Betsy sniffed. "Well, I must say, Mr. Cale has been mighty absent these past two days for a man just returned to his wife after ten years."

"He *is* trying very hard to unearth my relations." She had told Betsy everything, confident that her servant would not betray her. What she hadn't expected was that Betsy might become suspicious of Victor.

Then again, the woman considered Isa and Amalie family; she would protect them to the death. She agreed that Victor was handsome and brave—and the profusion of dahlias had swayed her a bit—but she hadn't liked that he'd been so ready to distrust Isa ten years ago. Betsy was nothing if not loyal.

"If you'll finish up this packing for me," Isa said, "I'll see why Rupert is here."

She got her answer as soon as she walked into the parlor, where Rupert was compulsively straightening her paintings on the walls. That was always a sign he was agitated.

"Good morning, Rupert. I thought you would be well on your way to Kinlaw Castle with your mother by now."

He faced her with a grim set to his mouth. "I'm not going."

"What? You can't do that! It's *your* house party. You have to go."

"No, I don't," he said sullenly. "I'm the baron. I can do as I please. People already think me half-mad anyway, so who cares if I choose not to go?"

"I care," she said.

"That's not true," he said in a voice of deep betrayal. "You lied to me. You told me you were a widow, and you're not."

She sighed. "I take it that Mr. Cale has spoken to your mother."

"Yes. Just this morning." He scowled. "And she delighted in telling me all about how you and Mr. Cale have been married for ten years. Ten years! Why didn't you say anything?"

Lord help her. She'd been dreading this ever since their last encounter. "Because I couldn't. Back when I believed the awful lies my family told me about my husband, I was afraid that he might find me, so I became Sofie Franke. When he *did* find me, I learned that we had both been laboring under an enormous misapprehension. I've been trying to figure out how to tell you ever since."

Her explanation didn't seem to dampen his anger one bit. "I trusted you! I believed you to be a widow. I wanted to *marry* you."

She swallowed. This was so hard. "I'm sorry about that. I never realized that you saw me as a possible wife until this whole mess with Victor—Mr. Cale—happened."

"That's because you never saw *me* as a possible husband," he said petulantly. "It's because I don't understand women, isn't it? Because I'm not a man about town, and I buy walking shoes instead of flowers and—"

"No, Rupert, of course not." Stepping forward, she put her hand on his arm, relieved that he didn't pull away. "I'm older than you, and far beneath you in station. I never dreamed that you would consider me a suitable wife. I assumed that we were friends. Good friends, but no more."

He wouldn't look at her, but his frown softened a fraction. "We *are* good friends, aren't we?"

"We will *always* be good friends. You are the kindest, sweetest man I know."

"More even than Mr. Cale?"

She suppressed a laugh. Victor was many things—forceful, ardent, seductive—but "sweet" wasn't one of them.

A quick glance at the dahlias filling the parlor made her amend that. He did have his sweet moments.

"You and Mr. Cale are very different men," she said earnestly. "I like you both in different ways."

"But you *love* him."

She caught her breath. Did she? She had once. Could she again? "The point is that I don't love you, which is neither of our faults, but just the way things are." She smiled at him. "And you don't really love me, either, do you?"

He frowned. "I don't know. I don't understand love. I like being with you. But then, I like being with lots of people."

"Mary Grace?" she ventured.

A blush filled his cheeks. "She's so beautiful, with her red curls and freckles. And so *tall*. Tall women are elegant, don't you think?"

She would never have described Mary Grace as elegant, but now that she thought about it, the girl had potential to be so. If Isa gave her a few tips. "I certainly do."

His face fell. "But she couldn't possibly like me. Ladies who are young don't understand me any better than I do them."

"Ah, but Mary Grace isn't the typical young lady, any more than you are the typical young gentleman. Give her a chance. She might surprise you." She patted his arm. "And she speaks of you as if you're the cleverest, finest fellow in the land."

"She *does?*" he said, his blush deepening.

Isa nodded. "And I know she's really been looking forward to the house party, solely because you invited her personally. If you don't go, and you disappoint all those people who are expecting you, she might not think quite so well of you."

That point seemed to perturb him.

Isa heard a knock at the door and then low voices in the hall. "That's probably her right now, since her great-uncle is driving us out there." She cast him a sly smile. "Of course, if you brought your curricle, she could ride with *you*, and Mr. Gordon and I could just follow behind you."

That obviously flummoxed him. "I . . . I suppose that would be all right." He steadied his shoulders. "*If* I go, I mean."

"Come now, lad, you have to go," a voice said from the door.

Isa caught her breath. Her husband was here at last!

Tensing, Rupert faced Victor and scowled. "Why do *you* care if I go?"

"Because I'm going, too. And while I may not really be your cousin, I could use your friendship." When Rupert looked skeptical, he added, "From what my wife has told me, you've learned that I've only been part of English society for a few months. I still find that world difficult to navigate. It would mean a great deal to me if you would help me figure out how to behave."

Rupert snorted. "You don't need me for that. You're a duke's cousin."

"I wasn't born knowing I was a duke's cousin. And I certainly wasn't raised as one."

When Rupert looked surprised, Victor glanced to her, and she smiled her encouragement.

With a heavy breath, he explained, "My father was a soldier, so I grew up on the fields of battle. I know how to load a cannon, but not a dealer's box for faro. I learned how to hunt for food, not for sport. I've never even been on a fox hunt."

"You don't say!" Rupert exclaimed, clearly shocked.

"I can drive a sword through a man's heart, but not dance. I write reports, not verses. All the songs I know are too vulgar for the company of ladies, and I know no sonnets at all. Every time someone of high rank enters a room, I still need a friend to explain how I am to address them."

Irritability crept into Victor's voice. "And could someone please tell me what it means to 'smell of April and May'? I can only assume it has something to do with flowers."

"It means that two people are courting. Even I know that, cousin!" Rupert caught himself with a frown. "Sorry. I keep forgetting you're *not* my cousin."

"No, but I hope you're my friend," Victor said earnestly. "Because I will certainly need one to make it through this house party, since your mother insists that I attend."

"She's good at insisting." Rupert's tone turned sullen. "She's good at ruining my life, too. It looks as if she's managed to separate me from Mrs. Franke—I mean, Mrs. Cale—after all."

Victor gave a tight smile. "Your mother didn't do that. My marriage to Isa ten years ago did. And you didn't want to make a bigamist of her, did you?"

Rupert shot Isa a furtive glance. "She would never have married me anyway. She made that very clear just now."

"She *couldn't* have married you without breaking the law," Victor countered. "But it's just as well. Because Mr. Gordon drove up with Mary Grace as I was arriving, and she's waiting for us outside. Waiting for *you*. I daresay she would be very unhappy to see you married to anyone."

Rupert gazed at Victor for a long moment, then sighed. "Oh, all right, I'll go to the house party. But only on one condition."

"What's that?" Victor asked.

"You take my curricle, and you let me drive your phaeton there."

"It's not my—" Victor caught himself. "Of course." Even as Isa was wondering if she should warn Victor about Rupert's driving, Victor asked, "But why?"

Rupert colored. "Miss Gordon is sure to be impressed with a phaeton."

Isa doubted that Mary Grace knew a phaeton from a dogcart, but if it made Rupert happy, why not?

"Ah." Victor stepped forward and held out his hand. "Well, then, we have a bargain."

Rupert stared down at Victor's hand and hesitated. When he shook Victor's hand, Isa let out a long breath. A friendship between Victor and Rupert would go a long way toward making her deception a bit more palatable in Edinburgh society once it became widely known.

Victor turned to her. "If Lochlaw is driving Miss Gordon up to Kinlaw Castle, there's no point in Mr. Gordon driving you there. You can ride in Lochlaw's curricle with me."

"That would be wonderful, thank you," she said and took the arm he offered.

"Is the estate far?" Victor asked as he headed for the door. "Will we need a picnic basket?"

"It's a couple of hours away," she told him. "And I'm sure they'll have a big dinner waiting for us when we arrive."

"Wait!" Rupert cried from behind them, his voice

sounding panicked. "What do I say to Miss Gordon?"

"About what?" Isa asked.

"About anything." Rupert came up to her. "I don't know how to talk to women."

Isa smiled at him. "You talked to me perfectly well. And I didn't even understand all the nonsense about atomic theory, whereas she finds it fascinating. So why not start there?"

"I don't think you'll have to speak much, anyway," Victor said dryly. "A lovely bouquet of roses showed up at her house this morning, courtesy of the Baron Loch-law. She'll be happy just to sit beside you and blush."

Rupert's eyes went wide. "But I didn't send her any flowers."

"I know," Victor said with a wink at Isa.

When Rupert still looked perplexed, Isa said gently, "Victor is saying that *he* did." She shot her husband an arch glance. "It was the least he could do, after deceiving you at the florist two days ago."

"Ohhh." Rupert glanced at Victor, his gaze friendlier this time. "Thank you, old fellow!" Then he cocked his head. "Are you *sure* you need my help at the house party?"

Victor chuckled. "Trust me, it wasn't my brief sojourn in society that taught me the fine effects of sending flowers." He patted Isa's hand. "I learned that from my wife years ago. All women like flowers."

"Do they?" Rupert said. "I shall have to remember that."

Isa had no doubt that Mary Grace would make sure

he did. "One other thing you should remember." She flashed him an encouraging smile. "You are the Baron of Lochlaw and a fine young man. Both Victor and I think so. Don't let your mother's machinations keep you from having a life of your own, on your own terms."

Rupert gazed at her uncertainly for a moment, then nodded. "All the same, I don't think Mother will approve of my riding out to the house party on my own instead of in the carriage with her, even if it is in a phaeton."

"Which is precisely why you should do it," Victor said, clearly suppressing a smile. "It will show her that you mean to behave as you please from now on."

"Yes!" Rupert said, squaring his shoulders. "It certainly will."

When they walked outside, Rupert surprised Isa by taking their advice to heart. He very graciously asked Mr. Gordon's permission to drive Mary Grace in the phaeton, as long as Victor and Isa were right behind them. Then, true to Victor's prediction, he escorted the furiously blushing young woman to the duke's equipage.

As the four of them set out for Kinlaw Castle, Isa breathed in the crisp autumn air and thanked God that the day was so cloudless and clear that she could see for miles. That was a good thing, since only a madman could have kept pace with Rupert.

Victor let out a curse as Rupert pulled ahead, the phaeton careening a bit on the road in front of them. "Why didn't you warn me that Lochlaw drives like a cavalry officer vaulting into battle?"

"I thought about it, but I was afraid he wouldn't go otherwise. And that would have sorely disappointed Mary Grace."

"She might have preferred disappointment to death."

Isa laughed. "Oh, he'll get them there in one piece. He always manages to avoid accident, though I don't know how." She touched Victor's arm. "Thank you for being so sweet to him."

Victor merely grunted and increased the speed of his horses. The carriages were still far enough apart that both couples could talk without overhearing each other, which was good, since Isa had a number of questions for her husband.

"Did you find Jacoba and Gerhart?" she asked.

"Regrettably, no, but I did discover where they'd been staying. They'd rented rooms in the Old Town. I tracked them that far the night I left here. By the time I got there, they were gone—without paying the rent, which lends credence to your sister's claim that they need money."

Isa snorted. "They always need money. It doesn't mean I'm going to give them any."

"I wasn't suggesting that you would." He maneuvered the curricle far more smoothly than Rupert ever had. "I'm just saying that Jacoba wasn't lying about that. Though I suspect we were right about Gerhart's not really being sick. The man who'd leased rooms to them said that he saw no signs of illness in the man staying there. So that was probably just a lie to squeeze money out of you."

She stared blindly at the mud flats they were passing. "Do you think they're gone for good?"

"I doubt it." His face looked grim. "But until I have some whiff of where they've landed, there's naught I can do about it."

"Perhaps they gave up."

He eyed her askance. "And perhaps this curricle will fly up to the moon tonight, but somehow I don't expect that. They're not going to stop until they get what they want. And I'm not going to stop until I get *them*."

That was what worried her. But it wasn't the only thing. "Did Lady Lochlaw really insist that you attend the house party?"

"Actually, now that I've separated you from Lochlaw, she has hired me to do something else that required my attendance. It seems that she worries about all the 'strange science people' her son has invited. She wants someone '*braw* and manly' standing about to keep them in line."

Isa smiled in spite of herself. "That sounds like Lady Lochlaw."

"That's the reason she gave. But I think the real reason is that she wants to rub poor Lochlaw's nose in the fact that you and I are together."

"Oh, dear. Then she is *not* going to be happy to discover that her son has new plans of his own."

"No, I don't think she is." He grinned at her. "And you'll enjoy this: She also wants me to keep people from stealing her jewels."

A laugh escaped her. "I suppose it's a good thing she doesn't know anything about our past."

"I daresay it will be a very interesting week at Kinlaw Castle."

To put it mildly. "So are we presenting ourselves at this affair as Mr. and Mrs. Cale?"

He cast her a sidelong glance. "Might as well. You've told Gordon and Lochlaw, and I've told the baroness. But with all these people knowing, do you think Amalie will get wind of it before we can tell her?"

"I doubt it; not in Carlisle. But just in case, I've already sent a letter explaining as much as I could to her headmistress. And I told her that we would come there as soon as we could get away. So if Amalie does, by some chance, hear gossip about us, the headmistress will know how to handle it."

His jaw was rigid. "I hate that I've missed so much of my daughter's life."

"I hate it, too." She covered his hand with hers. "But we will make up for lost time as best we can."

A terse nod was his only response.

Time to change the subject. "So I gather that Lady Lochlaw wasn't upset by the news that we're married."

"She took it quite well, though not entirely because it meant that her son was no longer in danger from you." He shot her a bemused glance. "It seems that she chose to see our marriage as an explanation for why I rebuffed her attempts to . . . er . . ."

"Get you into her bed?" Isa said archly.

"Exactly. She'd convinced herself that I ought to

have happily joined her there, so my lack of interest had damaged her pride. My marriage gave her a plausible reason for why I didn't let her seduce me, which much relieved her."

"Well, your marriage *ought* to be the reason," Isa said with a sniff. "I don't approve of other women seducing you, any more than you approve of other gentlemen courting me."

He chuckled. "I wouldn't bed that woman even if I were free and she were the last female on earth."

That surprised her. "Why not? She's very beautiful."

"If you can call a shark beautiful, *lieveke*. Whoever takes on that woman will be regularly picking teeth out of his flesh."

She smothered a laugh. "Glad to see that there's something we agree on."

He was silent a long moment. "We agree on a great many things, I expect. We just haven't had much of a chance to find out what those things are."

"And will we have the chance now?" she asked softly. "Your new cousin may not approve of me. He may not wish you to continue the marriage."

"I don't give a bloody damn!" Then Victor softened his tone. "He doesn't get a say in it, but honestly, I think he'll just be happy for me."

"Even if I . . . take you away from him?"

He shot her a sharp glance. "What do you mean?"

"Well, I have a thriving business here. And you . . . that is . . . I don't know what—"

"You're worried I have no income," he said tightly.

"It's not that. I just—"

"It *is* that. And I don't blame you for worrying." His voice chilled a fraction. "As Jacoba so eloquently put it, back then I didn't have 'two guilders to rub together.' And I had only a temporary post. But that has changed, I promise you. For one thing, my cousin gives me a generous allowance, although I would prefer that we not have to rely on that."

"Especially considering our circumstances. If people ever find out about our past in Amsterdam, your cousin won't be so eager to offer you a generous allowance."

"I doubt that. If the duke can embrace me after what my father did to his family—"

When he broke off, Isa said, "What do you mean?"

Victor muttered a low oath. "Just that you're not the only one who has . . . scurrilous relations."

She laid her hand on Victor's thigh. "Tell me."

He sighed. "I suppose I might as well. You'll probably hear all about it once you meet Dom and Tristan anyway."

"And we have a long drive ahead of us." When he remained silent, she prodded, "What could your father possibly have done to hurt a wealthy and powerful duke's family?"

He stared into the distance, his face rigid. "A great many things, it seems. His first crime was to have an affair with Max's mother and give *her* syphilis, which she then gave to Max's father. It was probably what led to Max's father going mad, like mine."

She sucked in a breath. She'd completely forgotten what Mr. Gordon had said about the duke's family coming to Edinburgh years ago, in search of a cure for the man's madness.

"But the second—and worst—of Father's crimes came after he retired as a naval officer. He discovered that Max's mother had actually borne a child from their affair. His name was Peter, and he was heir to the dukedom." Victor's voice grew unsteady. "So Father kidnapped him and carried him back home to Belgium. That was the last time Max ever saw his older brother alive."

18

ISA GASPED. "KIDNAPPED him!" She couldn't believe this—how much more had he been hiding from her all these years? "You mean you have a half brother somewhere? Who is also brother to the present duke?"

"*Half* brother to the present duke, as best anyone can be certain. And I don't have him anymore. He's dead. He'd been dead for four years by the time I met you."

"Why didn't you tell me about him?" she asked, unable to keep the hurt from her voice.

"I would have had to tell you about Father, too, which I didn't want." He stared blindly at the road. "Father claimed that Peter was his bastard by a whore. When the boy came to us at five, I was only four, so I always just knew him as my big brother."

A brief smile touched his lips. "We were two peas in a pod, both of us rough-and-tumble, ready to stage mock battles with sticks for rifles and rocks for cannonballs." His voice turned haunted. "It was Peter who kept me going during the years of Father's madness;

Peter who always talked of fighting Boney. It was for Peter that I ran off to join the army."

He gripped the reins so tightly his knuckles were white. "Because he'd died in the same fire that took my mad father in Gheel when I was sixteen."

"Oh, Victor," she murmured, rubbing his knee for comfort. "I'm so sorry."

He squeezed her hand, his eyes looking misty. "Manton's Investigations didn't just 'find me' in Antwerp, Isa. Max's family had learned about the fire, and had known for years that a boy who resembled Peter had died with Father. But they didn't know that Father also had a wife and son. So when Tristan and I began working together, and he noticed a handkerchief I had that was distinctive to Max's family, he decided, based on some things I'd said, that perhaps Peter wasn't dead after all. That *I* might be Peter."

She sucked in a breath. "I take it that you were deemed not to be."

"Yes. Tristan was very cagey about his suspicions, so I didn't know what he thought until I met with Max." His tone hardened. "That's when I learned that Father was an even viler bastard than I'd thought. That he'd torn my poor cousin's brother from him, and caused the madness and death of Max's father."

He cast her a brittle glance. "You and I are not very different, are we? My father was an adulterer and a kidnapper, and your sister and brother-in-law are thieves. Our families have mucked up our lives considerably."

She tucked her hand into the crook of his elbow.

"Yes, but Papa was a fine man who taught me everything I know about jewels. And your cousin must be a good man, if he can overlook your father's crimes to take you into the family."

Victor nodded. "There's no one left but the two of us. He was so happy to have family that he didn't care how I came to be his cousin. That's how I know that Max won't blame you for your family troubles. Because he's been through that sort of trouble himself."

Reaching over, he squeezed her hand briefly. "I think you'll like him. And I know he will like you." He arched an eyebrow. "His wife will be ecstatic. She resembles you a bit; she's willful, impudent, a bit wild."

"I'm not wild!"

He lowered his voice to a husky murmur. "You certainly were the night before last."

Her cheeks heated. "It's not very gentlemanly of you to point that out."

"But I'm not really a gentleman." He sobered. "I wasn't raised as one, in any case."

"Even though your father was a duke's son?"

"He was also a criminal who didn't want to be found. That's why he joined the army as an enlisted man, why he avoided people of rank, why he lived a lower-class life with my mother. It was all designed to hide his true lineage. Yes, he made sure that Peter and I had a good education, and he spoke and thought like a gentleman. But I didn't know I was a gentleman's son until I came to England."

Her heart went out to him. "That must have been . . . quite a change."

"To say the least." He managed a smile. "My cousin has been the soul of kindness; he treats me like a brother. But I don't like taking an allowance from him; it seems wrong. That's why I would prefer to work for Manton's Investigations. And I have some experience in that area as well."

Her breath burned her throat. "But what will happen if it comes out that you were connected to the theft of royal diamonds? Manton's Investigations will have to wash its hands of you, if only to protect its reputation."

He stiffened. "That's why we must make sure that your family is dealt with *before* it comes out. Every story can be made to end well, as long as the principals agree on how the story is to be told. That's why you've heard none of this about my father and Max's half brother—because the truth never made it to the papers."

"That might have worked for you and a wealthy duke, who both had much to hide, but you're mad if you think you can get my family to lie for us. They'll only keep quiet out of fear that they'll be prosecuted themselves. And they still may find a way to implicate us without implicating themselves."

"We'll see," he said noncommittally, though his expression was grim.

A thick silence fell between them.

He was up to something. She felt sure of it. "Are you

planning something you haven't told me? Do you know their whereabouts after all?"

"Not yet. But I will."

"I'm glad you're so sure," she said sarcastically. "You just told me that until they land somewhere, you can't find them. And you can't do anything while the house party is going on. So unless you mean to have someone else—" Then she groaned. "Victor, please tell me that you didn't write to your Bow Street Runner friends in London."

When he said nothing to that, a chill passed down her spine. "Victor! We said that we wouldn't—"

"*You* said, Isa." He stared resolutely ahead to where the horses clopped along at a slower pace than that of her racing heart. "I didn't agree, as you'll recall."

"I had good reason for what I said! Until we find my sister and brother-in-law, we are still suspects in a theft! I'm still the one who made the parure, and you're still the one who left the strongbox long enough for thieves to get into it. What do you think your friends will make of that?"

He glared at her. "They won't judge us, I promise you."

"How do you know?"

"Because Tristan is the reason I found my family. He risked much to reunite me with them. He's not going to do anything to hurt me."

"But you don't know if he'll hurt *me*. He has no loyalty to me."

"He will," he said firmly. "You're my wife."

"And due to me, you've suffered. Your friends may not take that as well as you have."

"Have faith in me for once. The way I always have faith in you."

She snorted. "Not enough to consult me on your decisions or abide by my wishes." Her blood thundered in her ears. "Did you go to Carlisle, too, after you promised not to? Did you lead Jacoba and Gerhart to Amalie?"

"Of course not!" he said, outrage in his tone. "I made you a promise, and I uphold my promises. But I never promised to keep my friends out of this. And I won't, do you hear me? We *need* them, damn it. You'll just have to trust me on this. *If* you're capable of that."

For him, it was a matter of trust, but for her it was so much more. She'd acquiesced to everything her family wanted when she was young, and she'd transferred that acquiescence to her husband after she married. It had nearly destroyed her life.

But after she'd been on her own, she'd begun to trust her own instincts, and her instincts were screaming that they should keep their past as secret as possible. So it didn't sit well with her when he stepped in to take over her life as if she should have no say.

"Isa," he said quietly. "You know damned well that if we don't resolve this problem with Gerhart and Jacoba, they will come back one day—perhaps when Amalie is about to get married, or you're heavy with our second child—whenever we least expect it. And they will attempt to wreak havoc again. I know better than anyone that family secrets rarely remain buried."

He was right. But that didn't lessen her terror of what might happen when he opened the Pandora's box of their past for the world to see.

When she didn't answer, he took her gloved hand and lifted it to his lips for a kiss. "It's too late to stop Tristan and Dom from coming, *lieveke*. I sent them an express yesterday, and if I know them, they'll be here before the house party is over."

He hesitated, then added, "But I didn't tell them why I needed them, only that it was urgent. So if, by the time they arrive, you're still uncomfortable with their involvement, I'll keep silent about why we're seeking your relations. How's that?"

A lump stuck in her throat. He was trying. He really was trying. "That's all I ask—that you consider what I want, before you go off and follow your own instincts."

He sighed. "I'll do my best. But it's been a long time since I had a wife."

"I know. And a long time since I had a husband."

They finally smiled at each other, and were silent awhile.

Then she brought up what she'd been thinking about during their discussion of income earlier. "Is there no possibility of us living in Edinburgh? Perhaps you could do some investigative work here."

His expression was thoughtful. "I suppose it's possible." He glanced over at her. "But I've just begun to know my family. I would like to know them better if I can. And there's no reason you can't open a shop in London. You might make more money there."

She eyed him askance. "I'm sure your cousin will be delighted to have one of his relations in trade."

"That's a good point. We'll have to see how that will sit with him. Then again, his wife's family runs Manton's Investigations, so he obviously doesn't stand on ceremony as much as a duke generally does."

His cousin sounded more intriguing by the moment. Perhaps he wouldn't look down on her so much after all.

"There's another, more important consideration," he put in. "Amalie could go to school in London, and then you wouldn't have to send her away."

Isa hadn't thought of that. "That is indeed an important consideration. And one that might just tip the balance." She glanced at him. "I miss her so, when she's gone."

He met her gaze with a smile, and her heart flipped over. Perhaps everything could work out after all. Assuming that her relations stopped plaguing them.

Victor was right: They couldn't go on with the past hanging over their heads. They had to resolve the problem of Jacoba and Gerhart before it destroyed their lives again.

19

THREE DAYS INTO the house party, Victor roused to the feel of his wife's soft hand stroking his hard cock.

Instantly awake, he murmured, "You've become inordinately fond of this game."

A provocative smile curved her lips. "And I suppose you haven't?"

"I didn't say that." He leaned over to kiss her deeply.

He never tired of kissing her, never tired of taking her. Perhaps one day he would, but it had become an unrelenting obsession as he made up for all the years without her.

Rolling her beneath him, he lifted her nightdress to enter her and found her wet, warm, and willing, which only fired his desire more. When she rose to his thrusts with great enthusiasm, it spurred him into madness.

Her new boldness intoxicated him. In his youth, he'd loved her shy blushes, but now that he wasn't so young anymore, he loved having a lusty bed partner.

Some time later, they'd both found their release and lay there breathing hard, entangled in each other's arms. He buried his face in her neck to kiss the rapid pulse at her throat. God, who'd have guessed a month ago that he'd be spending his nights in the arms of his wife again? It still seemed like a miracle.

After a few moments, she left the bed to dress. He sat up and leaned back against the bedstead to watch. Strange how he'd forgotten so many little things about her—the way she'd never liked to linger in bed, the way she did her ablutions . . . the way her hips swayed as she walked.

When that made him harden, he swore. He had to curb his randy urges before he wore the poor woman out and drove her away again.

No, he hadn't driven her away, he reminded himself. He must stop thinking like that. She wanted him, had always wanted him. Hell, if she hadn't balked at his having a mad kidnapper of a father and a tavern wench mother, nothing was going to drive her off. What a fool he'd been, to keep so many secrets from her when they'd married. Perhaps if he hadn't, they wouldn't have lost so much time together.

"Well?" she asked as she shimmied into her corset. "Are you going to get up?"

"I suppose I must, if I'm to play lady's maid," he drawled.

She lifted an eyebrow. "I could always call for a servant and let her get a look at you lying there in the altogether."

Chuckling, he left the bed. That was something the old Isa would *never* have said. Her lack of modesty around him was another new thing that he enjoyed.

"Remind me—what does Lady Lochlaw have planned for us today?" he asked as he laced her up.

"I suppose, since the day has dawned fair for a change, we'll finally get to play that Scottish game called 'golf' that Rupert loves so much."

He groaned. "I hate games. They're pointless."

"I think it sounds fun. It involves hitting a ball with a club into a series of holes along a lengthy course." She cast him a teasing glance. "If you really don't want to play, you can always just walk around holding my club for me."

"I'd rather you hold *my* club," he said, pressing his budding erection against her from behind.

"No more of that, now. Rupert wants us on the lawn by nine. He's afraid it will rain before we can complete a full game."

Victor snorted. "What a pity that would be." But he began to dress. If Lochlaw wanted them on the lawn, then her ladyship would want *him* on the lawn, and he did owe the woman for not blaming Manton's Investigations for his subterfuges.

Isa finished dressing before he did, so he told her to go on. He knew she liked a hearty breakfast, whereas he almost never ate it.

He was heading downstairs when a servant met him with a note. Tristan and Dom had arrived in Edinburgh. The servant asked if there was any answer, and

Victor wrote a reply asking the two men to come to the estate as soon as possible. Then he charged the servant with getting the note to them in all haste. Isa wasn't going to be happy to hear this.

When he reached the lawn, he saw the others heading for the course that ranged over a flat portion of the estate bounded by woods. Good. There'd be no chance to speak to Isa alone for a while. She deserved a few hours of fun before she had to start worrying about Jacoba and Gerhart again.

The morning passed more quickly than he'd expected. After a while, he began to enjoy watching as his wife attempted futilely to master the game. Every time she missed, she muttered to herself, then complained about her faulty club. She was a sore loser, his wife, another thing he hadn't known about her.

She also had quite an arm on her, for she kept striking the little leather ball too hard. Indeed, when she came up to hit it this time, she knocked it so far that it sailed over the green area around the hole and into the nearby woods.

When he laughed and she glared at him, he couldn't resist teasing, "You've confused this game with archery, Mrs. Cale. The object isn't to hit a tree."

"I did that on purpose," she said, tipping up her chin. "It's more of a challenge to hit it out of the woods."

He snorted. "If you can even find it in there."

She planted her hands on her hips. "Care to place a wager on that? If I hit the ball back onto the course from the woods, you have to take my place and show me you can do better at this than I."

"And if you don't?" he asked.

"I'll make you *banketstaaf*," she said with a smile.

"Will you lick your fingers when you're done?"

Color rose in her cheeks. "Victor! Don't be rude!"

But he saw her smiling as she began the long trek toward the other end of the course.

As she'd watched them banter, Miss Gordon had worn a guarded expression. But when Isa paused to look back, then stuck her tongue out at him, the young woman burst into laughter. It pleased Victor to see Miss Gordon coming out of her shell under Isa's encouragement. She was even wearing those ridiculous purple walking shoes Lochlaw had bought.

"Can't you do something about this?" said a female voice at his elbow.

Lady Lochlaw. Damnation.

He shot her a sideways glance. Though her evening gowns were provocatively low-cut, the baroness had the good sense to dress fairly modestly during the day. But she flirted so outrageously with the male guests that several of the wives were beginning to grumble. Even Isa had made a few arch remarks regarding the baroness.

Not that he blamed her. Lady Lochlaw was shameless.

"About what?" he said smoothly, though he had a pretty good idea of the source of her disgruntlement.

"My son. And that . . . that daughter of a trades-man."

"Ah, you mean Miss Gordon."

"Of course I mean Miss Gordon. Don't be impudent." She glanced over to where Lochlaw was showing Miss Gordon the proper way to hold a golf club, and Miss Gordon was gazing up at him adoringly. "It won't even do me any good to hire you to find out all her dark secrets. A chit like that is too young to have any."

"I should hope so." He watched as Isa disappeared into the woods after her ball. "I understand why you didn't like your son taking up with an older woman you believed to be a widow. But why don't you approve of a young, well-bred maiden?"

"Well-bred—hah!"

He decided to give Lochlaw a little help. "You do know that she has quite a substantial dowry, don't you?"

The baroness blinked. "Isn't she the granddaughter of your wife's partner?"

"Great-niece. Her father, Mr. Gordon's nephew, is Alistair Gordon."

She gaped at him. "The coffee merchant who owns half of New Town?"

"The very one." He suppressed a smirk at her astonished expression. "She's merely very fond of her great-uncle, so she enjoys hanging about his shop."

"That's the most ridiculous thing I've ever heard,"

Lady Lochlaw said with a sniff. "What is the world coming to? Young women 'hanging about' in shops, indeed. What is her family thinking?"

"That it's better for her to make herself useful to her relations than to sit bored at home? I don't know. You'll have to ask them." He cast her a covert glance. "But your son likes her. Shouldn't that be all that matters?"

She stiffened her shoulders. "I can see that being related to a duke has taught you nothing."

He chuckled. "Not enough to suit your ladyship, apparently."

Waving away a midge buzzing around her head, she murmured, "How substantial is this dowry anyway?"

"Somewhere in the vicinity of twenty thousand pounds, I believe."

She sucked in a sharp breath. "That *is* a nice dowry." Gazing over at her son, she frowned. "Still, my boy could have any young lady of rank he wants. Lady Zoe, for example, would be perfect. Her father is the Earl of Olivier. Granted, she can be a bit too opinionated for my tastes, but she's an even greater heiress than Miss Gordon."

He glanced over to where the exotic-looking Lady Zoe was arguing about methods of crop planting, of all things, with some poor gentleman. "Ah, but does she know about atomic theory?"

"Pish posh," the baroness said with a dismissive wave of her hand, "who cares about that?"

"Your son."

"Nonsense. He will grow out of it. My point is, with so many eligible females about, why must he always fix on the unsuitable ones?"

Lady Lochlaw wouldn't like hearing that she'd brought it on herself by trying to fit her square peg of a son into a round hole. Any young man would balk at that.

"Think of it this way," Victor offered. "A quiet and malleable woman like Miss Gordon will be more likely to allow you to 'guide' her actions once they marry. If you make an ally of her, you might have a say in your son's life yet."

Though he doubted it. Miss Gordon had some experience with avoiding a scheming mother. With Lochlaw to bolster her confidence and him to bolster hers, they might prove more formidable together than they'd been apart.

And if they didn't, they'd simply remove themselves as far away from their mothers as they could.

Lady Lochlaw was tapping her chin. "He does have to marry; we must have an heir, after all. And I've had no luck in coaxing him to marry a lady of my choosing." As she spotted her son headed toward her, she added in a whisper, "But don't tell him I am even thinking of allowing it. That will surely make him throw his latest *chère amie* over for some washerwoman, just to spite me."

Somehow Victor doubted that. Anyone could see

from looking at Lochlaw and Miss Gordon that they had eyes only for each other.

"Cale!" Lochlaw called out as he approached. "We're going on to the next part of the course. Did you see which way your wife went?"

A sudden unease settled in his gut as he scanned the area. "The last time I saw her, she was heading into the woods after her ball."

"Well, she hasn't returned, and we're ready to move on. Those woods are pretty deep; she'll never find it in there. I could have told her that."

And Isa was stubborn enough to look for it until dark, just so she could show him up. "I'll go fetch her. She can't have gone far."

Perhaps it was the arrival of Dom and Tristan that had him on edge, or perhaps it was just that his life felt unsettled. But as he headed for the spot where he'd last seen her, his sense of unease wouldn't leave him.

✦ ✦ ✦

ISA WANDERED THROUGH the beeches, feeling a bit silly as she peered through the underbrush for her ball. Pray God there were no snakes or ferocious beasts about. She'd lived in cities all her life; she wasn't comfortable with wild creatures.

She should have just abandoned the stupid ball. What had she been thinking, to wander into the woods after it?

A sigh escaped her. She'd been thinking to win

her wager against Victor. He'd been far too quiet until she'd hit the ball into the woods. It was time to jolly him out of whatever memories had thrown him into a pensive mood. She enjoyed her glimpses of the joking Victor; she saw that side of him far too seldom.

The sound of footsteps in the brush made her smile. He had come after her!

But before she could turn to tease him, she was grabbed roughly around the waist from behind and a forearm was shoved up against her throat so hard she could scarcely breathe. "Good morning, Isa," said a voice that she remembered only too well.

Gerhart!

She fought him and tried to scream, but she couldn't get a breath to do so.

"Hold still, damn it!" Gerhart growled in Dutch as he increased the pressure on her throat until spots formed before her eyes. "If you want to see your daughter again, you'd best keep still."

Her heart dropped, and she froze. Then she began to shake.

"That's better," he murmured, releasing his hold a fraction. "We don't have much time. Victor will come looking for you any moment, so listen to me and listen well. Amalie is with Jacoba."

Terror gripped her. How did he know Amalie's name?

He'd probably known from the beginning. What a fool she was! Jacoba had spoken of following her to the cottage after Amalie left, and Isa had believed her. But if the Hendrixes had followed Victor into town, there was no reason they couldn't have then followed Isa to her cottage while Amalie was still there. Or when she took Amalie to school.

"Do you understand?" he growled.

Her throat was on fire, but she managed to rasp, "Yes."

"So don't be screaming or trying to summon your husband. Jacoba knows that if I don't come back by evening, she's to move the girl elsewhere. And you'll never see your daughter again."

The thought made her blood run cold. He relaxed his grip, and she dragged air into her lungs. "How . . . where . . ."

"We took her out of that school in Carlisle." His low chuckle made her skin crawl. "Or I should say, *you* took her out. Jacoba can still mimic your handwriting well enough, and all it needed was a letter from you saying that you were sending your sister and brother-in-law to fetch her."

His voice hardened. "We sent it from Edinburgh the day after you tossed my wife out of your house like you were too good for her. Well, you're not. You're the same as us, no matter how fine your friends are now."

The fact that he knew where her daughter was in school lent credence to his claim, but surely the school would never have given Amalie over to strangers. "I don't believe you," she ventured.

"I thought you might say that." He held something up before her face. It took a second for her to make out what it was in the dim forest light, but as soon as she saw the glitter of the hatpin with its fleur-de-lis, her heart faltered.

"I see that you recognize it. She said that you made it for her, that it's paste. But you told her you'd give her one with real gold and jewels if she takes good care of this one."

Lord help her, they really did have Amalie! Her poor baby! What must she be thinking? Was she all right? Surely Jacoba wouldn't hurt her own niece. How could she?

"It's just to prove that we have her," Gerhart went on. "No harm will come to her as long as you do what we say, do you hear?"

She could barely breathe for the hold about her neck, and she couldn't think at all, but somehow she managed to nod.

"I swear if you do this one thing for us, we'll never trouble you again."

When she snorted, he jerked his forearm back into her throat so hard that she reeled.

"It would pay you to be nicer to me just now," he hissed in her ear. "I can make sure you pass out; I learned that as a wrestler. I can have you unconscious in a heartbeat if I wish. Do you understand?"

Her throat felt seared by an iron, and she nodded. She understood perfectly well that he was a villain, and she'd tell him so if she could just breathe once more.

He relaxed his hold again, and she gulped air.

"Now, listen well," he ordered. "I want you to bring me the Lochlaw diamonds. I don't care how you get them—I just want them in my hands by nightfall."

"Why don't you just let me give you money? Or jewels from my shop?" she rasped.

"Because the moment we're away, you'll have the authorities after us for kidnapping." He pressed his mouth to her ear, and his beard scratched her cheek. "But not if you've stolen the diamonds. Then you'll have no choice but to keep quiet about it."

She groaned. That was how he'd always worked— turning her into a thief like him, so he could control her. "I don't know the first thing about stealing," she rasped.

"That's not my concern. You can put a fake in their place if you want. We heard in town that you were the one to clean them, so you must have a good idea of what they look like. Or you can just steal them. I don't care, though I'm sure you'd rather stay free of the noose."

"Please, Gerhart, there's no time to create a copy," she protested, though she had no intention of making a copy *or* stealing the real necklace, if she could help it.

"As I said, not my concern. But her ladyship won't miss them until some ball or other, so after you take the real necklace and bring it to me, you'll have plenty of time to replace it with an imitation to save your neck.

Either way, I want the real diamonds by evening. Then, and only then, will I give you my niece."

"What if I can't get to the necklace?" she asked, her heart pounding painfully. "What if it's in a strong-box or—"

"Then your sister and I will be raising little Amalie." He taunted her, "I daresay she'll be a hard little worker in some trade. Of course, she'll always wonder what happened to her mama, but—"

Isa released a savage growl, and he choked off her air again.

Now his voice held an edge. "And don't be thinking to pawn off any fake jewels on me. You taught me how to tell paste from real well enough. So, at five o'clock this evening, you will take the Lochlaw diamonds and leave the estate—alone—to ride out along Strathridge Road. At some point along the route, I'll join you and we'll make the exchange—my niece for the diamonds."

Anger had her shaking even as she struggled for breath.

"Oh, and one more thing, *sister*. I advise you not to mention this little conversation to your husband. We both know he wouldn't approve of your stealing any diamonds, even to save your brat. And if I see him going off to town to summon the authorities or mount a rescue, if I get even a hint that he's following you this evening, I will never show myself, and you will never see your daughter again. Do you understand?"

When he lessened the pressure on her throat once more, she rasped, "I understand, you coward." She fought for breath to vent her rage, but could only manage a low whisper. "I understand very well that if you hurt Amalie in any way, I'll find you and cut your heart out."

He chuckled. "How bloodthirsty you've become, *Mausi*. Does Cale have to sleep with one eye open, after the way he abandoned you?"

"You know quite well he didn't abandon me!" she hissed.

"True. So perhaps it's *you* having to sleep with one eye open. I heard that Cale languished in gaol for weeks while the prince's guards were given free rein to go at him full bore, trying to learn the truth."

A chill froze her blood. "You *know* what happened to him after I left?"

"The friends who helped us leave Amsterdam told me." His voice turned snide. "You must have quite the hold on him. I heard that they starved and humiliated him, day after day, determined to make him break down and admit who committed the crime. And he still wouldn't point the finger at you, poor sod."

Oh, Victor, my love. "That 'poor sod' will see you dead before this is over," she warned in a harsh rasp. "And I'll see you hang for this if it's the last thing I do."

He tightened his grip on her throat again. "I wouldn't be planning on that if I were you, *sister*. Not if you want Amalie to ever meet her father." He mused aloud, "Perhaps we'll pass her off as our daughter. With those blond curls of hers, she certainly looks like Jacoba."

Impotent tears welled in her eyes.

Suddenly she heard the sounds of rustling brush. "Isa! Where are you?" Victor called. "Forget about that damned golf ball! I concede the wager."

"I must go," Gerhart whispered. "But I'll see you on the road at five o'clock. Don't forget."

Then he tightened his hold until everything went black.

When she came to, she was lying on her back on the ground staring up into Victor's worried face as he knelt beside her, chafing her hands.

"Are you all right?" he said hoarsely. "Did you faint?"

"I'm . . . fine," she rasped, her throat still too sore to do more than whisper. For half a second, she considered not telling him and just doing what Gerhart wanted, however she could.

But that impulse swiftly fled. Victor had a right to know. And she needed to tell him. "Gerhart was here. You must go after him!"

Shock lit Victor's face before he leapt to his feet in a fury. "Devil take it, I'll kill him for hurting you!"

"*No!*" she hissed, grabbing his leg. "Don't go near him! He's kidnapped Amalie, but he wouldn't say where he's got her. So just follow him. *That's all!*"

Victor paled. After briefly scanning the woods, he headed off at a run.

She lay there a moment, her breath coming in labored gasps. When she could breathe again, she struggled to her feet. Glancing around, she looked for anything

Gerhart might have left behind as a clue to Amalie's whereabouts, but all she found was her bonnet, which had been knocked off in the struggle with Gerhart. As she bent to pick it up, she spotted the fleur-de-lis hat-pin nearby, glittering in the leaves.

The tears she'd been holding back during her encounter with Gerhart now streamed down her face. She took the hatpin in her gloved hands and stared blindly into the woods.

"Hold on, dearling," she whispered. "We're coming for you. They won't get away with this."

Guilt settled in her belly like soured wine. She should have listened to Victor, and gone to get Amalie the second those two appeared in Edinburgh. No, she should never have let her daughter out of her sight in the first place. If only she'd kept her at home. If only—

The sounds of footsteps in the brush made her turn to find Rupert and Mary Grace approaching.

Rupert took in her tears and dirt-smeared skirts and his eyes widened. "What the deuce happened? We've been looking and looking for you." He surveyed her surroundings. "Where's Victor? He called out that he'd found you."

She thought fast. "I . . . I startled a vagrant who knocked me down. Victor went after him."

"A vagrant!" Rupert cried. "On the estate? No doubt it was a poacher. I shall speak to the gamekeeper at once."

"No, I'm all right," she said hastily. She had to talk to Victor, figure out what they were going to do before she involved Rupert. "I'm sure he's gone by now."

She hoped he was. And that Victor was tracking him.

"Perhaps you should go lie down in the house," Mary Grace said, hurrying to her side to take hold of her arm. "You look unwell, truly you do. And you're talking funny."

"Yes," she murmured. "I—I probably should go inside."

The rustling of brush coming from the direction Victor had headed made her heart sink. As soon as he came into view, panic seized her.

"You two go on," she urged Rupert and Mary Grace, wanting only to get rid of them now. "Victor's back. He can look after me."

"Did you find the poacher?" Rupert asked Victor.

"No," Victor said, his heart in his eyes as he looked at her. "He had a horse waiting; I heard it whinny and then hoofbeats as he rode away. By the time I got to the road, he was long gone. It's been so dry, I couldn't even tell which way he went. And he may not have taken the road at all."

"A poacher with a horse," Rupert mused aloud. "That's peculiar."

"Lochlaw," Victor said in a tight voice. "Could you hurry ahead to the house and make sure there's some wine waiting for Isa?"

"Oh! Of course! Come, Miss Gordon, let's go."

As soon as they were out of earshot, she grabbed Victor's arms. "He's gone? Disappeared?"

The howling in Victor's eyes mirrored that in her heart. "Yes," he snapped. "But he's a dead man. This time, nothing you say will keep me from murdering that bastard."

"I would rather see him hang." She cupped his cheeks in her hands. "But first, we must get Amalie back."

"And how are we to do that?"

Through a throat still raw from Gerhart's abuse, she told him what her evil brother-in-law wanted.

20

A SHORT WHILE later, Isa watched Victor change into his riding clothes in their bedchamber at Kinlaw Castle. She'd never seen him like this, so driven . . . so deadly cold.

He'd been like this from the moment she'd told him what Gerhart wanted. It worried her. Especially when he shoved a flintlock pistol into each greatcoat pocket.

"Victor, you must listen to me—"

"No!" His gaze turned desperate, trailing down over her neck, where bruises were surely showing already. "Forgive me for not protecting you, *lieveke*," he said hoarsely as he came up to cup her cheek. "The very thought of him hurting you—"

"It wasn't your fault."

"It was. I should have been there with you." He gave a shudder, then stiffened his stance and returned to stuffing items in his pockets. "Dom and Tristan are on their way here, and we will find that bastard and Amalie if we have to search all day."

Any discussion of not involving Manton's Investigations had ended once Amalie was taken.

"You couldn't find him before," she said. "What makes you think you can find them now?"

She regretted her words the instant Victor tensed. "This time I have help; surely Dom, Tristan, and I can run him to ground before evening." He took out a powder flask and checked its contents. "No matter what I have to do, I will set everything right and rid us of the Hendrixes forever."

"But if Gerhart sees the three of you searching," she cried, "he'll bolt, and I won't have the chance to get her back!"

Victor rounded on her so swiftly that she jumped, and he cursed under his breath. "You are not meeting alone with him ever again." His gaze dropped to her neck, and his mouth formed a grim line. "He could have killed you today. I would never have forgiven myself if he had."

She swallowed. "But he didn't. And he won't. Not as long as he thinks he can get something from me."

"You're not stealing the Lochlaw diamonds for that man!" he growled.

"I quite agree." She squared her shoulders. "I merely mean to borrow them."

He stared at her. "What the devil are you talking about?"

"Rupert adores Amalie. He will certainly loan me the necklace long enough to save her. Then you and your men can hunt Gerhart down for however long it takes to retrieve it."

"And what happens if I can't get it back before he sells the gems out of it, the way he did before? That necklace is a family heirloom. Lochlaw might not care if it disappears, but the baroness most certainly will."

"Rupert won't involve her," she said stoutly.

"The minute she needs to wear the necklace for some society affair and it's not to be found, she'll start pestering him about where it went. You know Lochlaw. He won't stand firm against her. He'll give you up, and next thing you know, Lady Lochlaw will have you prosecuted. She won't care why he 'loaned' them to you, especially once she hears about what happened in Amsterdam."

"We have no choice! Amalie is at stake!"

Stark fear showed in his face before he shuttered it. "Yes, but I'm not gaining our daughter only to lose her mother." He shoved the powder flask into his pocket. "I'll save you both without risking prison for either of us."

A knock came at the door and Victor hurried to open it. Isa heard a footman say, "Mr. Cale, there are three gentlemen downstairs waiting to speak to you. They say they're from London."

"Thank you, I've been expecting them. Tell them I'll be along in a moment."

The footman headed off as Isa said, "Three? Who is the third?"

"Probably my cousin, though I'm surprised they involved him." Victor faced Isa with a grim expression. "I have to go." When she walked toward him, he added, "Let me have a few moments alone with them, Isa."

She blinked. "Why?"

"Because I haven't told them anything about us yet. And I need to do that without you there to make them nervous."

Oh, Lord.

I heard that they starved and humiliated him, day after day, determined to make him break down and admit who committed the crime. And he still wouldn't point the finger at you, poor sod.

No—but he hadn't forgotten it, either.

Whatever he saw on her face made his expression soften. "I'll want you to come in afterward and answer their questions. But with two of us telling the tale, it will get too confusing and take too long. It will go more quickly if I prepare them first. All right?"

She gazed at him warily. "I suppose."

He sighed and closed the door. "Don't you trust me to save our daughter, Isa?"

"That's not it." She searched his face. "The question is whether you trust me."

A muscle throbbed in his jaw. "Of course I trust you."

"Then why won't you let me borrow the diamonds?" she asked. "And don't tell me it's because of Lady Lochlaw. You're cousin to a duke; Lochlaw is a baron. The two of them can prevail if something happens to those diamonds."

She shook her head. "No—it's because deep inside, some small part of you still worries that this is just another scheme. That my family and I have found a more creative way to trick you so we can commit another theft right under your nose."

Anger flared in his face. "That's absurd. I know you would never steal."

She smiled wanly. "Just a week ago, you were painting me a master criminal who wanted to steal the diamonds for herself."

"That was before I knew the truth!" he protested.

"It was also before you found out that I hid your daughter from you." She softened her voice. "I wouldn't blame you for not trusting me. Not after what Gerhart told me about what they did to you in Amsterdam. He heard of it from his friends."

Every inch of him went rigid. "You can't believe anything Gerhart says."

"I wouldn't generally, but I know something happened to you after I left, something that turned you bitter and angry. Something more than my seeming abandonment."

When Victor turned away with an oath, she added in a whisper, "Is it true the prince's guard starved you? Humiliated you? That you were in gaol for weeks, being tormented?"

"It's all in the past. None of it matters now."

"All of it matters!" She grabbed him by the arm. "It's still a thorn in your heart, making you wary of me, making you do things like call in your friends without consulting me, and refuse to let me take the diamonds. Because deep down, you're afraid it will all happen again—Jacoba and Gerhart and I destroying your life, fooling you—"

"Damn it, Isa, that's not true!" He released a shaky breath, then continued in a more controlled tone, "We don't have time for this. You'll just to have to believe me when I say that the only ones I distrust are Gerhart and Jacoba." He pulled free of her and opened the door. "I'll send for you when we're ready for you."

"Victor—"

"No arguing right now, Isa. I have to go." He walked out and left her.

You'll just have to believe me when I say that the only ones I distrust are Gerhart and Jacoba.

She wanted to believe him, to be sure that the past wasn't influencing his decisions. But how could she, after what had happened to him? What if the real reason he refused to try giving Gerhart the diamonds was some lingering distrust of her?

She had to do *something*. If Victor wouldn't involve Rupert, she would. Because she was not going to let Gerhart have her baby.

She headed for the door. Catching sight of herself in the mirror, she winced to see the purplish bruises ringing her throat. It was no wonder Victor wasn't thinking rationally right now, if this was what he had seen. She didn't *think* the sight of them would turn Rupert irrational, too, but right now she needed both men to be sensible.

Determinedly, she jerked out a scarf and wrapped it about her neck. Then she went off to find Rupert.

✦ ✦ ✦

VICTOR HURRIED DOWN the stairs with Isa's words ringing in his ears. Was she right? *Did* he still distrust her, somewhere in the part of his soul he never wanted to probe? Where the ghosts of his inquisitors resided?

Your wife is too clever for the likes of you. She knows you can never provide her with the riches she craves.

He thought he'd silenced those voices once he knew the truth, but perhaps she was right. Perhaps he never could.

Forcing that uneasy thought away, he joined his friends. He trusted her. He did. And now it was time to lay everything out for them, and make sure they trusted her, too. Because they had to help him. He couldn't do it alone.

To his surprise, Dom and Tristan had brought Dr. Percy Worth with them, the man who had cured Victor's pneumonia when he was near death on the ship a few months ago. The doctor had become the de facto physician to the Duke's Men, so Victor wasn't surprised that they'd wanted him along. He hadn't said what his emergency was; they might have thought he was injured.

He was glad to see the man. He and Isa would need all the help they could get.

It took far too long to tell them everything that had happened, right up to the kidnapping. They asked a number of questions, and when they fell quiet at the end of his tale, it worried him.

Then Dom rose from his chair. "You do know how insane this all sounds."

"Probably as insane as my turning out to be the long-lost cousin of a duke," Victor said dryly. "Or you, a viscount's son, being forced to become the owner of an investigative agency." When Dom grimaced at that, Victor glanced at Tristan. "Or you ending up as an agent for the French police after stealing your half brother's horse." Victor crossed his arms over his chest. "Life is full of insanity. And just because it sounds insane doesn't mean it didn't happen."

Tristan stared at him. "We're not questioning whether it happened, but whether it happened the way your wife says it did. She *could* have conspired with her family to steal those diamonds years ago and set you up to be blamed for it. And she could very well be colluding with her family now to do it again."

"You wouldn't think that if you'd seen her throat," Victor ground out.

He'd hardly been able to look at her once the bruises had begun showing, so dark against the pale skin of her neck. Just the sight of them had made his heart stop and his belly roil. And when he thought of the terror she must be feeling—the terror *he* was feeling—

Damn it all to hell. Amalie was out there somewhere, confused and afraid, and that bastard Gerhart meant to profit from it. When Victor caught up to him, he would kill him with his bare hands.

"If I had time," he went on, "I could lay out for you every instance that proves her innocence—the interviews I conducted, the claims of her servants, the things Lochlaw and his mother observed. But that will have to wait." He steadied his gaze on them, resolute. "My daughter is in that bastard's clutches and I mean to find her, with or without your help."

"You have our help, sir," Dr. Worth put in. "You know that you do. But the girl might not even be yours."

Victor bristled at that. They were as bad as his inquisitors, thinking him some fool. "She was born almost exactly nine months to the day after we married. I asked Gordon where she was christened, then checked the birth records."

He'd had to talk to the man while he was hunting down Gerhart, in case Gordon had encountered the pair without knowing who they were. And Victor hadn't been able to resist asking about Amalie's birth. Then he'd endured Gordon's lecture over it, a lecture he'd known he richly deserved. It had been his last little stab of distrust of her.

Hadn't it?

Of course it had. "Don't you think I probed every part of her story until I was sure of the truth of it? I am no longer a young idiot to be taken in by wild tales." He choked down his temper. "I trust her. So you are going to have to trust *me* that I am right about her. If you can't do that, tell me now. Because I need you on my side if we are to rout Gerhart."

A knock sounded at the drawing room door, and he let out a curse. What now? The door opened and Isa sailed in with Lochlaw in tow.

Victor scowled. "I told you I'd send for you."

"Forgive me," she said tightly, "but I find myself unable to wait on your leisure when our daughter is in danger."

He ought to be glad she managed to stay away *this* long. "What's he doing here?" Victor demanded, his gaze flicking to the baron.

Lochlaw flushed but stood his ground. "Let me help," he said earnestly. "Amalie is a sweet girl. The diamonds are nothing to me next to that."

"Damn it, Isa," Victor cried, "you *told* him?"

"Yes, I told him! I told him everything."

"Even about us and Amsterdam?" Victor said, incredulous.

She nodded. "I figured he should know what he's getting into."

Lochlaw stepped forward. "Look here, Cale, I don't care about what happened in the past. I know that your wife is a good person."

"Yes, but you are not the only person in this household."

"It doesn't matter," Isa said. "I don't care if you never recover the necklace and Lady Lochlaw tries to send me to prison. I don't care if they hang me. I have to see Amalie safe from them once and for all! I *have* to!"

Tristan exchanged a shuttered glance with his companions as he rose. "And my friends and I mean to make sure that you do, Mrs. Cale."

Stifling an oath, Victor made introductions all around.

As soon as he was done, Isa told the men, "Please talk some sense into my husband. He thinks he can find them on his own, but Gerhart is sure to whisk her away if he has any inkling of your involvement." She leveled a hurt glance on Victor. "I don't even care if you never trust me or believe me again. I can't risk our daughter!"

And in that moment, when he saw the fear and worry in her face and realized that he'd helped to put them there, he knew: She was wrong about him. His inquisitors were wrong. *Everyone* was wrong.

The problem ran far deeper than any supposed remnant of distrust of her. And he had to make her see that if they were to save Amalie.

21

"Gentlemen, would you please give me and my wife a moment alone?"

Isa caught her breath, the words filling her with dread . . . until she saw Victor's eyes. He was staring at her with a melting tenderness that calmed her fears.

As soon as the other men moved into the hall, he came up to her. "You asked if what Gerhart said about me was true. And the answer is yes. They did starve and humiliate me. They told me you were using me, that you were a thief who only married me because I was the guard."

He dragged in a harsh breath. "Apparently the jeweler, who knew Mother, had told them about my father, so they used that, too. They played on my self-doubts by pointing out that I was a nobody with a mad father, that I would never be able to give you the things you wanted, that I couldn't take care of you. They said anything to break me down, so that I would admit you were the thief."

Hearing her fears so clearly voiced made sobs rise in her throat. "Gerhart said that he heard you wouldn't give me up. Why not, after all of that?"

A brilliant smile crossed his lips. "Because, my dearest, there was a part of me deep inside that screamed that they were wrong. A part of me that denied it. A part of me that trusted you when even logic said I shouldn't." His eyes darkened. "But after my time in gaol, I buried that part so deep I almost forgot it was there. As did you. Still, it never went away."

He grabbed her hands. "Ten years ago, when we let Gerhart and Jacoba and the prince's guard play on our fears about ourselves, we lost sight of the truth. That we loved each other. Deeply. Intensely. With every part of our souls."

She was crying now, and he reached up to brush the tears from her eyes. "Tell me, Isa. Do you still love me?"

Through her sobs, she managed to whisper, "Yes." She did love him. She couldn't conceive of *not* loving him.

"And I love you. More than life, more than breath. That's why I trust you; why I know bone-deep that every word you've told me is true. I know it the same way I know that you regret the past, that you never betrayed me . . . that you would die to keep our daughter safe." He laid her hands against his chest. "I know it in here. Your good character resonates deep in my heart."

He loved her—he truly did! And he believed in her. The past truly was the past.

"What *really* kept us apart for so long, what we both

forgot," he went on, "is that we are stronger together. Separately, we remember our weaknesses and our self-doubts and we falter." He clutched her hands tightly. "Don't you see, my love? Gerhart said those things to make you doubt yourself, to make you worry about my trusting you. Jacoba mentioned our daughter so I would get angry at you and doubt my budding trust of you."

As he spoke, her vision of the past shifted. Like a jeweler cleaving a gem, Jacoba had known just where to score the stone so she could crack it with one blow. She'd known how to play on Isa's fears—and Victor's. And they'd let those fears drive them apart.

"Even my inquisitors knew just where to stick the knife to make me falter," Victor was saying. "They didn't have to lift one hand to me. All they had to do was appeal to the part of me that didn't feel good enough for you—the part that was ashamed of my parents and my childhood and worried about my ability to care for you."

His voice turned fierce. "But they couldn't touch the part of me that loved you. And Jacoba and Gerhart couldn't touch the part of you that loved *me*. So we can't let them touch it now. We have to hold firm to what we know, what we believe: that together we can save our daughter. That we are good, strong people who can do anything we put our minds to."

Lifting her hands to his lips, he kissed them softly. "That our love for each other is the rock upon which everything depends. As long as we cling to that rock, they cannot drown us, no matter how hard they try. As long as we cling to that rock, we *will* save Amalie."

"Oh, Victor," she whispered. "We *have* to save her. I don't know if even our love could survive the loss of her."

"Our love can survive anything," he vowed. "But let's make sure that it doesn't have to survive that, shall we?"

He kissed her lips then, and she took solace from the sweetness of it. When he drew back, his eyes burned into hers. "Believe in me, *lieveke*. Believe in yourself. And we *will* get through this."

He released her hands. "Now, let's make a plan to save our daughter." Striding to the door, he opened it. "Come in, gentlemen. We must figure out what to do."

As the men filed back in, Isa could tell that they'd been discussing matters in the hall. It reassured her that they radiated the same bold confidence as Victor. Mr. Manton and Mr. Bonnaud were used to dealing with the likes of Gerhart and Jacoba. She only hoped they were as successful in getting her daughter back as they'd been in finding Victor.

Mr. Manton faced Victor. "It seems to me that if the baron is willing to offer the diamonds—"

"No," Victor said firmly. "Gerhart is setting a trap, just as he did last time. If we play the game his way, he'll win and we'll be left with nothing."

"So we don't play the game his way," Mr. Bonnaud said. "We play it ours. We have a few advantages. He doesn't know that more Duke's Men are here, or that the baron is in on the scheme." He nodded at Isa. "And he vastly underestimates the determination of a lioness to protect her cub."

Victor smiled warmly at her. "Very true. Gerhart also expects Isa to be a mouse—one more advantage we have." He glanced at Rupert. "I know what Gerhart said about not following her, but is there any chance we can do so from off the road?"

"It's heavily wooded," Rupert said. "I fear that if you stayed close enough to keep sight of her, you'd be heard by him. Strathridge Road isn't traveled very much."

"Which is probably why he chose it," Dom said. "Still, with three more men involved than Gerhart expects, we can lie in wait at intervals alongside the road."

"I could charge the servants with helping—" Rupert began.

"No," Victor said sharply. "The moment we involve the servants—or the other guests—there are too many people to control. Someone will spook him."

"All right," Rupert said. "Most of the road runs along the river, so he's likely to come from the side away from that. I can also tell you the best places to hide. I know every inch of those woods from gathering plants for my experiments."

"That's something else Gerhart won't expect," Tristan pointed out. "He'll assume that Victor knows the terrain as little as he."

"So if his lordship can show us a couple of hours beforehand where to station ourselves along it," Dom said, "we can divide the road up among the five of us, so we can search for Gerhart after the exchange is made. We might even get lucky and see where he enters it from the woods."

"True, but you're missing the point," Victor said. "All of this presumes that we let Isa meet him and give him the diamonds. But even if we caught him with them, he'd just claim that he had no idea they were stolen. He'll say that his loving sister-in-law brought them to him as a gift. He'll say that Isa did ask him and Jacoba to fetch Amalie, and that they were coming to bring her to Isa when Isa decided to meet them on the road."

Dragging his fingers through his hair, Victor began to pace. "It's not as if Isa can deny that they're her family. And the authorities won't want to believe that Amalie's own aunt and uncle kidnapped her. There's no note, no evidence to prove Isa's story other than those bruises on her neck, and she could have made those herself. It's her word against his that he kidnapped Amalie."

Rupert's gaze shot to her in alarm. "What bruises on your neck?"

"Never mind," Isa murmured.

At that, Dr. Worth inexplicably narrowed his gaze on her.

"Gerhart will invent some story to save his own skin and make sure Isa gets blamed for it," Victor went on. "If pressed, he'll drag out the theft from years ago and blame that on her, too."

"And you, if he can manage it." Isa glanced to the other men. "That's how Gerhart works." When she saw them exchange veiled glances, her heart sank. "I know you gentlemen have no reason to believe me anything but a schemer and a thief. I'm not sure *I* would believe me. But—"

"Actually," Dr. Worth interrupted, "I do believe you." He gestured to the scarf around her neck. "A schemer would be making the most of those bruises you're covering up, using them to whip us into a frenzy so she could get what she wanted. But a woman with a heart and a conscience wouldn't want to distress her admirers—or her husband—any further."

"What bruises?" Rupert cried. "Did your brother-in-law *hurt* you, Mrs. Cale?"

"See what I mean?" Dr. Worth said with a smile.

Tears stung Isa's eyes. "Thank you," she whispered. "Whatever you can do to regain my daughter will be much appreciated. But I don't see any way around giving Gerhart the diamonds. Believe me, I wish I did."

Mr. Bonnaud rubbed his chin. "It's a pity we can't get him to steal them himself. It would be hard for him to deny being caught in the act of theft."

"That *would* be convenient," Victor said, "because then every claim Gerhart made after that would be deemed untrustworthy. The preponderance of old evidence he might bring to bear against Isa would work against him instead."

"Unfortunately, Gerhart is too much a coward to do his own stealing," Isa said bitterly. "Even in Amsterdam, he sent my sister to the shop rather than going himself. He prefers to throw the blame for crimes on other people."

"Exactly," Victor said, but he sounded distracted as he wandered over to the fireplace.

"I wouldn't be at all surprised if he didn't even take

part in opening the strongbox beyond making the false keys," Isa went on. "He always—"

"That's it!" Victor whirled to face Rupert. "Where does your mother keep the diamonds?"

"In . . . in her jewelry case. Why?"

"Could it be breached easily? Broken into?"

Rupert scowled. "You don't have to break into it. I'm *giving* you the jewelry."

"Just answer the question, damn it!" Victor growled.

The poor lad blinked. "It has a key, but Mother hides that in her bureau. I suppose the case could be smashed open if someone really wanted to steal anything, but here in the country, with all the servants about—"

"Someone would almost definitely be caught," Victor said gleefully. "Or at least seen fleeing with the gems."

Mr. Bonnaud's eyes lit up. "So if Gerhart can be seen running off with them by someone other than you two—or us—then when we capture him on the road, we won't have to mention any kidnapping. We'll merely be part of a group of men apprehending him for the theft he just committed."

"Desperate men do desperate things, after all," Mr. Manton said, a slow smile curving up his lips. "Everything that has happened can be recast to fit our tale. Gerhart assaulted Mrs. Cale in the woods when she wouldn't give him money. He grew desperate after that, and ran into the manor to steal the diamonds."

Victor got excited. "We can point out that his wife

showed up at Isa's home to get money from her a few days ago. Isa's servant can testify that Isa threw Jacoba out for it."

"And if he starts claiming that Mrs. Cale stole those diamonds in Amsterdam," Mr. Bonnaud said eagerly, "Victor's claims otherwise will sound more believable in light of Gerhart's clear theft of the diamonds now."

"The timing will have to be precise," Mr. Manton warned. "We'll have to work fast."

"But—" Isa began, not following the conversation at all.

"I know," Victor said, ignoring her. "Fortunately, with Lochlaw involved, we can shape events to our satisfaction. He'll make sure the right people are in the right places at the right time."

Isa stared at them. "But I don't see—"

"And since no one needs to actually lay their eyes on the diamonds," Mr. Manton said, "your wife can already have them in her possession while everything is happening."

"Yes," Victor said, "she'll have a part to play as well. Because she has to have a firm alibi for the theft."

Isa scowled. "I don't—"

"As do you," Mr. Manton pointed out.

"Will all of you just be quiet!" Isa finally cried. When she'd got their attention, she said, "I don't understand you. How can you possibly get Gerhart to steal the diamonds?"

"We can't," Victor said, grinning at her. "But we don't have to. We just have to make it *look* like he did."

He turned to Mr. Bonnaud. "Ready to do a bit of play-acting, old chap?"

◆ ◆ ◆

BY TWO O'CLOCK, Victor and Isa were ready for their "alibi" performance. As they headed out to the banks of the river that ran along one end of the Kinlaw Castle grounds, Victor could tell she was nervous, but it didn't matter.

They had to do this. It was the only way he could think of to save Amalie and her. He hated that she still had to meet with Gerhart, but there was no way around it. He could only pray that Lochlaw was right, and they'd be able to keep her well in sight from certain vantage points along Strathridge Road.

"Victor, I'm not so sure about this part of the plan," she murmured.

"You don't think Tristan can steal the diamonds?"

"I'm sure he can, but what if someone gets a good look at him? He's at least ten years younger than Gerhart, and their faces aren't remotely similar. Though I suppose the false beard does help."

"Trust me, Isa," Victor said as he escorted her down the stairs. "Tristan's disguise will hold up from a distance."

"Yes, but what if—"

"Tristan is experienced at slipping into and out of tight spots. He's not going to let anyone see him closely but Miss Gordon, and she's already been coached in what to say."

They'd had to involve the young woman since they needed one reliable "witness" to the "theft" who could raise the alarm.

"Yes, but she's related to my partner," Isa said. "Don't you think the authorities will find her testimony suspicious?"

"Not when she's also a close friend to the baron whose diamonds are being stolen." He smiled faintly at her. "And I daresay by the time any trial comes about, she will be an even closer friend to the baron, which will make it even more convincing."

Her hand tightened on his arm. "I'm worried about Rupert, too. He's not used to lying; he doesn't do it well. This will be hard for him."

"That's why his involvement is limited to getting his guests and servants where we need them." And so far Lochlaw had done his part rather well. He'd already gathered the guests for an afternoon tea by the river, and he'd made such a fuss over the preparations that all the house servants were out here attending to everyone.

"And you're assuming that Gerhart won't see any of this—"

"The part of the river we're going to is on the opposite side of the estate from Strathridge Road; that's why we chose it. Gerhart can't be in two places at once. It's also why the timing is so crucial. We want him to be already waiting for you near the road when our 'theft' takes place."

"Oh, Victor, this could go wrong in so many ways."

He halted to gaze solemnly at her. "Yes, it could. But

it won't." He covered her hand and squeezed. "Have faith, my love. Your friends and mine won't fail us. That's something else Gerhart isn't considering: He can't conceive of people who care so much for each other that money doesn't matter. He'll never expect us to have so many friends on our side."

That must have settled her nerves some, for she gazed up at him, her heart in her eyes. "I love you, Victor."

"I love you, too. And we're going to get our daughter back, I swear." He cast her a hard glance. "Just remember, *don't* give the diamonds to Gerhart until you have her in your hands. I don't trust him."

"Don't worry. That's one rule I can easily follow."

"I assume that Lochlaw has already given the necklace to you," he said.

"It's in my . . . er . . . corset cups. I figured I couldn't lose it there." She slanted a self-deprecating look at him. "I have plenty of room, after all."

"Not that much room." Then something dawned on him. "Your breasts—they're bigger because of Amalie. God, I'm such a dolt. That should have occurred to me."

She lifted an eyebrow. "Men don't usually question the reasons for such enhancements. You're no different from any other man in that respect."

They fell silent as they neared the crowd by the river, where the baron was already introducing Dom as the owner of Manton's Investigations and Dr. Worth as a friend of his. Dom took over from there, explaining that his partner, Mr. Bonnaud, had been forced to return to Edinburgh to deal with some business. Since

Lochlaw wasn't a good liar, they'd figured it was best to give him very few lies to tell.

So Dom chatted amiably about their reason for coming to Scotland—a new case Victor had found them. Tristan had already made sure to be seen riding toward Edinburgh, before he'd circled back to the remote hunting cottage on the estate. He should be there now, donning an oversize coat, which Lochlaw had unearthed from old clothes in the manor attic, and padding it out with extra shirts. He was also using greasepaint to draw on a false beard and tucking his hair up under a wide-brimmed beaver hat to complete his Gerhart disguise.

Miss Gordon glanced at Isa. "I do wish I'd had the forethought to wear a scarf out here, like you. I find it rather chilly."

"Shall I have a servant fetch your shawl?" Lochlaw asked, forgetting his role.

Fortunately, Miss Gordon was more adept at deception. "Oh no, my lord, I think a brisk walk back to the house will warm me. Besides, I don't know which one I wish to wear."

When she smiled shyly at him, Lochlaw looked momentarily dazzled. Then he seemed to remember his part, for he straightened and said, "Oh, right. You ladies do like to . . . look your best."

"As long as you're heading back, Mary Grace," Isa said to smooth over the moment, "would you mind fetching my shawl as well? I believe I left it in her ladyship's sitting room."

"I don't mind a bit," Miss Gordon said and, with a last veiled glance at Victor, hurried off toward the house.

Victor pulled out his pocket watch and glanced at it. Damnation. How was he to make polite conversation for another fifteen minutes with his blood pumping and his hands itching to throttle Gerhart?

Lady Zoe walked up to Dom. "You're one of the Duke's Men, aren't you?"

When Dom grimaced, Victor had to choke back a laugh.

"Some call us that, yes," Dom said tightly. "But we don't work for the Duke of Lyons all the time, you know. That was just some silly nickname the press gave us after one case."

"Yes, but it was a rather spectacular case," she said. "You were the talk of my town for weeks, especially since you and Mr. Bonnaud are Yorkshire-born, and your father's estate is only a few hours distant from Highthorpe. We were all terribly impressed by how you found Mr. Cale and saved the dukedom."

"Yes, it was very clever of them, wasn't it?" Victor put in before Dom could say anything to ruin the young lady's enthusiasm. It was actually a good thing she knew of Manton's Investigations. It would make everything easier when the trouble started. "Dom, why don't you tell Lady Zoe about that case you took in Lancashire, the one with the innkeeper who'd disappeared?"

Though Dom lifted an eyebrow at him, he launched into the tale, which thoroughly engrossed the other guests, too. Victor listened with only half an ear, aware that any minute now, Tristan would be slipping into Lady Lochlaw's boudoir and breaking open the jewelry case.

He cast a quick eye over the crowd. Thank God Lady Lochlaw seemed to have no desire to leave the party. If she headed for the house, it would muck up their plan considerably.

Though Dom dragged out his tale a long time, Dr. Worth was forced to jump in and ask more questions to keep it going. Victor wanted to growl his frustration. What the devil was taking Tristan so long?

Isa squeezed his arm, clearly impatient, too.

And then he heard it—Miss Gordon screaming as she ran across the wide lawn to the riverside. "Help, someone, help!"

Lochlaw leapt into action. "What is it, Miss Gordon?" he called.

"There was a strange man in her ladyship's sitting room!" she cried as she approached them, all out of breath. "I—I think I took him . . . by surprise. It looked as if he'd broken . . . open a case of some kind."

Lady Lochlaw's eyes went wide. "My jewelry! Oh, Lord!"

As if on cue, Tristan sprinted away from the side of the house farthest from them. As the guests looked on in horror, he jumped dramatically atop a horse he'd had waiting there and rode off into the woods.

"Mr. Manton and I will catch him, my lady!" Victor cried as he and Dom sprang for the house. "Don't you worry!"

Behind him, he heard the baron telling his mother

that they should leave this to the investigators. But Victor had known there would be male guests, and perhaps even servants, who would want to join the chase, so he'd charged Dr. Worth with staying behind to urge caution and keep the other guests from jumping in.

Victor and Dom ran toward the house, both of them calling for horses as they neared the stables. The minute the grooms came running out with mounts, they jumped on and rode off for the woods in the direction Tristan had gone.

They rode hard for several minutes until they came to the cottage where Tristan was awaiting them. Dom and Victor pulled up in front. "Did anyone see you?" Dom asked.

"No one but Miss Gordon," Tristan said as his horse danced a little, still blowing hard. "And by the way, she's a pretty thing, isn't she?"

"Don't even think it," Victor said with a roll of his eyes. "She's Lochlaw's."

"I was merely commenting that she is an attractive—"

"Quiet!" Dom ground out, and they all fell silent, listening. The sound of an approaching horse made Victor curse. Someone had managed to follow them despite Dr. Worth's efforts.

When the horse burst into the clearing with Lady Zoe atop it, Dom began to curse, too. Spotting them, she drew the horse up short, her eyes going wide.

"Who the bloody hell are you?" Tristan growled, the only one of them who hadn't met her.

She screamed, turned her horse before any of them could react, and spurred it into a gallop back the way she'd come. Tristan thought quicker than any of them and was off after her before Victor could even blink.

A short while later, he returned with the lady sitting across the saddle in front of him. He had one hand on the reins and the other across her mouth, but he was having a devil of a time controlling her. As soon as he pulled up, she started fighting him in truth.

"Stop it, damn you!" Tristan cried and pulled his pistol from his coat pocket. "Don't make me shoot you!"

She froze, her eyes widening in terror as she gazed at Victor.

"Put that thing away, for God's sake," Victor ordered. "You're frightening the poor woman."

"Good," Tristan said blithely. "She shouldn't be running after a— Ow!" He jerked his hand from her mouth. "That 'poor woman' bit me!"

"It's no more than you deserve," Lady Zoe cried as she slid from the horse and backed away from the three of them, looking as if she'd bolt any second. "I can't believe you're all really thieves!"

Muttering a curse, Victor got off his horse and walked toward her. "This is not what you think, Lady Zoe."

"What are you going to do to me?" she demanded.

Tristan dismounted. "I still say shooting her is the best course," he drawled as he stalked her.

"Shut up," Dom growled. "You're only making it worse."

"How can I make it worse? Now we have a witness we don't need."

Lady Zoe was shaking her head. "I won't tell anyone, I swear. I only wanted to see the great Duke's Men in action." Her voice hardened. "I didn't know you were all conspiring with this . . . this . . ."

"Tristan Bonnaud, at your service," he said with a mock bow. "And I'm only occasionally a thief."

Her eyes went wide. "*You're* the famous Mr. Bonnaud?"

Tristan broke into a grin. "You've heard of me. How flattering."

She snorted. "You're ruder than I imagined." She planted her hands on her hips. "And fatter."

His grin vanished. "I'm in disguise." He swept her with a rakish glance. "But I'd be happy to show you my true form later, after this is done and we—"

"Stop flirting, Tristan," Victor snapped. "We don't have time for this." He approached the young woman warily. "Lady Zoe, we're in the midst of a very secret, very important operation. There was no theft. We're only making it *appear* that there was a theft in order to save my daughter."

"Your daughter!" She narrowed her gaze on him. "Mrs. Cale said she was at school."

"She was. Until someone kidnapped her from there. I don't have time to explain it all right now. Just trust me when I say that his lordship knows all, and he's part of it." He bore down on her swiftly. "But it is absolutely essential that you not speak of this to anyone."

A calculating expression crossed her face. "I see."

"I mean it. When events unfold, you'll understand why, but for now, I really need you to stay out of this and keep our secret. Do you think you could do that for me? The lives and futures of my wife and my little girl are at stake."

She glanced from him to Dom and Tristan. "I suppose I could keep quiet." Then she lifted her chin. "But I will expect something in exchange."

That caught Victor by surprise.

"How much do you want for your silence?" Dom asked in a hard voice.

"Not money!" She eyed them all warily. "A favor."

Victor blinked. "What kind of favor?"

"You'll know when I come to claim it."

As Dom muttered an oath under his breath, Tristan snorted. "I still say we should just shoot her and be done—"

"Shut up, Tristan!" Victor and Dom said in unison.

Then Victor thrust his hand out to Lady Zoe. "A favor. It's a deal. You have my word."

With a furtive glance at Tristan, she shook his hand.

"We need to go," Dom told Victor. He glanced at Lady Zoe. "We have to be somewhere shortly, my lady. Can you get back to the house on your own?"

"She got here on her own, didn't she?" Tristan said dryly.

Lady Zoe shot him a foul glance. "I'll be fine." She stalked off in the direction of where her horse was probably wandering, then paused at the edge of the clearing to look back at them. "Don't forget. The Duke's Men owe me a favor."

"Yes, my lady, we know," Victor said.

As she disappeared into the woods, Dom sighed. "Something tells me that we are going to regret that bargain."

"I won't," Victor said. "I'll pay it in blood if I have to." He headed for his horse. "Come on. We don't have much time before Lochlaw is to meet us near Strathridge Road. And five o'clock will be here sooner than we think."

22

AT A QUARTER to five, Isa slipped out by the garden door, where Mary Grace was waiting for her with a horse she'd requested for herself from the stables. Everyone had been told that Isa was frantic over her husband's disappearance in pursuit of the thief, and had gone to her rooms to watch for him out of her window. If anyone tried to see her, Dr. Worth was to hold them at bay by saying she had fallen sick from worry and needed to be left alone, that he was tending her and she needed rest.

"Good luck," Mary Grace whispered as she handed over the reins. "I'll be waiting here for your return." She blushed. "And his lordship's."

Rupert had told his guests that he was joining the search for the thief. Then he'd ridden off into the woods to meet with Victor and the others on the road.

Now she must do her part. Isa reached Strathridge Road in a few minutes, then rode down it with her pulse pounding madly. Gerhart was here somewhere.

She could feel him watching her, feel his eyes on her.

Her only consolation was that he had Amalie with him. That was all that mattered.

She listened for sounds of the men in the woods but heard nothing, which reassured her. If she couldn't hear them, then Gerhart couldn't, either.

As she rode along, she started to worry. How far down the road had the men positioned themselves? What if Gerhart made her go miles and miles? It would be dusk soon. Surely he didn't mean to do all of this in the dark.

Then she heard the clopping of horse's hooves, and she tensed. Before she could turn to look, a voice ordered in Dutch, "Keep your eyes ahead, Isa."

Gerhart.

Her heart felt as if it would beat right out of her chest. She scanned the woods lining the road ahead of her, wondering where Victor and the others might be. Had they come this far? Were they watching her now? Or had she outstripped them?

Even if they were nearby, they'd agreed not to approach Gerhart as long as he had Amalie under his control, since it would be too easy for him to ride off with her before he could be caught. Too easy for him to hurt her.

Her hands tightened on the reins. Pray God he wasn't *that* much a villain.

"Listen carefully," Gerhart went on in a low voice. "I want you to hand the diamonds back to me."

She frowned. "Not until I see Amalie."

"You'll see her soon enough," he growled, "but only if I get the damned diamonds now! Hand them over, or I swear I'll leave you here on the road, and you'll never see her again!"

Did he think her a complete fool? Her temper rising, she turned in the saddle to see Gerhart riding just behind her. But there was no sign of Amalie.

Her blood ran cold. "Where's my daughter?"

Gerhart scowled at her. "I know your husband has to be around here somewhere," he clipped out as he spurred his horse to come up beside her. "I'm not fool enough to bring her with me."

"You said for me not to tell him, so I didn't," she lied. "I kept my side of the bargain. Now keep yours, curse you!"

His gaze narrowed on her. "Not until you give me the diamonds. If you do it now, I'll go fetch her and bring her back to you. If you don't, I'll assume you don't have them and we'll be done. And little Amalie will be ours to raise."

Victor's voice sounded in her ears: *Just remember, don't give the diamonds to Gerhart until you have her in your hands. I don't trust him.*

Neither did she.

"That wasn't our agreement," she said, slowing her horse. "I'm not giving you *anything* until I see my daughter."

"You try my patience, Isa."

"And you try mine!" she spat. "How can I even be

sure you *have* her? You didn't give me enough time to find out from the school if she was gone. It's possible you and Jacoba got into the school to talk with her by telling them you were her relations. You could have got the hatpin from her then. For all I know, she's *still* at school, and this is just another way you and my sister are trying to get money out of me!"

His face went cold. "Are you willing to risk it?" A snide look crossed his face. "Can you imagine what your husband will say when he learns that you bartered your daughter's future for a handful of diamonds?"

That twisted the knife in her chest. But she dared not take the chance that he would keep the diamonds and Amalie, too. That necklace was the only thing she could rely on to get her what she wanted.

And she could rely on Victor. He was here somewhere; she knew it in her bones. He would never let Gerhart get away with this.

"Either you give me Amalie," she said firmly, "or I ride off with the diamonds. The choice is yours."

He blinked, clearly shocked that she was standing up to him. Then his face clouded over. "Fine," he snapped. "Let your daughter's future be on your head."

He spurred his horse into a gallop and rode past her down the road. For half a second, she sat frozen. Did he really mean to end this now?

Perhaps she *should* agree to his terms. Wouldn't it be better to take the chance that he would keep his word, rather than risk the possibility of Amalie disappearing forever and Victor and his men never being able to find her?

Separately, we remember our weaknesses and our self-doubts and we falter . . . Gerhart said those things to make you doubt yourself . . . We have to hold firm to what we know, what we believe: that together we can save our daughter.

Believe in yourself.

She did. And her every instinct cried that Gerhart was bluffing—that if she gave up the diamonds now, she would never see her daughter again.

Turning her horse, she rode back in the opposite direction. Her heart was hammering in her chest; her blood ran like sludge through her veins. *Oh God oh God oh God,* she prayed, *please don't let this be the end. Please let me be right about Gerhart.*

After what seemed like an eternity, she heard hoofbeats behind her and Gerhart rode up alongside her. She'd won this round!

Gerhart glowered at her. "Follow me," he ordered. "I'll bring you to her. But if you don't have those diamonds on you, I'll make you both regret it."

She had no doubt of that.

Whirling the horse back around, he set off at a gallop. She followed, fear gripping her chest. The men had their horses with them in the woods, but they couldn't follow through the dense growth on horseback, and they dared not follow on the road unless they kept far enough behind for Gerhart not to see them. Which meant they'd have to stay far enough behind not to see *her.*

So how would they find her, especially if he left the road?

She squared her shoulders. She would simply have to lead them to her.

♦ ♦ ♦

VICTOR WAS FIT to be tied. Isa had ridden past his spot what seemed like hours ago, though it had probably been a few minutes. She'd been alone. And just seeing her perched on the horse, back straight and face bloodless, roused his every protective instinct.

Where the devil was that bastard Gerhart? Would he show? Or had he figured out that they were up to something?

The longer he stood there, the more terror gripped him. For the first time, he understood what Max's father must have felt when his son had disappeared. How fitting that Victor should suffer the same. Though it hardly seemed fair that he—or his innocent daughter—should be punished for his father's sins.

He wouldn't let that happen, damn it! He would hunt Gerhart to the ends of the earth first.

Several more minutes ticked past. Then he heard a vaguely birdlike cry. He thanked God for his training as a soldier; otherwise, he wouldn't have recognized Lochlaw's birdcall as the same signal they'd agreed upon. He could only pray that Gerhart hadn't noticed it.

Moving as swiftly through the woods as he could with his horse, he came upon Lochlaw pacing in his designated spot. "Thank God!" the young man cried when Victor reached him. "Your wife rode past with some fellow just a short while ago. He was in front of her, and she was following him." He cast Victor an anxious look. "Neither of them had Amalie."

Victor's heart stopped. "Damn that bastard! I knew we couldn't trust him." Creeping up to the road, he gazed down it, but there was no sign of anyone.

Within moments, Tristan and Dom, who'd also heard the cry, were at his side. Lochlaw began telling them what he'd seen as Victor brought his horse onto the road.

When Victor mounted, Dom grabbed his reins. "You don't want to be seen by him."

"I know," Victor said. "But I can't let him get too far ahead of us either, or we'll never find him. He has my wife and child, damn it!"

"You don't know that for certain," Tristan said quietly as he brought his own horse up onto the road. "Lochlaw saw no sign of a girl. Perhaps this really *was* all about the diamonds. Perhaps Amalie is still in school, and your wife is just joining her family with a fortune in stolen jewels."

Victor cast him a hard stare. "I thought you believed her."

Tristan's expression was pitying. "Those diamonds are worth at least seventeen thousand pounds. You said that yourself."

"It doesn't matter," Victor said. "She's not stealing them. That much I know." He snatched his reins from Dom. "So you two can help me, or you can sit here. But I'm going after my family."

Lochlaw thrust out his chin and mounted his own horse. "So am I."

"Either way," Dom pointed out to Tristan, "we have to retrieve the jewels, old man."

Leaving them to climb onto their mounts, Victor spurred his horse forward, but he'd only gone a few feet when he spotted something white fluttering in the growth beside the road. "Hold up," he said. Halting his horse, he climbed down to find Isa's fichu caught on a thistle.

Had it flown off in her mad dash after Gerhart? No, that couldn't be. He'd seen her pin it on securely this morning. So what the devil—

Ah. A slow smile curved his lips. "Come on," he told the others, jumping back onto his horse. "My wife is leaving us a map."

They rode silently, four abreast, scanning the road as they went. First they found a ribbon, part of the trim from Isa's gown. Then a garter. Then some lace that had clearly been ripped from her petticoat.

After that, however, the articles of clothing stopped. "Devil take it," Victor muttered as they pulled up after riding awhile without seeing anything. "She must have run out of things to discard."

"I only saw one garter," Tristan said. "I believe most women wear two."

"Good point," Victor said. "We must have missed something. We should retrace our steps and broaden our search to beyond the road."

Within moments, they'd found a scarf caught on a branch next to a half-hidden track through the woods. But it was on the side of the road near the river.

Victor's heart sank. They were headed to the river? That didn't bode well.

He rode swiftly down the cart track, leaving the others to follow. The fact that she'd left her scarf worried him. Gerhart could notice such a thing. God only knew what he would do then.

Fear for her spurred Victor on. He didn't have to go far before he spotted her other garter on a tree branch. And shortly after that, he heard voices arguing ahead. Reining in his horse, he tied it off and drew out his pistol as he crept closer on foot, not wanting any noise to alert Gerhart to his presence.

Then again, Gerhart was shouting so loudly, Victor wasn't sure the man could hear anything. He caught snatches—"Jacoba, you'd best . . . now . . . the child will"—before he got near enough to see what was going on.

And it struck him with terror. In a small clearing near the bank of the river, Isa faced down Gerhart, who stood clutching a golden-haired girl against him.

His own girl. Amalie—oh God.

Gerhart had one arm about the child's middle and his forearm clamped against her throat, as he must have done with Isa earlier in the day, and it was all Victor could do not to vault into the clearing to knock the bastard down and throttle him to death.

But he knew better than to let emotion guide him right now. Too much was at stake. Before Victor could reach him, the former wrestler could easily break Amalie's neck. And Victor's gun was no use with Gerhart holding the girl so close. He dared not risk hitting his daughter.

Fighting for calm, Victor tried to determine how best to proceed.

"Gerhart, I did everything you asked," Isa choked out. "You have the diamonds now. Just let Amalie go! Don't hurt my baby!"

"He won't hurt her," Jacoba said, sounding anxious. "You won't, will you, my love?"

"He hurt *me*," Isa snapped. "How do you think I got these bruises on my neck?"

Jacoba looked shocked. "Gerhart, you didn't . . . you wouldn't . . ."

"Stay out of this, Jacoba. The girl will be fine as long as Isa does what I say," Gerhart growled. "I just need the child a while longer."

"Please, Uncle Gerhart," Amalie squeaked in a girlish voice that made Victor's heart twist. "I don't want to go in the boat!"

Then Victor spotted a dilapidated skiff, half hidden

by the trees, pulled up on the bank. God rot him, Gerhart meant to go out on the river in that thing. And take Amalie with him!

He would beat the bastard to a bloody pulp!

"Listen to me, my dearest," Jacoba said, clearly unsettled by her niece's pleas. "We don't need either of them anymore. Just give Amalie back to Isa. We can be well away in moments. It's not as if my sister can stop us once we're on the river."

"Perhaps not, but her damned husband is bound to be lurking about." He dragged Amalie back toward the skiff. "Clearly she left her scarf somewhere to show him the way, and I daresay he'll find her soon enough. Having the girl with us will just ensure that he lets us get away."

"And then what?" Isa cried.

"We'll leave her in a safe place—assuming we aren't pursued."

"But Gerhart—" Jacoba began.

"Come over here and get in the damned boat!" he cried.

Victor felt rather than saw Dom, Tristan, and Lochlaw edge up beside him. The baron couldn't hold back a gasp when he saw the scene, but fortunately Gerhart was too intent on dealing with Isa and Jacoba to notice. Casting Lochlaw a warning glance, Victor pressed his finger to his lips.

Tristan jerked his head in the direction of the boat. Guessing what he intended, Victor nodded. As Tristan and Dom slid through the woods toward the river, Victor indicated to the baron to stay put.

Time for a distraction. Gerhart wasn't expecting anyone other than him, and he meant to keep it that way while Dom and Tristan got into position.

Victor watched, heart pounding, until the other two men reached the riverbank and slipped into the water. Then, dragging in a deep breath, he walked out into the clearing with his pistol drawn.

23

⁂

ISA NEARLY HAD heart failure when she saw her husband enter the clearing. What was Victor doing? Gerhart would *never* release Amalie now!

"Let her go, Gerhart!" Victor ordered. "Or I swear I'll shoot you where you stand!"

Gerhart paled, but his grip on Amalie tightened. "You don't dare. Not while I've got your precious daughter in my arms."

Amalie's face clouded in confusion. "Mama?" she said, staring at Isa. "What does Uncle Gerhart mean—daughter?"

"We'll talk about it later, dearest," Isa said, forcing calm into her voice. "For now, just do whatever your uncle says." She scowled at him. "Surely you won't hurt your own niece. What kind of monster are you?"

Gerhart's face was implacable. "This is what happens when you don't follow my rules, Isa."

Fear made her light-headed, and only through strength of will did she not faint. "I have no control over my husband, as you should well know by now."

"Then your daughter will suffer for it."

When Isa uttered an unintelligible cry, Victor stiffened and called over to Jacoba. "Look at your sister, damn it," he said, never taking his eyes from Gerhart. "Look at what your husband is doing to her. She's your blood, for God's sake. Do you really mean to tear her child from her?"

Jacoba watched him with indecision in her face. "It's not my fault! You shouldn't have come. If you don't let us leave, we'll both hang!"

"I swear that you won't," Victor said. "Not if he releases the child right *now*."

Isa wanted to scream. Her sister would never go against Gerhart. She'd abandoned Isa for him long ago; why did Victor think that was going to change?

Something moved just beyond Isa's vision, and she glanced over to see Mr. Manton in the water, his head just showing above the surface past the boat. When he was sure she'd seen him, he moved behind the skiff.

Isa's blood thundered in her veins. So *that* was why Victor was drawing Jacoba's attention. Whatever the men were planning, he clearly had a hand in it.

She swallowed tears. He wouldn't let their daughter be hurt by Gerhart. He wouldn't! She had to trust to that.

"Jacoba, come over here now!" Gerhart ordered. "Or I swear, I'll leave you here to be hanged!"

"Do as he says," Isa said quietly to her sister. "I don't want my girl alone with him." And whatever the men were up to, it clearly involved getting Gerhart and Jacoba into the boat or the river or something.

Jacoba looked wary, but she hurried toward her husband. Together the pair crept back to the skiff, dragging Amalie with them. Gerhart ordered Jacoba to shove the vessel off. Then he followed her into the river, still holding Amalie.

"Get in the boat," he ordered Jacoba.

Once she was in it, Gerhart seemed to realize that he might have trouble holding onto Amalie and climbing into the boat at the same time. So he hefted her onto his shoulders, obviously confident that Victor wouldn't dare to shoot him as long as he was holding up Amalie.

Pushing the boat as he went, Gerhart backed into the water. The current was already catching the vessel. All he would have to do was toss Amalie into it and hold on to it while the water swept them downstream out of reach.

That had obviously occurred to Mr. Manton, too, for Isa saw him moving through the water behind Gerhart. Thankfully, Jacoba was too intent on Victor to notice.

But Isa wasn't taking any chances. "Curse it, Gerhart, she can't swim!"

"Then you'd best not let your husband shoot me, aye?" he cried.

"Stop!" Amalie called in a panic, gripping Gerhart's head as he backed shoulder-deep into the water. "Stop . . . stop . . . *stop* . . ."

Then everything happened at once.

Mr. Manton rose up to snatch Amalie off Gerhart's shoulders from behind as Mr. Bonnaud lunged into Gerhart from the side, knocking him off his feet. While Mr. Bonnaud struggled to subdue Gerhart, Jacoba screamed and jumped out of the boat to help her husband.

Isa was already running for her baby, who was screaming, too, and fighting Mr. Manton as he carried her to the shore. Within moments he'd handed Amalie to Isa, who immediately began sobbing and clutching her baby to her.

Mr. Manton waded back to help Mr. Bonnaud with Gerhart and Jacoba, but before he could join the fray, Gerhart broke free and lunged for the shore.

He didn't get far, for his way was blocked by Victor, standing with a gun trained at his head.

Gerhart froze, his eyes going wide.

"Give me one good reason not to kill you," Victor ground out. "Because I damned well can't think of any."

When Gerhart seemed incapable of speech, Isa caught her breath. The coldness in Victor's eyes and the stiffness of his stance told her that her soldier husband was on the verge of committing murder right then and there.

And she would have let him, too—if not for their daughter. "Victor," she called out, "think of Amalie." The last thing their little girl needed to see, after what she'd been through, was her uncle being shot dead before her eyes.

That reminder was all it took. Victor hesitated long enough for Mr. Bonnaud to seize Gerhart from behind. Then Victor lowered his pistol, and Isa let out the breath she hadn't realized she was holding.

As the three men restrained Gerhart and Jacoba, Isa cuddled her baby close. "Everything's all right now, dearest," she murmured into her daughter's tangled curls.

"Oh, Mama," Amalie cried, clinging so tightly to Isa's neck that she could scarcely breathe. "I'm *so* glad you came! I was so *scared*."

"I know, baby, I know." Isa showered kisses over her daughter's sweet cheeks and brow and hair.

"I don't like Uncle Gerhart," Amalie said. "He's *mean*."

"He didn't hurt you, did he?" Isa asked hoarsely, glaring over to where Gerhart was struggling against his captors.

"Only when he grabbed my neck."

That brought it all back again, and Isa had to check her baby's throat and arms and everything to be sure she really was all right. But she wasn't going to feel perfectly at ease until Dr. Worth could examine Amalie and determine that she was unhurt.

Then Rupert entered the clearing. "Glad to see that you're safe, Amalie."

"Lord Lochlaw!" Amalie cried, lighting up at the sight of a familiar face.

"Rupert helped to rescue us," Isa explained.

"Did he *really*?" Amalie slipped out of her mother's arms to run over and give him a hug.

Rupert turned a bright red as he ruffled her hair.

"Well, I only did a little bit. Your father and his friends did most of it."

Amalie gaped up at him, then raced back to gape at her mother. "M-my father?"

Oh, dear. Everything was happening so fast.

Isa pointed over to where Victor and Mr. Manton were searching Gerhart's clothing while he fought their attempts. "You see that tall man there, the one in the blue coat? That's your papa."

Amalie blinked. "You told me my papa was dead," she accused.

Now came the hard part. "That's because I thought he was lost to us—but he wasn't. Your Uncle Gerhart and Aunt Jacoba lied to me about him. And lied to him about me." She smoothed Amalie's hair from her eyes. "But he found us anyway. It just took him a long time."

"Is that why Uncle Gerhart kept calling you Isa instead of Sofie? Because of the lying?"

Isa sighed. "Yes, dearest. I . . . I came to Scotland to start a new life, so I changed my name. My real name is Isabella Cale."

Amalie frowned and stared down at the ground. "You could have told me."

"I didn't tell *anyone*, not even Mr. Gordon. I was afraid that Uncle Gerhart and Aunt Jacoba would find us and hurt us if they ever learned where we'd gone. You can see that I was right to be worried. But now that they're going to gaol, I don't have to worry anymore, so I'll be returning to my real name. And your father will call me Isa, as he used to."

Turning to watch as Victor found the diamonds and removed them from Gerhart's pocket, Amalie cocked her head to one side. "What's my papa's name?"

"Victor Cale."

A troubled expression crossed her face. "Does that mean that I have to change my name, too?"

"I honestly don't know," Isa said. It was the first time she'd thought of it. "I believe we christened you Amalie Franke, so I don't know how that works. I'll have to find out."

"I don't want to change my name!"

"Well, then. We'll see."

Amalie looked unsure of how she felt about that answer. "Will he be coming to live with us?"

"Either that, or we'll be going to live with him."

"So . . . I'll have a papa like other girls?"

"Yes."

Amalie digested that in silence, obviously still unsettled by all of the information being thrown at her. But before she could ask any more questions, Isa heard Victor say, "This is for my wife."

Isa looked over in time to see him land his fist on Gerhart's jaw.

"And *this* is for my daughter, damn you!" Victor said as he punched Gerhart in the stomach until Gerhart doubled over.

Gerhart started cursing, then straightened carefully. "You think you've won," he choked out, "but if you accuse me of kidnapping, I'll deny it. She's my niece, and the school has a letter from your wife saying that we were to fetch her." He wiped away the blood trickling from the corner of his mouth. "I'll say that you and your friends are just trying to separate your wife from her family."

"I know what you'll say," Victor growled. "And that's why we're not apprehending you for kidnapping, much as I want to. We're apprehending you for theft."

"Ah, but Isa was the one to steal that necklace." Gerhart smiled smugly. "Knowing her, she left a fake in its place, so the authorities will see that I speak the truth. And when I tell them that she helped you steal the royal diamonds in Amsterdam, you'll both land in prison."

Rupert walked over to Gerhart. "Whatever are you talking about, sir? Mrs. Cale had nothing to do with any theft. You were seen stealing my diamonds just this afternoon. I have a whole raft of houseguests who witnessed your desperate act."

"What the hell? I didn't steal a damned thing," Gerhart spat. "And if you're thinking of paying them all off to lie—"

"No need to pay anyone off," Victor said with a cold smile. "A burly man with dark hair and a beard was seen by several people—servants *and* guests—running from the manor house after the jewel case was broken into." He glanced at Mr. Bonnaud. "That reminds me; I need your coat. Though I think your trousers look close enough to Gerhart's to pass."

"Excellent," Mr. Bonnaud said as he slipped off his overly large coat. "The trousers are mine. It's only the coat that doesn't fit me."

Victor flashed Gerhart a triumphant look. "But I daresay it fits my brother-in-law well enough."

It took a minute for Gerhart to realize that they were setting him up as the thief, but when he did, he began fighting them, to no avail. He could hardly withstand three men bent on forcibly removing his coat and replacing it with Mr. Bonnaud's.

And once they had the coat on, they tied him up so that no matter how much he struggled, he was well and truly caught. Then Mr. Bonnaud's wide-brimmed beaver hat was clamped atop his head, and they were done.

Amalie grabbed Isa's hand. "What are they doing, Mama?"

"Making sure that your Uncle Gerhart can never hurt you—or any of the rest of us—ever again, dearest."

Victor stepped back to view their handiwork. "He'll do, don't you think, Dom?"

"Oh, excellent." Mr. Manton cast Mr. Bonnaud a mocking glance. "You two could be twins."

"Don't say that," his brother grumbled. "I had a devil of a time getting that black junk off my face before we headed here."

Rupert cast Gerhart a hard look. "I'm absolutely certain that's the man I saw riding away. And I'm sure Miss Gordon will confirm it. Besides, we found the stolen necklace on him, so there you are. All the proof we need."

"You won't get away with this!" Gerhart cried as Mr. Bonnaud and Mr. Manton dragged him over to Mr. Manton's horse. "I'll tell everyone what I've seen and what you're trying to do. And so will my wife, damn you all!"

"Will she?" Victor snapped. "I doubt that." He turned to Jacoba, who was staring after Gerhart with a heartsick expression. "It's time you consider yourself, sister," he said coldly. "Your husband is lost to you. He will almost certainly hang for the theft of those diamonds; it's a capital crime. Right now you're only guilty of being his accomplice to the diamond theft. But if we haul you back to Amsterdam and start building a case against you two for *those* thefts, you're likely to find yourself on the gallows with him. Unless . . ."

"Unless?" Jacoba whispered.

"You speak the truth about what happened to those diamonds in Amsterdam. If you testify that Isa and I had nothing to do with it, I will make sure that your sentence is commuted to transportation. I have enough influence to keep you from the gallows."

Jacoba cast Isa a pleading glance, but Isa could barely stand to look at her.

"It's your choice, Jacoba," Victor said. "Transportation or the gallows. If you take your chances on a trial, I will use all the influence I have to see you both prosecuted equally for stealing. And you *will* hang with him."

"Don't be a fool, Jacoba," Isa said. "He's not worth it."

With a sigh, Jacoba looked at Victor. "All right. I'll tell the truth."

And for the first time in ten years, Isa finally felt free.

✦ ✦ ✦

THE NEXT FEW hours tried Victor's patience. He hated having to put Isa into Lochlaw's care even temporarily when they left the clearing, but he and Dom had been seen setting out to capture Gerhart, and now they had to be seen bringing him and Jacoba in. But only after Lochlaw had whisked Isa back into the manor through the garden door by which she'd left.

Meanwhile, Tristan was keeping Amalie under wraps at the hunting cottage until Victor and Isa could head back to Edinburgh with Dom, ostensibly so that they could consult with lawyers about her wretched family caught in this horrible crime. Along the way, Tristan and Dr. Worth would join them, driving the phaeton while Dom drove Isa and Victor and Amalie in Dom's coach.

They had no choice in that, either. If Amalie made a miraculous appearance at the house party, it would destroy their plan to undermine Gerhart's claims.

Well into the evening, Victor had to lie about the capture while Isa had to pretend to be shocked by the fact that her brother-in-law was a thief. She had to act horrified by the nasty claims he was making against her. Her bruises contributed to Victor's and Isa's story of Gerhart's desperation for money, especially with Dr. Worth there to speak of the damage done to her throat. And her presence among the other guests during the theft vindicated her of stealing.

Everyone played his part to perfection. Victor had a

moment's worry when Lady Zoe came into the room, but she kept quiet as she'd promised, and the moment passed.

Now he was relieved to finally be in the carriage on his way back to Edinburgh with Isa. Traveling at night was never ideal, but the moon was full and the weather was fine.

The only problem was that Amalie had just joined them, and he had no idea how to deal with her. What did one say to a nine-year-old girl who'd just discovered that her mother had been living a lie, her father wasn't dead, and her relations were decidedly corrupt?

He only wished he could see her better. She sat curled up against her mother on the opposite side of the coach, her golden hair limned with moonlight. What was she thinking?

"So," he said, feeling the weight of this moment, "your mother tells me that you do very well with your studies."

"Yes, sir," she murmured.

"Do you like your school?"

She glanced up at her mother, who nodded. "Yes, sir," she mumbled. "It's very nice."

"But surely you would like to live at home with your mother while you go to school, if it could be arranged."

"That would be fabulous!" she exclaimed, then caught herself. "I mean, yes, sir, I would."

The word *fabulous* grabbed his attention. Isa had described their daughter as flamboyant, but this was the first glimpse he'd had of that side of her. Perhaps it was time he ventured into uncharted waters and pried a bit more of the flamboyant out of her.

"Of course, you might not like living in London." Remembering what Isa had told him over the past few days about Amalie's interests, Victor added, "All those fancy ladies prancing about in the latest fashions from Paris. I'm sure that would bore you."

"No, it wouldn't!" she cried "I *like* fancy ladies. Do they wear big hats?"

He bit back a smile. "The biggest. It's a problem for us gentlemen; we get poked in the eye with oyster feathers whenever we help ladies into their carriages."

She snorted. "They're not *oyster* feathers, sir. They're *ostrich* feathers."

"Are you sure? I could have sworn that they grew out of pearls. That's why they're white, isn't it?"

This time he got a giggle out of her. "Pearls don't grow things. That's ridiculous."

"Your father enjoys teasing sometimes," Isa put in, "but only if he really, really likes you. I think he must like you a great deal."

Victor's throat tightened. "Yes. I do. And I hope that one day you can like me, too. Even if I don't know a damn—" He winced. "A *single* thing about female fashions." Or not cursing in front of young ladies.

Amalie sat quiet for so long that he began to despair. Then she said in a small voice, "I could teach you. About female fashions, I mean."

"I would enjoy that immensely." Right now, he would enjoy anything that got his daughter to feel more comfortable with him. "And in exchange, I will teach you how to swim. If you'd like."

She cocked her head, and he could almost imagine her searching his face. "I would rather learn how to shoot a gun."

"All right," he said, willing to do anything to gain her favor.

"Victor!" Isa cried. "You are *not* going to teach our daughter how to shoot!"

"Fine," he said, then uttered a dramatic sigh. "It's probably just as well. I'm told that guns are hopelessly out of fashion in Paris, and you can't really wear one on your big hat. Oyster feathers work much better."

"Papa!" Amalie cried, half laughing. "They're *ostrich* feathers!"

His heart flipped over in his chest. She'd called him "papa." He'd never heard anything so sweet. "Right," he said. "So, what's the name of those long lacy things that the ladies wear around their necks?"

For the next hour she regaled him with explanations and descriptions of every "fabulous" gown and hat and pair of slippers she'd ever seen, while he showed his ignorance about all things "fashionable." After a bit, he thought perhaps she'd begun to catch on that he wasn't *quite* as ignorant as he pretended, but by then she apparently didn't care, either.

Because by then, she'd started asking questions about the past and the future. About how they would go on. He and Isa answered as best they could, until her head began to nod and she began to yawn.

After she fell asleep, Isa laid her down on the seat and crossed to sit beside him. Victor slid his arm about her shoulders. "She's as wonderful as her mother," he murmured, feeling a painful tightness in his chest as he gazed on his daughter. *Their* daughter. "You did well with her."

Isa leaned her head on his shoulder. "I'm sorry for the years you lost with her, sorry that—"

"No more apologies." He stared down at the wife he was only beginning to know; the woman he would cherish until death closed his eyes and stopped his breath. "We both made mistakes, but we both paid for them in spades. Fate has given us a second chance, so it's time we let our mistakes go. We love each other, and we love her. That should be all we need to start our new life, don't you think?"

Isa stretched up to brush a kiss to his lips, and her smile made his blood heat and his heart swell. "I think that sounds perfectly fabulous."

EPILOGUE

London
December 1828

WHEN ISA ARRIVED at the Duke of Lyons's town house to join the duke and duchess and Victor for dinner there, she was feeling rather blue. But she didn't wish to put a damper on the evening, so she pasted a smile to her lips as she knocked.

To her surprise, her husband opened the door and he was alone. Usually the place swarmed with footmen and maids.

When he greeted her with a kiss, then took her coat, she teased, "Do tell me you haven't left Manton's Investigations to take a position as Max's footman."

"I doubt Max would approve of footmen who kissed the guests. I just wanted a moment alone with you." He searched her face. "How was Jacoba?"

She should have known her husband would see through her determined good cheer. "How do you think? Her husband is dead, and she's off to the Australian colonies in a few weeks."

"You're not regretting that we held firm on seeing her prosecuted."

"Absolutely not. She helped her evil husband take our daughter! I can never forgive that, and she knows it. But seeing her there in Newgate, with the other women, and knowing that she would soon be half a world away ..."

"Made you remember when times were good."

She nodded. "When I was little, she was the one who coddled me, warmed chocolate for me to drink, and took care of my sore throats. I hate that Gerhart twisted her into someone I no longer recognized."

"So do I, for your sake."

Taking in a deep breath, she forced her frown from her brow. "Well, enough about that. I shall try to put it behind me for the evening. I don't want to make Max and Lisette gloomy, too."

A strange expression passed over his face. "I'm sure they'll understand if your spirits are low."

They walked down the hall toward the drawing room, arm in arm. It had taken a while for her to grow accustomed to the palatial mansion that was the duke's town house, but after two months in London, having put Amalie into school and settled into her new home with Victor, she'd begun to feel very comfortable.

Soon she would have to decide whether to set up a new jeweler's shop in London, now that she'd sold her share of the Edinburgh shop to Mr. Gordon. But at the moment she was content to get to know her husband and his new family, to spend time mending the past.

They entered the drawing room and she halted. This was no intimate family dinner with Max and Lisette. Dom and Tristan were both here, along with Mr. Gordon, Dr. Worth, Mary Grace, and Rupert.

Barreling out of the crowd came Amalie, dressed in her latest and most fashionable gown. "Mama, Mama, you've come at last!"

Amalie was supposed to be having dinner with a little friend from school! "How did you get here?" Isa exclaimed, then glanced at Victor. "What's going on?"

"It's the tenth anniversary of our wedding, my love," Victor said softly.

Flummoxed, she swiftly dredged her memory and realized he was right. "Oh, dear—I'm so sorry, Victor. I utterly forgot."

"What with the trial and Jacoba, it's a wonder you even remember your own name. But I couldn't let it pass without a celebration." He nodded to where the duke and duchess stood smiling. "And since we wouldn't be together again if not for my relations and the Duke's Men, I thought you wouldn't mind if they were included."

As everyone crowded round her, she somehow managed, "Thank you. You're all so kind," and then promptly burst into tears. When Victor looked a little alarmed, she choked out, "This is the loveliest thing anyone has ever done for me."

His face cleared. "That's all right then," he said gruffly, clearly a little choked up himself.

As he offered her his handkerchief, Amalie pushed her way through to the front. "You haven't even seen the cake yet, Mama. It has fleurs-de-lis all over it!"

"Spiders, you mean," Rupert teased her as he came up to kiss Isa on the cheek, then murmured, "I do hope you'll be at *our* wedding anniversary celebration in a little more than ten years."

As Mary Grace slid up beside him, blushing as always, Isa broke into a broad smile. "You're engaged?" Not that she was terribly surprised, though she had expected Lady Lochlaw to make more of a fuss about it.

"Miss Gordon has made me the happiest of men," Rupert said as he took the young woman's hand. "I hope you'll all three be at the wedding."

"Of course!" Isa hugged them both. "We wouldn't miss it!"

After they moved aside, Tristan pushed in to grab her hand and kiss it with a little flourish. When Victor scowled at him, he laughed. "Your husband neglected to tell you the real reason he's having this celebration— so you won't be angry when he informs you that he has a case in Devonshire next week, and will be gone for at least two weeks."

Isa laughed. "He already told me."

"Nice try," Victor said smugly. "But a clever husband never pulls the wool over his wife's eyes—not unless he wants to have it shoved down his throat. Just a bit of advice for when *you* are married."

Tristan's smile looked forced. "Why should I marry, when there are plenty of ripe peaches waiting to be plucked in the drawing rooms of London?"

"Better be careful," Victor said. "Peaches have stones, and you might just find yourself choking on them."

"Excellent advice," Dr. Worth said as he came up to shake her hand. "A pity that Bonnaud is unlikely to pay it any mind."

When Tristan laughed, Dom moved up beside him. "Yes, Victor, good luck with trying to knock any sense into my younger brother. He likes to live dangerously."

"Anything else is boring," Tristan shot back. He grinned at the doctor. "Besides, I've got Worth here to patch me up if I get into trouble. Come on, Doctor, let's see if we can find some."

As the young doctor allowed Tristan to pull him away, Dom shook his head.

Isa had really grown to like the man after Victor had begun working with him. Tristan could be fun to tease, but he was also exasperating; Dom was as solid as the rock of Gibraltar.

He smiled at her. "We're delighted that you caught Lochlaw's eye and drew Victor to Edinburgh. The man deserves some happiness." He glanced at Victor. "And . . . well . . . we've been thinking about asking you if you might like to do some work for us from time to time. Looking at chemical compositions and evaluating gems for our clients to see if they're real."

"They could also use some help in the office," Lisette put in. She laid a hand on her noticeably rounded belly.

"I'm afraid I'm not going to be much good to them anymore. I simply have too much to do."

The duke slid his hand about her waist and gazed down at her fondly. "My wife has decided that our nursery needs a complete overhaul, now that we're intent on filling it."

"Oh, do you have a baby, Your Grace?" Amalie exclaimed. "I *love* babies!"

"You love everything," Lisette said fondly and ruffled her hair. "We don't have a baby now, but we will soon, and you are welcome to come help with it whenever you wish."

"Papa, did you hear that? I can help with the baby!"

"Yes, lambkin, I heard," Victor said. "*Everyone* in the town house heard."

They all laughed. The trial of their lives was trying to teach Amalie not to be quite so boisterous.

"So, what do you say?" Dom asked Isa. "Would you be interested in helping us from time to time? At least until you decide what to do with your jewelry business?"

"Actually, that sounds intriguing," Isa said. "We can try it for a bit, anyway."

A footman came in to announce that dinner was served. As everyone moved toward the door, Victor murmured something to Lisette, who took Amalie's hand and drew her off. Then Victor halted Isa with a hand and called out to the others, "We'll be there in a moment."

For his pains he got lots of sly looks from his friends, who had now become her friends, too. He stoically ignored them. As soon as the others were gone, he pulled out a little box.

"Since we were too poor to afford a ring for you all those years ago, I decided to remedy that situation." He opened the box, and she was surprised to see a ring with several gems in a line.

She caught her breath. Lapis, iris, emerald, *vermeille*, emerald, kyanite, emerald. *Lieveke*.

Tears clogged her throat. "Oh, Victor, it's *beautiful*!"

"They're real gems, too," he said. "Mr. Gordon had a devil of a time finding a gem to use for *k*, but Lochlaw suggested the kyanite, and there you are."

He slid the ring onto her finger, where it fit perfectly.

"I will forever be grateful to Lochlaw," Victor went on as he kissed her hand, "and not just for the kyanite either, but because he brought you back to me."

She covered his hand with hers. "Yes. Although sometimes, when I'm being whimsical, I fancy that our lonely hearts grew tired of waiting for us to find each other, and simply called out in the night until they got their answer. And that's what really brought us together."

"I like that," he said as he drew her into his arms. Then he kissed her so sweetly that for a moment she was eighteen again, sneaking off to be with her bold young soldier.

When he drew back, all the love in the world shone in his eyes. "Because I know for certain that my heart will always hear yours."

AUTHOR'S NOTE

I DIDN'T MAKE Isa and Mr. Gordon up out of whole cloth. They're partly inspired by Alsatian jeweler Georg Friedrich Strass, who invented the imitation diamond (which is why the glass for faux gems is called *strass* after him). He made a small fortune selling imitation gems. The other inspiration was a story I came across in a Regency-era English magazine, about a swindler in Paris who created such amazing faux diamonds that he managed to amass two million francs selling them as real diamonds before he was caught. Out of those two things Isa was born.

I state that Victor is Belgian even though Belgium wasn't officially a country at the time my books were set. That's because everyone still referred to the region as Belgium. There are whole books from this period and earlier discussing travel to "Belgium" at a time when Belgium wasn't officially a country. I assume the region was known as that before it was officially named that.

I'm not a legal expert, so I could only assess Dutch law to the extent that I could find it written in English and could understand the legalese, but everything I read stated that at this time a divorce could be obtained for desertion of the wife, without requiring the wife's presence. If that's not true, mea culpa!

And yes, atomic theory has been around since 1808, when chemist John Dalton published *A New System of Chemical Philosophy*. So Rupert was not ahead of his time!

Turn the page for a sneak peek
at the third book in the Duke's Men series
from *New York Times* bestselling author
Sabrina Jeffries!

HOW THE SCOUNDREL SEDUCES

Coming soon from Pocket Books

1

London
January 1829

WHEN THE HACKNEY halted, Lady Zoe Keane drew her veil aside and peered out the murky window to survey the building standing opposite Covent Garden Theater.

This couldn't be Manton's Investigations. It was too plain and ordinary for the famous Duke's Men, for pity's sake! No horses standing at the ready to dash off to danger? No imposing sign with gilt lettering?

"Are you sure this is their offices?" she asked Ralph, her footman, as he helped her out.

"Aye, milady. It's the address you gave me: twenty-nine Bow Street."

When the brittle cold needled her cheeks, she adjusted her veil over her face. She mustn't be recognized entering an office full of men, and certainly not *this* office. "It doesn't look right somehow."

"Or safe." He glanced warily at the rough neighborhood. "If your father knew I'd brought you to such a low part of town he'd kick me out the door, he would."

"No, indeed. I would *never* allow that." As Mama used to say, a lady got what she wanted by speaking with authority . . . even if her knees were knocking beneath her wool gown. "Besides, how will he find out? You accompanied me on my walk in St. James's Park, that's all. He'll never learn any different."

He mustn't, because he would almost certainly guess *why* she'd sought out an investigator. Then, like the former army major that he was, he would institute draconian measures to keep her close. She couldn't let that happen just when she was beginning to learn the truth. She wouldn't!

"I shan't be here long," she added. "We'll easily arrive home in time for dinner, and no one will be the wiser."

"If you say so, milady."

"I do appreciate this, you know. I'd never wish for you to get into trouble."

He sighed. "I know, milady."

She meant it, too. She liked Ralph, who'd served as her personal footman ever since Mama's death last winter. From the beginning, he'd felt sorry for Zoe, "the poor motherless lass." And if sometimes she used that to her advantage rather shamelessly, it was only because she had no choice. Time was running out. She'd already had to wait *months* for Papa to bring her and Aunt Flo to London so she could maneuver this secret meeting in the first place.

They climbed to the top of the steps, and Ralph

knocked on the door. It took forever for someone to come. She adjusted her cloak, shifted her reticule to her other hand, stamped snow off her boots.

At last the door swung open, to reveal a gaunt fellow wearing an antiquated suit of bottle-green silk and a puce waistcoat, who appeared to be headed out the door.

"Mr. Shaw!" she cried, both startled and delighted to see him again so soon.

He peered at her veiled face. "Do I know you, madam?"

"It's 'your ladyship,' if you please," Ralph corrected him.

As Mr. Shaw bristled, Zoe jumped in. "We haven't been introduced, sir, but I saw you in *Much Ado About Nothing* last night and thought you were *marvelous*. I've never witnessed an actor play Dogberry so feelingly."

His demeanor softened. "And who might you be?"

"I'm Lady Zoe Keane, and I'm scheduled to meet with the Duke's Men at three p.m."

It wasn't *too* much of a lie. A few months ago she'd caught the well-known investigators orchestrating a pretend theft in order to capture a kidnapper. In exchange for her silence, they'd agreed to do her a favor at some future date.

That date was now.

She only hoped they'd remember. Mr. Dominick Manton, the owner, and Mr. Victor Cale, one of his men, both seemed responsible fellows who would honor their promises.

Mr. Tristan Bonnaud, however . . .

She tensed. That bullying scoundrel had caught her by surprise, and she *hated* that. Why, he hadn't even wanted to agree to the bargain! No telling what he would do if things were left to him.

"Have you just been here to see the investigators?" she asked Mr. Shaw, wondering why he continued to block their way in.

He grimaced. "Alas, no. I am employed here. Acting is my second profession at present. My first one is as butler and sometime clerk to Mr. Manton."

Oh, dear. She only hoped he wasn't privy to his employer's meeting schedule. "In that case, perhaps you should announce me." When he stiffened, she added hastily, "I would be most honored. What a pity that I didn't expect you to be here, for then I would have brought my playbill for you to autograph."

Given how he arched his eyebrows, that was probably laying it on a bit thick. "What a pity indeed," he said. But thankfully he ushered them inside anyway.

Removing her cloak and veiled hat, she surveyed the foyer. This was more like what she'd expected: simple but elegant mahogany furniture; a beautiful, if inexpensive, Spanish rug; and nice damask draperies of a pale yellow. The decor could still use a bit of dash—perhaps some ancient daggers on the walls for effect, but then she always liked more dash than other people.

Besides, the newspapers told enough daring tales about the Duke's Men to make up for any lack of dash in their offices. It was said that they could find anyone. She dearly hoped that was true.

"I don't believe any of the gentlemen are present at the moment." Mr. Shaw kept eyeing the front door with a peculiar expression of longing. "They must have forgotten your appointment. Perhaps you should return later."

"Oh, but that's impossible!" she burst out.

When his gaze swung to hers, newly suspicious, she cringed. Why must she always speak the first thing that came into her head? No matter how she tried to behave as Mama had taught her, sometimes her mouth just did whatever it wanted, and to hell with the consequences.

She winced. Not *hell*. Ladies didn't so much as think the word *hell*, not even ladies whose papas used the word regularly while teaching their daughters how to manage the estates they would one day inherit.

Sucking in a breath, she added sweetly, "I can't imagine that the famous Duke's Men would forget an appointment. Perhaps they came in the back."

After all the risks she'd taken to meet with them, the thought of being thwarted just because they were all out investigating made her want to scream.

He sighed "Wait here. I'll see if anyone's in." He darted up the stairs like a spider up a web.

As soon as he was out of earshot, Ralph grumbled, "Still don't see why you want to consult with investigators. Your father would gladly find out whatever you wish to know."

Oh, no, he wouldn't. She'd already determined that. "Don't worry. It's nothing that will get you into any trouble."

It was only the entirety of her future, but she wasn't about to go into that with Ralph. None of the servants could ever know of this.

The door opened behind her. "Well, well, what have we here?"

She froze. She would recognize that voice anywhere. Oh, botheration, why did it have to be *him*?

Steadying herself for battle, she faced Mr. Bonnaud . . . only to be struck speechless by the sight of him.

This wasn't the Mr. Bonnaud she'd encountered in the woods near Kinlaw when she'd extracted her promise from the Duke's Men. That fellow had been barrel-chested, thick waisted, and rough looking, with a floppy hat and a beard that hid most of his face.

Belatedly she remembered his saying on that day that he was wearing a disguise. She hadn't believed him.

She did now. Because the man before her wasn't re-motely burly or bearded or badly dressed. He was lean and handsome and garbed almost fashionably, if one could call a sober riding coat of dark gray wool, a plain black waistcoat, tight buff trousers, and scuffed boots fashionable.

Not that any woman would care about his clothes when his broad shoulders and his muscular thighs filled them out so well. Heaven help her.

Then he removed his top hat of gray beaver to reveal a profusion of thick black curls worthy of a Greek god, and she had to suck down a sigh. Though Mr. Bon-naud's face wasn't remotely Mediterranean—his nose was too narrow and his jaw too finely crafted—the combination of his features with his hair was stunning. Absolutely stunning.

No wonder his name was so often linked to beautiful actresses and dancers. With those fierce blue eyes and that seducer's shapely mouth, he probably spent half his time in bed with willing females.

The images that rose in her mind made her curse her wild imagination. Ladies weren't supposed to think about *that* either.

He looked closely at her, and recognition leapt in those splendid eyes. "Lady Zoe," he said, bowing.

"Good afternoon, Mr. Bonnaud."

He crooked up one eyebrow. "Finally decided to call in your favor, did you?"

With a furtive glance at Ralph, who watched the exchange most avidly, she said, "I wish to consult with you and your companions, yes."

Just then Mr. Shaw returned. "Ah, there you are, Mr. Bonnaud. Is Mr. Manton with you?"

"He's tying up some loose ends, but he said he'd be along shortly."

Mr. Shaw nodded to her. "This lady claims to have an appointment with the . . . er . . . Duke's Men."

She watched Mr. Bonnaud warily, preparing herself for anything. So when he had the audacity to wink at her, it took her off guard—and sent a little thrill along her spine that was too annoying for words.

"She does indeed," he said, eyes agleam. "A rather long-standing one. Don't worry, Shaw—I can see you're impatient to be off to rehearsal. I'll take care of her ladyship."

"Thank you, sir," Mr. Shaw said, then rushed out the door.

Mr. Bonnaud gestured to the stairs. "Shall we adjourn to the office?"

Ralph jumped up, and Zoe said hastily, "Wait down here for me, Ralph."

"But my lady—"

She handed him her hat and cloak. "I've already met Mr. Bonnaud and his fellow investigators, and I promise they can be trusted."

Or some of them could, though it looked for now as if she was stuck with the one she wasn't sure about. Not that it mattered. She was desperate enough to settle for Mr. Bonnaud.

Lifting her skirts, she headed for the stairs, feeling the man fall into step behind her. Only when they were past the landing and well out of sight and earshot of Ralph did she say in a low voice, "I prefer to wait until the head of the Duke's Men is also present before proceeding."

"Do you?" he drawled. "Then let me give you a piece of advice. If you want to get on Dom's good side, stop calling us 'The Duke's Men.' He hates when people refer to the business he built himself as if it were an extension of His Grace's empire."

How odd. "One would think he'd relish his connection to a duke."

Mr. Bonnaud snorted. "Not everyone is as enamored of your sort as you might think, my lady."

The contempt in his voice irritated her, especially

given her reasons for being here. "Is that why you tried to shoot me the last time we met?" It still rankled that he'd not only managed to rattle her but had kept rattling her even after it became clear he was no threat.

"I didn't try to shoot you," he said. "I only *threatened* to shoot you."

"Three times. And the first time, you waved your pistol in my face."

"It wasn't loaded."

She paused on the stairs to glare down at him. "So you *deliberately* put me in fear for my life?"

He smirked at her. "Served you right. You shouldn't have been galloping after men who were reputedly in pursuit of a thief."

The heat rising in her cheeks made her scowl. She had nothing to be embarrassed about, curse it! "I had good reason for that."

He took another step up, putting him far too close. "Do tell."

Staring into his eyes was only marginally less alarming than staring down the barrel of his pistol had been months ago. And good heavens, he was tall. Even standing two steps below her, he met her gaze easily.

It did something rather startling to her insides.

She tipped up her chin. "I'm not saying anything until your brother is here. Just in case you threaten to shoot me again."

Amusement leapt in his gaze. "I only do that when you're interfering in matters beyond your concern."

"You don't understand. I had to—"

"Quiet," he ordered, cocking his head to one side.

Just as she was about to protest his arrogance, she heard sounds of conversation below.

"Dom is here." Mr. Bonnaud nodded toward the top of the stairs. "So unless you want him to think we were dallying in the staircase, I suggest we continue up."

She blinked at him. "Dallying? *Dallying*, mind you?" She turned to march up the last few steps. "As if I would ever, in a million years, dally with you." She wouldn't. Really, she wouldn't!

His low chuckle behind her put the lie to her words. "Never say never, my lady. A vow like that is sure to come back to bite you in the arse. Which would be a shame, given that you have such a fine one."

Oh, Lord, he was staring at her bottom.

Wait, how *dare* he stare at her bottom?

The second they moved into a long hallway, she turned to give him a firm setdown. Then she froze at the sight of his smug expression. He was deliberately trying to provoke her, the sly devil, just as when he threatened to shoot her.

This time she wouldn't let him succeed. She cast him a pitying smile. "And here I'd heard that you were so witty and charming toward the fair sex, Mr. Bonnaud. How disappointing to discover you have only the coarsest notion of how to compliment a lady."

To her enormous satisfaction, that wiped the smugness right off his face. "The operative word is 'lady.'" He bore down on her, an edge in his voice. "And since you seem to be a lady in name only, given your penchant for sticking your nose where it doesn't belong—"

"Lady Zoe?" Mr. Manton appeared at the top of the stairs. He glanced from her to Mr. Bonnaud, who instantly went rigid.

She couldn't resist a smile of triumph. It was rather satisfying to watch *him* caught off guard for once.

Turning to his half brother, she offered her hand. "Mr. Manton. How good to see you again."

Sparing a veiled glance for Mr. Bonnaud, he shook her hand. "Under much better circumstances than last time, fortunately."

All too aware of Mr. Bonnaud's hard gaze on her, she smiled brightly. "I was delighted to hear that you and your fellow investigators routed the true villains eventually." There, that sounded perfectly cordial and ladylike and all the things Mr. Bonnaud said she wasn't. "I was also pleased to learn that they were given the justice they deserved."

"Indeed they were. We much appreciate your discretion in that matter, too, I assure you."

Her pulse pounded. "So you remember your promise."

"Of course. What's more, I'm pleased to honor it." He gestured toward a nearby open doorway. "Why don't we discuss the matter in my study?"

"Thank you." As he led her in the room, she felt his brother fall into step behind her, no doubt staring at her "fine" arse again.

Let him stare. Now that she knew he only did it to provoke her, she refused to let it bother her. It's not as if he meant anything by it. He *did*, after all, have a string of beauties trailing after him throughout London, and she wasn't widely acclaimed a beauty herself.

Oh, men flirted with her often enough, but that was to be expected. She was rich, after all, and her inheritance was substantial. She would much rather they flirted with her because they found her interesting, but barring that, she wouldn't mind being admired for her more feminine attributes.

Unfortunately, English gentlemen weren't generally attracted to olive-skinned women with foreign-looking features, no matter how much Mama had always praised her "exotic" appearance. And her aunt, Mama's sister, despaired of her clothing choices, claiming that they had a bit *too* much dash for good society.

Zoe sighed. Even if by some chance Mr. Bonnaud didn't mind any of that and actually found her attractive, it didn't matter. He hardly seemed the marrying sort. And she had too much at stake to be interested in the other sort—scoundrels and rakes and rogues. No matter *how* handsome and daring they were.

"So," Mr. Manton said as he gestured to a chair and took his own seat behind the desk, "what do you want from me and my fellow investigators?"

Having circled around to lean against the wall nearest the desk, Mr. Bonnaud leveled her with his disapproving stare. But at least he wasn't smirking at her anymore.

She looked at Mr. Manton, and the enormity of what she was about to reveal hit her. For half a second, she reconsidered her decision. If the Duke's Men ever let slip even a tenth of what she was about to tell them, her future would be over and her family's estate, Windborough, would be lost forever.

"My lady?" Mr. Manton prodded. "Why are you here?"

Then again, it might be lost forever if she *didn't* involve them. Truly, she had no choice.

She gripped her reticule in her hands and fought for calm. "I need you to find my real parents."

"Dorinda and the Doctor"

A Short Story by
Sabrina Jeffries

1

Early on a fine Monday morning, Mrs. Dorinda Nunley let herself in through the side door of Dr. Percy Worth's abode, which he leased from Dorinda's distant relation, the Duke of Lyons. Lisette, the duke's new wife, had sent her over here with the key to set the place to rights while the doctor was out of town, but it still felt oddly intimate to invade his domain.

At least she wasn't entering the living areas. This part was his office, though apparently he didn't see patients in it. No need, for they were all members of the *ton*, not surprising for a physician who was presently the toast of London.

After removing her bonnet, Dorinda set it on a nearby highboy and surveyed the place. Clearly the man spent little time here, or else how could he abide such clutter? There were boxes only half-unpacked from when he'd taken up residence eight months ago after years as a ship's doctor. A full skeleton lay crumpled upon a chair, and jars and vials were jumbled up on a table, as if he rifled through them whenever he needed something.

Well, when she was done with this place, he would never have to hunt for anything again. She hated to admit it, but she was secretly looking forward to making herself useful to him. Though she disliked doctors as a rule, he'd been nothing but amiable to her, and for that he deserved to have an orderly place of business. Even if it *did* remind her of a difficult time in her life.

Setting her shoulders, she headed for the table and nearly tripped over a black satchel. She stared at it dumbly. It looked like the one he carried sometimes when he came to see how the duchess was faring in her pregnancy. But why would it be *here*? He was supposed to be—

Just at that moment the door swung open, and awareness dawned. Before she could so much as squeak a warning, the good doctor entered the room, wearing nothing but a half-open banyan and a pair of drawers.

He stopped short, his dark-brown eyes widening. "Mrs. Nunley?"

Oh dear oh dear oh dear. "Good morning, Dr. Worth," she said inanely.

Heaven help her, she'd never seen the doctor in dishabille. She'd never even seen him in shirtsleeves. She'd always thought the doctor very attractive with that finely carved jaw and expressive mouth, but she'd never guessed what lay beneath his clothes. Of its own accord, her gaze swept down to take in his chiseled chest and lean stomach and the thin line of hair leading down to—

She jerked her mortified gaze up to meet his astonished one. "What are you doing here?" she blurted out.

Amusement leapt into his face as he discreetly pulled his banyan closed. "I live here. And you?"

This couldn't be happening! "Her Grace said you were going to the country to attend a countess in her birthing," she babbled. "You're not supposed to be here!"

"Which is why you felt free to stop by and look around?" he asked, a smile crooking up one corner of his mouth.

To her horror, her cheeks heated like a foolish schoolgirl's. "Don't be absurd." But she was the absurd one. She should never have come so early. She should have knocked. She shouldn't have been caught gawking at a half-naked man.

Especially this particular half-naked man. She'd spent too much of her seven-year marriage enduring the arrogant doctors her husband had charged with curing her "barrenness" to find a physician remotely attractive. Yet she did, and had for months now. It was most annoying. And when his gaze lingered on her mouth, making her swallow hard, she wanted to turn tail and run.

Or stand still and let him catch her. She grimaced. What a ridiculous thought! He wasn't interested in "catching" her. Was he? Then he lifted his gaze from her mouth, and she cursed her dullness. He wanted an explanation, of course.

"The duchess has been so kind to me since Edgar died that I asked if she needed assistance with anything, and she sent me here to help organize your office. She said she offered to do it for you while you were out of town, but now found that she couldn't manage it."

Dr. Worth frowned. "That's odd. I sent Her Grace a note only yesterday that I had to cancel my trip because the countess's babe had arrived early. The duchess answered, too, inviting me to dine tonight. I wonder why she would—"

When he broke off with a laugh, Dorinda gaped at him.

Eyes gleaming, he crossed his arms over his chest. "It appears that Her Grace is playing matchmaker. She's grown tired of merely telling me I need a wife and is now trying to arrange one for me."

"But . . . but . . . I mean, surely she would never—"

"Send you over here at the crack of dawn when she *knew* I was home?"

"You can't blame her for the early hour," she said with a blush. "I thought you were gone and I didn't know how much time I would need, so I came early."

"The point is, she deliberately threw us together." He shoved back a lock of hair that was as coarse and straight and black as her own hair was feathery and curly and blond, then gave her a sweeping, rather heated glance. "For obvious reasons."

When that sent her pulse into a tumbling roll, she stiffened. "I can't believe it. Lisette *knows* I have no intention of marrying again." Unless it was to a man who wanted no children. Certainly never to an up-and-coming physician probably looking to start a family.

No matter how handsome he might be. Or how much he reminded her that she hadn't shared a man's bed in some time. Lord help her.

"Ah," he said tightly, "but a woman newly in love ignores such statements. The duchess is so happy she can't imagine anyone else not wanting what she has."

"It was still very wrong and presumptuous." She sighed. "I shall just have to be firmer with her. She and the duke have been so kind to me that I wanted to do whatever I could to repay them. But . . . that is . . ."

"Gratitude only extends so far," he finished for her. His gaze swept her again, with an awareness that made her feel naked. Until it hardened and snapped back to meet hers with a physician's usual cool arrogance. "And the great-granddaughter of a duke needn't stoop to marry a younger son of a silk merchant."

The hint of defensive pride in his voice struck a chord in her. "I'm a destitute widow, sir," she said quietly. "If anything, I'm too low for a man of your great renown. And I wouldn't make a good wife for any man, given—"

No, she couldn't talk about that with him, of all people. "In any case, if I'd had any inkling of what Lisette was really plotting, I would never have gone along with it. Indeed, I didn't mean to impose upon you even this long. Forgive me, sir."

She turned for the door, but before she could reach it, he said, "Wait."

That one word sent a thrill down her spine that she hadn't felt since the days Edgar had courted her. "Under the circumstances, I should probably go."

He stepped nearer. "She'll just try again. The duchess can be stubborn about 'helping' her friends. And she has a soft spot for you. I suspect you remind her of her mother, who was equally left in the lurch by a negligent lord."

Dorinda hadn't thought of it that way. All she knew was that Lisette had insisted on the duke's taking her in after hearing of the dire straits in which Edgar had left her. Edgar had married her in a last-ditch effort to keep his property from being entailed away. When she'd repeatedly failed to give him an heir, he'd begun drinking even more heavily than usual, which was how he'd ended up stumbling into the Thames one night and drowning.

She faced the doctor warily. "So how do you propose that I stop her nonsense?"

"Not you. *We*. It will take both of us to show her why it won't work." His crooked grin made her heart turn over in her chest. "You'll be at dinner at their house tonight, too, won't you?"

"Yes." She frowned. "Oh dear, that's probably why she's always inviting you to dine. I should have realized what she was up to long before this. I'm so sorry—I'm sure it's very annoying for you. You probably have a hundred women wanting to meet the doctor who saved the life of the duke's cousin."

"Slightly fewer than a hundred," he said dryly. "Honestly, you mustn't blame yourself for this. Her Grace can be very sly." He began to pace. "But we will put her in her place, don't worry. Tonight we'll attend, look at each other with adoring eyes, pretend to have fallen in with her plan . . . and then pull the rug out from under her."

"How on earth can we manage that?"

He eyed her intently. "We'll get into a row at dinner over whatever couples usually argue over, and I'll storm out. Or you. Whichever will upset her more. Then she'll see what her meddling has wrought, and leave us be."

Dorinda considered that. "I suppose it *could* work. Lisette is always trying to keep the peace between the members of the Duke's Men; she wouldn't like seeing two of her friends quarrel as a result of her machinations."

"Precisely." A twinkle appeared in his eye. "It might be fun, actually. As long as we can keep straight faces while we do it."

His teasing never ceased to take her by surprise. Edgar's doctors had all been stiff and dour, behaving as if she were some recalcitrant child who needed punishing for not spitting out an heir as she should.

Of course, Dr. Worth would probably be the same if he were treating her. Fortunately, he was not. So perhaps this would be all right. Besides, she had to do *something*, besides confiding her embarrassing secret, to keep Lisette from pursuing her matchmaking.

"Very well," she said. "That sounds like an excellent plan. Though we should agree on what to argue over beforehand."

"We certainly should." A calculating look crossed his face. "And we can discuss it while you're organizing my office."

The swift increase in her pulse alarmed her. "You still want me to?"

"Of course. You're here. You offered." He swept his hand about to indicate the mayhem. "As you can see, I need the help."

"You certainly do," she said, then winced at her frankness. "I—I mean—"

"Trust me, I know. Why do you think I asked for the duchess's aid?" His voice softened. "And I've noticed how much she relies on you in managing the duke's household. I doubt she's ever been taxed with quite that large an endeavor, while you're obviously well accustomed to taking such matters in hand."

Gratified by the fact that he'd noticed, she murmured, "Well, Edgar did have a large estate." A rather tumbledown estate, which his nephew inherited, since she couldn't give him an heir. "But what will people say if I remain here alone with you?"

"Nothing, I should hope. You're a widow, not some maiden miss. I doubt anyone even saw you come in, and if they did, the cat's out of the bag anyway. Might as well make the best of it."

He flashed her another disarming grin. "Besides, since you're living at the duke's right now, Her Grace would surely notice if you return there so quickly. If we are to fool her tonight, she has to believe you spent the day with me."

"That's true." And the idea of spending the day with him sounded perfectly wonderful.

Yet oh so dangerous.

Tamping down the quiver that went through her, she stared pointedly at his chest, where the banyan had fallen open again to reveal a smattering of dark curls. "I'm happy to stay and help, but—"

"Oh! Right." He pushed back that errant lock of hair again. "None of my informal bachelor attire, eh?" He grinned as he turned for the door. "I'll just go change into something more suitable. And I'll put on the kettle."

She gaped at him. "You know how to make tea?"

He eyed her askance. "I served on a ship for years, remember? If I wanted tea there, I had to make it myself. Would you like some?"

Edgar would have fallen through the floor before he made tea for her. "That would be lovely, Dr. Worth, thank you."

"Percy," he said. "If we're to be convincing tonight, we should use each other's Christian names."

"Of course." When he just continued to stare at her, she murmured, "You should call me Dorinda."

"Dorinda," he repeated, with an odd glint in his eye, and a shiver went down her spine.

She'd always hated her name because it was so different, but when he said it, it sounded as shimmering as the poetry from which it was taken.

"I'll be back shortly, Dorinda," he said. "Make yourself at home." Then he disappeared through the door.

For a moment, she could only stare after him. The last thing she needed was to "make herself at home" here. But, as he said, she was here already, so she might as well improve his office situation. And if in the process she got to know the doctor—Percy—a bit better, what could it hurt?

Ignoring all the many, *many* ways it could hurt, she hurried to the table and set to work.

✦ ✦ ✦

PERCY DRESSED SWIFTLY. He couldn't believe it— the widow he'd been coveting for months was standing in his office at this very moment.

Thank you, Duchess.

Her Grace was giving him a chance. Granted, it was a small one, only a day to convince Mrs. Nunley—Dorinda—that he and she were well suited, but it was more than he'd had heretofore.

Of course, he had to get past that nonsense of hers about not remarrying. He couldn't fathom why a woman so pretty and accomplished would take such a notion into her head, but he meant to banish it for good.

Especially now that he knew she might fancy him. All this time he'd thought himself alone in his interest, but her presence here—and their bit of conversation—had led him to reconsider. So did the way she'd stared at his bared chest with decided fascination . . .

His pulse began to pound. Dorinda was *not* the type of woman who should remain alone the rest of her life. Somehow he must make her see that.

Tying his cravat, he regarded himself critically in the mirror. At least he *looked* like a gentleman now, and not some ill-bred oaf who wandered about his lodgings half-dressed. Still, he hoped she spoke the truth when she said she didn't care about the difference in their social standing. Doctors were considered gentlemen, but just barely. Compared to a duke's great-granddaughter . . .

He set his shoulders. That didn't matter. As she herself had pointed out, he had risen in consequence of late while she had fallen. That made them equals. And she'd never stood on ceremony with him. Just the fact that she'd come here to help him proved that she wasn't toplofty.

A glance at the mantel clock told him there were

twelve hours until he was expected at the Lyons town house for dinner. Dorinda would need a couple of hours to get back there to dress, so that left him with ten hours total. It wasn't much to work with, given that they were supposed to have a falling-out at dinner.

He wished he hadn't proposed that, but he'd been scrambling for a way to keep her here and hadn't thought it through.

Well, no matter. By dinnertime, he meant to have shown her that she belonged with him. That they would make a good match. That Her Grace had proven wise beyond her years when she'd thrown them together.

The kettle began to boil, and he headed over to make tea in his battered teapot. Since he lacked a tea tray, he set his two cups onto a large medical tome, added the pot, and then shoved the door open with his elbow so he could carry the whole contraption into the office.

Then he froze. The widow stood on a low stool before his cupboard, and the sun coming in through the transom highlighted the golden ringlets fringing her elegant neck.

God, but she was beautiful—an intoxicating hand ful of a female who never failed to make his heart race and his blood heat. Then she reached up to arrange the books that had previously been stacked haphazardly on the top shelf, and he thought he might lose his mind.

Because not only did the position tighten all the parts of her amber-colored gown about her shapely figure, but with her skirts hiked up, he could see the lower part of her legs perfectly. And what shapely legs they were, too, in their creamy silk stockings. He stood there gaping at them, imagining what it would be like to smooth his hands up those lovely calves, past her knees to—

"You're back," she said brightly and hopped down from the stool, forcing him to choke back a regretful groan. "I thought it might be good to start with the top shelves so we could see how much room we have for the other, more useful items on the lower ones. Don't you think?"

"I wouldn't know." He was still trying to banish that lovely image of her atop the stool. "Organization is not my . . . er . . . strong suit. I keep meaning to hire a maid of all work to come in and take care of such matters, but I've had no time to interview anyone."

"You really must take the time," she chided him. "A doctor with a cluttered office will be eyed askance by any female patient who comes here."

He smiled. "Female patients don't come here; I go to them. Besides, you're not eyeing me askance."

"I'm not your patient, thank God."

His smile vanished. "Why 'thank God'? I'll have you know that—"

"Forgive me, I didn't mean it that way. I just . . . have been at the mercy of doctors too many times to wish to be anyone's patient."

He was about to ask for an explanation, but she hurried to take the book from him and instantly changed the subject. "Good Lord, have you no tea tray?"

"I've had no need of one until now. I live here alone, remember?" Though he hoped to change that state of affairs shortly.

He watched as she set the book on the table and poured the tea. She glanced at him with one pretty eyebrow raised. "No sugar? Or milk?"

"No. Sorry. I drink it without."

With a roll of her eyes, she sipped some tea, then set down her cup. "We shall definitely have to arrange for you to hire a maid of all work. Or a cook or someone who can keep your pantry stocked."

"And buy me a tea tray," he added cheerily, encouraged by her use of the word *we*.

"Trust me, I'm already making a list of necessary purchases." Reminded once again of how competent she was in running a household, he watched as she critically surveyed the table's jumbled contents. "I suggest you organize these by function. We can put the astringents—elixir of vitriol, alum, and Peruvian bark—together, then the purges, then the emollients and so on. Don't you think?"

Astringents? She *knew* what those were? "Clearly you really *have* spent a great deal of time in doctors' offices. But I thought your husband was in perfect health until he met his untimely death. How do you know the function of what's in those jars? Were you once sickly? You certainly don't look it now."

She paled. "I had a great many ill relations," she mumbled, then turned deliberately toward the cupboard. "Now, about these shelves . . ."

Percy watched her retreat with a narrowed gaze. How very odd. He could swear that she had no ill relations—the duke's family was small. So why hide the reason for her medical knowledge? Might that be why she behaved so strangely with him, one moment friendly and open and the next wary and closed?

Well, whatever it was, he meant to get to the bottom of it. Because the first step in gaining her affections was clearly going to be gaining her trust.

2

DORINDA OPENED A box and tried to look interested in its contents, but her blood was still in a wild
riot over what she'd nearly revealed. And how quickly
he'd pounced on it, turning very physician-like.

She shuddered. She liked him much better when he
was teasing her. Or carrying that ridiculous excuse for a
tea tray. Or wearing the banyan that revealed more than it
concealed of his surprisingly firm and well-sculpted body.

There's no reason you can't just have an affair with him,
you know. You're a widow. It's practically expected of you to
take a lover.

Percy reached past her to remove an instrument from
the box she was staring blindly into, and just the feel of
him so close set her senses reeling. Oh Lord. Clearly it
had been far too long since she'd shared a man's bed.

"I suppose we should decide what we're going to
argue about," he murmured beside her.

"Wh-what?" she asked, still caught up in wicked
thoughts of him in her bed.

He smiled down at her. "For tonight. For when we argue at dinner."

Oh, *that*. "Certainly! Of course."

He turned the instrument around, as if checking for damage. "You'll have to be the one to figure it out, since I've never been married or even engaged," he said conversationally. "What sort of things did you and your husband fight over?"

Trying to still the clamoring in her blood at having him so close, she pulled more medical implements from the box. "Oh, the usual. Which of our families to spend Christmas with. How the dining room should be renovated. Where we should go for a holiday."

Why she wasn't willing to drink mare's milk just because Edgar had heard that it would help her produce the requisite son. She grimaced.

"None of those will work, since they only pertain to already married couples," Percy pointed out. "What did you argue about during your courtship?"

"I don't remember us arguing then," she said truthfully.

He gaped at her. "Never?"

She shrugged. "We didn't court long enough to argue. I was Edgar's second wife, you see, so he was in something of a hurry to marry, and I was happy to oblige him." Little had she known that he was in a hurry because he needed the heir that his previous wife hadn't lived long enough to bear him.

"I see," Percy clipped out. "So you were very much in love."

"At the beginning, I suppose." She'd thought it was love at the time, in any case. But now she wondered if she'd just been in love with the idea of being lady of the manor and thus escaping her stultifying life of balls and parties. She was not a terribly social person.

"But not later?" he probed.

She'd said too much. "Come to think of it, there *was* something we argued about during our courtship: which season was better, spring or summer."

"You're joking," he said. "That's the silliest thing I ever heard."

A smile crossed her face. "Isn't it, though? I made the mistake of telling him one night that I preferred summer because my eyes continually water in spring, and he told me that I was being absurd. He said I *ought* to prefer spring because summer was too hot. He argued the point until I conceded it just to get him to stop plaguing me about it."

Percy shook his head. "Arguing over one's preference for a season is ludicrous. Might as well argue over the best color. If we choose to fight about *that*, Her Grace will laugh us right out of the dining room."

"True." Sifting back through old memories, she carried the box of implements to the cupboard shelves and began to lay them out. "We did used to fight over whether ladies should use rouge."

"They shouldn't, of course," he said firmly.

She bristled. "And why not? Sometimes a lady needs a bit of color in her cheeks in the dead of winter."

"I've no objection to that, but most rouges contain lead." Frowning, he walked up to take the empty box from her. "You might brighten your cheeks, but only until you kill yourself."

That took the wind right out of her sails. "There's lead in rouge?"

"Some of it. The men who make such potions don't tell you when those pretty pots of rouge contain poison along with their unguents," he said with fierce conviction. Then he shot her a long glance. "So why did your husband disapprove of rouge if not because of the lead in it?"

"He thought it was the mark of a whore."

"Ah. Seems a bit harsh."

"Exactly! But he was a man of strong opinions."

"Forgive my frankness, madam, but he sounds like an arse."

She blinked, then burst into laughter. No one had ever put it quite that way before. "He was, actually. Sometimes."

He fixed her with a dark gaze. "All the same, I'm glad he stopped you from using rouge, no matter what his reasons. I would rather have you here with me, looking a bit pale, than in the grave with color on your cheeks."

What a lovely thing to say. And there was such intensity in his eyes that it quite stole the breath from her.

Dangerous. Very, *very* dangerous.

She jerked her gaze from his. "Well, we can't argue over rouge then either, now that I know about the poison. That would make me look ridiculous."

"You couldn't look ridiculous if you tried," he said softly.

A profound pleasure coursed through her that made her chide herself for being so susceptible to his flatteries. They *were* merely flatteries, weren't they? "But we still have nothing to argue over."

He stared at her another long moment, then said tightly, "We could argue over my coarse ways."

She snorted. "What coarse ways? You're always a perfect gentleman."

"With no tea tray and no sugar to offer a lady," he pointed out.

"That hardly signifies," she said. "Bachelors are all that way, gentlemen or no."

That provoked another heart-stopping smile from him. "Especially doctors. It's hard to care about the mundane when you deal with life and death every day."

"I would imagine so." She stared at him. "What made you become a doctor?"

"My mother had consumption when I was a boy." His eyes clouded over. "I had no sisters, so it fell to me to take care of her. When she died a lingering death, I swore that one day I'd find a cure for it." He forced a smile. "So far, no luck, but I keep trying."

"I'm sorry," she said, her heart aching for him.

"Don't be. I miss her, but her death led me on a path I might not have chosen on my own, and I cannot regret that." He took in a deep breath. "Now, we still must decide what to argue over."

She allowed him to change the subject, sensing that he would not welcome pity. "That gets harder by the moment since we seem to agree on everything." She thought a moment. "I suppose we could argue about what exercise is best: walking or riding."

Percy shrugged. "Either one keeps the constitution in good order. What is there to argue about?"

"Trust me, Edgar found plenty. He used to insist that a brisk walk was far superior to a long ride." Especially since he always fretted that riding might keep her from conceiving.

"That's absurd."

"I quite agree," she said, secretly pleased that Percy saw things as she did. "Besides, people must choose whatever activity comes naturally to them. And I'm a natural at riding. I love it more than anything."

"So do I." Percy opened another box. "Though I suppose I could pretend not to. One of us must, if we're to argue over it."

"Then I should be the one to pretend I like walking. I heard Edgar extol the virtues of a brisk walk often enough that I know exactly what to say."

"Good, because I have no trouble waxing rhapsodic about riding. There's something about racing along in the wind that reminds me of being at sea, hurtling through the waves in pursuit of some new land."

The wistfulness in his voice clutched at her heart. "Do you miss it? Being at sea, I mean."

"Sometimes." He gazed off at the lone window. "I miss how brilliantly the stars shone, unobscured by the smoke and fog of London. I miss the rocking of the ocean." He winked at her. "Though I don't miss being thrown out of my bunk whenever seas were rough."

"Oh my, that must have been jarring."

"And occasionally downright hazardous, since I sat on my bunk to shave."

"Good Lord! You never cut yourself, did you?"

His eyes warmed. "Thank you for the concern, but no. Though it didn't take me long to realize why so many seamen grow beards."

She gazed up at his clean-shaven chin. "I can hardly imagine you in a beard. I'll bet it made you feel very piratical."

"Oh, very," he said with a grin. "I considered adding a skull-and-crossbones hat and a gold hoop in my ear, but I was afraid a drunk sailor might accidentally shoot me in the passageway one night, so I settled for saying 'Arr' and 'Ahoy, matey' from time to time."

"But no parrot on your shoulder?" she teased.

"Absolutely not. Parrots chatter too much. I like my sleep."

"It doesn't sound as if you got any," she said lightly, "what with being tossed out of your bunk and staring at the stars and encountering drunk sailors in passageways."

"Not to mention playing cards into the wee hours, which we did whenever the ship was becalmed. It was either that or go mad from boredom." His gaze turned serious again. "Still, at least at sea a man need never be alone. Even here in London, with all its people, I sometimes feel very lonely. That's when I wish I could just walk down a passageway to find a friend striking up a fiddle or playing a game of loo."

Lonely. How well she knew the feeling. Lisette and

the duke were wonderful people, but sometimes they saw only each other, and she was left wishing for what could never be.

"You could go to a club," she said. "That's what my husband did nearly every night." Then Edgar would stumble in during the wee hours of the morning stinking of brandy and wanting to bed her.

"Did he?" His voice lowered to a ragged rasp. "I can't imagine why. What possible entertainment could a club provide that would compare to an evening spent with you?"

The words hung in the air between them. And when his gaze locked on her mouth, she had to fight the sudden leap of desire in her veins. "I never guessed you were such a flatterer, Dr. Worth," she managed to whisper.

"Percy, remember?" He reached up to cup her chin in his warm hand. "And it's not flattery, sweetheart. It's the truth."

Sweetheart. Even Edgar had never called her that. Or touched her with such feeling.

Anticipation shivered deliciously down her spine when Percy's eyes darkened and he bent his head toward hers. In that moment she knew that if she just kept standing there like a dolt, he would kiss her.

She wanted him to. Oh, how she wanted it! But she couldn't let him. Not if she were to keep her sanity.

Stepping back from him, she turned toward the table and said, "I suppose we really should tackle this jumble here."

A muttered curse escaped him, and she wondered if

he would press his advantage and take her in his arms anyway, like some bold buccaneer. If he did, she didn't know how she would resist him.

Though she *must*. He might be an attractive, fascinating fellow tempting her into madness, but he was also a doctor used to healing people. He wouldn't simply accept that she was barren. And she would never again put up with some pompous physician admonishing her to "just relax" or "take cold baths" or even "do whatever your husband wishes." Never again.

As the silence spun out behind her, she stared down at the jars and picked out the purges, the elixir of vitriol, the alum, and the Peruvian bark—all supposed "cures" for barrenness that made her violently ill.

Remembering that gave her the strength to resist him. She squared her shoulders and forced a brightness into her tone that she didn't feel. "So tell me, Doctor, what was it like to travel the world? Did you visit any interesting places?"

There, that was a safe subject.

At first he didn't answer. One moment passed, then two as she held her breath and prayed. At last he said, in a cool voice, "Morocco. And the West Indies. Not to mention . . ."

When he launched into a recitation of the many places he'd visited, it was all she could do not to sag against the table in relief. Because the last thing she needed was a man like Percy courting her. He was too perceptive, too intriguing . . . too irresistibly dangerous, like the bright and pretty rouge that hid poison. If he swept her into his orbit, she would never have the power to leave it.

And she hated feeling trapped. Men had certain expectations of women that she could never fulfill. So she would be better off not taking up with Percy.

Still, as the day went on, she wished she *could*. Because no other man had ever shared so many of her opinions and views of the world. She'd never met a man who could laugh at himself and make her do the same.

A man who tempted her to consider the unthinkable.

It was all she thought about while they organized his office. Especially with him so clearly pursuing her. It wasn't just the provocative things he said. It was his many probing questions about her past. And his sly touches—a brush of his hand here, a bump of his shoulder there.

It was the way he watched her, like a sleek cormorant ready to pluck her up and devour her whole if she was fool enough to come up for air.

She should swim away, just put an end to this farce and leave. That would be the sensible thing. A pity that she wasn't feeling very sensible today. Besides, they were almost done. In an hour she would *have* to leave to dress for dinner.

The thought depressed her.

Determinedly she opened a box, then shuddered to find it filled with daunting instruments, including a nasty-looking saw. "Shall we put all these in a drawer?" She held up the saw. "So the sight of them doesn't alarm your patients?"

"Might as well. I had more use for an amputation saw at sea than I ever do on land." He cast her a quick smile. "Not too many lords and ladies get their limbs crushed while navigating slippery decks in a storm."

"I should hope not." She loaded the instruments into a cupboard drawer, then turned to watch as he pushed furniture around now that all the boxes were out of the way. Sweat beaded his wide brow, and he stopped to wipe it on his sleeve. At her insistence, he'd removed his coat earlier to keep from soiling it, and the sight of him in shirtsleeves made her heart catch in her throat.

"That's the last box," she said inanely.

He stared hard at her. "I see that."

She should leave. But she didn't want to. Despite spending the day in a doctor's office, this had been more fun than she'd had in a very long while. Wouldn't it be lovely if Percy proved *not* to care about her barrenness? If she could . . . perhaps . . . spend more wonderful days like this with him?

Glancing around, desperate for any excuse to stay longer, she pointed to the skeleton. "We still have to figure out where to put that."

"*That*," he said decisively, "belongs precisely where it is."

"Slumped in a chair?" she said with a chuckle.

"He isn't slumped. He's sitting." He walked over to the chair and hauled the skeleton up beside him. "It's hard to get a skeleton to stay seated, you know. And Seymour can be rather obstinate."

"*Seymour?*" A laugh sputtered out of her. "You call your skeleton Seymour?"

"Of course," he said lightly. "What else does one call a skeleton?"

"Yorick?" she offered.

"No, no, Yorick is only for skulls. A full skeleton requires a more auspicious name." He carefully arranged the skeleton so that it actually looked as if it was seated. "He has no clothes, after all, with which to display his dignity."

She cocked her head. "How do you know it's not a she? Perhaps its name is Priscilla. Or Elizabeth."

"Absolutely not," he said, glancing down at the lower half. "The pelvis is too small and it's shaped wrong, besides. This skeleton could never bear a child."

The words came out of nowhere, as if Fate was determined to remind her of everything that had gone wrong in her marriage.

She stiffened, then anger roiled up in her, tinged with despair. "And of course that's the essential thing," she said bitterly. "That a woman be able to bear a child."

When he looked startled, she knew she should stop, but now that the words had been loosed, she couldn't seem to hold them back. "God forbid that a woman be valued for her skills as a wife or her intelligence or her ability to dance. Oh no, she is good for only one thing—bearing that essential son so that *he* can inherit what she is never allowed to."

He came toward her. "Sweetheart, I'm sorry, but I cannot fathom why you're upset."

"Don't call me 'sweetheart'!" she cried. The futility of it all swamped her, making her despair. "I can never be that to you."

"I don't understand," he said hoarsely. "I don't see what children have to do with—"

"I'm barren, blast it! I can't bear you or any other man the requisite 'heir and a spare'!" Tears clogged her throat, and she fought them back. "S-so all your lovely words about s-spending nights with me . . . all our wonderful conversations a-and the way you make me feel . . ." She cast him a hopeless glance. "They're all for naught, don't you see? I can never be that woman for you, no matter how much I want to be."

Then, to her horror, she burst into tears.

3

FOR HALF A second, Percy stood immobile, stunned into silence. Not since his mother's illness had he seen a woman cry so deeply, and he'd forgotten how wrenching it could be.

Then, cursing himself for a fool, he hurried to draw her in his arms. "Shh, shh, it's all right, it'll be all right," he murmured against her hair, falling back on the soothing words his father had offered whenever his mother couldn't abide the chest pain and the wracking coughs.

But he knew only too well that nothing could really soothe Dorinda. Her hurt ran deeper than he could reach. God, why hadn't he recognized the source of it sooner? He should have seen the signs—her comments about doctors, her vacillating responses to his advances . . . the fact that she'd earlier recited every sort of half-baked cure used to treat barrenness.

With a groan, he fumbled for his handkerchief, alarmed by the tears spilling down her cheeks. "There, now, don't go on so." At least she was letting him hold her, even though he was an oblivious dolt. At least she trusted him enough to show him her aching heart. He pressed his handkerchief into her hand. "Steady on, sweetheart, take a breath. You'll make yourself sick."

"Oh, w-what does it m-matter?" she managed as she pulled back from him, dabbing at her face with his handkerchief. "I'm that h-horribly useless thing to a man—a w-woman who can't b-bear children."

The pain in her words struck him to the heart. He caught her hands in his. "Anyone who thinks that a woman is good for only that is a fool. I certainly don't think any such silly thing."

Though she eyed him skeptically, she didn't yank her hands away. "*Every* husband wants a wife who can bear him sons." She dragged in a shivering breath. "Why do you think I visited so many doctors? Edgar would have done anything to ensure that I carried his child."

He choked back the words, *More evidence that he was an arse.* This was probably not the moment to make that point. "Yes, but I'm sure he valued you for your other fine attributes."

"If he did, I saw no evidence of it," she said bitterly. "Before he died, that was all he could talk about—my 'flaw.'"

"That is *not* a flaw in you," he growled, wishing he could go back in time and thrash the hell out of her late husband. Instead he settled for trying to undo some of the damage the arse had done. "It's just . . . part of life. And he was a fool if he cared only about your ability to give him children. A good wife is worth far more than that."

She stared at him with reddened eyes. "He wasn't alone in his thinking. Every doctor he sent me to felt the same."

"Then they were fools, too. And obviously not very attentive to the lessons they'd surely learned in their practice of medicine."

That made her blink. "What lessons?"

"I've been present at a number of birthings, sweetheart. And in the few tragic cases where a man was forced to choose between the life of his unborn child and the life of his wife, he always chose his wife." He squeezed her hands. "Always."

She stiffened. "Because a wife can produce more babies."

"No. Because a man carefully picks the woman he wishes to be his companion for life. He can't get that from his children. So given the choice between the real woman of his heart and a potential child of his blood, he will choose his heart over his blood every time."

"Not every man," she said, though there was more uncertainty in her voice now. "Not Edgar. I think he would have tried any cure, no matter how outrageous, no matter what it did to me, as long as it got him his heir."

The very thought of what she must have gone through trying "any cure" chilled him to the bone. "That wasn't about children; that was about pride and money. If he only cared about those, then he didn't deserve you." He caught her head in his hands. "Because if I had a woman as fine as you for my wife, I swear I would never torment her with astringents and purges and mare's milk."

Her eyes went wide, confirming the sort of dubious remedies her husband and his quacks had been subjecting her to. It made him want to howl.

It made him want to show her what he already saw—that she was so much more than a brood mare.

"You don't know what you'd do if you were desperate," she pointed out. "No matter how much I protested, there was always another doctor who gave him new hope that I could be fixed, who offered new guaranteed cures. So if you and I were married for years and I still hadn't managed to—"

He pressed a finger to her lips to silence her. "I would *never* risk your health in some fool attempt to circumvent nature." He skimmed his finger along her luscious, perfect mouth. "I don't know if you're barren, but neither do I care. You're a beautiful, intelligent woman with a heart as wide as the sky at sea, and a courage deep enough to withstand Fate's many arrows. That's all that matters to me."

Then he kissed her, for lack of any other way to express the fullness in his heart. He kissed her long and hard, half expecting her to thrust him away for his impudence.

So when she curled her fingers into his sleeves and kissed him back instead, his blood soared. He deepened the kiss at once, ravaging her mouth with his tongue, reveling in the soft silk of her.

She tore her lips from his. "Percy . . . oh, Lord, Percy . . . you don't know what you're doing."

With an exultant laugh, he looped one arm about

her waist and dragged her close. "Of course I do. I'm reminding you that I find you desirable just as you are." Nuzzling her cheek to drink in the honeyed scent of her, he skimmed his hands up her ribs. "I'm doing what I've wanted to do for months—hold you and kiss you and worship every inch of you with my mouth and hands and tongue."

She drew back to gape at him. "But you never let on . . . I never guessed that you—"

"I thought it was hopeless." He stared into her lovely face, encouraged by her expression of wonder and surprise. "I thought you must still be mourning your husband. That you saw me as only the friend of your friends. Until today." He lowered his voice to a husky murmur. "Until you showed up here in the early morning to help me organize my office."

She colored so fetchingly, he wanted to kiss her again. "That was because of Lisette. I would never have—"

"No?" He pressed kisses into her fragrant hair. "You could have asked her to assign you some other task. Or once you arrived and I showed up half-dressed, you could have screamed and run out."

"I am . . . far too sensible for that," she said, though she swayed against him, rousing his blood to new heights.

He chuckled. "Yes, you are." Taking a chance, he slid one hand up to cup her breast. When she sucked in a ragged breath in response, he added, "But there was more to it than that. The moment you stared at me in my banyan, you let me see that you wanted me. Perhaps as much as I want you."

Fixing her with a heated glance, he kneaded her breast in slow circles through her gown. "You do want me, don't you? I did not imagine that."

She stared at him with a sudden wildness in her eyes, then reached down to raise his other hand to her other breast. "No. You did not imagine that."

God save him, he was in trouble now. Not that he minded. Any trouble involving the Widow Nunley was well worth it.

Dorinda was thinking much the same thing as Percy took her mouth with a savage abandon that made her ache to do all manner of wicked things. With him. To him.

She wanted to believe his tender words. She wanted to trust that he really didn't care about her ability to give him children. Perhaps she shouldn't, but she couldn't help herself. His hands were all over her, reminding her that she was desirable, reminding her that she *desired* . . . to be with him, to be touched by him, to take him into her bed. She'd forgotten the lushness of desire, how it made a woman yearn and hope and *feel*.

He thumbed her nipples so deliciously through her walking gown and soft stays that she wanted to rip her clothes off to have his hands on her naked body. Meanwhile, his magical mouth trailed a path of fire down her neck to her throat, which it branded with hot, eager kisses.

Next thing she knew, he was unfastening her walking dress to better expose her bosom, and she was helping him.

"I want you, sweetheart," he said. "Now. But if you don't—"

"I do," she whispered, pushing her fears firmly aside. "Take me, Percy. *Please.*"

Meanwhile, she urged his head down to her breasts, for she thought she'd die if she didn't feel his mouth there. When he obliged her by unearthing one taut nipple and seizing it with his teeth, she buried her hands in his thick, silken hair and clutched him to her.

The next several moments were a blur of kisses and caresses and words of urgent need as they yanked off each other's clothes, eager to banish the barriers between them. When she was stripped down to her shift and he to his drawers, he paused to give her a look as dark as sin and twice as hot. "Are you sure about this?" he growled, even as his gaze scoured every part of her.

Her answer was to shimmy out of her shift and drop it to the floor.

His eyes turned a sultry black as they took in her nakedness. Then he hauled her into his arms for a long, heated kiss that inflamed her senses.

Emboldened by his unabashed desire for her, she slid her hands into his drawers and shoved them off so that he was naked against her from head to hips to heels.

"Oh, God, sweetheart," he gasped as he filled his hands with her breasts, "you are even more than I had guessed."

"More . . . what?" she managed, exulting in the feel of his hands on her, of his flesh hardening against her belly.

"More beautiful, more warm . . . more woman. More everything."

While she was still smiling at those silky words, he dragged her to a nearby chair and dropped onto it, then pulled her to stand in front of him. When she gaped at him, he grinned. "You said you like to ride."

"Ride?"

He cocked his head. "Have you never been on top to make love?"

She shook her head. "Edgar always said there was only one way to do it if we wanted to conceive."

His face darkened. "Edgar was an arse. There are many ways to make love, and I mean for us to try them all."

He began stroking her body, finding all the secret places that yearned for him and caressing them until she turned to putty in his hands.

So this was what he'd meant by wanting to worship her. Good Lord in heaven, it was pure sacrilege, the way he roused her. And she didn't care one whit. She only wanted more and more and more . . .

"*Please*, Percy, please . . ."

Satisfaction leapt in his face as he pulled her to straddle him. "Time for you to ride, sweetheart." He urged her over his member, then impaled her on the hot, hard flesh.

"Ohhh, yes," she whispered, reveling in the fullness of him. "That's . . . *amazing*." When he squirmed urgently beneath her, she began to move, up and down, finding her own rhythm.

How wonderful! She loved this—being in control. Having Percy—*her* Percy—beneath her.

His breath came hard and fast, like his answering thrusts. "I think you lied . . . about never doing this . . . Dorinda. You're very . . . good."

She gave a giddy laugh. "I told you. I'm a natural . . . at riding."

"Thank God."

After that, there were no more words. They were too caught up in the steady beat of their ride, which quickened and darkened and intensified until she could feel the world rushing past her, feel the rushing build in her loins and her blood and her heart.

And as she crashed through into bliss, he cried out beneath her and found his own release, spilling himself inside her. In that moment everything she thought she knew about men shattered, and she knew, really *knew*.

He was the only man she could ever marry. Because she feared she might well be in love with him.

If that was true, then God help her.

4

PERCY COULDN'T BELIEVE it. Dorinda was his at last, every warm, beautiful inch of her. She still sat sprawled across him, her body wrapped about his like a fragrant cloak, and he wished he could keep her there forever.

He glanced beyond her, then laughed.

"What?" she murmured sleepily.

"I think Seymour is jealous."

She roused to glance behind her. "How can you tell?"

"He's slumped in his chair again." They must have been vigorous enough that the vibrations along the floor had shaken him back down into that position. "Clearly he's disappointed that I'm the one who has you in his arms and not he."

She laughed. "I don't know—it looks to me as if he's hiding his face in embarrassment. Poor Seymour got to *see more* than he bargained for."

He groaned. "That's the worst pun I've ever heard."

"He's practically stiff with indignation."

"Please stop," he said.

Her eyes twinkled. "Or perhaps he's just looking on the floor for a skeleton key."

A laugh escaped him, despite himself. "You're amazing, do you know that?"

"Because I make bad jokes?"

"About a skeleton. Which most women would regard with horror and loathing."

"Most women haven't spent as much time in doctors' offices as I have."

That sobered him. "Does it bother you? Being here among the medicines and the nasty implements?"

She brushed a kiss to his lips. "Not when you're here."

His heart caught in his throat. "Marry me."

Her eyes went wide. "That's . . . rather precipitous, isn't it?"

"Hardly. I've known you for five months and lusted after you for four and three-quarters. I would have asked you for your hand three months ago if you hadn't been still in mourning. And if I'd thought I had any hope of your consenting."

She dropped her gaze to his chest. "What about my inability to give you children?"

"Doesn't matter," he said. "Besides, don't let those quacks tell you that it's only the fault of a woman if a couple can't bear children. It's perfectly possible that your husband was the problem. You may not even be barren at all."

Her eyes met his, suddenly wary. It stymied him. He'd thought he was giving her good news.

"I think I'd better go," she murmured.

He blinked. "Why?"

Slipping from his grasp, she left him to go pull on her shift. "If I don't return in enough time to dress for dinner, they will realize something is amiss."

"Let them. Once we tell them we're marrying—"

"I haven't agreed to that," she said sharply.

He leapt to his feet. "What's wrong, Dorinda?" he demanded as she shimmied into her stays.

"Nothing." She presented her back to him. "Will you please do me up?"

Gritting his teeth, he did as she asked. He'd gone awry with her somehow, but he wasn't sure where. "Are you saying you do not want to marry me?"

"We can talk about it later." Swiftly she pulled on her front-fastening gown and did it up. "Right now I have to go."

"Damn it, Dorinda," he bit out, grabbing her by the arm and forcing her to face him. "What is this all about?"

Her eyes filled with tears. "Please, Percy," she said, "if you care for me at all, let me go. I have to leave!"

There was such panic in her face, in her voice, that it chilled his blood. He released her arm at once. "Of course," he said. "Whatever you wish."

"Thank you," she whispered. "I'll see you at dinner."

He watched numbly as she finished dressing, then headed out the door. For a long time, he just stood there, staring at the emptiness she'd left behind.

Then anger seized him. He did not deserve this.

She'd been perfectly eager to lie with him in his bed until he mentioned marriage, and then she'd run off.

She did tell you she meant never to marry again.

Yes, but that was only because of her worry that no man would want a barren wife. He'd already made it clear that he didn't care. Why, just now when she'd asked about it, he'd told her again that he didn't care. He'd even pointed out that she might not be barren at all. That ought to have given her new hope, not sent her running out into—

There was always another doctor who gave him new hope that I could be fixed . . .

And just like that, he understood.

Oh God. He was a fool. Here she'd just unburdened herself about the years of misery her late husband had put her through trying to ensure that she conceived and then Percy had gone and made her think he would do the same. That he wouldn't accept the "inevitable."

That he'd lied when he said he didn't care if she could bear him a son.

He dropped into the chair. *Had* he lied? *Did* he care? Clearly he hadn't examined that point thoroughly enough. But if he were to have any chance with her, he had to be sure of how he felt about being married to a woman who could not give him children.

Because there was always the possibility that she *was* barren. And if he couldn't accept that, couldn't accept her for who she was, then he had no business courting her.

✦ ✦ ✦

By the time Dorinda was dressed for dinner, she'd already made up her mind to sever all ties to Percy, whatever it took. She'd believed him when he'd said her barrenness didn't matter, but he'd been lying. Or at least lying to himself. Clearly it *did* matter or he wouldn't have started discussing the possibility that she might *not* be barren. And talking like a doctor, too, with a doctor's certainty that everything could be fixed with the right nostrum or food or way of life.

She didn't *want* to be fixed. She wanted children, yes, but not at that price. So tonight she would have to make that clear. And there was only one way to do that, one way to be sure that he wouldn't plague her and prevaricate until he wore her down and got what he wanted.

It was a coward's way, but after her marriage to Edgar, she *was* a coward. She couldn't go through all of that again, even if it meant cutting herself off from the man who'd made her feel alive for the first time in a long while.

You're a beautiful, intelligent woman with a heart as wide as the sky at sea, and a courage deep enough to withstand Fate's many arrows. That's all that matters to me.

He was wrong. She wasn't brave. Not enough for that, anyway.

She made sure she waited until right before dinner would be served to go down to the drawing room, so Percy would have no time to get her alone. Thank God she had, too, for it was clear from the way he looked at her that he would have tried.

But before he could do more than greet her, Lisette,

a stickler for promptness, announced that dinner was served and hurried them all toward the dining room.

Leaving the duke talking with Percy, the duchess fell behind to take Dorinda's arm. "Do forgive me for being so shatter-brained this morning. I completely forgot to tell you that the doctor was still in town after all." Lisette cast her a sly glance. "I hope it wasn't too much of a shock."

"Of course not," Dorinda said, determined to follow Percy's original plan for the evening. "It was actually very . . . enlightening."

"Was it, indeed?" Lisette's eyes lit up as they entered the drawing room and the duke came over to accompany her to her chair. "You'll have to tell me all about it later."

Dorinda forced a smile. She ought to, if only to shame the woman into minding her own business. But Percy's way was gentler, and it wouldn't force Dorinda into having to reveal the shame of her barrenness to the duchess.

Percy approached to lead her to her chair. "We need to talk," he murmured as he laid his hand on the small of her back.

"No. We don't." She hurried ahead to take her seat, then added loudly, "Thank you, Dr. Worth."

She could feel his presence behind her, feel him looming over her. But thankfully he must have known that she dared not speak more of it in front of the duchess. Still, she let out a long breath when he left her side and went to sit opposite her in his usual seat at the long, impressive table.

Normally, there were more people at these dinners

than just the four of them. Sometimes Mr. Cale and his wife came, sometimes the Duke's Men attended, and sometimes all of them at once. Lisette was far more social than Dorinda, and His Grace indulged his wife shamelessly.

Besides, the duke seemed to enjoy having people around. By all accounts, he'd lived a very lonely life before Lisette came along. The same sort of lonely life that stretched before Dorinda.

She winced. It didn't matter. Better a lonely life than a life spent trying to meet a man's impossible expectations.

But, oh, it was so hard to look at him and know that this was their last night together, that she had to avoid him from now on. He was wearing one of the two evening coats he seemed to own, and a cravat that was woefully under-starched. He needed a wife—badly. And she wanted desperately to be the one to marry him.

As soon as the soup was served, Lisette smiled knowingly at Dorinda. "So, Dr. Worth told me that you were kind enough to work on organizing his office anyway."

"He asked me to," Dorinda said. "How could I refuse?"

"Especially after she saw what a state it was in," Percy put in. "She could tell at once that only an expert could take my mess in hand." Percy's gaze locked with hers. "I'm surprised she didn't just run screaming from the place the minute she saw the chaos. But then, the widow isn't the sort to run from trouble. She meets it head-on."

She stiffened at the note of rebuke in his voice. He didn't understand. He would never understand. "Sometimes meeting trouble head-on is the wrong approach. Some sorts of trouble can't be set to rights, and it's best just to avoid them."

"Clearly you don't have enough faith in your abilities," he countered. "You set things beautifully to rights in my office. And within a remarkably short time, too."

"Indeed?" Eyes gleaming, Lisette took a sip of soup and surveyed them both. "It mustn't have been *too* short a time, for Dorinda came home only an hour ago."

"Have you been spying on me?" Dorinda said pointedly. When Lisette blinked, then colored, Dorinda cursed her quick tongue. "But you're right—it did take me the entire day."

"Which enabled us to become better acquainted," Percy said. "I have you to thank for that, Your Grace. I'm very grateful I had the chance to come to know your cousin so thoroughly."

The lovely words, so typical of him, made her heart twist in her chest. Until belatedly she caught the double entendre in the words "know your cousin so thoroughly." She stifled a snort. "Dr. Worth has a skeleton in his office," she said blithely, determined to change the subject. "His name is Seymour."

"I've met the indomitable Seymour," the duke put in. A smile crossed his lips. "I trust he did not give you any trouble."

"Only once," Percy said quietly, "when he fell into a slump, jealous of me for having the company of the beautiful Dorinda."

Lisette exchanged a meaningful glance with her

husband at Percy's use of Dorinda's Christian name.

Dorinda could have strangled Percy for that. "Poor Seymour wasn't jealous." She glared at Percy. "He was probably just tired of being jerked this way and that to suit various doctors' whims."

Percy gazed steadily at her. "Or perhaps he was kicking himself for being so oblivious to what was really going on."

"I doubt that," Dorinda snapped. "He was probably just yearning for a place to breathe. Or even a spot of *exercise*." She cast Percy a triumphant look. "Perhaps he wanted a brisk walk in the clear air, where no one has any expectations of him."

"We *are* still talking about a skeleton, aren't we?" Lisette said, looking bewildered.

"I daresay you could use some exercise yourself, Dr. Worth," Dorinda went on. "It's very invigorating."

The duke was watching them now, too, with eyes narrowed.

Dorinda couldn't mistake the stiffening of Percy's shoulders before he shot her a fiercely determined glance. "I prefer riding, myself. There's no more wonderful exercise, in my opinion."

Tamping down a quick stab of disappointment that he'd taken her meaning and was going along with their original plan, she said stoutly, "Riding is too dangerous. Walking is much safer."

"Nonsense." The sudden softening in his eyes caught her off guard. "I suppose you're thinking of those doctors who claim that a woman will hurt her chances to have children if she rides. But it's not true."

She caught her breath, pain slicing through her. He would bring that up *here*? Before her friends?

"Of course it isn't true," Lisette put in, blithely unaware of the tension in the room as she shot her husband a coy glance. "I used to ride all the time, and clearly it didn't stop me from . . . well . . . you know."

"I wasn't thinking of the dangers to a woman's conceiving," Dorinda said through gritted teeth. "I was thinking of how often a rider sometimes takes a wild leap and ends up broken."

"Well, of course riders must be careful—" the duke began.

"Better to take a wild leap than to cower in a corner, wouldn't you say?" Percy snapped, his gaze hot on her.

"I don't want to cower in a corner," Dorinda shot back. "I want to walk. Alone. For exercise. Because it is better for my health than *riding*."

He stared her down. "Come now, Dorinda, I know that you enjoy riding. I've heard you speak of it in glowing terms." With a stubborn gleam in his eye, he added, "And not just riding horses, either. All kinds of riding. Why, just this afternoon—"

She leapt to her feet. She had to put a stop to this before he ruined her reputation before her friends! "Dr. Worth, may I have a word with you in the drawing room, please?"

Triumph lit his face. "Certainly," he drawled as he rose. "I'd like a word with you as well."

"Is everything all right?" Lisette called out anxiously as Dorinda marched off without waiting to see if Percy followed.

To her surprise, it was the duke who answered. "Leave them be, dearling. You've done enough."

"But Max—"

Dorinda didn't hear the rest. She was already halfway down the hall. She could feel Percy hot on her heels, and she braced herself for a fight.

As soon as they'd both entered the drawing room and he'd closed the door, she whirled on him. "You refuse to let it go. You refuse to just—"

"Yes, I do," he interrupted as he approached. "I can't let it go. I love you, Dorinda."

The words caught her entirely off guard. For a moment, her heart soared. But then she realized that it changed nothing and her heart plummeted. Curse the man! She should have known he would pull out a dirty trick like that.

"Even if you don't love me now," he went on, "perhaps in time—"

"Of course I love you!" she burst out, unable to pretend otherwise, not when her heart was breaking. "Do you think I would let just any man make love to me? But there's no point to it. I can't have children and that's what you want—children. Don't try to tell me that you don't, because no matter what you say, I know the truth."

"You're right," he said softly. "I do want children. I won't deny it. I just need to know one thing. Do *you* want them?"

The cruelty of that question made her want to cry. "Yes, of course!" she choked out. "But not if it means torture and horrible remedies and—"

"It doesn't." Walking up, he seized her hands in his

and wouldn't let go. "I shouldn't have left you with any fear that it might. I handled our last discussion very badly; I admit that. But I meant what I said before. I would never put a woman I loved through that."

"You claim that now, but—"

"Let me finish. After you left, I thought about everything you'd told me. I thought about what I wanted, and I realized that I do want children. I do want to make a family with you." When she stiffened, he added hastily, "But I don't care if our children come from your womb or from the foundling hospital down the street. As long as you don't care, we can take in urchins from Spitalfields."

She stared at him, stunned, and he drew her closer. "It's *you* I want, you whom I need in my life. And I will do whatever I must to convince you of that."

Try as she might to resist them, the tender words crept under her defenses to steal around her heart. He would take in foundlings? Or urchins? For *her*? "You'd still have no real heir. The laws of England don't allow for true adoption."

"Why does that matter?" He cupped her head in his hands. "It's not as if I have a large entailed estate or a title that must go to my male heirs. I can still leave my possessions to whatever children we do take in. As long as we have a child to love and hold, to raise and teach, we'll have exactly what we want."

Tears started in her eyes that she tried fruitlessly to contain. He was offering her hope, for the first time, that her life did not have to be as Edgar had dictated it. She could be what she pleased . . . with him.